Dorothy L. Sayers

The greatest detective novelist of the Golden Age was born in Oxford in 1893. She was one of the first women to be awarded a degree by Oxford University and she was a copywriter in an advertising agency from 1922 to 1929. Her aristocratic detective Lord Peter Wimsey became one of the world's most popular fictional heroes.

Dorothy L. Sayers also became famous for her religious plays, notably *The Man Born to Be King*, which was broadcast controversially during the war years, and her translation of Dante's *Divine Comedy*. She died in 1957.

Hodder & Stoughton is the publisher of all her detective stories and four new Lord Peter Wimsey novels by Jill Paton Walsh. *Thrones, Dominations* and *A Presumption of Death* are based closely on Dorothy L. Sayers' own work. Hodder & Stoughton's Sceptre imprint is the publisher of the revised and updated version of the definitive biography, *Dorothy L. Sayers: Her Life and Soul* by Barbara Reynolds.

Christopher Fowler

Christopher Fowler is the award-winning author of over thirty novels and twelve short story collections, and the *Bryant & May* mystery novels, which record the adventures of two Golden Age detectives investigating impossible London crimes. He is a five-time British Fantasy Award-winner, and has also won the Edge Hill prize for *Old Devil Moon*, the Last Laugh prize for *The Victoria Vanishes*, the Green Carnation Award for *Paperboy* and the E-Dunnit Award for *Bryant & May and the Invisible Code*. After living in France and the USA he now lives in King's Cross, London, and Barcelona.

DOROTHY L. SAYERS

LORD PETER VIEWS THE BODY

WITH AN INTRODUCTION BY CHRISTOPHER FOWLER

HODDER

First published in Great Britain in 1928 by Victor Gollancz Ltd
First published in paperback by New English Library in 1974

This edition published in 2016 by Hodder & Stoughton
An Hachette UK company

6

A CIP catalogue record for this title is available from the British Library

Paperback ISBN 978 1 473 62132 9
Ebook ISBN 978 1 848 94376 6

Typeset by Hewer Text UK Ltd, Edinburgh
Printed and bound by Clays Ltd, Elcograf S.p.A.

Hodder & Stoughton policy is to use papers that are natural, renewable
and recyclable products and made from wood grown in sustainable
forests. The logging and manufacturing processes are expected to
conform to the environmental regulations of the country of origin.

Hodder & Stoughton Ltd
Carmelite House
50 Victoria Embankment
London EC4Y 0DZ

www.hodder.co.uk

When you think of Golden Age crime fiction what comes to mind? Bodies in libraries, country house murders, butlers and maids, gentleman thieves, dowager duchesses losing their pearls? These images can't help but spring to mind when we look at the twentieth century's greatest crime writers. We think of Agatha Christie as the queen of the whodunit and Margery Allingham as the mistress of elegant wordplay, but then there's the Dorothy Problem. In his book *Snobbery with Violence* Colin Watson isolates it; how do you celebrate something that can be seen, in its worst form, as the most class-ridden and backward-looking of all crime genres? The deference of servants and coppers to the titled interferers who solve crimes can be most off-putting.

Dorothy L. Sayers came up with the most archetypal Golden Age detective of them all, a genuinely aristocratic investigator with a sidekick manservant, but luckily for us she built her own solution into that question; Lord Peter Wimsey tips his hat and winks to you from his name onwards. He is charm personified, so disarmingly likeable and generous of spirit that it would be a curmudgeon indeed who finds him unappealing.

But if that was all Sayers brought to the table, her books would not still be finding readers. Rather than employ a cut-out character to pick his way through the plot mechanics, she breathes life into Wimsey in a way that few of her peers ever managed. Her noble hero is flesh and blood. While he has the unattractive physical excesses of a limited gene pool, straw hair, a sloping forehead, a lean arched nose, a foolish smile, a fondness for primrose PJs, he is reason personified. Wimsey listens to everyone from the poacher to the vicar, and takes them all seriously. He uses his breeding and knowledge to help others, and he's an enemy to cads and chancers. What's more, his life is messy; no arrogant loner, he has friends, relatives and eventually a wife. He's tangled up in the times and engages directly with the hot topics of the period, including ethics, women's roles and the after-effects of war.

Sayers was attacked by a handful of academics who found Wimsey too perfect, her tales too fond of British stereotypes and her plots too self-consciously intelligent, but since when was it wrong for crime fiction to reach toward comment on the human condition? Besides, the books are intended to be imaginative, erudite and romantic, not grittily realistic. The criticism was misplaced; the stories are never more delightful than when they're at their most English. Mysteries set in town are fine, but the countryside is where Sayers excels. Her descriptions of nature are always evocative: 'the rain streamed down remorselessly over the laurel leaves, stiff and shiny as mackintoshes.' In her story 'The Undignified Melodrama of the Bone of Contention' she makes the kind of observations I love, explaining that under-attendance at church is partly due to field workers not wishing to walk mud into the vestry, or that funerals need good weather otherwise they spoil the locals' enjoyment of them. Villagers need something to talk about, especially if it involves death.

I first encountered Sayers in a way that could have put me off for life, reading *The Nine Tailors* too young. For her critics the problem is that virtually the whole of the book's first half is about campanology, the art of bell-ringing. What they failed to realise was that this becomes one of the great enjoyments in reading Sayers. She seizes upon a subject and really digs into it with gusto. After you've read that novel you'll know what a Kent Treble Bob Major is, but more importantly the weight of her research makes the story far more enjoyable. Who doesn't like a well-written essay on something they knew little about?

Sometimes a detail completes a story. In her short fiction, Sayers pursues these with a kind of delirious energy. In 'The Fascinating Problem of Uncle Meleager's Will' there's a crossword puzzle to fill in (I found it impossible, even with the author's helpful notes). In 'The Entertaining Episode of the Article in Question' she not only hides a clue in the title, but prints the page holding the puzzle's answer in untranslated French, which is cheeky to say the least. She assumes her readers have questing minds and will do some work. She's no slouch at suspense, either, capturing the reckless thrill of early driving, the tension of courtrooms, the eeriness of omens on country backroads.

The plots are delicious, of course, and the characters charming, but Sayers is ultimately lifted by something that P.G. Wodehouse had in spades; a sense of joyfulness in her prose. Only Wimsey would nickname somebody 'Gherkins'. Only Wimsey would delay his appearance until we're well into the story, seemingly wandering in on a whim. Only Wimsey would get involved in a lengthy discussion about the years of vintage wines or the rules of poker. No one else's mysteries are so wide-ranging in in their subject matter.

Too much modern crime fiction dwells in degradation and pain. Sayers acknowledges tragedy but has grander schemes in mind – to entertain and enlighten with suspense, subtlety and a sense of humour. Be warned, though. Once you make friends with Wimsey you'll want to get better acquainted. Sayers' crime fiction output was not prodigious. Quantity is not the issue here, but quality; something that for all its period glory has proved to be timeless.

Christopher Fowler, May 2016

THE STORIES

THE ABOMINABLE HISTORY OF THE
MAN WITH COPPER FINGERS

The Egotists' Club is one of the most genial places in London. It is a place to which you may go when you want to tell that odd dream you had last night, or to announce what a good dentist you have discovered. You can write letters there if you like, and have the temperament of a Jane Austen, for there is no silence room, and it would be a breach of club manners to appear busy or absorbed when another member addresses you. You must not mention golf or fish, however, and, if the Hon. Freddy Arbuthnot's motion is carried at the next committee meeting (and opinion so far appears very favourable), you will not be allowed to mention wireless either. As Lord Peter Wimsey said when the matter was mooted the other day in the smoking-room, those are things you can talk about anywhere. Otherwise the club is not specially exclusive. Nobody is ineligible *per se*, except strong, silent men. Nominees are, however, required to pass certain tests, whose nature is sufficiently indicated by the fact that a certain distinguished explorer came to grief through accepting, and smoking, a powerful Trichinopoly cigar as an accompaniment to a '63 port. On the other hand, dear old Sir Roger Bunt (the coster millionaire who won the £20,000 ballot offered by the *Sunday Shriek*, and used it to found his immense catering business in the Midlands) was highly commended and unanimously elected after declaring frankly that beer and a pipe were all he really cared for in that way. As Lord Peter said again: 'Nobody minds coarseness, but one must draw the line at cruelty.'

On this particular evening, Masterman (the cubist poet) had brought a guest with him, a man named Varden. Varden had started life as a professional athlete, but a strained heart had obliged him to cut short a brilliant career, and turn his handsome face and remarkably beautiful body to account in the service of the cinema screen. He had come to London from Los Angeles to stimulate publicity for his great new film, *Marathon*, and turned out to be quite a pleasant, unspoiled person – greatly to the relief of the club, since Masterman's guests were apt to be something of a toss-up.

There were only eight men, including Varden, in the brown room that evening. This, with its panelled walls, shaded lamps, and heavy blue curtains was perhaps the cosiest and pleasantest of the small smoking-rooms, of which the club possessed half a dozen or so. The conversation had begun quite casually by Armstrong's relating a curious little incident which he had witnessed that afternoon at the Temple Station, and Bayes had gone on to say that that was nothing to the really very odd thing which had happened to him, personally, in a thick fog one night in the Euston Road.

Masterman said that the more secluded London squares teemed with subjects for a writer, and instanced his own singular encounter with a weeping woman and a dead monkey, and then Judson took up the tale and narrated how, in a lonely suburb, late at night, he had come upon the dead body of a woman stretched on the pavement with a knife in her side and a policeman standing motionless near by. He had asked if he could do anything, but the policeman had only said, 'I wouldn't interfere if I was you, sir; she deserved what she got.' Judson said he had not been able to get the incident out of his mind, and then Pettifer told them of a queer case in his own medical practice, when a totally unknown man had led him to a house in Bloomsbury where there was a woman suffering from strychnine poisoning. This man had helped him in the most intelligent manner all night, and, when the patient was out of danger, had walked straight out of the house and never reappeared; the odd thing being that, when he (Pettifer) questioned the woman, she answered in great surprise that she had never seen the man in her life and had taken him to be Pettifer's assistant.

'That reminds me,' said Varden, 'of something still stranger that happened to me once in New York – I've never been able to make out whether it was a madman or a practical joke, or whether I really had a very narrow shave.'

This sounded promising, and the guest was urged to go on with his story.

'Well, it really started ages ago,' said the actor, 'seven years it must have been – just before America came into the war. I was twenty-five at the time, and had been in the film business a little over two years. There was a man called Eric P. Loder, pretty well known in New York at that period, who would have been a very fine sculptor if he hadn't had more money than was good for him, or so I understood from the people who go in for that kind of thing. He used to exhibit a good deal and had a lot of one-man shows of his stuff to which the highbrow people went – he did a good many bronzes, I believe. Perhaps you know about him, Masterman?'

'I've never seen any of his things,' said the poet, 'but I remember some photographs in *The Art of Tomorrow*. Clever, but rather over-ripe. Didn't he go in for a lot of that chryselephantine stuff? Just to show he could afford to pay for the materials, I suppose.'

'Yes, that sounds very like him.'

'Of course – and he did a very slick and very ugly realistic group called Lucina, and had the impudence to have it cast in solid gold and stood in his front hall.'

'Oh, that thing! Yes – simply beastly I thought it, but then I never could see anything artistic in the idea. Realism, I suppose you'd call it. I like a picture or a statue to make you feel good, or what's it there for? Still, there was something very attractive about Loder.'

'How did you come across him?'

'Oh, yes. Well, he saw me in that little picture of mine, *Apollo comes to New York* – perhaps you remember it. It was my first star part. About a statue that's brought to life – one of the old gods, you know – and how he gets on in a modern city. Dear old Reubenssohn produced it. Now, there was a man who could put a thing through with consummate artistry. You couldn't find an atom of offence from beginning to end, it was all so tasteful, though in the first part one didn't have anything to wear except a sort of scarf – taken from the classical statue, you know.'

'The Belvedere?'

'I dare say. Well. Loder wrote to me, and said as a sculptor he was interested in me, because I was a good shape and so on, and would I come and pay him a visit in New York when I was free. So I found out about Loder, and decided it would be good publicity, and when my contract was up, and I had a bit of time to fill in, I went up east and called on him. He was very decent to me, and asked me to stay a few weeks with him while I was looking around.

'He had a magnificent great house about five miles out of the city, crammed full of pictures and antiques and so on. He was somewhere between thirty-five and forty, I should think, dark and smooth, and very quick and lively in his movements. He talked very well; seemed to have been everywhere and have seen everything and not to have any too good opinion of anybody. You could sit and listen to him for hours; he'd got anecdotes about everybody, from the Pope to old Phineas E. Groot of the Chicago Ring. The only kind of story I didn't care about hearing from him was the improper sort. Not that I don't enjoy an after-dinner story – no sir, I wouldn't like you to think I was a prig – but he'd tell it with his eye upon you as if he suspected you of having something to do with it. I've known women do that, and I've seen men do it to women and seen the women squirm, but he was the only man that's ever given *me* that feeling. Still, apart from that, Loder was the most fascinating fellow I've ever known. And, as I say, his house surely was beautiful, and he kept a first-class table.

'He liked to have everything of the best. There was his mistress, Maria Morano. I don't think I've ever seen anything to touch her, and when you work for the screen you're apt to have a pretty exacting standard of female beauty. She was one of those big, slow, beautifully moving creatures, very placid, with a slow, wide smile. We don't grow them in the States. She'd come from the South – had been a cabaret dancer he said, and she didn't contradict him. He was very proud of her, and she seemed to be devoted to him in her own fashion. He'd

5

show her off in the studio with nothing on but a fig-leaf or so – stand her up beside one of the figures he was always doing of her, and compare them point by point. There was literally only one half inch of her, it seemed, that wasn't absolutely perfect from the sculptor's point of view – the second toe of her left foot was shorter than the big toe. He used to correct it, of course, in the statues. She'd listen to it all with a good-natured smile, sort of vaguely flattered, you know. Though I think the poor girl sometimes got tired of being gloated over that way. She'd sometimes hunt me out and confide to me that what she had always hoped for was to run a restaurant of her own, with a cabaret show and a great many cooks with white aprons, and lots of polished electric cookers. 'And then I would marry,' she'd say, 'and have four sons and one daughter,' and she told me all the names she had chosen for the family. I thought it was rather pathetic. Loder came in at the end of one of these conversations. He had a sort of a grin on, so I dare say he'd overheard. I don't suppose he attached much importance to it, which shows that he never really understood the girl. I don't think he ever imagined any woman would chuck up the sort of life he'd accustomed her to, and if he was a bit possessive in his manner, at least he never gave her a rival. For all his talk and his ugly statues, she'd got him, and she knew it.

'I stayed there getting on for a month altogether, having a thundering good time. On two occasions Loder had an art spasm, and shut himself up in his studio to work and wouldn't let anybody in for several days on end. He was rather given to that sort of stunt, and when it was over we would have a party, and all Loder's friends and hangers-on would come to have a look at the work of art. He was doing a figure of some nymph or goddess, I fancy, to be cast in silver, and Maria used to go along and sit for him. Apart from those times, he went about everywhere, and we saw all there was to be seen.

'I was fairly annoyed, I admit, when it came to an end. War was declared, and I'd made up my mind to join up when that happened. My heart put me out of the running for trench service, but I counted on getting some sort of a job, with perseverance, so I packed up and went off.

'I wouldn't have believed Loder would have been so genuinely sorry to say good-bye to me. He said over and over again that we'd meet again soon. However, I did get a job with the hospital people, and was sent over to Europe, and it wasn't until 1920 that I saw Loder again.

'He'd written to me before, but I'd had two big pictures to make in '19, and it couldn't be done. However, in '20 I found myself back in New York, doing publicity for *The Passion Streak*, and got a note from Loder begging me to stay with him, and saying he wanted me to sit for him. Well, that was advertisement that he'd pay for himself, you know, so I agreed. I had accepted an engagement to go out with Mystofilms Ltd in *Jake of Dead Man's Bush* – the dwarfmen picture, you know, taken on the spot among the Australian bushmen. I wired them that I would join them at Sydney the third week in April, and took my bags to Loder's.

'Loder greeted me very cordially, though I thought he looked older than when I last saw him. He had certainly grown more nervous in his manner. He was – how shall I describe it? – more *intense* – more real, in a way. He brought out his pet cynicisms as if he thoroughly meant them, and more and more with that air of getting at you personally. I used to think his disbelief in everything was a kind of artistic pose, but I began to feel I had done him an injustice. He was really unhappy, I could see that quite well, and soon I discovered the reason. As we were driving out in the car I asked after Maria.

' "She has left me," ' he said.

'Well, now you know, that really surprised me. Honestly, I hadn't thought the girl had that much initiative. "Why," I said, "has she gone and set up in that restaurant of her own she wanted so much?"

' "Oh! she talked to you about restaurants, did she?" said Loder. "I suppose you are one of the men that women tell things to. No. She made a fool of herself. She's gone."

'I didn't quite know what to say. He was so obviously hurt in his vanity, you know, as well as in his feelings. I muttered the usual things, and added that it must be a great loss to his work as well as in other ways. He said it was.

'I asked him when it had happened and whether he'd finished the nymph he was working on before I left. He said, "Oh, yes, he'd finished that and done another – something pretty original, which I should like."

'Well, we got to the house and dined, and Loder told me he was going to Europe shortly, a few days after I left myself, in fact. The nymph stood in the dining-room, in a special niche let into the wall. It really was a beautiful thing, not so showy as most of Loder's work, and a wonderful likeness of Maria. Loder put me opposite it, so that I could see it during dinner, and, really, I could hardly take my eyes off it. He seemed very proud of it, and kept on telling me over and over again how glad he was that I liked it. It struck me that he was falling into a trick of repeating himself.

'We went into the smoking-room after dinner. He'd

had it rearranged, and the first thing that caught one's eye was a big settee drawn before the fire. It stood about a couple of feet from the ground, and consisted of a base made like a Roman couch, with cushions and a highish back, all made of oak with a silver inlay, and on top of this, forming the actual seat one sat on, if you follow me, there was a great silver figure of a nude woman, fully life-size, lying with her head back and her arms extended along the sides of the couch. A few big loose cushions made it possible to use the thing as an actual settee, though I must say it never was really comfortable to sit on respectably. As a stage prop. for registering dissipation it would have been excellent, but to see Loder sprawling over it by his own fireside gave me a kind of shock. He seemed very much attached to it, though.

' "I told you," he said, "that it was something original."

'Then I looked more closely at it, and saw that the figure actually was Maria's, though the face was rather sketchily done, if you understand what I mean. I suppose he thought a bolder treatment more suited to a piece of furniture.

'But I did begin to think Loder a trifle degenerate when I saw that couch. And in the fortnight that followed I grew more and more uncomfortable with him. That personal manner of his grew more marked every day, and sometimes, while I was giving him sittings, he would sit there and tell one the most beastly things, with his eyes fixed on one in the nastiest way, just to see how one would take it. Upon my word, though he certainly did me uncommonly well, I began to feel I'd be more at ease among the bushmen.

'Well, now I come to the odd thing.'

9

Everybody sat up and listened a little more eagerly.

'It was the evening before I had to leave New York,' went on Varden. 'I was sitting—'

Here somebody opened the door of the brown room, to be greeted by a warning sign from Bayes. The intruder sank obscurely into a large chair and mixed himself a whisky with extreme care not to disturb the speaker.

'I was sitting in the smoking-room,' continued Varden, 'waiting for Loder to come in. I had the house to myself, for Loder had given the servants leave to go to some show or lecture or other, and he himself was getting his things together for his European trip and had had to keep an appointment with his man of business. I must have been very nearly asleep, because it was dusk when I came to with a start and saw a young man quite close to me.

'He wasn't at all like a housebreaker, and still less like a ghost. He was, I might almost say, exceptionally ordinary-looking. He was dressed in a grey English suit, with a fawn overcoat on his arm, and his soft hat and stick in his hand. He had sleek, pale hair, and one of those rather stupid faces, with a long nose and a monocle. I stared at him, for I knew the front door was locked, but before I could get my wits together he spoke. He had a curious, hesitating, husky voice and a strong English accent. He said, surprisingly:

' "Are you Mr Varden?"

' "You have the advantage of me," I said.

'He said, "Please excuse my butting in; I know it looks like bad manners, but you'd better clear out of this place very quickly, don't you know."

' "What the hell do you mean?" I said.

'He said, "I don't mean it in any impertinent way, but you must realise that Loder's never forgiven you, and I'm afraid he means to make you into a hatstand or an electric-light fitting, or something of that sort."

'My God! I can tell you I felt queer. It was such a quiet voice, and his manners were perfect, and yet the words were quite meaningless! I remembered that madmen are supposed to be extra strong, and edged towards the bell – and then it came over me with rather a chill that I was alone in the house.

' "How did you get here?" I asked, putting a bold face on it.

' "I'm afraid I picked the lock," he said, as casually as though he were apologising for not having a card about him. "I couldn't be sure Loder hadn't came back. But I do really think you had better get out as quickly as possible."

' "See here," I said, "who are you and what the hell are you driving at? What do you mean about Loder never forgiving me? Forgiving me what?"

' "Why," he said, "about – you *will* pardon me prancing in on your private affairs, won't you – about Maria Morano."

' "*What* about her, in the devil's name?" I cried. "What do you know about her, anyway? She went off while I was at the war. What's it to do with me?"

' "Oh!" said the very odd young man, "I beg your pardon. Perhaps I have been relying too much on Loder's judgement. Damned foolish; but the possibility of his being mistaken did not occur to me. He fancies you were Maria Morano's lover when you were here last time."

' "Maria's lover?" I said. "Preposterous! She went off with her man, whoever he was. He must know she didn't go with me."

' "Maria never left the house," said the young man,

"and if you don't get out of it this moment, I won't answer for *your* ever leaving, either."

' "In God's name," I cried, exasperated, "what do you mean?"

'The man turned and threw the blue cushions off the foot of the silver couch.

' "Have you ever examined the toes of this?" he asked.

' "Not particularly," I said, more and more astonished. "Why should I?"

' "Did you ever know Loder make any figure of her but this with that short toe on the left foot?" he went on.

'Well, I did take a look at it then, and saw it was as he said – the left foot had a short second toe.

' "So it is," I said, "but, after all, why not?"

' "Why not, indeed?" said the young man. "Wouldn't you like to see why, of all the figures Loder made of Maria Morano, this is the only one that has the feet of the living woman?"

'He picked up the poker.

' "Look!" he said.

'With a lot more strength than I should have expected from him, he brought the head of the poker down with a heavy crack on the silver couch. It struck one of the arms of the figure neatly at the elbow-joint, smashing a jagged hole in the silver. He wrenched at the arm and brought it away. It was hollow, and, as I am alive, I tell you there was a long, dry arm-bone inside it!'

Varden paused, and put away a good mouthful of whisky.

'Well?' cried several breathless voices.

'Well,' said Varden, 'I'm not ashamed to say I went out of that house like an old buck-rabbit that hears the man with the gun. There was a car standing just outside, and the driver opened the door. I tumbled in, and then it came over me that the whole thing might be a trap, and I tumbled out again and ran till I reached the trolley-cars. But I found my bags at the station next day, duly registered for Vancouver.

'When I pulled myself together I did rather wonder what Loder was thinking about my disappearance, but I could no more have gone back into that horrible house than I could have taken poison. I left for Vancouver next morning, and from that day to this I never saw either of those men again. I've still not the faintest idea who the fair man was, or what became of him, but I heard in a roundabout way that Loder was dead – in some kind of an accident, I fancy.'

There was a pause. Then:

'It's a damned good story, Mr Varden,' said Armstrong – he was a dabbler in various kinds of handiwork, and was, indeed, chiefly responsible for Mr Arbuthnot's motion to ban wireless – 'but are you suggesting there was a complete skeleton inside that silver casting? Do you mean Loder put it into the core of the mould when the casting was done? It would be awfully difficult and dangerous – the slightest accident would have put him at the mercy of his workmen. And that statue must have been considerably over life-size to allow of the skeleton being well covered.'

'Mr Varden has unintentionally misled you, Armstrong,' said a quiet, husky voice suddenly from the shadow behind Varden's chair. 'The figure was not silver, but electro-plated on a copper base deposited direct on the body. The lady was Sheffield-plated, in fact. I fancy the soft parts of her must have been digested away with pepsin, or some preparation of the kind, after

13

the process was complete, but I can't be positive about that.'

'Hullo, Wimsey,' said Armstrong, 'was that you came in just now? And why this confident pronouncement?'

The effect of Wimsey's voice on Varden had been extraordinary. He had leapt to his feet, and turned the lamp so as to light up Wimsey's face.

'Good evening, Mr Varden,' said Lord Peter. 'I'm delighted to meet you again and to apologise for my unceremonious behaviour on the occasion of our last encounter.'

Varden took the proffered hand, but was speechless.

'D'you mean to say, you mad mystery-monger, that *you* were Varden's Great Unknown?' demanded Bayes. 'Ah, well,' he added rudely, 'we might have guessed it from his vivid description.'

'Well, since you're here,' said Smith-Hartington, the *Morning Yell* man, 'I think you ought to come across with the rest of the story.'

'Was it just a joke?' asked Judson.

'Of course not,' interrupted Pettifer, before Lord Peter had time to reply. 'Why should it be? Wimsey's seen enough queer things not to have to waste his time inventing them.'

'That's true enough,' said Bayes. 'Comes of having deductive powers and all that sort of thing, and always sticking one's nose into things that are better not investigated.'

'That's all very well, Bayes,' said his lordship, 'but if I hadn't just mentioned the matter to Mr Varden that evening, where would he be?'

'Ah, where? That's exactly what we want to know,'

14

demanded Smith-Hartington. 'Come on, Wimsey, no shirking; we must have the tale.'

'And the whole tale,' added Pettifer.

'And nothing but the tale,' said Armstrong, dexterously whisking away the whisky-bottle and the cigars from under Lord Peter's nose. 'Get on with it, old son. Not a smoke do you smoke and not a sup do you sip till Burd Ellen is set free.'

'Brute!' said his lordship plaintively. 'As a matter of fact,' he went on, with a change of tone, 'it's not really a story I want to get about. It might land me in a very unpleasant sort of position – manslaughter probably, and murder possibly.'

'Gosh!' said Bayes.

'That's all right,' said Armstrong, 'nobody's going to talk. We can't afford to lose you from the club, you know. Smith-Hartington will have to control his passion for copy, that's all.'

Pledges of discretion having been given all round, Lord Peter settled himself back and began his tale.

'The curious case of Eric P. Loder affords one more instance of the strange manner in which some power beyond our puny human wills arranges the affairs of men. Call it Providence – call it Destiny—'

'We'll call it off,' said Bayes; 'you can leave out that part.'

Lord Peter groaned and began again.

'Well, the first thing that made me feel a bit inquisitive about Loder was a casual remark by a man at the Emigration Office in New York, where I happened to go about that silly affair of Mrs Bilt's. He said, "What on earth is Eric Loder going to do in Australia? I should have thought Europe was more in his line."

15

' "Australia?" I said, "you're wandering, dear old thing. He told me the other day he was off to Italy in three weeks' time."

' "Italy, nothing," he said, "he was all over our place today, asking about how you got to Sydney and what were the necessary formalities, and so on."

' "Oh," I said, "I suppose he's going by the Pacific route, and calling at Sydney on his way." But I wondered why he hadn't said so when I'd met him the day before. He had distinctly talked about sailing for Europe and doing Paris before he went on to Rome.

'I felt so darned inquisitive that I went and called on Loder two nights later.

'He seemed quite pleased to see me, and was full of his forthcoming trip. I asked him again about his route, and he told me quite distinctly he was going via Paris.

'Well, that was that, and it wasn't really any of my business, and we chatted about other things. He told me that Mr Varden was coming to stay with him before he went, and that he hoped to get him to pose for a figure before he left. He said he'd never seen a man so perfectly formed. "I meant to get him to do it before," he said, "but war broke out, and he went and joined the army before I had time to start."

'He was lolling on that beastly couch of his at the time, and, happening to look round at him, I caught such a nasty sort of glitter in his eye that it gave me quite a turn. He was stroking the figure over the neck and grinning at it.

' "None of your efforts in Sheffield plate, I hope," said I.

' "Well," he said, "I thought of making a kind of companion to this, *The Sleeping Athlete*, you know, or something of that sort."

' "You'd much better cast it," I said. "Why did you put the stuff on so thick? It destroys the fine detail."

'That annoyed him. He never liked to hear any objection made to that work of art.

' "This was experimental," he said. "I mean the next to be a real masterpiece. You'll see."

'We'd got to about that point when the butler came in to ask should he make up a bed for me, as it was such a bad night. We hadn't noticed the weather particularly, though it had looked a bit threatening when I started from New York. However, we now looked out, and saw that it was coming down in sheets and torrents. It wouldn't have mattered, only that I'd only brought a little open racing car and no overcoat, and certainly the prospect of five miles in that downpour wasn't altogether attractive. Loder urged me to stay, and I said I would.

'I was feeling a bit fagged, so I went to bed right off. Loder said he wanted to do a bit of work in the studio first, and I saw him depart along the corridor.

'You won't allow me to mention Providence, so I'll only say it was a very remarkable thing that I should have woken up at two in the morning to find myself lying in a pool of water. The man had stuck a hot-water bottle into the bed, because it hadn't been used just lately, and the beastly thing had gone and unstoppered itself. I lay awake for ten minutes in the deeps of damp misery before I had sufficient strength of mind to investigate. Then I found it was hopeless – sheets, blankets, mattress, all soaked. I looked at the arm-chair, and then I had a brilliant idea. I remembered there was a lovely great divan in the studio, with a big skin rug and a pile of cushions. Why not finish the night there? I took the little electric torch which always goes about with me, and started off.

'The studio was empty, so I supposed Loder had finished and trotted off to roost. The divan was there, all right, with a screen drawn partly across it, so I rolled myself up under the rug and prepared to snooze off.

'I was just getting beautifully sleepy again when I heard footsteps, not in the passage, but apparently on the other side of the room. I was surprised, because I didn't know there was any way out in that direction. I lay low, and presently I saw a streak of light appear from the cupboard where Loder kept his tools and things. The streak widened, and Loder emerged, carrying an electric torch. He closed the cupboard door very gently after him, and padded across the studio. He stopped before the easel and uncovered it; I could see him through a crack in the screen. He stood for some minutes gazing at a sketch on the easel, and then gave one of the nastiest gurgly laughs I've ever had the pleasure of hearing. If I'd ever seriously thought of announcing my unauthorised presence, I abandoned all idea of it then. Presently he covered the easel again, and went out by the door at which I had come in.

'I waited till I was sure he had gone, and then got up – uncommonly quietly, I may say. I tiptoed over to the easel to see what the fascinating work of art was. I saw at once it was the design for the figure of *The Sleeping Athlete*, and as I looked at it I felt a sort of horrid conviction stealing over me. It was an idea which seemed to begin in my stomach, and work its way up to the roots of my hair.

'My family say I'm too inquisitive. I can only say that wild horses wouldn't have kept me from investigating

18

that cupboard. With the feeling that something absolutely vile might hop out at me – I was a bit wrought up, and it was a rotten time of night – I put a heroic hand on the door knob.

'To my astonishment, the thing wasn't even locked. It opened at once, to show a range of perfectly innocent and orderly shelves, which couldn't possibly have held Loder.

'My blood was up, you know, by this time, so I hunted round for the spring-lock which I knew must exist, and found it without much difficulty. The back of the cupboard swung noiselessly inwards, and I found myself at the top of a narrow flight of stairs.

'I had the sense to stop and see that the door could be opened from the inside before I went any farther, and I also selected a good stout pestle which I found on the shelves as a weapon in case of accident. Then I closed the door and tripped with elf-like lightness down that jolly old staircase.

'There was another door at the bottom, but it didn't take me long to fathom the secret of that. Feeling frightfully excited, I threw it boldly open, with the pestle ready for action.'

'However, the room seemed to be empty. My torch caught the gleam of something liquid, and then I found the wall-switch.

'I saw a biggish square room, fitted up as a workshop. On the right-hand wall was a big switchboard, with a bench beneath it. From the middle of the ceiling hung a great flood-light, illuminating a glass vat, fully seven feet long by about three wide. I turned on the flood-light, and looked down into the vat. It was filled with a dark brown liquid which I recognised as the usual compound of cyanide and copper-sulphate which they use for copper-plating.

The rods hung over it with their hooks all empty, but there was a packing-case half-opened at one side of the room, and, pulling the covering aside, I could see rows of copper anodes – enough of them to put a plating over a quarter of an inch thick on a life-size figure. There was a smaller case, still nailed up, which from its weight and appearance I guessed to contain the silver for the rest of the process. There was something else I was looking for, and I soon found it – a considerable quantity of prepared graphite and a big jar of varnish.

'Of course, there was no evidence, really, of anything being on the cross. There was no reason why Loder shouldn't make a plaster cast and Sheffield-plate it if he had a fancy for that kind of thing. But then I found something that *couldn't* have come there legitimately.

'On the bench was an oval slab of copper about an inch and a half long – Loder's night's work, I guessed. It was an electrotype of the American Consular seal, the thing they stamp on your passport photograph to keep you from hiking it off and substituting the picture of your friend Mr Jiggs, who would like to get out of the country because he is so popular with Scotland Yard.

'I sat down on Loder's stool, and worked out that pretty little plot in all its details. I could see it all turned on three things. First of all, I must find out if Varden was proposing to make tracks shortly for Australia, because, if he wasn't, it threw all my beautiful theories out. And, secondly, it would help matters greatly if he happened to have dark hair like Loder's, as he has, you see – near enough, anyway, to fit the description on a passport. I'd only seen him in that Apollo Belvedere thing, with a fair wig on. But I knew if I hung about I should see him presently when he came to stay with Loder. And, thirdly, of course, I had to discover if Loder was likely to have any grounds for a grudge against Varden.

'Well, I figured out I'd stayed down in that room about as long as was healthy. Loder might come back at any moment, and I didn't forget that a vatful of copper sulphate and cyanide of potassium would be a highly handy means of getting rid of a too-inquisitive guest. And I can't say I had any great fancy for figuring as part of Loder's domestic furniture. I've always hated things made in the shape of things – volumes of Dickens that turn out to be a biscuit-tin, and dodges like that; and, though I take no overwhelming interest in my own funeral, I should like it to be in good taste. I went so far as to wipe away any finger-marks I might have left behind me, and then I went back to the studio and rearranged that divan. I didn't feel Loder would care to think I'd been down there.

'There was just one other thing I felt inquisitive about. I tiptoed back through the hall and into the smoking-room. The silver couch glimmered in the light of the torch. I felt I disliked it fifty times more than ever before. However, I pulled myself together and took a careful look at the feet of the figure. I'd heard all about that second toe of Maria Morano's.

'I passed the rest of the night in the arm-chair after all.

'What with Mrs Bilt's job and one thing and another, and the enquiries I had to make, I had to put off my interference in Loder's little game till rather late. I found out that Varden had been staying with Loder a few months before the beautiful Maria Morano had vanished. I'm afraid I was rather stupid about that, Mr Varden. I thought perhaps there *had* been something.'

'Don't apologise,' said Varden, with a little laugh. 'Cinema actors are notoriously immoral.'

'Why rub it in?' said Wimsey, a trifle hurt. 'I apologise. Anyway, it came to the same thing as far as Loder was concerned. Then there was one bit of evidence I had to get to be absolutely certain. Electro-plating – especially such a ticklish job as the one I had in mind – wasn't a job that could be finished in a night; on the other hand, it seemed necessary that Mr Varden should be seen alive in New York up to the day he was scheduled to depart. It was also clear that Loder meant to be able to prove that a Mr Varden had left New York all right, according to plan, and had actually arrived in Sydney. Accordingly, a false Mr Varden was to depart with Varden's papers and Varden's passport furnished with a new photograph duly stamped with the Consular stamp, and to disappear quietly at Sydney and be retransformed into Mr Eric Loder, travelling with a perfectly regular passport of his own. Well, then, in that case, obviously a cablegram would have to be sent off to Mystofilms Ltd., warning them to expect Varden by a later boat than he had arranged. I handed over this part of the job to my man, Bunter, who is uncommonly capable. The devoted fellow shadowed Loder faithfully for getting on for three weeks, and at length, the very day before Mr Varden was due to depart, the cablegram was sent from an office in Broadway, where, by a happy providence (once more) they supply extremely hard pencils.'

'By Jove!' cried Varden, 'I remember now being told something about a cablegram when I got out, but I never connected it with Loder. I thought it was just some stupidity of the Western Electric people.'

'Quite so. Well, as soon as I'd got that, I popped along

to Loder's with a picklock in one pocket and an automatic in the other. The good Bunter went with me, and, if I didn't return by a certain time, had orders to telephone for the police. So you see everything was pretty well covered. Bunter was the chauffeur who was waiting for you, Mr Varden, but you turned suspicious – I don't blame you altogether – so all we could do was to forward your luggage along to the train.

'On the way out we met the Loder servants *en route* for New York in a car, which showed us that we were on the right track, and also that I was going to have a fairly simple job of it.

'You've heard all about my interview with Mr Varden. I really don't think I could improve upon his account. When I'd seen him and his traps safely off the premises, I made for the studio. It was empty, so I opened the secret door, and, as I expected, saw a line of light under the workshop door at the far end of the passage.'

'So Loder was there all the time?'

'Of course he was. I took my little pop-gun tight in my fist and opened the door very gently. Loder was standing between the tank and the switchboard, very busy indeed – so busy he didn't hear me come in. His hands were black with graphite, a big heap of which was spread on a sheet on the floor, and he was engaged with a long, springy coil of copper wire, running to the output of the transformer. The big packing-case had been opened, and all the hooks were occupied.

' "Loder!' I said.

'He turned on me with a face like nothing human. "Wimsey!" he shouted, "what the hell are you doing here?"

' "I have come," I said, "to tell you that I know how

the apple gets into the dumpling." And I showed him the automatic.

'He gave a great yell and dashed at the switchboard, turning out the light, so that I could not see to aim. I heard him leap at me – and then there came in the darkness a crash and a splash – and a shriek such as I never heard – not in five years of war – and never want to hear again.

'I groped forward for the switchboard. Of course, I turned on everything before I could lay my hand on the light, but I got it at last – a great white glare from the floodlight over the vat.

'He lay there, still twitching faintly. Cyanide, you see, is about the swiftest and painfullest thing out. Before I could move to do anything, I knew he was dead – poisoned and drowned and dead. The coil of wire that had tripped him had gone into the vat with him. Without thinking, I touched it, and got a shock that pretty well staggered me. Then I realised that I must have turned on the current when I was hunting for the light. I looked into the vat again. As he fell, his dying hands had clutched at the wire. The coils were tight round his fingers, and the current was methodically depositing a film of copper all over his hands, which were blackened with the graphite.

'I had just sense enough to realise that Loder was dead, and that it might be a nasty sort of look-out for me if the thing came out, for I'd certainly gone along to threaten him with a pistol.

'I searched about till I found some solder and an iron. Then I went upstairs and called in Bunter, who had done his ten miles in record time. We went into the smoking-room and soldered the arm of that cursed figure into place again, as well as we could, and then we took everything back into the workshop. We cleaned off every finger-print and removed every trace of our presence. We left the light and the switchboard as they were, and returned to New York by an extremely roundabout route. The only thing we brought away with us was the facsimile of the Consular seal, and that we threw into the river.

'Loder was found by the butler next morning. We read in the papers how he had fallen into the vat when engaged on some experiments in electro-plating. The ghastly fact was commented upon that the dead man's hands were thickly coppered over. They couldn't get it off without irreverent violence, so he was buried like that.

'That's all. Please, Armstrong, may I have my whisky-and-soda now?'

'What happened to the couch?' enquired Smith-Hartington presently.

'I bought it in at the sale of Loder's things,' said Wimsey, 'and got hold of a dear old Catholic priest I knew, to whom I told the whole story under strict vow of secrecy. He was a very sensible and feeling old bird; so one moonlight night Bunter and I carried the thing out in the car to his own little church, some miles out of the city, and gave it Christian burial in a corner of the graveyard. It seemed the best thing to do.'

THE ENTERTAINING EPISODE OF THE
ARTICLE IN QUESTION

The unprofessional detective career of Lord Peter Wimsey was regulated (though the word has no particular propriety in this connection) by a persistent and undignified inquisitiveness. The habit of asking silly questions – natural, though irritating, in the immature male – remained with him long after his immaculate man, Bunter, had become attached to his service to shave the bristles from his chin and see to the due purchase and housing of Napoleon brandies and Villar y Villar cigars. At the age of thirty-two his sister Mary christened him Elephant's Child. It was his idiotic enquiries (before his brother, the Duke of Denver, who grew scarlet with mortification) as to what the Woolsack was really stuffed with that led the then Lord Chancellor idly to investigate the article in question, and to discover, tucked deep within its recesses, that famous diamond necklace of the Marchioness of Writtle, which had disappeared on the day Parliament was opened and been safely secreted by one of the cleaners. It was by a continual and personal badgering of the Chief Engineer at 2LO on the question of 'Why is Oscillation and How is it Done?' that his lordship incidentally unmasked the great Ploffsky gang of Anarchist conspirators, who were accustomed to converse in code by a methodical system of howls, superimposed (to the great annoyance of listeners in British and European stations) upon the London wave-length and duly relayed by 5XX over a radius of some five or six hundred miles. He annoyed persons of more leisure than decorum by suddenly taking into his head to descend to the Underground by way of the stairs, though the only exciting thing he ever actually found there were the bloodstained boots of the Sloane Square murderer; on the other hand when the drains were taken up at Glegg's Folly, it was by hanging about and hindering the plumbers at their job that he accidentally made the discovery which hanged that detestable poisoner, William Girdlestone Chitty.

Accordingly, it was with no surprise at all that the reliable Bunter, one April morning, received the announcement of an abrupt change of plan.

They had arrived at the Gare St Lazare in good time to register the luggage. Their three months' trip to Italy had been purely for enjoyment, and had been followed by a pleasant fortnight in Paris. They were now intending to pay a short visit to the Duc de Sainte-Croix in Rouen on their way back to England. Lord Peter paced the Salle des Pas Perdus for some time, buying an illustrated paper or two and eyeing the crowd. He bent an appreciative eye on a slim, shingled creature with the face of a Paris *gamin*, but was forced to admit to himself that her ankles were a trifle on the thick side; he assisted an elderly lady who was explaining to the bookstall clerk that she wanted a map of Paris and not a *carte postale*, consumed a quick cognac at one of the little green tables at the far end, and then decided he had better go down and see how Bunter was getting on.

In half an hour Bunter and his porter had worked themselves up to the second place in the enormous queue – for, as usual, one of the weighing-machines was out of order. In front of them stood an agitated little group – the young woman Lord Peter had noticed in the Salle des Pas Perdus, a sallow-faced man of about thirty, their porter, and the registration official, who was peering eagerly through his little *guichet*.

'Mais je te répète que je ne les ai pas,' said the sallow man heatedly. 'Voyons, voyons. C'est bien toi qui les as pris, n'est-ce pas? Eh bien, alors, comment veux-tu que je les aie, moi?'

'Mais non, mais non, je te les ai bien donnés là-haut, avant d'aller chercher les journaux.'

'Je t'assure que non. Enfin, c'est évident! J'ai cherché partout, que diable! Tu ne m'as rien donné, du tout, du tout.'

'Mais, puisque je t'ai dit d'aller faire enrégistrer les bagages! Ne faut-il pas que je t'aie bien remis les billets? Me prends-tu pour un imbécile? Va! On n'est pas dépourvu de sens! Mais regarde l'heure! Le train part à 11 h. 20 m. Cherche un peu, au moins.'

'Mais puisque j'ai cherché partout – le gilet, rien! Le jacquet rien, rien! Le pardessus – rien! rien! rien! C'est toi—'

Here the porter, urged by the frantic cries and stamping of the queue, and the repeated insults of Lord Peter's porter, flung himself into the discussion.

'P't-être qu' m'sieur a bouté les billets dans son pantalon,' he suggested.

'Triple idiot!' snapped the traveller, 'je vous le demande – est-ce qu'on a jamais entendu parler de mettre des billets dans son pantalon? Jamais—'

The French porter is a Republican, and, moreover, extremely ill-paid. The large tolerance of his English colleague is not for him.

'Ah!' said he, dropping two heavy bags and looking

round for moral support. 'Vous dîtes? En voilà du joli! Allons, mon p'tit, ce n'est pas parce qu'on porte un faux col qu'on a le droit d'insulter les gens.'

The discussion might have become a full-blown row, had not the young man discovered the missing tickets – incidentally, they were in his trousers-pocket after all – and continued the registration of his luggage, to the undisguised satisfaction of the crowd.

'Bunter,' said his lordship, who had turned his back on the group and was lighting a cigarette, 'I am going to change the tickets. We shall go straight on to London. Have you got that snapshot affair of yours with you?'

'Yes, my lord.'

'The one you can work from your pocket without anyone noticing?'

'Yes, my lord.'

'Get me a picture of those two.'

'Yes, my lord.'

'I will see to the luggage. Wire to the Duc that I am unexpectedly called home.'

'Very good my lord.'

Lord Peter did not allude to the matter again till Bunter was putting his trousers in the press in their cabin on board the *Normannia*, Beyond ascertaining that the young man and woman who had aroused his curiosity were on the boat as second-class passengers, he had sedulously avoided contact with them.

'Did you get that photograph?'

'I hope so, my lord. As your lordship knows, the aim from the breast-pocket tends to be unreliable. I have made three attempts, and trust that one at least may prove to be not unsuccessful.'

'How soon can you develop them?'

'At once, if your lordship pleases. I have all the materials in my suit case,'

'What fun!' said Lord Peter, eagerly tying himself into a pair of mauve silk pyjamas. 'May I hold the bottles and things?'

Mr Bunter poured 3 ounces of water into an 8-ounce measure, and handed his master a glass rod and a minute packet.

'If your lordship would be so good as to stir the contents of the white packet slowly into the water,' he said, bolting the door, 'and, when dissolved, add the contents of the blue packet.'

'Just like a Seidlitz powder,' said his lordship happily. 'Does it fizz?'

'Not much, my lord,' replied the expert, shaking a quantity of hypo crystals into the hand-basin.

'That's a pity,' said Lord Peter. 'I say, Bunter, it's no end of a bore to dissolve.'

'Yes, my lord,' returned Bunter sedately. 'I have always found that part of the process exceptionally tedious, my lord.'

Lord Peter jabbed viciously with the glass rod.

'Just you wait,' he said, in a vindictive tone, 'till we get to Waterloo.'

Three days later Lord Peter Wimsey sat in his book-lined sitting-room at 110A Piccadilly. The tall bunches of daffodils on the table smiled in the spring sunshine, and nodded to the breeze which danced in from the open window. The door opened, and his lordship glanced up from a handsome edition of the Contes de La Fontaine, whose handsome hand-coloured Fragonard plates he was examining with the aid of a lens.

'Morning, Bunter. Anything doing?'

'I have ascertained, my lord, that the young person in question has entered the service of the elder Duchess of Medway. Her name is Célestine Berger.'

'You are less accurate than usual, Bunter. Nobody off the stage is called Célestine. You should say "under the name of Célestine Berger". And the man?'

'He is domiciled at this address in Guildford Street, Bloomsbury, my lord.'

'Excellent, my Bunter. Now give me *Who's Who*. Was it a very tiresome job?'

'Not exceptionally so, my lord.'

'One of these days I suppose I shall give you something to do which you *will* jib at,' said his lordship, 'and you will leave me and I shall cut my throat. Thanks. Run away and play. I shall lunch at the club.'

The book which Bunter had handed his employer indeed bore the words *Who's Who* embossed upon its cover, but it was to be found in no public library and in no bookseller's shop. It was a bulky manuscript, closely filled, in part with the small print-like handwriting of Mr Bunter, in part with Lord Peter's neat and altogether illegible hand. It contained biographies of the most unexpected people, and the most unexpected facts about the most obvious people. Lord Peter turned to a very long entry under the name of the Dowager Duchess of Medway. It appeared to make satisfactory reading, for after a time he smiled, closed the book, and went to the telephone.

'Yes – this is the Duchess of Medway. Who is it?'

The deep, harsh old voice pleased Lord Peter. He could see the imperious face and upright figure of what had been the most famous beauty in the London of the 'sixties.

31

'It's Peter Wimsey, duchess.'

'Indeed, and how do you do, young man? Back from your Continental jaunting?'

'Just home – and longing to lay my devotion at the feet of the most fascinating lady in England.'

'God bless my soul, child, what do you want?' demanded the duchess. 'Boys like you don't flatter an old woman for nothing.'

'I want to tell you my sins, duchess.'

'You should have lived in the great days,' said the voice appreciatively. 'Your talents are wasted on the young fry.'

'That is why I want to talk to you, duchess.'

'Well, my dear, if you've committed any sins worth hearing I shall enjoy your visit.'

'You are as exquisite in kindness as in charm. I am coming this afternoon.'

'I will be at home to you and no one else. There.'

'Dear lady, I kiss your hands,' said Lord Peter, and he heard a deep chuckle as the duchess rang off.

'You may say what you like, duchess,' said Lord Peter from his reverential position on the fender-stool, 'but you are the youngest grandmother in London, not excepting my own mother.'

'Dear Honoria is the merest child,' said the duchess. 'I have twenty years more experience of life, and have arrived at the age when we boast of them. I have every intention of being a great-grandmother before I die. Sylvia is being married in a fortnight's time, to that stupid son of Attenbury's.'

'Abcock?'

'Yes. He keeps the worst hunters I ever saw, and

doesn't know still champagne from sauterne. But Sylvia is stupid, too, poor child, so I dare say they will get on charmingly. In my day one had to have either brains or beauty to get on – preferably both. Nowadays nothing seems to be required but a total lack of figure. But all the sense went out of society with the House of Lords' veto. I except you, Peter. You have talents. It is a pity you do not employ them in politics.'

'Dear lady, God forbid.'

'Perhaps you are right, as things are. There were giants in my day. Dear Dizzy. I remember so well, when his wife died, how hard we all tried to get him – Medway had died the year before – but he was wrapped up in that stupid Bradford woman, who had never even read a line of one of his books, and couldn't have understood 'em if she had. And now we have Abcock standing for Mid-hurst, and married to Sylvia!'

'You haven't invited me to the wedding, duchess dear. I'm so hurt,' sighed his lordship.

'Bless you, child, *I* didn't send out the invitations, but I suppose your brother and that tiresome wife of his will be there. You must come, of course, if you want to. I had no idea you had a passion for weddings.'

'Hadn't you?' said Peter. 'I have a passion for this one. I want to see Lady Sylvia wearing white satin and the family lace and diamonds, and to sentimentalise over the days when my fox-terrier bit the stuffing out of her doll.'

'Very well, my dear, you shall. Come early and give me your support. As for the diamonds, if it weren't a family tradition, Sylvia shouldn't wear them. She has the im-pudence to complain of them.'

'I thought they were some of the finest in existence.'

'So they are. But she says the settings are ugly and old-fashioned, and she doesn't like diamonds, and they won't go with her dress. Such nonsense. Whoever heard of a girl not liking diamonds? She wants to be something romantic and moonshiny in pearls. I have no patience with her.'

'I'll promise to admire them,' said Peter – 'use the privilege of early acquaintance and tell her she's an ass and so on. I'd love to have a view of them. When do they come out of cold storage?'

'Mr Whitehead will bring them up from the Bank the night before,' said the duchess, 'and they'll go into the safe in my room. Come round at twelve o'clock and you shall have a private view of them.'

'That would be delightful. Mind they don't disappear in the night, won't you?'

'Oh, my dear, the house is going to be over-run with policemen. Such a nuisance. I suppose it can't be helped.'

'Oh, I think it's a good thing,' said Peter. 'I have rather an unwholesome weakness for policemen.'

On the morning of the wedding-day, Lord Peter emerged from Bunter's hands a marvel of sleek brilliance. His primrose-coloured hair was so exquisite a work of art that to eclipse it with his glossy hat was like shutting up the sun in a shrine of polished jet; his spats, light trousers, and exquisitely polished shoes formed a tone-symphony in monochrome. It was only by the most impassioned pleading that he persuaded his tyrant to allow him to place two small photographs and a thin, foreign letter in his breast-pocket. Mr Bunter, likewise immaculately attired, stepped into the taxi after him. At noon precisely they were deposited beneath the striped awning which adorned the door of the Duchess of Medway's house in

Park Lane. Bunter promptly disappeared in the direction of the back entrance, while his lordship mounted the steps and asked to see the dowager.

The majority of the guests had not yet arrived, but the house was full of agitated people, flitting hither and thither, with flowers and prayer-books, while a clatter of dishes and cutlery from the dining-room proclaimed the laying of a sumptuous breakfast. Lord Peter was shown into the morning-room while the footman went to announce him, and here he found a very close friend and devoted colleague, Detective-Inspector Parker, mounting guard in plain clothes over a costly collection of white elephants. Lord Peter greeted him with an affectionate handgrip.

'All serene so far?' he enquired.

'Perfectly O.K.'

'You got my note?'

'Sure thing. I've got three of our men shadowing your friend in Guildford Street. The girl is very much in evidence here. Does the old lady's wig and that sort of thing. Bit of a coming-on disposition, isn't she?'

'You surprise me,' said Lord Peter. 'No' – as his friend grinned sardonically – 'you really do. Not seriously? That would throw all my calculations out.'

'Oh, no! Saucy with her eyes and her tongue, that's all.'

'Do her job well?'

'I've heard no complaints. What put you on to this?'

'Pure accident. Of course I may be mistaken.'

'Did you receive any information from Paris?'

'I wish you wouldn't use that phrase,' said Lord Peter peevishly. 'It's so of the Yard – yardy. One of these days it'll give you away.'

'Sorry,' said Parker. 'Second nature, I suppose.'

'Those are the things to beware of,' returned his lordship, with an earnestness that seemed a little out of place. 'One can keep guard on everything but just those second-nature tricks.' He moved across to the window, which overlooked the tradesmen's entrance. 'Hullo!' he said, 'here's our bird.'

Parker joined him, and saw the neat, shingled head of the French girl from the Gare St Lazare, topped by a neat black bandeau and bow. A man with a basket full of white narcissi had rung the bell, and appeared to be trying to make a sale. Parker gently opened the window, and they heard Célestine say with a marked French accent, 'No, nossing today, sank you.' The man insisted in the monotonous whine of his type, thrusting a big bunch of the white flowers upon her, but she pushed them back into the basket with an angry exclamation and flirted away, tossing her head and slapping the door smartly to. The man moved off muttering. As he did so a thin, unhealthy-looking lounger in a check cap detached himself from a lamp-post opposite and mouched along the street after him, at the same time casting a glance up at the window. Mr Parker looked at Lord Peter, nodded, and made a slight sign with his hand. At once the man in the check cap removed his cigarette from his mouth, extinguished it, and, tucking the stub behind his ear, moved off without a second glance.

'Very interesting,' said Lord Peter, when both were out of sight. 'Hark!'

There was a sound of running feet overhead – a cry – and a general commotion. The two men dashed to the door as the bride, rushing frantically downstairs with her bevy of bridesmaids after her, proclaimed in a hysterical shriek: 'The diamonds! They're stolen! They're gone!'

Instantly the house was in an uproar. The servants and the caterers' men crowded into the hall; the bride's father burst out from his room in a magnificent white waistcoat and no coat; the Duchess of Medway descended upon Mr Parker, demanding that something should be done; while the butler, who never to the day of his death got over the disgrace, ran out of the pantry with a corkscrew in one hand and a priceless bottle of crusted port in the other, which he shook with all the vehemence of a town-crier ringing a bell. The only dignified entry was made by the dowager duchess, who came down like a ship in sail, dragging Célestine with her, and admonishing her not to be so silly.

'Be quiet, girl,' said the dowager. 'Anyone would think you were going to be murdered.'

'Allow me, your grace,' said Mr Bunter, appearing suddenly from nowhere in his usual unperturbed manner, and taking the agitated Célestine firmly by the arm. 'Young woman, calm yourself.'

'But what is to be *done*?' cried the bride's mother. 'How did it happen?'

It was at this moment that Detective-Inspector Parker took the floor. It was the most impressive and dramatic moment in his whole career. His magnificent calm rebuked the clamorous nobility surrounding him.

'Your grace,' he said, 'there is no cause for alarm. Our measures have been taken. We have the criminals and the gems, thanks to Lord Peter Wimsey, from whom we received inf—'

'Charles!' said Lord Peter in an awful voice.

'Warning of the attempt. One of our men is just

bringing in the male criminal at the front door, taken red-handed with your grace's diamonds in his possession.' (All gazed round, and perceived indeed the check-capped lounger and a uniformed constable entering with the flower-seller between them.) 'The female criminal, who picked the lock of your grace's safe, is – here! No you don't,' he added, as Célestine, amid a torrent of apache language which nobody, fortunately, had French enough to understand, attempted to whip out a revolver from the bosom of her demure black dress. 'Célestine Berger,' he continued, pocketing the weapon. 'I arrest you in the name of the law, and I warn you that anything you say will be taken down and used as evidence against you.'

'Heaven help us,' said Lord Peter; 'the roof would fly off the court. And you've got the name wrong, Charles. Ladies and gentlemen, allow me to introduce to you Jacques Lerouge, known as Sans-culotte – the youngest and cleverest thief, safe-breaker, and female impersonator that ever occupied a dossier in the Palais de Justice.'

There was a gasp. Jacques Sans-culotte gave vent to a low oath and cocked a *gamin* grimace at Peter.

'C'est parfait,' said he; 'toutes mes félicitations, mi-lord, what you call a fair cop, hein? And now I know him,' he added, grinning at Bunter, 'the so-patient Eng-lishman who stand behind us in the queue at St Lazare. But tell me, please, how you know me, that I may correct it, *next time.*'

'I have mentioned to you before, Charles,' said Lord Peter, 'the unwisdom of falling into habits of speech: They give you away. Now, in France, every male child is brought up to use masculine adjectives about himself. He says: Que *je suis* beau. But a little girl has it rammed home to her that she is female; she must say: Que je suis belle! It must make it beastly hard to be a female impersonator. When I am at a station and I hear an excited young woman say to her companion, "Me prends-tu pour *un* imbécile" – the masculine article arouses curiosity. And that's that!' he concluded briskly. 'The rest was merely a matter of getting Bunter to take a photograph and communicating with our friends of the Sûreté and Scotland Yard.'

Jacques Sans-culotte bowed again.

'Once more I congratulate milord. He is the only Englishman I have ever met who is capable of appreciating our beautiful language. I will pay great attention in future to the article in question.'

With an awful look, the Dowager Duchess of Medway advanced upon Lord Peter.

'Peter,' she said, 'do you mean to say you *knew* about this, and that for the last three weeks you have allowed me to be dressed and undressed and put to bed by a *young man*?'

His lordship had the grace to blush.

'Duchess,' he said humbly, 'on my honour I didn't know absolutely for certain till this morning. And the police were so anxious to have these people caught red-handed. What can I do to show my penitence? Shall I cut the privileged beast to pieces?'

The grim old mouth relaxed a little.

'After all,' said the dowager duchess, with the delightful consciousness that she was going to shock her daughter-in-law, 'there are very few women of my age who could make the same boast. It seems that we die as we have lived, my dear.'

For indeed the Dowager Duches of Medway had been notable in her day.

'You look a little worried, Bunter,' said his lordship kindly to his manservant. 'Is there anything I can do?'

The valet's face brightened as he released his employer's grey trousers from the press.

'Perhaps your lordship could be so good as to think,' he said hopefully, 'of a word in seven letters with S in the middle, meaning two.'

'Also,' suggested Lord Peter thoughtlessly.

'I beg your lordship's pardon. T-w-o. And seven letters.'

'Nonsense!' said Lord Peter. 'How about that bath?'

'It should be just about ready, my lord.'

Lord Peter Wimsey swung his mauve silk legs lightly over the edge of the bed and stretched appreciatively. It was a beautiful June that year. Through the open door he saw the delicate coils of steam wreathing across a shaft of yellow sunlight. Every step he took into the bathroom was a conscious act of enjoyment. In the husky light tenor he carolled a few bars of '*Maman, dîtes-moi.*' Then a thought struck him, and he turned back.

'Bunter!'

'My lord?'

'No bacon this morning. Quite the wrong smell.'

'I was thinking of buttered eggs, my lord.'

'Excellent. Like primroses The Beaconsfield touch,' said his lordship approvingly.

His song died into a rapturous crooning as he settled into the verbena-scented water, His eyes roamed vaguely over the pale blue-and-white tiles of the bathroom walls.

Mr Bunter had retired to the kitchen to put the coffee on the stove when the bell rang. Surprised, he hastened back to the bedroom. It was empty. With increased surprise, he realised that it must have been the bathroom bell. The words 'heart-attack' formed swiftly in his mind, to be displaced by the still more alarming thought, 'No soap.' He opened the door almost nervously.

'Did you ring, my lord?' he demanded of Lord Peter's head, alone visible.

'Yes,' said his lordship abruptly; 'Ambsace.'

'I beg your lordship's pardon?'

'Ambsace. Word of seven letters. Meaning two. With S in the middle. Two aces. Ambsace.'

Bunter's expression became beatified.

'Undoubtedly correct,' he said, pulling a small sheet of paper from his pocket, and entering the word upon it in pencil. 'I am extremely obliged to your lordship. In that case the "indifferent cook in six letters ending with *red*" must be Alfred.'

Lord Peter waved a dismissive hand.

On re-entering his bedroom, Lord Peter was astonished to see his sister Mary seated in his own particular chair and consuming his buttered eggs. He greeted her with a friendly acerbity, demanding why she look him up at that unearthly hour.

'I'm riding with Freddy Arbuthnot,' said her ladyship, 'as you might see by my legs, if you were really as big a Sherlock as you make out.'

'Riding,' replied her brother, 'I had already deduced,

though I admit that Freddy's name was not writ large, to my before-breakfast eye, upon the knees of your breeches. But why this visit?'

'Well, because you were on the way,' said Lady Mary, 'and I'm booked up all day, and I want you to come and dine at the Soviet Club with me tonight.'

'Good God, Mary, why? You know I hate the place. Cooking's beastly, the men don't shave, and the conversation gets my goat. Besides, last time I went there, your friend Goyles plugged me in the shoulder. I thought you'd chucked the Soviet Club.'

'It isn't me. It's Hannah Marryat.'

'What, the intense young woman with the badly bobbed hair and the brogues?'

'Well, she's never been able to afford a good hairdresser. That's just what I want your help about.'

'My dear child, I can't cut her hair for her. Bunter might. He can do most things.'

'Silly. No. But she's got – that is, she used to have – an uncle, the very rich, curmudgeony sort, you know, who never gave anyone a penny. Well, he's dead, and they can't find his will.'

'Perhaps he didn't make one.'

'Oh, yes, he did. He wrote and told her so. But the nasty old thing hid it, and it can't be found.'

'Is the will in her favour?'

'Yes.'

'Who's the next of kin?'

'She and her mother are the only members of the family left.'

'Well, then, she's only got to sit tight and she'll get the goods.'

'No – because the horrid old man left two wills, and, if

she can't find the latest one, they'll prove the first one. He explained that to her carefully.'

'Oh. I see. H'm. By the way I thought the young woman was a Socialist.'

'Oh, she is. Terrifically so. One really can't help admiring her. She has done some wonderful work—'

'Yes, I dare say. But in that case I don't see why she need be so keen on getting uncle's dollars.'

Mary began to chuckle.

'Ah! but that's where Uncle Meleager—'

'Uncle *what*?'

'Meleager. That's his name. Meleager Finch.'

'Oh!'

'Yes – well, that's where he's been so clever. Unless she finds the new will, the old will comes into force and hands over every penny of the money to the funds of the Primrose League.'

Lord Peter gave a little yelp of joy.

'Good for Uncle Meleager! But, look here, Mary, I'm a Tory, if anything. I'm certainly not a Red. Why should I help to snatch the good gold from the Primrose Leaguers and hand it over to the Third International? Uncle Meleager's a sport. I take to Uncle Meleager.'

'Oh, but Peter, I really don't think she'll do that with it. Not at present, anyway. They're awfully poor, and her mother ought to have some frightfully difficult operation or something, and go and live abroad, so it really is ever so important they should get the money. And perhaps Hannah wouldn't be quite so Red if she'd ever had a bean of her own. Besides, you could make it a condition of helping her that she should go and get properly shingled at Bresil's.'

'You are a very cynically-minded person,' said his lordship. 'However, it would be fun to have a go at

Uncle M. Was he obliging enough to give any clues for finding the will?'

'He wrote a funny sort of letter, which we can't make head or tail of. Come to the club tonight and she'll show it to you.'

'Right-ho! Seven o'clock do? And we could go on and see a show afterwards. Do you mind clearing out now? I'm going to get dressed.'

Amid a deafening babble of voices in a low-pitched cellar, the Soviet Club meets and dines. Ethics and sociology, the latest vortices of the Whirligig school of verse, combine with the smoke of countless cigarettes to produce an inspissated atmosphere, through which flat, angular mural paintings dimly lower upon the revellers. There is painfully little room for the elbows, or indeed for any part of one's body. Lord Peter – his feet curled under his chair to avoid the stray kicks of the heavy brogues opposite him – was acutely conscious of an unbecoming attitude and an overheated feeling about the head. He found it difficult to get any response from Hannah Marryat. Under her heavy ill-cut fringe her dark eyes gloomed sombrely at him. At the same time he received a strong impression of something enormously vital. He had a sudden fancy that if she were set free from self-defensiveness and the importance of being earnest, she would exhibit unexpected powers of enjoyment. He was interested, but oppressed. Mary, to his great relief, suggested that they should have their coffee upstairs.

They found a quiet corner with comfortable chairs.

'Well, now,' said Mary encouragingly.

'Of course you understand,' said Miss Marryat mournfully, 'that if it were not for the monstrous injustice of

Uncle Meleager's other will, and mother being so ill, I shouldn't take any steps. But when there is £250,000, and the prospect of doing real good with it—'

'Naturally,' said Lord Peter, 'it isn't the money you care about, as the dear old bromide says, it's the principle of the thing. Right you are! Now supposin' we have a look at Uncle Meleager's letter.'

Miss Marryat rummaged in a very large handbag and passed the paper over.

This was Uncle Meleager's letter, dated from Sienna twelve months previously:

'My dear Hannah, – When I die – which I propose to do at my own convenience and not at that of my family – you will at last discover my monetary worth. It is, of course, considerably less than you had hoped, and quite fails, I assure you, adequately to represent my actual worth in the eyes of the discerning. I made my will yesterday, leaving the entire sum, such as it is, to the Primrose League – a body quite as fatuous as any other in our preposterous state, but which has the advantage of being peculiarly obnoxious to yourself. This will will be found in the safe in the library.

'I am not, however, unmindful of the fact that your mother is my sister, and you and she my only surviving relatives. I shall accordingly amuse myself by drawing up today a second will, superseding the other and leaving the money to you.

'I have always held that woman is a frivolous animal. A woman who pretends to be serious is wasting her time and spoiling her appearance. I consider that you have wasted your time to a really shocking extent. Accordingly, I intend to conceal this will, and that in

45

such a manner that you will certainly never find it unless by the exercise of a sustained frivolity.

'I hope you will contrive to be frivolous enough to become the heiress of your affectionate

'UNCLE MELEAGER'

'Couldn't we use that letter as proof of the testator's intention, and fight the will?' asked Mary anxiously.

''Fraid not,' said Lord Peter. 'You see, there's no evidence here that the will was ever actually drawn up. Though I suppose we could find the witnesses.'

'We've tried,' said Miss Marryat, 'but, as you see, Uncle Meleager was travelling abroad at the time, and he probably got some obscure people in some obscure Italian town to witness it for him. We advertised, but got no answer.'

'H'm. Uncle Meleager doesn't seem to have left things to chance. And, anyhow, wills are queer things, and so are the probate and divorce wallahs. Obviously the thing to do is to find the other will. Did the clues he speaks of turn up among his papers?'

'We hunted through everything. And, of course, we had the whole house searched from top to bottom for the will. But it was quite useless.'

'You've not destroyed anything, of course. Who were the executors of the Primrose League will?'

'Mother and Mr Sands, Uncle Meleager's solicitor. The will left mother a silver teapot for her trouble.'

'I like Uncle Meleager more and more. Anyhow, he did the sporting thing. I'm beginnin' to enjoy this case like anything. Where did Uncle Meleager hang out?'

'It's an old house down at Dorking. It's rather quaint. Somebody had a fancy to build a little Roman villa sort of thing there, with a verandah behind, with columns and a pond in the front hall, and statues. It's very decent there just now, though it's awfully cold in the winter, with all those stone floors and stone stairs and the skylight over the hall! Mother said perhaps you would be very kind and come down and have a look at it.'

'I'd simply love to. Can we start tomorrow? I promise you we'll be frivolous enough to please even Uncle Meleager, if you'll do your bit, Miss Marryat. Won't we, Mary?'

'Rather! And, I say, hadn't we better be moving if we're going to the Pallambra?'

'I never go to music halls,' said Miss Marryat ungraciously.

'Oh, but you must come tonight,' said his lordship persuasively. 'It's so frivolous. Just think how it would please Uncle Meleager.'

Accordingly, the next day found the party, including the indispensable Mr Bunter, assembled at Uncle Meleager's house. Pending the settlement of the will question, there had seemed every reason why Mr Finch's executrix and next-of-kin should live in the house, thus providing every facility for what Lord Peter called the 'Treasure-hunt'. After being introduced to Mrs Marryat, who was an invalid and remained in her room, Lady Mary and her brother were shown over the house by Miss Marryat, who explained to them how carefully the search had been conducted. Every paper had been examined, every book in the library scrutinised page by page, the walls and chimneys tapped for hiding-places, the boards taken up, and so forth, but with no result.

'Y'know,' said his lordship, 'I'm sure you've been going the wrong way to work. My idea is, old Uncle

Meleager was a man of his word. If he said frivolous, he meant really frivolous. Something beastly silly. I wonder what it was.'

He was still wondering when he went up to dress. Bunter was putting studs in his shirt. Lord Peter gazed thoughtfully at him, and then enquired:

'Are any of Mr Finch's old staff still here?'

'Yes, my lord. The cook and the housekeeper. Wonderful old gentleman they say he was, too. Eighty-three, but as up-to-date as you please. Had his wireless in his bedroom, and enjoyed the Savoy bands every night of his life. Followed his politics, and was always ready with the details of the latest big law-cases. If a young lady came to see him, he'd like to see she had her hair shingled and the latest style in fashions. They say he took up cross-words as soon as they came in, and was remarkably quick at solving them, my lord, and inventing them. Took a £10 prize in the *Daily Yell* for one, and was wonderfully pleased to get it, they say, my lord, rich as he was.'

'Indeed.'

'Yes, my lord. He was a great man for acrostics before that, I understood them to say, but, when cross-words came in, he threw away his acrostics and said he liked the new game better. Wonderfully adaptable, if I may say so, he seems to have been for an old gentleman.'

'Was he, by Jove?' said his lordship absently, and then, with sudden energy:

'Bunter, I'd like to double your salary, but I suppose you'd take it as an insult.'

The conversation bore fruit at dinner.

'What,' enquired his lordship, 'happened to Uncle Meleager's cross-words?'

'Cross-words?' said Hannah Marryat, knitting her

heavy brows. 'Oh, those puzzle things! Poor old man, he went mad over them. He had every newspaper sent him, and in his last illness he'd be trying to fill the wretched things in. It was worse than his acrostics and his jig-saw puzzles. Poor old creature, he must have been senile, I'm afraid. Of course, we looked through them, but there wasn't anything there. We put them all in the attic.'

'The attic for me,' said Lord Peter.

'And for me,' said Mary. 'I don't believe there was anything senile about Uncle Meleager.'

The evening was warm, and they had dined in the little viridarium at the back of the house, with its tall vases and hanging baskets of flowers and little marble statues.

'Is there an attic here?' said Peter. 'It seems such a – well, such an un-attic thing to have in a house like this.'

'It's just a horrid, poky little hole over the porch,' said Miss Marryat, rising and leading the way. 'Don't tumble into the pond, will you? It's a great nuisance having it there, especially at night. I always tell them to leave a light on.'

Lord Peter glanced into the miniature impluvium, with its tiling of red, white, and black marble.

'That's not a very classic design,' he observed.

'No. Uncle Meleager used to complain about it and say he must have it altered. There was a proper one once, I believe, but it got damaged, and the man before Uncle Meleager had it replaced by some local idiot. He built three bay windows out of the dining-room at the same time, which made it very much lighter and pleasanter, of course, but it looks awful. Now, this tiling is all right; uncle put that in himself.'

She pointed to a mosaic dog at the threshold, with the

motto, 'Cave canem,' and Lord Peter recognised it as a copy of a Pompeian original.

A narrow stair brought them to the 'attic', where the Wimseys flung themselves with enthusiasm upon a huge heap of dusty old newspapers and manuscripts. The latter seemed the likelier field, so they started with them. They consisted of a quantity of cross-words in manuscript – presumably the children of Uncle Meleager's own brain. The square, the list of definitions, and the solution were in every case neatly pinned together. Some (early efforts, no doubt) were childishly simple, but others were difficult, with allusive or punning clues; some of the ordinary newspaper type, others in the form of rhymed distichs. They scrutinised the solutions closely, and searched the definitions for acrostics or hidden words, unsuccessfully for a long time.

'This one's a funny one,' said Mary, 'nothing seems to fit. Oh! it's two pinned together. No, it isn't – yes, it is – it's only been pinned up wrong. Peter, have you seen the puzzle belonging to these clues anywhere?'

'What one's that?'

'Well, it's numbered rather funnily, with Roman and Arabic numerals, and it starts off with a thing that hasn't got any numbers at all:

'Truth, poor girl, was nobody's daughter;
She took off her clothes and jumped into the water.'

'Frivolous old wretch!' said Miss Marryat.

'Friv – here, gimme that!' cried Lord Peter. 'Look here, I say, Miss Marryat, you oughtn't to have overlooked this.'

'I thought it just belonged to that other square.'

'Not it. It's different. I believe it's our thing. Listen:

> 'Your expectation to be rich
> Here will reach its highest pitch.

That's one for you, Miss Marryat. Mary, hunt about. We *must* find the square that belongs to this.'

But, though they turned everything upside-down, they could find no square with Roman and Arabic numerals.

'Hang it all!' said Peter, 'it must be made to fit one of these others. Look! I know what he's done. He's just taken a fifteen-letter square, and numbered it with Roman figures one way and Arabic the other. I bet its fits into that one it was pinned up with.'

But the one it was pinned up with turned out to have only thirteen squares.

'Dash it all,' said his lordship, 'we'll have to carry the whole lot down, and work away at it till we find the one it *does* fit.'

He snatched up a great bundle of newspapers, and led the way out. The others followed, each with an armful. The search had taken some time, and the atrium was in semi-darkness.

'Where shall I take them?' asked Lord Peter, calling back over his shoulder.

'Hi!' cried Mary; and, 'Look where you're going!' cried her friend.

They were too late. A splash and a flounder proclaimed that Lord Peter had walked, like Johnny Head-in-Air, over the edge of the impluvium, papers and all.

'You ass!' said Mary.

His lordship scrambled out, spluttering, and Hannah Marryat suddenly burst out into the first laugh Peter had ever heard her give.

'Truth, they say, was nobody's daughter,
   She took off her clothes and fell into the water'

she proclaimed.

'Well, I couldn't take my clothes off with you here, could I?' grumbled Lord Peter. 'We'll have to fish out the papers. I'm afraid they've got a bit damp.'

Miss Marryat turned on the lights, and they started to clear the basin.

'Truth, poor girl –' began Lord Peter, and suddenly, with a little shriek, began to dance on the marble edge of the impluvium.

'One, two, three, four, five, six—'

'Quite, quite demented,' said Mary. 'How shall I break it to mother?'

'Thirteen, fourteen, *fifteen*!' cried his lordship, and sat down, suddenly and damply, exhausted by his own excitement.

'Feeling better?' asked his sister acidly.

'I'm well. I'm all right. Everything's all right. I *love* Uncle Meleager. Fifteen squares each way. Look at it. *Look* at it. The truth's in the water. Didn't he say so. Oh, frabjous day! Calloo! callay! I chortle. Mary, what became of those definitions?'

'They're in your pocket, all damp,' said Mary.

Lord Peter snatched them out hurriedly.

'It's all right, they haven't run,' he said. 'Oh, *darling* Uncle Meleager. Can you drain the impluvium, Miss Marryat, and find a bit of charcoal. Then I'll get some dry clothes on and we'll get down to it. Don't you see? *There's* your missing cross-word square – on the floor of the impluvium!'

It took, however, some time to get the basin emptied, and it was not till next morning that the party, armed with sticks of charcoal, squatted down in the empty impluvium to fill in Uncle Meleager's cross-word on the marble tiles. Their first difficulty was to decide whether the red squares counted as stops or had to be filled in, but, after a few definitions had been solved, the construction of the puzzle grew apace. The investigators grew steadily hotter and more thickly covered with charcoal, while the attentive Mr Bunter hurried to and fro between the atrium and the library, and the dictionaries piled up on the edge of the impluvium.

'Truth, poor girl, was nobody's daughter;
She took off her clothes and jumped into the water.'

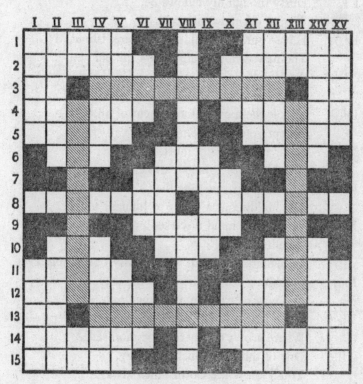

Across.

I.1.   Foolish or wise, yet one remains alone,
          'Twixt Strength and Justice on a heavenly throne.

XI.1.   O to what ears the chink of gold was sweet!
          The greed for treasure brought him but defeat.

'That's a hint to us,' said Lord Peter.

I.2.   One drop of vinegar to two of oil
          Dresses this curly head sprung from the soil.

X.2.   Nothing itself, it needs but little more
          To be that nothingness the Preacher saw.

I.3.   Dusty though my fellows be,
          We are a kingly company.

IV.3.   Have your own will, though here, I hold,
          The new is *not* a patch upon the old.

XIV.3.   Any loud cry would do as well,
          Or so the poet's verses tell.

I.4.   This is the most unkindest cut of all,
          Except your skill be mathematical.

X.4.   Little and hid from mortal sight.
          I darkly work to make all light.

I.5.   The need for this (like that it's cut off short)
          The building of a tower to humans taught.

XI.5.   'More than mind discloses and more than men
             believe'
          (A definition by man whom Pussyfoot doth grieve).

II.6.   Backward observe her turn her way,
          The way of wisdom, wise men say.

VII 6.   Grew long ago by river's edge
          Where grows to-day the common sedge.

XII.6.   One of three by which, they say,
          You'll know the Cornishmen alway.

VI.7. Blow upon blow; five more the vanquished Roman
          shows;
       And if the foot slip one, on crippled feet one goes.

I.8.   By this Jew's work the whole we find,
       In a glass clearly, darkly in the mind.

IX.8. Little by little see it grow
       Till cut off short by hammer-blow.

VI.9. Watch him go, heel and toe,
       Across the wide Karroo!

II.10. In expectation to be rich
       Here you reach the highest pitch.

VII.10. Of this, concerning nothing, much—
       Too often do we hear of such!

XII.10. O'er land and sea, passing on deadly wings,
       Pain to the strong, to weaklings death it brings.

I.11. Requests like these, however long they be,
       Stop just too soon for common courtesy.

XI.11. Caesar, the living dead salute thee here,
       Facing for thy delight tooth, claw, and spear.

I.12. One word had served, but he in ranting vein
       'Lend me your ears' must mouth o'er Caesar
          slain.

X.12. Helical circumvolution
       Adumbrates correct solution.

I.13. One that works for Irish men
       Both by word and deed and pen.

'That's an easy one,' said Miss Marryat.

IV.13. Seven out of twelve this number makes complete
       As the sun journeys on from seat to seat.

XIV.13. My brothers play with planets; Cicero,
       Master of words, my master is below.

I.14.   Free of her jesses let the falcon fly,
           With sight undimmed into the azure sky.

X.14.   And so you dine with Borgia? Let me lend
           You this as a precaution, my poor friend.

I.15.   Friendship carried to excess
           Got him in a horrid mess.

XI.15.   Smooth and elastic and, I guess,
           The dearest treasure you possess.

Down

1.I.   If step by step the Steppes you wander through
           Many of those in this, of these in those you'll
              view.

'Bunter,' said Lord Peter, 'bring me a whisky-and-soda!'

11.I.   If me without my head you do,
           Then generously my head renew,
           Or put it to my hinder end—
           Your cheer it shall nor may nor mend.

1.II.   Quietly, quietly, 'twixt edge and edge,
           Do this unto the thin end of the wedge.

10.II.   'Something that hath a reference to my state?'
           Just as you like, it shall be written straight.

1.III.   When all is read, then give the world its due,
           And never need the world read this of you.

'That's a comfort,' said Lady Mary. 'It shows we're on the right lines.'

4.III.   Sing Nunc Dimittis and Magnificat—
           But look a little farther back than that.

14.III.   Here in brief epitome
           Attribute of royalty.

1.IV.   Lo! at a glance
          The Spanish gipsy and her dance.

10.IV.   Bring me skin and a needle or a stick—
          A needle does it slowly, a stick does it quick.

1.V.   It was a brazen business when
          King Phalaris made these for men.

11.V.   This king (of whom not much is known),
          By Heaven's mercy was o'erthrown.

2.VI.   'Bid 'ov και μη 'ov farewell?' Nay, in this
          The sterner Roman stands by that which is.

7.VI.   This the termination is
          Of many minds' activities.

12.VI.   I mingle on Norwegian shore,
          With ebbing water's backward roar.

6.VII.   I stand, a ladder to renown,
          Set 'twixt the stars and Milan town.

1.VIII.   Highest and lowliest both to me lay claim,
          The little hyssop and the king of fame.

'That makes that point about the squares clear,' said Mary.
'I think it's even more significant,' said her brother.

9.VIII.   This sensible old man refused to tread
          The path to Hades in a youngster's stead.

6.IX.   Long since, at Nature's call, they let it drop,
          Thoughtlessly thoughtful for our next year's
               crop.

2.X.   To smallest words great speakers greatness give;
          Here Rome propounded her alternative.

7.X.   We heap up many with toil and trouble,
          And find that the whole of our gain is a bubble.

12.X.   Add it among the hidden things—
          A fishy tale to light it brings.

1.XI.   'Lions,' said a Gallic critic, 'are not these.'
Benevolent souls – they'd make your heart's blood
   freeze.

11.XI.   An epithet for husky fellows.
That stand, all robed in greens and yellows.

1.XII.   Whole without holes behold me here,
My meaning should be wholly clear.

10.XII.   Running all around, never setting foot to floor,
If there isn't one in this room, there may be one next
   door.

1.XIII.   Ye gods! think also of that goddess' name
Whose might two hours on end the mob proclaim.

4.XIII.   The Priest uplifts his voice on high,
The choristers make their reply.

14.XIII.   When you've guessed it, with one voice
You'll say it was a golden choice.

1.XIV.   Shall learning die amid a war's alarms?
I, at my birth, was clasped in iron arms.

10.XIV.   At sunset see the labourer now
Loose all his oxen from the plough.

1.XV.   Without a miracle it cannot be—
At this point, Solver, bid him pray for thee!

11.XV.   Two thousand years ago and more
(Just as we do to-day),
The Romans saw these distant lights—
But, oh? How hard the way!

The most remarkable part of the search – or so Lord
Peter thought – was its effect on Miss Marryat. At first
she hovered disconsolately on the margin, aching with
wounded dignity, yet ashamed to dissociate herself from
people who were toiling so hard and so cheerfully in her
cause.

'I think that's so-and-so,' Mary would say hopefully.

And her brother would reply enthusiastically, 'Holed it in one, old lady. Good for you! We've got it this time, Miss Marryat' – and explain it.

And Hannah Marryat would say with a snort:

'That's just the childish kind of joke Uncle Meleager *would* make.'

Gradually, however, the fascination of seeing the squares fit together caught her, and, when the first word appeared which showed that the searchers were definitely on the right track, she lay down flat on the floor and peered over Lord Peter's shoulder as he grovelled below, writing letters in charcoal, rubbing them out with his handkerchief and mopping his heated face, till the Moor of Venice had nothing on him in the matter of blackness. Once, half scornfully, half timidly, she made a suggestion; twice, she made a suggestion; the third time she had an inspiration. The next minute she was down in the mêlée, crawling over the tiles flushed and excited, wiping important letters out with her knees as fast as Peter could write them in, poring over the pages of Roget, her eyes gleaming under her tumbled black fringe.

Hurried meals of cold meat and tea sustained the exhausted party, and towards sunset Peter, with a shout of triumph, added the last letter to the square.

They crawled out and looked at it.

'All the words can't be clues,' said Mary. 'I think it must be just those four.'

'Yes, undoubtedly. It's quite clear. We've only got to look it up. Where's a Bible?'

Miss Marryat hunted it out from the pile of reference books. 'But that isn't the name of a Bible book,' she said. 'It's those things they have at evening service.'

'That's all you know,' said Lord Peter. 'I was brought up religious, I was. It's Vulgate, that's what that is. You're quite right, of course, but, as Uncle Meleager says, we must "look a little further back than that". Here you are. Now, then.'

'But it doesn't say what chapter.'

'So it doesn't. I mean, nor it does.'

'And, anyhow, all the chapters are too short.'

'Damn! Oh! Here, suppose we just count right on from the beginning – one, two, three—'

'Seventeen in chapter one, eighteen, nineteen – this must be it.'

Two fair heads and one dark one peered excitedly at the small print, Bunter hovering decorously on the outskirts.

'O my dove, that art in the clefts of the rock, in the covert of the steep place.'

'Oh, dear!' said Mary, disappointed, 'that does sound rather hopeless. Are you sure you've counted right? It might mean *anything*.'

Lord Peter scratched his head.

'This is a bit of a blow,' he said. 'I don't like Uncle Meleager half as much as I did. Old beast!'

'After all our work!' moaned Mary.

'It must be right,' cried Miss Marryat. 'Perhaps there's some kind of an anagram in it. We can't give up now!'

'Bravo!' said Lord Peter. 'That's the spirit. 'Fraid we're in for another outburst of frivolity, Miss Marryat.'

'Well, it's been great fun,' said Hannah Marryat.

'If you will excuse me,' began the deferential voice of Bunter.

'I'd forgotten you, Bunter,' said his lordship. 'Of

course you can put us right – you always can. Where have we gone wrong?'

'I was about to observe, my lord, that the words you mention do not appear to agree with my recollection of the passage in question. In my mother's Bible, my lord, it ran, I fancy, some-what differently.'

Lord Peter closed the volume and looked at the back of it.

'Naturally,' he said, 'you are right again, of course. This is a Revised Version. It's your fault, Miss Marryat. You *would* have a Revised Version. But can we imagine Uncle Meleager with one? No. Bring me Uncle Meleager's Bible.'

'Come and look in the library,' cried Miss Marryat, snatching him by the hand and running. 'Don't be so dreadfully calm.'

On the centre of the library table lay a huge and venerable Bible – reverend in age and tooled leather binding. Lord Peter's hands caressed it, for a noble old book was like a song to his soul. Sobered by its beauty, they turned the yellow pages over.'

'In the clefts of the rocks, in the secret places of the stairs.'

'Miss Marryat,' said his lordship, 'if your Uncle's will is not concealed in the staircase, then – well, all I can say is, he's played a rotten trick on us,' he concluded lamely.

'Shall we try the main staircase, or the little one up to the porch?'

'Oh, the main one, I think. I hope it won't mean pulling it down. No. Somebody would have noticed if Uncle Meleager had done anything drastic in that way. It's probably quite a simple hiding-place. Wait a minute. Let's ask the housekeeper.'

Mrs Meakers was called, and perfectly remembered that about nine months previously Mr Finch had pointed out to her a 'kind of a crack like' on the under surface of the staircase, and had had a man in to fill it up. Certainly, she could point out the exact place. There was the mark of the plaster filling quite clear.

'Hurray!' cried Lord Peter. 'Bunter – a chisel or something. Uncle Meleager, Uncle Meleager, we've *got* you! Miss Marryat, I think yours should be the hand to strike the blow. It's your staircase, you know – at least, if we find the will, so if any destruction has to be done it's up to you.'

Breathless they stood round, while with a few blows the new plaster flaked off, disclosing a wide chink in the stonework. Hannah Marryat flung down hammer and chisel and groped in the gap.

'There's something,' she gasped. 'Lift me up; I can't reach. Oh, it is! it is; it *is* it!' And she withdrew her hand, grasping a long, sealed envelope, bearing the superscription:

Positively the LAST Will and Testament of Meleager Finch

Miss Marryat gave a yodel of joy and flung her arms round Lord Peter's neck.

Mary executed a joy-dance. 'I'll tell the world,' she proclaimed.

'Come and tell mother!' cried Miss Marryat.

Mr Bunter interposed.

'Your lordship will excuse me,' he said firmly, 'but your lordship's face is all over charcoal.'

'Black but comely,' said Lord Peter, 'but I submit to

your reproof. How clever we've all been. How topping everything is. How rich you are going to be. How late it is and how hungry I am. Yes, Bunter, I will wash my face. Is there anything else I can do for anybody while I feel in the mood?'

'If your lordship would he so kind,' said Mr Bunter, producing a small paper from his pocket, 'I should be grateful if you could favour me with a South African quadruped in six letters, beginning with Q.'

NOTE: *The solution of the cross-word will be found at the end of the book.*

THE FANTASTIC HORROR OF THE
CAT IN THE BAG

The Great North Road wound away like a flat, steel-grey ribbon. Up it, with the sun and wind behind them, two black specks moved swiftly. To the yokel in charge of the hay-waggon they were only two of 'they dratted motor-cyclists', as they barked and zoomed past him in rapid succession. A little farther on, a family man, driving delicately with a two-seater side-car, grinned as the sharp rattle of the o.h.v. Norton was succeeded by the feline shriek of an angry Scott Flying-Squirrel. He, too, in bachelor days, had taken a side in that perennial feud. He sighed regretfully as he watched the racing machines dwindle away northwards.

At that abominable and unexpected S-bend across the bridge above Hatfield, the Norton man, in the pride of his heart, turned to wave a defiant hand at his pursuer. In that second, the enormous bulk of a loaded charabanc loomed down upon him from the bridgehead. He wrenched himself away from it in a fierce wobble, and the Scott, cornering melodramatically, with left and right foot-rests alternately skimming the tarmac, gained a few triumphant yards. The Norton leapt forward with wide-open throttle. A party of children, seized with sudden panic, rushed helter-skelter across the road. The Scott lurched through them in drunken swerves. The road was clear, and the chase settled down once more.

It is not known why motorists, who sing the joys of the

open road, spend so much petrol every weekend grinding their way to Southend and Brighton and Margate, in the stench of each other's exhausts, one hand on the horn and one foot on the brake, their eyes starting from their orbits in the nerve-racking search for cops, corners, blind turnings, and cross-road suicides. They ride in a baffled fury, hating each other. They arrive with shattered nerves and fight for parking places. They return, blinded by the headlights of fresh arrivals, whom they hate even worse than they hate each other. And all the time the Great North Road winds away like a long, flat, steel-grey ribbon – a surface like a race-track, without traps, without hedges, without side-roads, and without traffic. True, it leads to nowhere in particular; but, after all, one pub is very much like another.

The tarmac reeled away, mile after mile. The sharp turn to the right at Baldock, the involute intricacies of Biggleswade, with its multiplication of sign-posts, gave temporary check, but brought the pursuer no nearer. Through Tempsford at full speed, with blowing horn and exhaust, then, screaming like a hurricane past the R.A.C. post where the road forks in from Bedford. The Norton rider again glanced back; the Scott rider again sounded his horn ferociously. Flat as a chessboard, dyke and field revolved about the horizon.

The constable at Eaton Socon was by no means an anti-motor fiend. In fact, he had just alighted from his push-bike to pass the time of day with the A.A. man on point duty at the cross-roads. But he was just and God-fearing. The sight of two maniacs careering at seventy miles an hour into his protectorate was more than he could be expected to countenance – the more, that the local magistrate happened to be passing at that very moment in a pony-trap. He advanced to the middle of the road, spreading his arms in a majestic manner. The Norton rider looked, saw the road beyond complicated by the pony-trap and a traction-engine, and resigned himself to the inevitable. He flung the throttle-lever back, stamped on his squealing brakes, and skidded to a standstill. The Scott, having had notice, came up mincingly, with a voice like a pleased kitten.

'Now, then,' said the constable, in a tone of reproof, 'ain't you got no more sense than to come drivin' into the town at a 'undred miles an hour. This ain't Brooklands, you know. I never see anything like it. 'Ave to take your names and numbers, if *you* please. You'll bear witness, Mr Nadgett, as they was doin' over eighty.'

The A.A. man, after a swift glance over the two sets of handlebars to assure himself that the black sheep were not of his flock, said, with an air of impartial accuracy. 'About sixty-six and a half, I should say, if you was to ask me in court.'

'Look here, you blighter,' said the Scott man indignantly to the Norton man, 'why the hell couldn't you stop when you heard me hoot? I've been chasing you with your beastly bag nearly thirty miles. Why can't you look after your own rotten luggage?'

He indicated a small, stout bag, tied with string to his own carrier.

'That?' said the Norton man, with scorn. 'What do you mean? It's not mine. Never saw it in my life.'

This bare-faced denial threatened to render the Scott rider speechless.

'Of all the –' he gasped. 'Why, you crimson idiot, I saw it fall off, just the other side of Hatfield. I yelled and blew like fury. I suppose that overhead gear of yours makes so

66

much noise you can't hear anything else. I take the trouble to pick the thing up, and go after you, and all you do is to race off like a lunatic and run me into a cop. Fat lot of thanks one gets for trying to be decent to fools on the road.'

'That ain't neither here nor there,' said the policeman. 'Your licence, please, sir.'

'Here you are,' said the Scott man, ferociously flapping out his pocket-book. 'My name's Walters, and it's the last time I'll try to do anybody a good turn, you can lay your shirt.'

'Walters,' said the constable, entering the particulars laboriously in his note-book, 'and Simpkins. You'll 'ave your summonses in doo course. It'll be for about a week 'ence, on Monday or thereabouts, I shouldn't wonder.'

'Another forty bob gone west,' growled Mr Simpkins, toying with his throttle. 'Oh, well, can't be helped, I suppose'

'Forty bob?' snorted the constable. 'What do *you* think? Furious driving to the common danger, that's wot it is. You'll be lucky to get off with five quid apiece.'

'Oh, blast!' said the other, stamping furiously on the kick-starter. The engine roared into life, but Mr Walters dexterously swung his machine across the Norton's path.

'Oh, no, you don't,' he said viciously. 'You jolly well take your bleeding bag, and no nonsense. I tell you, I *saw* it fall off.'

'Now, no language,' began the constable, when he suddenly became aware that the A.A. man was staring in a very odd manner at the bag and making signs to him.

''Ullo,' he demanded, 'wot's the matter with the – bleedin' bag did you say? 'Ere, I'd like to 'ave a look at that 'ere bag, sir, if you don't mind.'

'It's nothing to do with me,' said Mr Walters, handing it over. 'I saw it fall off and –' His voice died away in his throat, and his eyes became fixed upon one corner of the bag, where something damp and horrible was seeping darkly through.

'Did you notice this 'ere corner when you picked it up?' asked the constable. He prodded it gingerly and looked at his fingers.

'I don't know – no – not particularly,' stammered Walters. 'I didn't notice anything. I – I expect it burst when it hit the road.'

The constable probed the split seam in silence, and then turned hurriedly round to wave away a couple of young women who had stopped to stare. The A.A. man peered curiously, and then started back with a sensation of sickness.

'Ow, Gawd!' he gasped. 'It's curly – it's a woman's.'

'It's not me,' screamed Simpkins. 'I swear to heaven it's not mine. This man's trying to put it across me.'

'Me?' gasped Walters. 'Me? Why you filthy, murdering brute, I tell you I saw it fall off your carrier. No wonder you blinded off when you saw me coming. Arrest him, constable. Take him away to prison—'

'Hullo, officer!' said a voice behind them. 'What's all the excitement? you haven't seen a motor-cyclist go by with a little bag on his carrier, I suppose?'

A big open car with an unnaturally long bonnet had slipped up to them, silent as an owl. The whole agitated party with one accord turned upon the driver.

'Would this be it, sir?'

The motorist pushed off his goggles, disclosing a long, narrow nose and a pair of rather cynical-looking grey eyes.

'It looks rather –' he began; and then, catching sight of the horrid relic protruding from one corner, 'In God's name, he enquired, 'what's that?'

'That's what we'd like to know, sir,' said the constable grimly.

'H'm,' said the motorist, 'I seem to have chosen an uncommonly suitable moment for enquirin' after my bag. Tactless. To say now that it is not my bag is simple, though in no way convincing. As a matter of fact, it is not mine, and I may say that, if it had been, I should not have been at any pains to pursue it.'

The constable scratched his head.

'Both these gentlemen –' he began.

The two cyclists burst into simultaneous and heated disclaimers. By this time a small crowd had collected, which the A.A. scout helpfully tried to shoo away.

'You'll all 'ave to come with me to the station,' said the harassed constable. 'Can't stand 'ere 'oldin' up the traffic. No tricks, now. You wheel them bikes, and I'll come in the car with you, sir.'

'But supposing I was to let her rip and kidnap you,' said the motorist, with a grin. 'Where'd you be? Here,' he added, turning to the A.A. man, 'can you handle this outfit?'

'You bet,' said the scout, his eye running lovingly over the long sweep of the exhaust and the rakish lines of the car.

'Right. Hop in. Now, officer, you can toddle along with the other suspects and keep an eye on them. Wonderful head I've got for detail. By the way, that foot-brake's on the fierce side. Don't bully it, or you'll surprise yourself.'

The lock of the bag was forced at the police-station in

the midst of an excitement unparalleled in the calm annals of Eaton Socon, and the dreadful contents laid reverently upon a table. Beyond a quantity of cheese-cloth in which they had been wrapped, there was nothing to supply any clue to the mystery.

'Now,' said the superintendent, 'what do you gentlemen know about this?'

'Nothing whatever,' said Mr Simpkins, with a ghastly countenance, 'except that this man tried to palm it off on me.'

'I saw it fall off this man's carrier just the other side of Hatfield,' repeated Mr Walters firmly, 'and I rode after him for thirty miles trying to stop him. That's all I know about it, and I wish to God I'd never touched the beastly thing.'

'Nor do I know anything about it personally,' said the car-owner, 'but I fancy I know what it is.'

'What's that?' asked the superintendent sharply.

'I rather imagine it's the head of the Finsbury Park murder – though, mind you, that's only a guess.'

'That's just what I've been thinking myself,' agreed the superintendent, glancing at a daily paper which lay on his desk, its headlines lurid with the details of that very horrid crime, 'and, if so, you are to be congratulated, constable, on a very important capture.'

'Thank you, sir,' said the gratified officer, saluting.

'Now I'd better take all your statements,' said the superintendent. 'No, no; I'll hear the constable first. Yes, Briggs?'

The constable, the A.A. man, and the two motor-cyclists having given their versions of the story, the superintendent turned to the motorist.

'And what have you got to say about it?' he enquired. 'First of all, your name and address.'

The other produced a card, which the superintendent copied out and returned to him respectfully.

'A bag of mine, containing some valuable jewellery, was stolen from my car yesterday, in Piccadilly,' began the motorist. 'It is very much like this, but has a cipher lock. I made enquiries through Scotland Yard, and was informed today that a bag of precisely similar appearance had been cloak-roomed yesterday afternoon at Paddington, main line. I hurried round there, and was told by the clerk that just before the police warning came through the bag had been claimed by a man in motor-cycling kit. A porter said he saw the man leave the station, and a loiterer observed him riding off on a motor-bicycle. That was about an hour before. It seemed pretty hopeless, as, of course, nobody had noticed even the make of the bike, let alone the number. Fortunately, however, there was a smart little girl. The smart little girl had been dawdling round outside the station, and had heard a motor-cyclist ask a taxi-driver the quickest route to Finchley. I left the police hunting for the taxi-driver, and started off, and in Finchley I found an intelligent boy-scout. He had seen a motor-cyclist with a bag on the carrier, and had waved and shouted to him that the strap was loose. The cyclist had got off and tightened the strap, and gone straight on up the road towards Chipping Barnet. The boy hadn't been near enough to identify the machine – the only thing he knew for certain was that it wasn't a Douglas, his brother having one of that sort. At Barnet I got an odd little story of a man in a motor-coat who had staggered into a pub with a ghastly white face and drunk two double brandies and gone out and ridden off furiously. Number? – of course not. The barmaid told me. *She* didn't notice the number. After that it was a tale of furious driving all along the road. After Hatfield, I got the story of a road-race. And here we are.'

'It seems to me, my lord,' said the superintendent, 'that the furious driving can't have been all on one side.'

'I admit it,' said the other, 'though I do plead in extenuation that I spared the women and children and hit up the miles in the wide, open spaces. The point at the moment is—'

'Well, my lord,' said the superintendent, 'I've got your story, and, if it's all right, it can be verified by enquiry at Paddington and Finchley and so on. Now, as for these two gentlemen—'

'It's perfectly obvious,' broke in Mr Walters, 'the bag dropped off this man's carrier, and, when he saw me coming after him with it, he thought it was a good opportunity to saddle me with the cursed thing. Nothing could be clearer.'

'It's a lie,' said Mr Simpkins. 'Here's this fellow has got hold of the bag – I don't say how, but I can guess – and he has the bright idea of shoving the blame on me. It's easy enough to *say a* thing's fallen off a man's carrier. Where's the proof? Where's the strap? If his story's true, you'd find the broken strap on my 'bus. The bag *was* on *his* machine – tied on, tied on, tight.'

'Yes, with string,' retorted the other. 'If I'd gone and murdered someone and run off with their head, do you think I'd be such an ass as to tie it on with a bit of twopenny twine? The strap's worked loose and fallen off on the road somewhere; that's what's happened to that.'

'Well, look here,' said the man addressed as 'my lord', 'I've got an idea for what it's worth. Suppose, superintendent, you turn out as many of your men as you think adequate to keep an eye on three desperate criminals, and we all tool down to Hatfield together. I can take two in my 'bus at a pinch, and no doubt you have a police car. If this thing *did* fall off the carrier, somebody beside Mr Walters may have seen it fall.'

'They didn't,' said Mr Simpkins.

'There wasn't a soul,' said Mr Walters, 'but how do *you* know there wasn't, eh? I thought you didn't know anything about it.'

'I mean, it didn't fall off, so nobody *could* have seen it,' gasped the other.

'Well, my lord,' said the superintendent, 'I'm inclined to accept your suggestion, as it gives us a chance of enquiring into your story at the same time. Mind you, I'm not saying I doubt it, you being who you are. I've read about some of your detective work, my lord, and very smart I considered it. But, still, it wouldn't be my duty not to get corroborative evidence if possible.'

'Good egg! Quite right,' said his lordship. 'Forward the light brigade. We can do it easily in – that is to say, at the legal rate of progress it needn't take us much over an hour and a half.'

About three-quarters of an hour later, the racing car and the police car loped quietly side by side into Hatfield. Henceforward, the four-seater, in which Walters and Simpkins sat glaring at each other, took the lead, and presently Walters waved his hand and both cars came to a stop.

'It was just about here, as near as I can remember, that it fell off,' he said. 'Of course, there's no trace of it now.'

'You're quite sure as there wasn't a strap fell off with

73

it?' suggested the superintendent, 'because, you see, there must 'a' been something holding it on.'

'Of course there wasn't a strap,' said Simpkins, white with passion. 'You haven't any business to ask him leading questions like that.'

'Wait a minute,' said Walters slowly. 'No, there was no strap. But I've got a sort of recollection of seeing something on the road about a quarter of a mile farther up.'

'It's a lie!' screamed Simpkins. 'He's inventing it.'

'Just about where we passed that man with the side-car a minute or two ago,' said his lordship. 'I told you we ought to have stopped and asked him if we could help him, superintendent. Courtesy of the road, you know, and all that.'

'He couldn't have told us anything,' said the superintendent. 'He'd probably only just stopped.'

'I'm not so sure,' said the other. 'Didn't you notice what he was doing? Oh, dear, dear, where were your eyes? Hullo! here he comes.'

He sprang out into the road and waved to the rider, who, seeing four policemen, thought it better to pull up.

'Excuse me,' said his lordship. 'Thought we'd just like to stop you and ask if you were all right, and all that sort of thing, you know. Wanted to stop in passing, throttle jammed open, couldn't shut the confounded thing. Little trouble, what?'

'Oh, yes, perfectly all right, thanks, except that I would be glad if you could spare a gallon of petrol. Tank came adrift. Beastly nuisance. Had a bit of a struggle. Happily, Providence placed a broken strap in my way and I've fixed it. Split a bit, though, where that bolt came off. Lucky not to have an explosion, but there's a special cherub for motor-cyclists.'

'Strap, eh?' said the superintendent. 'Afraid I'll have to trouble you to let me have a look at that.'

'What?' said the other. 'And just as I've got the damned thing fixed? What the –? All right, dear, all right' – to his passenger. 'Is it something serious, officer?'

'Afraid so, sir. Sorry to trouble you.'

'Hi!' yelled one of the policemen, neatly fielding Mr Simpkins as he was taking a dive over the back of the car. 'No use doin' that. You're for it, my lad.'

'No doubt about it,' said the superintendent triumphantly, snatching at the strap which the side-car rider held out to him. 'Here's his name on it, "J. SIMPKINS," written on in ink as large as life. Very much obliged to *you*, sir, I'm sure. You've helped us effect a very important capture.'

'No! *Who* is it?' cried the girl in the side-car. 'How frightfully thrilling! Is it murder?'

'Look in your paper tomorrow, miss,' said the superintendent, 'and you may see something. Here, Briggs, better put the handcuffs on him.'

'And how about my tank?' said the man mournfully. 'It's all right for you to get excited, Babs, but you'll have to get out and help push.'

'Oh, no,' said his lordship. 'Here's a strap. A *much* nicer strap. A really superior strap. And petrol. *And* a pocket-flask. Everything a young man ought to know. And, when you're in town, mind you both look me up. Lord Peter Wimsey, 110A Piccadilly. Delighted to see you any time. Chin, chin!'

'Cheerio!' said the other, wiping his lips and much mollified. 'Only too charmed to be of use. Remember it in my favour, officer, next time you catch me speeding.'

'Very fortunate we spotted him,' said the superintendent complacently, as they continued their way into Hatfield. 'Quite providential, as you might say.'

'I'll come across with it,' said the wretched Simpkins, sitting handcuffed in the Hatfield police-station. 'I swear to God I know nothing whatever about it – about the murder, I mean. There's a man I know who has a jewellery business in Birmingham. I don't know him very well. In fact, I only met him at Southend last Easter, and we got pally. His name's Owen – Thomas Owen. He wrote me yesterday and said he'd accidentally left a bag in the cloakroom at Paddington and asked if I'd take it out – he enclosed the ticket – and bring it up next time I came that way. I'm in transport service, you see – you've got my card – and I'm always up and down the country. As it, happened, I was just going up in that direction with this Norton, so I fetched the thing out at lunch-time and started off with it. I didn't notice the date on the cloak-room ticket. I know there wasn't anything to pay on it, so it can't have been there long. Well, it all went just as you said up to Finchley, and there that boy told me my strap was loose and I went to tighten it up. And then I noticed that the corner of the bag was split, and it was damp – and – well, I saw what you saw. That sort of turned me over, and I lost my head. The only thing I could think of was to get rid of it, quick. I remembered there were a lot of lonely stretches on the Great North Road, so I cut the strap nearly through – that was when I stopped for that drink at Barnet – and then, when I thought there wasn't anybody in sight, I just reached back and gave it a tug, and it went – strap and all; I hadn't put it through the slots. It fell off, just like a great weight dropping off my mind. I suppose Walters must just have come round into sight as it fell. I had to slow down a mile or two farther on for some sheep going into a field, and then I heard him hooting at me – and – oh, my God!'

He groaned, and buried his head in his hands.

'I see,' said the Eaton Socon superintendent. 'Well, that's your statement. Now, about this Thomas Owen—'

'Oh,' cried Lord Peter Wimsey, 'never mind Thomas Owen. He's not the man you want. You can't suppose that a bloke who'd committed a murder would want a fellow tailin' after him to Birmingham with the head. It stands to reason that was intended to stay in Paddington cloakroom till the ingenious perpetrator had skipped, or till it was unrecognisable, or both. Which, by the way, is where we'll find those family heirlooms of mine, which your engaging friend Mr Owen lifted out of my car. Now, Mr Simpkins, just pull yourself together and tell us who was standing next to you at the cloakroom when you took out that bag. Try hard to remember, because this jolly little island is no place for him, and he'll be taking the next boat while we stand talking.'

'I can't remember,' moaned Simpkins. 'I didn't notice. My head's all in a whirl.'

'Never mind. Go back. Think quietly. Make a picture of yourself getting off your machine – leaning it up against something—'

'No, I put it on the stand.'

'Good! That's the way. Now, think – you're taking the cloakroom ticket out of your pocket and going up – trying to attract the man's attention.'

'I couldn't at first. There was an old lady trying to cloakroom a canary, and a very bustling man in a hurry with some golfclubs. He was quite rude to a quiet little man with a – by Jove! yes, a hand-bag like that one. Yes, that's it.

The timid man had had it on the counter quite a long time, and the big man pushed him aside. I don't know what happened, quite, because mine was handed out to me just then. The big man pushed his luggage in front of both of us and I had to reach over it – and I suppose – yes, I must have taken the wrong one. Good God! Do you mean to say that that timid little insignificant-looking man was a murderer?'

'Lots of 'em like that,' put in the Hatfield superintendent.' 'But what was he like – come!'

'He was only about five foot five, and he wore a soft hat and a long, dust-coloured coat. He was very ordinary, with rather weak, prominent eyes, I think, but I'm not sure I should know him again. Oh, wait a minute! I do remember one thing. He had an odd scar – crescent-shaped – under his left eye.'

'That settles it,' said Lord Peter. 'I thought as much. Did you recognise the – the face when we took it out, superintendent? No? I did. It was Dahlia Dallmeyers, the actress, who is supposed to have sailed for America last week. And the short man with the crescent-shaped scar is her husband, Philip Storey. Sordid tale and all that. She ruined him, treated him like dirt, and was unfaithful to him, but it looks as though he had had the last word in the argument. And now, I imagine, the Law will have the last word with him. Get busy on the wires, superintendent, and you might ring up the Paddington people and tell 'em to let me have my bag, before Mr Thomas Owen tumbles to it that there's been a slight mistake.'

'Well, anyhow,' said Mr Walters, extending a magnanimous hand to the abashed Mr Simpkins, 'it was a top-hole race – well worth a summons. We must have a return match one of these days.'

*　　　*　　　*

Early the following morning a little, insignificant-looking man stepped aboard the trans-Atlantic liner *Volucria*. At the head of the gangway two men blundered into him. The younger of the two, who carried a small bag, was turning to apologise, when a light of recognition flashed across his face.

'Why, if it isn't Mr Storey!' he exclaimed loudly. 'Where are you off to? I haven't see you for an age.'

'I'm afraid,' said Philip Storey, 'I haven't the pleasure—'

'Cut it out,' said the other, laughing. 'I'd know that scar of yours anywhere. Going to the States?'

'Well, yes,' said the other, seeing that his acquaintance's boisterous manner was attracting attention. 'I beg your pardon. It's Lord Peter Wimsey, isn't it? Yes, I'm joining the wife out there.'

'And how is she?' enquired Wimsey, steering the way into the bar and sitting down at a table. 'Left last week, didn't she? I saw it in the papers.'

'Yes. She's cabled me to join her. We're – er – taking a holiday in – er – the lakes. Very pleasant there in summer.'

'Cabled you, did she? And so here we are on the same boat. Odd how things turn out, what? I only got my sailing orders at the last minute. Chasing criminals – my hobby, you know.'

'Oh, really?' Mr Storey licked his lips.

'Yes. This is Defective-Inspector Parker of Scotland Yard – great pal of mine. Yes. Very unpleasant matter, annoying and all that. Bag that ought to have been reposin' peacefully at Paddington turns up at Eaton Socon. No business there, what?'

He smacked the bag on the table so violently that the lock sprang open.

Storey leapt to his feet with a shriek, flinging his arms across the opening of the bag as though to hide its contents.

'How did you get that?' he screamed. 'Eaton Socon? It – I never—'

'It's mine,' said Wimsey quietly, as the wretched man sank back, realising that he had betrayed himself. 'Some jewellery of my mother's. What did you think it was?'

Detective Parker touched his charge gently on the shoulder.

'You needn't answer that,' he said. 'I arrest you, Philip Storey, for the murder of your wife. Anything that you say may be used against you.'

The *Zambesi*, they said, was expected to dock at six in the morning. Mrs Ruyslaender booked a bedroom at the Magnifical, with despair in her heart. A bare nine hours and she would be greeting her husband. After that would begin the sickening period of waiting – it might be days, it might be weeks, possibly even months – for the inevitable discovery.

The reception-clerk twirled the register towards her. Mechanically, as she signed it, she glanced at the preceding entry:

'Lord Peter Wimsey and valet – London – Suite 24.'

Mrs Ruyslaender's heart seemed to stop for a second. Was it possible that, even now, God had left a loophole? She expected little from Him – all her life He had shown Himself a sufficiently stern creditor. It was fantastic to base the frailest hope on this signature of a man she had never even seen.

Yet the name remained in her mind while she dined in her own room. She dismissed her maid presently, and sat for a long time looking at her own haggard reflection in the mirror. Twice she rose and went to the door – then turned back, calling herself a fool. The third time she turned the handle quickly and hurried down the corridor, without giving herself time to think.

A large golden arrow at the corner directed her to Suite 24. It was 11 o'clock, and nobody was within view. Mrs

Ruyslaender gave a sharp knock on Lord Peter Wimsey's door and stood back, waiting, with the sort of desperate relief one experiences after hearing a dangerous letter thump the bottom of the pillar-box. Whatever the adventure, she was committed to it.

The manservant was of the imperturbable sort. He neither invited nor rejected, but stood respectfully upon the threshold.

'Lord Peter Wimsey?' murmured Mrs Ruyslaender.

'Yes, madam.'

'Could I speak to him for a moment?'

'His lordship has just retired, madam. If you will step in, I will enquire.'

Mrs Ruyslaender followed him into one of those palatial sitting-rooms which the Magnifical provides for the wealthy pilgrim.

'Will you take a seat, madam?'

The man stepped noiselessly to the bedroom door and passed in, shutting it behind him. The lock, however, failed to catch, and Mrs Ruyslaender caught the conversation.

'Pardon me, my lord, a lady has called. She mentioned no appointment, so I considered it better to acquaint your lordship.'

'Excellent discretion,' said a voice. It had a slow, sarcastic intonation, which brought a painful flush to Mrs Ruyslaender's cheek. 'I never make appointments. Do I know the lady?'

'No, my lord. But – hem – I know her by sight, my lord. It is Mrs Ruyslaender.'

'Oh, the diamond merchant's wife. Well, find out tactfully what it's all about, and, unless it's urgent, ask her to call tomorrow.'

The valet's next remark was inaudible, but the reply was:

'Don't be coarse, Bunter.'

The valet returned.

'His lordship desires me to ask you, madam, in what way he can be of service to you.'

'Will you say to him that I have heard of him in connection with the Attenbury diamond case, and am anxious to ask his advice.'

'Certainly, madam. May I suggest that, as his lordship is greatly fatigued, he would be better able to assist you after he has slept.'

'If tomorrow would have done, I would not have thought of disturbing him tonight. Tell him, I am aware of the trouble I am giving—'

'Excuse me one moment, madam.'

This time the door shut properly. After a short interval Bunter returned to say, 'His lordship will be with you immediately, madam,' and to place a decanter of wine and a box of Sobranies beside her.

Mrs Ruyslaender lit a cigarette, but had barely sampled its flavour when she was aware of a soft step beside her. Looking round, she perceived a young man, attired in a mauve dressing-gown of great splendour, from beneath the hem of which peeped coyly a pair of primrose silk pyjamas.

'You must think it very strange of me, thrusting myself on you at this hour,' she said, with a nervous laugh.

Lord Peter put his head to one side.

'Don't know the answer to that,' he said. 'If I say, "Not at all," it sounds abandoned. If I say, "Yes, very," it's rude. Supposin' we give it a miss, what? and you tell me what I can do for you.'

Mrs Ruyslaender hesitated. Lord Peter was not what she had expected. She noted the sleek, straw-coloured hair, brushed flat back from a rather sloping forehead, the ugly, lean, arched nose, and the faintly foolish smile, and her heart sank within her.

'I – I'm afraid it's ridiculous of me to suppose you can help me,' she began.

'Always my unfortunate appearance,' moaned Lord Peter, with such alarming acumen as to double her discomfort. 'Would it invite confidence more, d'you suppose, if I dyed my hair black an' grew a Newgate fringe? It's very tryin', you can't think, always to look as if one's name was Algy.'

'I only meant,' said Mrs Ruyslaender, 'that I don't think *anybody* could possibly help. But I saw your name in the hotel book, and it seemed just a chance.'

Lord Peter filled the glasses and sat down.

'Carry on,' he said cheerfully; 'it sounds interestin'.'

Mrs Ruyslaender took the plunge.

'My husband,' she explained, 'is Henry Ruyslaender, the diamond merchant. We came over from Kimberley ten years ago, and settled in England. He spends several months in Africa every year on business, and I am expecting him back on the *Zambesi* tomorrow morning. Now, this is the trouble. Last year he gave me a magnificent diamond necklace of a hundred and fifteen stones—'

'The Light of Africa – I know,' said Wimsey.

She looked a little surprised, but assented. 'The necklace has been stolen from me, and I can't hope to conceal the loss from him. No duplicate would deceive him for an instant.'

She paused and Lord Peter prompted gently:

84

'You have come to me, I presume, because it is not to be a police matter. Will you tell me quite frankly why?'

'The police would be useless. I know who took it,'

'Yes?'

'There is a man we both know slightly – a man called Paul Melville.'

Lord Peter's eyes narrowed. 'M'm, yes, I fancy I've seen him about the clubs. New Army, but transferred himself into the Regulars. Dark. Showy. Bit of an ampelopsis, what?'

'Ampelopsis?'

'Suburban plant that climbs by suction. *You* know – first year, tender little shoots – second year, fine show – next year, all over the shop. Now tell me I am rude.'

Mrs Ruyslaender giggled. 'Now you mention it, he is *exactly* like an ampelopsis. What a relief to be able to think of him as that. . . . Well, he is some sort of distant relation of my husband's. He called one evening when I was alone. We talked about jewels, and I brought down my jewel-box and showed him the Light of Africa. He knows a good deal about stones. I was in and out of the room two or three times, but didn't think to lock up the box. After he left, I was putting the things away, and I opened the jeweller's case the diamonds were in – and they had gone!'

'H'm – pretty barefaced. Look here, Mrs Ruyslaender, you agree he's an ampelopsis, but you won't call in the police. Honestly, now – forgive me; you're askin' my advice, you know – is he worth botherin' about?'

'It's not that,' said the woman, in a low tone. 'Oh, no! But he took something else as well. He took – a portrait – a small painting set with diamonds.'

'Oh!'

'Yes. It was in a secret drawer in the jewel-box. I can't imagine how he knew it was there, but the box was an old casket, belonging to my husband's family, and I fancy he must have known about the drawer and – well, thought that investigation might prove profitable. Anyway, the evening the diamonds went, the portrait went too, and he knows I daren't try to get the necklace back because they'd both be found together.'

'Was there something more than just the portrait, then? A portrait in itself isn't necessarily hopeless of explanation. It was given you to take care of, say.'

'The names were on it – and – and an inscription which nothing, *nothing* could ever explain away. A – a passage from Petronius.'

'Oh, dear!' said Lord Peter, 'dear me, yes. Rather a lively author.'

'I was married very young,' said Mrs Ruyslaender, 'and my husband and I have never got on well. Then one year, when he was in Africa, it all happened. We were wonderful – and shameless. It came to an end. I was bitter. I wish I had not been. He left me, you see, and I couldn't forgive it. I prayed day and night for revenge. Only now – I don't want it to be through me!'

'Wait a moment,' said Wimsey, 'you mean that, if the diamonds are found and the portrait is found too, all this story is bound to come out.'

'My husband would get a divorce. He would never forgive me – or him. It is not so much that I mind paying the price myself, but—'

She clenched her hands.

'I have cursed him again and again, and the clever girl who married him. She played her cards so well. This would ruin them both.'

86

'But if *you* were the instrument of vengeance,' said Wimsey gently, 'you would hate yourself. And it would be terrible to you because he would hate you. A woman like you couldn't stoop to get your own back. I see that. If God makes a thunderbolt, how awful and satisfying – if you help to make a beastly row, what a rotten business it would be.'

'You seem to understand,' said Mrs Ruyslaender. 'How unusual.'

'I understand perfectly. Though let me tell you,' said Wimsey, with a wry little twist of the lips, 'that it's sheer foolishness for a woman to have a sense of honour in such matters. It only gives her excruciating pain, and nobody expects it, anyway. Look here, don't let's get all worked up. You certainly shan't have your vengeance thrust on you by an ampelopsis. Why should you? Nasty fellow. We'll have him up – root, branch, and little suckers. Don't worry. Let's see. My business here will only take a day. Then I've got to get to know Melville – say a week. Then I've got to get the doings – say another week, provided he hasn't sold them yet, which isn't likely. Can you hold your husband off 'em for a fortnight, d'you think?'

'Oh, yes. I'll say they're in the country, or being cleaned, or something. But do you really think you can –?'

'I'll have a jolly good try, anyhow, Mrs Ruyslaender. Is the fellow hard up, to start stealing diamonds?'

'I fancy he has got into debt over horses lately. And possibly poker.'

'Oh! Poker player, is he? That makes an excellent excuse for gettin' to know him. Well, cheer up – we'll get the goods, even if he have to buy 'em. But we won't, if we can help it. Bunter!'

'My lord?' the valet appeared from the inner room.

'Just go an' give the "All Clear", will you?'

Mr Bunter accordingly stepped into the passage, and, having seen an old gentleman safely away to the bathroom and a young lady in a pink kimono pop her head out of an adjacent door and hurriedly pop it back on beholding him, blew his nose with aloud, trumpeting sound.

'Good night,' said Mrs Ruyslaender, 'and thank you.' She slipped back to her room unobserved.

'Whatever has induced you, my dear boy,' said Colonel Marchbanks, 'to take up with that very objectionable fellow Melville?'

'Diamonds,' said Lord Peter. 'Do you find him so, really?'

'Perfectly dreadful man,' said the Hon. Frederick Arbuthnot. 'Hearts. What did you want to go and get him a room here for? This used to be a quite decent club.'

'Two clubs?' said Sir Impey Biggs, who had been ordering a whisky, and had only caught the last word.

'No, no, one heart.'

'I beg your pardon. Well, partner, how about spades? Perfectly good suit.'

'Pass,' said the Colonel. 'I don't know what the Army's coming to nowadays.'

'No trumps,' said Wimsey. 'It's all right, children. Trust your Uncle Pete. Come on, Freddy, how many of those hearts are you going to shout for?'

'None, the Colonel havin' let me down so 'orrid,' said the Hon. Freddy.

'Cautious blighter. All content? Righty-ho! Bring out your dead, partner. Oh, very pretty indeed. We'll make it a slam this time. I'm rather glad to hear that expression of opinion from you, Colonel, because I particularly want you and Biggy to hang on this evening and take a hand with Melville and me.'

'What happens to me?' enquired the Hon. Freddy.

'You have an engagement and go home early, dear old thing. I've specially invited friend Melville to meet the redoubtable Colonel Marchbanks and our greatest criminal lawyer. Which hand am I supposed to be playin' this from? Oh, yes. Come on, Colonel – you've got to hike that old king out some time, why not now?'

'It's a plot,' said Mr Arbuthnot, with an exaggerated expression of mystery. 'Carry on, don't mind me.'

'I take at you have your own reasons for cultivating the man,' said Sir Impey.

'The rest are mine, I fancy. Well, yes, I have. You and the Colonel would really do me a favour by letting Melville cut in tonight.'

'If you wish it,' growled the Colonel, 'but I hope the impudent young beggar won't presume on the acquaintance.'

'I'll see to that,' said his lordship. 'Your cards, Freddy. Who had the ace of hearts? Oh! I had it myself, of course. Our honours. . . . Hullo! Evenin', Melville.'

The ampelopsis was rather a good-looking creature in his own way. Tall and bronzed, with a fine row of very persuasive teeth. He greeted Wimsey and Arbuthnot heartily, the Colonel with a shade too much familiarity, and expressed himself delighted to be introduced to Sir Impey Biggs.

'You're just in time to hold Freddy's hand,' said Wimsey; 'he's got a date. Not his littly paddy-paw, I don't mean – but the dam' rotten hand he generally gets dealt him. Joke.'

'Oh, well,' said the obedient Freddy, rising, 'I s'pose I'd better make a noise like a hoop and roll away. Night, night, everybody.'

Melville took his place, and the game continued with varying fortunes for two hours, at the end of which time Colonel Marchbanks, who had suffered much under his partner's eloquent theory of the game, was beginning to wilt visibly.

Wimsey yawned.

'Gettin' a bit bored, Colonel? Wish they'd invent somethin' to liven this game up a bit.'

'Oh, Bridge is a one-horse show, anyway,' said Melville. 'Why not have a little flutter at poker, Colonel? Do you all the good in the world, What d'you say, Biggs?'

Sir Impey turned on Wimsey a thoughtful eye, accustomed to sizing-up the witnesses. Then he replied:

'I'm quite willing, if the others are.'

'Damn good idea,' said Lord Peter. 'Come now, Colonel, be a sport. You'll find the chips in that drawer, I think. I always lose money at poker, but what's the odds so long as you're happy. Let's have a new pack.'

'Any limit?'

'What do *you* say, Colonel?'

The Colonel proposed a twenty-shilling limit. Melville, with a grimace, amended this to one-tenth of the pool. The amendment was carried and the cards cut, the deal falling to the Colonel.

Contrary to his own prophecy, Wimsey began by winning considerably, and grew so garrulously imbecile in the process that even the experienced Melville began to wonder whether this indescribable fatuity was the cloak of ignorance or the mask of the hardened poker-player. Soon, however, he was reassured. The luck came over to his side, and he found himself winning hands down, steadily from Sir Impey and the Colonel, who played cautiously and took little risk – heavily from Wimsey, who appeared reckless and slightly drunk, and was staking foolishly on quite impossible cards.

'I never knew such luck as yours,' Melville,' said Sir Impey, when that young man had scooped in the proceeds from a handsome straight-flush.

'My turn tonight, yours tomorrow,' said Melville, pushing the cards across to Biggs, whose deal it was.

Colonel Marchbanks required one card. Wimsey laughed vacantly and demanded an entirely fresh hand; Briggs asked for three; and Melville, after a pause for consideration, took one.

It seemed as though everybody had something respectable this time – though Wimsey was not to be depended upon, frequently going the limit upon a pair of jacks in order, as he expressed it, to keep the pot a-boiling. He became particularly obstinate now, throwing his chips in with a flushed face, in spite of Melville's confident air.

The Colonel got out, and after a short time Biggs followed his example. Melville held on till the pool mounted to something under a hundred pounds, when Wimsey suddenly turned restive and demanded to see him.

'Four kings,' said Melville.

'Blast you!' said Lord Peter, laying down four queens. 'No holdin' this feller tonight, is there? Here, take the ruddy cards, Meville, and give somebody else a look in, will you.'

He shuffled them as he spoke, and handed them over.

91

Melville dealt, satisfied the demands of the other three players, and was in the act of taking three new cards for himself, when Wimsey gave a sudden exclamation, and shot a swift hand across the table.

'Hullo! Melville,' he said, in a chill tone which bore no resemblance to his ordinary speech, 'what exactly does this mean?'

He lifted Melville's left arm clear of the table and, with a sharp gesture, shook it. From the sleeve something fluttered to the table and glided away to the floor. Colonel Marchbanks picked it up, and in a dreadful silence laid the joker on the table.

'Good God!' said Sir Impey.

'You young blackguard!' gasped the Colonel, recovering speech.

'What the hell do you mean by this?' gasped Melville, with a face like chalk. 'How dare you! This is a trick – a plant –' A horrible fury gripped him. 'You dare to say that I have been cheating. You liar! You filthy sharper. You put it there. I tell you, gentlemen,' he cried, looking desperately round the table, 'he must have put it there.'

'Come, come,' said Colonel Marchbanks, 'no good carryin' on that way, Melville. Dear me, no good at all. Only makes matters worse. We all saw it, you know. Dear, dear, I don't know what the Army's coming to.'

'Do you mean you believe it?' shrieked Melville. 'For God's sake, Wimsey, is this a joke or what? Biggs – you've got a head on your shoulders – are you going to believe this half-drunk fool and this doddering old idiot who ought to be in his grave?'

'That language won't do you any good, Melville,' said Sir Impey. 'I'm afraid we all saw it clearly enough.'

'I've been suspectin' this some time, y' know,' said Wimsey. 'That's why I asked you two to stay tonight. We don't want to make a public row, but—'

'Gentlemen,' said Melville more soberly, 'I swear to you that I am absolutely innocent of this ghastly thing. Can't you believe me?'

'I can believe the evidence of my own eyes, sir,' said the Colonel, with some heat.

'For the good of the club,' said Wimsey, 'this couldn't go on, but – also for the good of the club – I think we should all prefer the matter to be quietly arranged. In the face of what Sir Impey and the Colonel can witness, Melville, I'm afraid your protestations are not likely to be credited.'

Melville looked from the soldier's face to that of the great criminal lawyer.

'I don't know what your game is,' he said sullenly to Wimsey, 'but I can see you've laid a trap and pulled it off all right.'

'I think, gentlemen,' said Wimsey, 'that, if I might have a word in private with Melville in his own room, I could get the thing settled satisfactorily, without undue fuss.'

'He'll have to resign his commission,' growled the Colonel.

'I'll put it to him in that light,' said Peter. 'May we go to your room for a minute, Melville?'

With a lowering brow, the young soldier led the way. Once alone with Wimsey, he turned furiously on him.

What do you want? What do you mean by making this monstrous charge. I'll take action for libel!'

'Do,' said Wimsey coolly, 'if you think anybody is likely to believe your story.'

He lit a cigarette, and smiled lazily at the angry young man.

'Well, what's the meaning of it, anyway?'

'The meaning,' said Wimsey, 'is simply that you, an officer and a member of this club, have been caught red-handed cheating at cards while playing for money, the witnesses being Sir Impey Biggs, Colonel Marchbanks, and myself. Now, I suggest to you, Captain Melville, that your best plan is to let me take charge of Mrs Ruyslaender's diamond necklace and portrait, and then just to trickle away quiet-like from these halls of dazzlin' light – without any questions asked.'

Melville leapt to his feet.

'My God!' he cried. 'I can see it now. It's blackmail.'

'You may certainly call it blackmail, and theft too,' said Lord Peter, with a shrug. 'But why use ugly names? I hold five aces, you see. Better chuck in your hand.'

'Suppose I say I never heard of the diamonds?'

'It's a bit late now, isn't it?' said Wimsey affably. 'But, in that case, I'm beastly sorry and all that, of course, but we shall have to make tonight's business public.'

'Damn you!' muttered Melville, 'you sneering devil.'

He showed all his white teeth, half springing, with crouched shoulders. Wimsey waited quietly, his hands in his pockets.

The rush did not come. With a furious gesture, Melville pulled out his keys and unlocked his dressing-case.

'Take them,' he growled, flinging a small parcel on the table; 'you've got me. Take 'em and go to hell.'

'Eventually – why not now?' murmured his lordship. 'Thanks frightfully. Man of peace myself, you know – hate unpleasantness and all that.' He scrutinised his booty carefully, running the stones expertly between

94

his fingers. Over the portrait he pursed up his lips. 'Yes,' he murmured, 'that *would* have made a row.' He replaced the wrapping and slipped the parcel into his pocket.

'Well, good night, Melville – and thanks for a pleasant game.'

'I say, Biggs,' said Wimsey, when he had returned to the card-room. 'You've had a lot of experience. What tactics d'you think one's justified in usin' with a blackmailer?'

'Ah!' said the KC. 'There you've put your fingers on Society's sore place, where the Law is helpless. Speaking as a man, I'd say nothing could be too bad for the brute. It's a crime crueller and infinitely worse in its results than murder. As a lawyer, I can only say that I have consistently refused to defend a blackmailer or to prosecute any poor devil who does away with his tormentor.'

'H'm,' replied Wimsey. 'What do you say, Colonel?'

'A man like that's a filthy pest,' said the little warrior stoutly. 'Shootin's too good for him. I knew a man – close personal friend, in fact – hounded to death – blew his brains out – one of the best. Don't like to talk about it.'

'I want to show you something,' said Wimsey.

He picked up the pack which still lay scattered on the table, and shuffled it together.

'Catch hold of these, Colonel, and lay 'em face downwards. That's right. First of all you cut 'em at the twentieth card – you'll see the seven of diamonds at the bottom. Correct? Now I'll call 'em. Ten of hearts, ace of spades, three of clubs, five of clubs, king of diamonds, nine, jack, two of hearts. Right? I could pick 'em all out, you see, except the ace of hearts, and that's here.'

He leaned forward and produced it dexterously from Sir Impey's breast-pocket.

'I learnt it from a man who shared my dug-out near Ypres,' he said. 'You needn't mention tonight's business, you two. There are crimes which the Law cannot reach.'

'I am afraid you have brought shocking weather with you, Lord Peter,' said Mrs Frobisher-Pym, with playful reproof. 'If it goes on like this they will have a bad day for the funeral.'

Lord Peter Wimsey glanced out of the morning-room window to the soaked green lawn and the shrubbery, where the rain streamed down remorselessly over the laurel leaves, stiff and shiny like mackintoshes.

'Nasty exposed business, standing round at funerals,' he agreed.

'Yes, I always think it's such a shame for the old people. In a tiny village like this it's about the only pleasure they get during the winter. It makes something for them to talk about for weeks.'

'Is it anybody's funeral in particular?'

'My dear Wimsey,' said his host, 'it is plain that you, coming from your little village of London, are quite out of the swim. There has never been a funeral like it in Little Doddering before. It's an event.'

'Really?'

'Oh dear, yes. You may possibly remember old Burdock?'

'Burdock? Let me see. Isn't he a sort of local squire, or something?'

'He was,' corrected Mr Frobisher-Pym. 'He's dead – died in New York about three weeks ago, and they're sending him over to be buried. The Burdocks have lived in the big house for hundreds of years, and they're all buried in the churchyard, except, of course, the one who was killed in the War. Burdock's secretary cabled the news of his death across, and said the body was following as soon as the embalmers had finished with it. The boat gets in to Southampton this morning, I believe. At any rate, the body will arrive here by the 6.30 from town.'

'Are you going down to meet it, Tom?'

'No, my dear. I don't think that is called for. There will be a grand turn-out of the village, of course. Joliffe's people are having the time of their lives; they borrowed an extra pair of horses from young Mortimer for the occasion. I only hope they don't kick over the traces and upset the hearse. Mortimer's horseflesh is generally on the spirited side.'

'But, Tom, we must show some respect to the Burdocks.'

'We're attending the funeral tomorrow, and that's quite enough. We must do that, I suppose, out of consideration for the family, though, as far as the old man himself goes, respect is the very last thing anybody would think of paying him.'

'Oh, Tom, he's dead.'

'And quite time too. No, Agatha, it's no use pretending that old Burdock was anything but a spiteful, bad-tempered, dirty-living old blackguard that the world's well rid of. The last scandal he stirred up made the place too hot to hold him. He had to leave the country and go to the States, and, even so, if he hadn't the money to pay the people off, he'd probably have been put in gaol. That's why I'm so annoyed with Hancock. I don't mind his

98

calling himself a priest, though clergyman was always good enough for dear old Weeks – who, after all, was a canon – and I don't mind his vestments. He can wrap himself up in a Union Jack if he likes – it doesn't worry *me*. But when it comes to having old Burdock put on trestles in the south aisle, with candles round him, and Hubbard from the "Red Cow" and Duggins's boy praying over him half the night, I think it's time to draw the line. The people don't like it, you know – at least, the older generation don't. It's all right for the young ones, I dare say; they must have their amusement; but it gives offence to a lot of the farmers. After all, they knew Burdock a bit too well. Simpson – he's people's warden, you know – came up quite in distress to speak to me about it last night. You couldn't have a sounder man than Simpson. I said I would speak to Hancock. I did speak to him this morning, as a matter of fact, but you might as well talk to the west door of the church.'

'Mr Hancock is one of those young men who fancy they know everything,' said his wife. 'A sensible man would have listened to you, Tom. You're a magistrate and have lived here all your life, and it stands to reason you know considerably more about the parish than he does.'

'He took up the ridiculous position,' said Mr Frobisher-Pym, 'that the more sinful the old man had been the more he needed praying for. I said, "I think it would need more praying than you or I could do to help old Burdock out of the place he's in now." Ha, ha! So he said, "I agree with you, Mr Frobisher-Pym; that is why I am having eight watchers to pray all through the night for him." I admit he had me there.'

'Eight people?' exclaimed Mrs Frobisher-Pym.

'Not all at once, I understand; in relays, two at a time.

99

"Well," I said, "I think you ought to consider that you will be giving a handle to the Noncomformists." Of course, he couldn't deny that.'

Wimsey helped himself to marmalade. Nonconformists, it seemed, were always searching for handles. Though what kind – whether door-handles, tea-pot handles, pump-handles, or starting-handles – was never explained, nor what the handles were to be used for when found. However, having been brought up in the odour of the Establishment, he was familiar with this odd dissenting peculiarity, and merely said:

'Pity to be extreme in a small parish like this. Disturbs the ideas of the simple fathers of the hamlet and the village blacksmith, with his daughter singin' in the choir and the Old Hundredth and all the rest of it. Don't Burdock's family have anything to say to it? There are some sons, aren't there?'

'Only the two, now. Aldine was the one that was killed, of course, and Martin is somewhere abroad. He went off after that row with his father, and I don't think he has been back in England since.'

'What was the row about?'

'Oh, that was a disgraceful business. Martin got a girl into trouble – a film actress or a typist or somebody of that sort – and insisted on marrying her.'

'Oh?'

'Yes, so dreadful of him,' said the lady, taking up the tale, 'when he was practically engaged to the Delaprime girl – the one with glasses, you know. It made a terrible scandal. Some horribly vulgar people came down and pushed their way into the house and insisted on seeing old Mr Burdock. I will say for him he stood up to them – he wasn't the sort of person you could intimidate. He told them the girl had only herself to blame, and they could sue Martin if they liked – *he* wouldn't be blackmailed on his son's account. The butler was listening at the door, naturally, and told the whole village about it. And then Martin Burdock came home and had a quarrel with his father you could have heard for miles. He said that the whole thing was a lie, and that he meant to marry the girl, anyway. I cannot understand how anybody could marry into a blackmailing family like that.'

'My dear,' said Mr Frobisher-Pym gently, 'I don't think you're being quite fair to Martin, or his wife's parents, either. From what Martin told me, they were quite decent people, only not his class, of course, and they came in a well-meaning way to find out what Martin's "intentions" were. You would want to do the same yourself, if it were a daughter of ours. Old Burdock, naturally, thought they meant blackmail. He was the kind of man who thinks everything can be paid for; and he considered a son of his had a perfect right to seduce a young woman who worked for a living. I don't say Martin was altogether in the right—'

'Martin is a chip off the old block, I'm afraid,' retorted the lady. 'He married the girl, anyway, and why should he do that, unless he had to?'

'Well, they've never had any children, you know,' said Mr Frobisher-Pym.

'That's as may be. I've no doubt the girl was in league with her parents. And you know the Martin Burdocks have lived in Paris ever since.'

'That's true,' admitted her husband. 'It was an unfortunate affair altogether. They've had some difficulty in tracing Martin's address, too, but no doubt he'll be coming back shortly. He is engaged in producing some film play, they tell me, so possibly he can't get away in time for the funeral.'

'If he had any natural feeling, he would not let a film play stand in his way,' said Mrs Frobisher-Pym.

'My dear, there are such things as contracts, with very heavy monetary penalties for breaking them. And I don't suppose Martin could afford to lose a big sum of money. It's not likely that his father will have left him anything.'

'Martin is the younger son, then?' asked Wimsey, politely showing more interest than he felt in the rather well-worn plot of this village melodrama.

'No, he is the eldest of the lot. The house is entailed, of course, and so is the estate, such as it is. But there's no money in the land. Old Burdock made his fortune in rubber shares during the boom, and the money will go as he leaves it – wherever that may be, for they haven't found any will yet. He's probably left it all to Haviland.'

'The younger son?'

'Yes. He's something in the City – a director of a company – connected with silk stockings, I believe. Nobody has seen very much of him. He came down as soon as he heard of his father's death. He's staying with the Hancocks. The big house has been shut up since old Burdock went to the States four years ago. I suppose Haviland thought it wasn't worth while opening it up till they knew what Martin was going to do about it. That's why the body is being taken to the church.'

'Much less trouble, certainly,' said Wimsey.

'Oh, yes – though, mind you, I think Haviland ought to take a more neighbourly view of it. Considering the position the Burdocks have always held in the place, the people had a right to expect a proper reception after the funeral. It's usual. But these business people think less of tradition than we do down here. And, naturally, since the Hancocks are putting Haviland up, he can't raise much objection to the candles and the prayers and things.'

'Perhaps not,' said Mrs Frobisher-Pym, 'but it would have been more suitable if Haviland had come to us, rather than to the Hancocks, whom he doesn't even know.'

'My dear, you forget the very unpleasant dispute I had with Haviland Burdock about shooting over my land. After the correspondence that passed between us, last time he was down here, I could scarcely offer him hospitality. His father took a perfectly proper view of it, I will say that for him, but Haviland was exceedingly discourteous to me, and things were said which I could not possibly overlook. However, we mustn't bore you, Lord Peter, with our local small-talk. If you've finished your breakfast, what do you say to a walk round the place? It's a pity it's raining so hard – and you don't see the garden at its best this time of year, of course – but I've got some cocker span'els you might like to have a look at.'

Lord Peter expressed eager anxiety to see the spaniels, and in a few minutes' time found himself squelching down the gravel path which led to the kennels.

'Nothing like a healthy country life,' said Mr Frobisher-Pym. 'I always think London is so depressing in the winter. Nothing to do with one's self. All right to run up for a day or two and see a theatre now and again, but how you people stick it week in and week out beats me. I must speak to Plunkett about this archway,' he added. 'It's getting out of trim.'

He broke off a dangling branch of ivy as he spoke. The plant shuddered revengefully, tipping a small shower of water down Wimsey's neck.

The cocker spaniel and her family occupied a comfortable and airy stall in the stable buildings. A youngish man in breeches and leggings emerged to greet the visitors, and produced the little bundles of puppyhood for their inspection. Wimsey sat down on an upturned bucket and examined them gravely one by one. The bitch, after cautiously reviewing his boots and grumbling a little, decided that he was trustworthy and slobbered genially over his knees.

'Let me see,' said Mr Frobisher-Pym, 'how old are they?'

'Thirteen days, sir.'

'Is she feeding them all right?'

'Fine, sir. She's having some of the malt food. Seems to suit her very well, sir.'

'Ah, yes. Plunkett was a little doubtful about it, but I heard it spoken very well of. Plunkett doesn't care for experiments, and, in a general way, I agree with him. Where is Plunkett, by the way?'

'He's not very well this morning, sir.'

'Sorry to hear that, Merridew. The rheumatics again?'

'No, sir. From what Mrs Plunkett tells me, he's had a bit of a shock.'

'A shock? What sort of a shock? Nothing wrong with Alf or Elsie, I hope?'

'No, sir. The fact is – I understand he's seen something, sir.'

'What do you mean, seen something?'

'Well, sir – something in the nature of a warning, from what he says.'

'A warning? Good heavens, Merridew, he mustn't get those sort of ideas in his head. I'm surprised at Plunkett; I always thought he was a very level-headed man. What sort of warning did he say it was?'

'I couldn't say, sir.'

'Surely he mentioned what he thought he'd seen.'

Merridew's face took on a slightly obstinate look.

'I can't say, I'm sure, sir.'

'This will never do. I must go and see Plunkett. Is he at the cottage?'

'Yes, sir.'

'We'll go down there at once. You don't mind, do you, Wimsey? I can't allow Plunkett to make himself ill. If he's had a shock he'd better see a doctor. Well, carry on, Merridew, and be sure you keep her warm and comfortable. The damp is apt to come up through these brick floors. I'm thinking of having the whole place re-set with concrete, but it takes money, of course. I can't imagine,' he went on, as he led the way past the greenhouse towards a trim cottage set in its own square of kitchen-garden, 'what can have happened to have upset Plunkett. I hope it's nothing serious. He's getting elderly, of course, but he ought to be above believing in warnings. You wouldn't believe the extraordinary ideas these people get hold of. Fact is, I expect he's been round at the "Weary Traveller", and caught sight of somebody's washing out on the way home.'

'Not washing,' corrected Wimsey mechanically. He had a deductive turn of mind which exposed the folly of the suggestion even while irritably admitting that the matter was of no importance. 'It poured with rain last night, and, besides, it's Thursday. But Tuesday and Wednesday were fine, so the drying would have been done then. No washing.'

'Well, well – something else then – a post, or old Mrs Gidden's white donkey. Plunkett does occasionally take a drop too much, I'm sorry to say, but he's a very good kennel-man, so one overlooks it. They're superstitious round about these parts, and they can tell some queer tales if once you get into their confidence. You'd be surprised how far off the main track we are as regards civilisation. Why, not here, but at Abbotts Bolton, fifteen miles off, it's as much as one's life is worth to shoot a hare. Witches, you know, and that sort of thing.'

'I shouldn't be a bit surprised. They'll still tell you about werewolves in some parts of Germany.'

'Yes, I dare say. Well, here we are.' Mr Frobisher-Pym rapped loudly with his walking-stick on the door of the cottage and turned the handle without waiting for permission.

'You there, Mrs Plunkett? May we come in? Ah! Good morning. Hope we're not disturbing you, but Merridew told me Plunkett was not so well. This is Lord Peter Wimsey – a very old friend of mine; that is to say, I'm a very old friend of *his*; ha, ha!'

'Good morning, sir; good morning, your lordship. I'm sure Plunkett will be very pleased to see you. Please step in. Plunkett, here's Mr Pym to see you.'

The elderly man who sat crouching over the fire turned a mournful face towards them, and half rose, touching his forehead.

'Well, now, Plunkett, what's the trouble?' enquired Mr Frobisher-Pym, with the hearty bedside manner adopted by country gentlefolk visiting their dependants. 'Sorry not to see you out and about. Touch of the old complaint, eh?'

'No, sir; no, sir. Thank you, sir. I'm well enough in myself. But I've had a warning, and I'm not long for this world.'

'Not long for this world? Oh, nonsense, Plunkett. You mustn't talk like that. A touch of indigestion, that's what you've got, I expect. Gives one the blues, I know. I'm sure I often feel like nothing on earth when I've got one of my bilious attacks. Try a dose of castor-oil, or a good old-fashioned blue pill and black draught. Nothing like it. Then you won't talk about warnings and dying.'

'No medicine won't do no good to *my* complaint, sir. Nobody as see what I've seed ever got the better of it. But as you and the gentleman are here, sir, I'm wondering if you'll do me a favour.'

'Of course, Plunkett, anything you like. What is it?'

'Why, just to draw up my will, sir. Old Parson, he used to do it. But I don't fancy this new young man, with his candles and bits of things. It don't seem as if he'd make it good and legal, sir, and I wouldn't like it if there was any dispute after I was gone. So as there ain't much time left me, I'd be grateful if you'd put it down clear for me in pen and ink that I wants my little bit all to go to Sarah here, and after her to Alf and Elsie, divided up equal.'

Of course I'll do that for you, Plunkett, any time you like. But it's nonsense to be talking about wills. Bless my soul, I shouldn't be surprised if you were to see us all underground.'

'No, sir. I've been a hale and hearty man, I'm not denying. But I've been called, sir, and I've got to go. It must come to all of us, I know that. But it's a fearful thing to see the death-coach come for one, and know that the dead are in it, that cannot rest in the grave.'

'Come now, Phunkett, you don't mean to tell me you believe in that old foolishness about the death-coach. I thought you were an educated man. What would Alf say if he heard you talking such nonsense?'

'Ah, sir, young people don't know everything, and

there's many more things in God's creation than what you'll find in the printed books.'

'Oh, well,' said Mr Frobisher-Pym, finding this opening irresistible, 'we know there are more things in heaven and earth, Horatio, than are dreamt of in your philosophy. Quite so. But that doesn't apply nowadays,' he added contradictorily. 'There are no ghosts in the twentieth century. Just you think the matter out quietly, and you'll find you've made a mistake. There's probably some quite simple explanation. Dear me! I remember Mrs Frobisher-Pym waking up one night and having a terrible fright, because she thought somebody'd been and hanged himself on our bedroom door. Such a silly idea, because I was safe in bed beside her – snoring, *she* said, ha, ha! – and, if anybody was feeling like hanging himself, he wouldn't come into our bedroom to do it. Well, she clutched my arm in a great state of mind, and when I went to see what had alarmed her, what do you think it was? My trousers, which I'd hung up by the braces, with the socks still in the legs! My word! and didn't I get a wigging for not having put my things away tidy!'

Mr Frobisher-Pym laughed, and Mrs Plunkett said dutifully, 'There now!' Her husband shook his head.

'That may be, sir, but I see the death-coach last night with my own eyes. Just striking midnight it was, by the church clock, and I see it come up the lane by the old priory wall.'

'And what were you doing out of bed at midnight, eh?'

'Well, sir, I'd been round to my sister's, that's got her boy home on leaf off of his ship.'

'And you'd been drinking his health, I dare say, Plunkett.' Mr Frobisher-Pym wagged an admonitory forefinger.

'No, sir, I don't deny I'd had a glass or two of ale, but not to fuddle me. My wife can tell you I was sober enough when I got home.'

'That's right, sir. Plunkett hadn't taken too much last night, that I'll swear to.'

'Well, what was it you saw, Plunkett?'

'I see the death-coach, same as I'm telling you, sir. It come up the lane, all ghostly white, sir, and never making no more sound than the dead – which it were, sir.'

'A waggon or something going through to Lymptree or Herriotting.'

'No, sir – 'tweren't a waggon. I counted the horses – four white horses, and they went by with never a sound of hoof or bridle. And that weren't—'

'Four horses! Come, Plunkett, you must have been seeing double. There's nobody about here would be driving four horses, unless it was Mr Mortimer from Abbotts Bolton, and he wouldn't be taking his horseflesh out at midnight.'

'Four horses they was, sir. I see them plain. And it weren't Mr Mortimer, neither, for he drives a drag, and this were a big, heavy coach, with no lights on it, but shinin' all of itself, with a colour like moonshine.'

'Oh, nonsense, man! You couldn't see the moon last night. It was pitch-dark.'

'No, sir, but the coach shone all moony-like, all the same.'

'And no lights? I wonder what the police would say to that.'

'No mortal police could stop that coach,' said Plunkett contemptuously, 'nor no mortal man could abide the sight on it. I tell you, sir, that ain't the worst of it. The horses—'

'Was it going slowly?'

'No, sir. It were going at a gallop, only the hoofs didn't touch the ground. There weren't no sound, and I see the black road and the white hoofs half a foot off of it. And the horses had no heads.'

'No heads?'

'No, sir.'

Mr Frobisher-Pym laughed.

'Come, come, Plunkett, you don't expect us to swallow that. No heads? How could even a ghost drive horses with no heads? How about the reins, eh?'

'You may laugh, sir, but we know that with God all things are possible. Four white horses they was. I see them clearly, but there was neither head nor neck beyond the collar, sir. I see the reins, shining like silver, and they ran up to the rings of the hames, and they didn't go no further. If I was to drop dead this minute, sir, that's what I see.'

'Was there a driver to this wonderful turn-out?'

'Yes, sir, there was a driver.'

'Headless too, I suppose?'

'Yes, sir, headless too. At least, I couldn't see nothing of him beyond his coat, which had them old-fashioned capes at the shoulders.'

'Well, I must say, Plunkett, you're very circumstantial. How far off was this – er – apparition when you saw it?'

'I was passing by the War Memorial, sir, when I see it come up the lane. It wouldn't be above twenty or thirty yards from where I stood. It went by at a gallop, and turned off to the left round the churchyard wall.'

'Well, well, it sounds odd, certainly, but it was a dark

night, and at that distance your eyes may have deceived you. Now, if you'll take my advice you'll think no more about it.'

'Ah, sir, it's all very well saying that, but everybody knows the man who sees the death-coach of the Burdocks is doomed to die within the week. There's no use rebelling against it, sir; it is so. And if you'll be so good as to oblige me over that matter of a will, I'd die happier for knowing as Sarah and the children was sure of their bit of money.'

Mr Frobisher-Pym obliged over the will, though much against the grain, exhorting and scolding as he wrote. Wimsey added his own signature as one of the witnesses, and contributed his own bit of comfort.

'I shouldn't worry too much about the coach, if I were you,' he said. 'Depend upon it, if it's the Burdock coach it'll just have come for the soul of the old squire. It couldn't be expected to go to New York for him, don't you see? It's just gettin' ready for the funeral tomorrow.'

'That's likely enough,' agreed Plunkett. 'Often and often it's been seen in these parts when one of the Burdocks was taken. But it's terrible unlucky to see it.'

The thought of the funeral seemed, however, to cheer him a little. The visitors again begged him not to think about it, and took their departure.

'Isn't it wonderful,' said Mr Frobisher-Pym, 'what imagination will do with these people? And they're obstinate. You could argue with them till you were black in the face.'

'Yes. I say, let's go down to the church and have a look at the place. I'd like to know how much he could really have seen from where he was standing.'

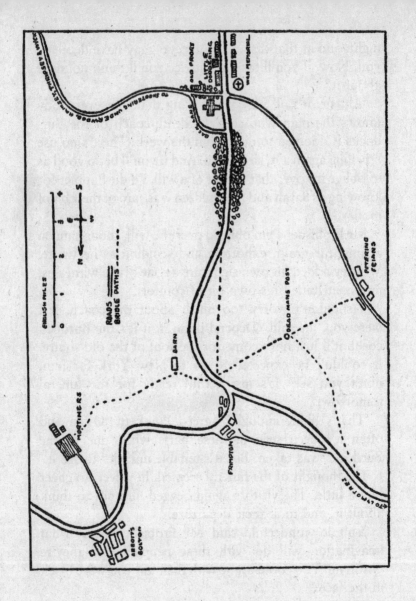

The parish church of Little Doddering stands, like so many country churches, at some distance from the houses. The main road from Herriotting, Abbotts Bolton, and Frimpton runs past the west gate of the churchyard – a wide God's acre, crowded with ancient stones. On the south side is a narrow and gloomy lane, heavily overhung with old elm-trees, dividing the church from the still more ancient ruins of Doddering Priory. On the main road, a little beyond the point where Old Priory Lane enters, stands the War Memorial, and from here the road runs straight on into Little Doddering. Round the remaining two sides of the churchyard winds another lane, known to the village simply as the Back Lane. This branches out from the Herriotting road about a hundred yards north of the church, connects with the far end of Priory Lane, and thence proceeds deviously to Shootering Underwood, Hamsey, Thripsey, and Wyck.

'Whatever it was Plunkett thinks he saw,' said Mr Frobisher-Pym, 'it must have came from Shootering. The Back Lane only leads round by some fields and a cottage or two, and it stands to reason anybody coming from Frimpton would have taken the main road, going and coming. The lane is in a very bad state with all this rain. I'm afraid even your detective ability, my dear Wimsey, would not avail to find wheel-marks on this modern tarmac.'

'Hardly,' said Wimsey, 'especially in the case of a ghostly chariot which gets along without touching the ground. But your reasoning seems perfectly sound, sir.'

'It was probably a couple of belated waggons going to market,' pursued Mr Frobisher-Pym, 'and the rest of it is superstition and, I am afraid, the local beer. Plunkett couldn't have seen all those details about drivers and harness and so on at this distance. And, if it was making no noise, how did he come to notice it at all, since he'd got past the turn and was walking in the other direction? Depend upon it, he heard the wheels and imagined the rest.'

'Probably,' said Wimsey,

'Of course,' went on his host, 'if the waggons really were going about without lights, it ought to be looked into. It is a very dangerous thing, with all these motor vehicles about, and I've had to speak severely about it before now. I fined a man only the other day for the very same thing. Do you care to see the church while we're here?'

Knowing that in country places it is always considered proper to see the church, Lord Peter expressed his eagerness to do so.

'It's always open nowadays,' said the magistrate, leading the way to the west entrance. 'The vicar has a idea that churches should be always open for private prayer. He comes from a town living, of course. Round about here the people are always out on the land, and you can't expect them to come into church in their working clothes and muddy boots. They wouldn't think it respectful, and they've other things to do. Besides, I said to him, consider the opportunity it gives for un-desirable conduct. But he's a young man, and he'll have to learn by experience.'

He pushed the door open. A curious, stuffy waft of stale incense, damp, and stoves rushed out at them as they entered – a kind of concentrated extract of Church of England. The two altars, bright with flowers and gilding, and showing as garish splashes among the heavy shadows and oppressive architecture of the little Norman building, sound the same note of contradiction; it was the warm and human that seemed exotic and unfamiliar; the cold and unwelcoming that seemed native to the place and people.

'This Lady-chapel, as Hancock calls it, in the south aisle, is new, of course,' said Mr Frobisher-Pym. 'It aroused a good deal of opposition, but the Bishop is lenient with the High Church party – too lenient, some people think – but, after all, what does it matter? I'm sure I can say my prayers just as well with two communion-tables as with one. And, I will say for Hancock, he is very good with the young men and the girls. In these days of motor-cycles, it's something to get them interested in religion at all. Those trestles in the chapel are for old Burdock's coffin, I suppose. Ah! Here is the vicar.'

A thin man in a cassock emerged from a door beside the high altar and came down towards them, carrying a tall, oaken candlestick in his hand. He greeted them with a slightly professional smile of welcome. Wimsey diagnosed him promptly as earnest, nervous, and not highly intellectual.

'The candlesticks have only just come,' he observed after the usual introductions had been made. 'I was afraid they would not be here in time. However, all is now well.'

He set the candlestick beside the coffin-trestles, and proceeded to decorate its brass spike with a long candle of unbleached wax, which he took from a parcel in a neighbouring pew.

Mr Frobisher-Pym said nothing. Wimsey felt it incumbent on him to express his interest, and did so.

'It is very gratifying,' said Mr Hancock, thus encouraged, 'to see the people beginning to take a real interest in

115

their church. I have really had very little difficulty in finding watchers for tonight. We are having eight watchers, two by two, from 10 o'clock this evening – till which time I shall be myself on duty – till six in the morning, when I come in to say Mass. The men will carry on till 2 o'clock, then my wife and daughter will relieve them, and Mr Hubbard and young Rawlinson have kindly consented to take the hours from four till six.'

'What Rawlinson is that?' demanded Mr Frobisher-Pym.

'Mr Graham's clerk from Herriotting. It is true he is not a member of the parish, but he was born here, and was good enough to wish to take his turn in watching. He is coming over on his motor-cycle. After all, Mr Graham has had charge of Burdock's family affairs for very many years, and no doubt they wish to show their respect in some way.'

'Well, I only hope he'll be awake enough to do his work in the morning, after gadding about all night,' said Mr Frobisher-Pym gruffly. 'As for Hubbard, that's his own look-out, though I must say it seems an odd occupation for a publican. Still, if he's pleased and you're pleased, there's no more to be said about it.'

You've got a very beautiful old church here, Mr Hancock,' said Wimsey, seeing that controversy seemed imminent.

'Very beautiful indeed,' said the vicar. 'Have you noticed that apse? It is rare for a village church to possess such a perfect Norman apse. Perhaps you would like to come and look at it.' He genuflected as they passed a hanging lamp which burned before a niche. 'You see, we are permitted Reservation. The Bishop –' He prattled cheerfully as they wandered up the chancel, digressing from time to time to draw attention to the handsome miserere seats ('Of course, this was the original Priory Church'), and a beautifully carved piscina and aumbry ('It is rare to find them so well preserved'). Wimsey assisted him to carry down the remaining candlesticks from the vestry, and, when these had been put in position, joined Mr Frobisher-Pym at the door.

'I think you said you were dining with the Lumsdens tonight,' said the magistrate, as they sat smoking after lunch. 'How are you going? Will you have the car?'

'I'd rather you'd lend me one of the saddle-horses,' said Wimsey. 'I get few opportunities of riding in town.'

'Certainly, my dear boy, certainly. Only I'm afraid you'll have rather a wet ride. Take Polly Flinders; it will do her good to get some exercise. You are quite sure you would prefer it? Have you got your kit with you?'

'Yes – I brought an old pair of bags down with me, and, with this raincoat, I shan't come to any harm. They won't expect me to dress. How far is it to Frimpton, by the way?'

'Nine miles by the main road, and tarmac all the way, I'm afraid, but there' a good wide piece of grass each side. And, of course, you can cut off a mile or so by going across the common. What time will you want to start?'

'Oh, about seven o'clock, I should think. And, I say, sir – will Mrs Frobisher-Pym think it very rude if I'm rather late back? Old Lumsden and I went through the war together, and if we get yarning over old times we may go on into the small hours. I don't want to feel I'm treating your house like a hotel, but—'

'Of course not, of course not! That's absolutely all right. My wife won't mind in the very least. We want you to enjoy your visit and do exactly what you like. I'll give you the key, and I'll remember not to put the chain up. Perhaps you wouldn't mind doing that yourself when you come in?'

'Rather not. And how about the mare?'

'I'll tell Merridew to look out for you; he sleeps over the stables. I only wish it were going to be a better night for you. I'm afraid the glass is going back. Yes. Dear, dear! It's a bad lookout for tomorrow. By the way, you'll probably pass the funeral procession at the church. It should be along by about then, if the train is punctual.'

The train, presumably, was punctual, for as Lord Peter cantered up to the west gate of the church he saw a hearse of great funereal pomp drawn up before it, surrounded by a little crowd of people. Two mourning coaches were in attendance; the driver of the second seemed to be having some difficulty with the horses, and Wimsey rightly inferred that this was the pair which had been borrowed from Mr Mortimer. Restraining Polly Flinders as best he might, he sidled into a respectful position on the edge of the crowd, and watched the coffin taken from the hearse and carried through the gate, where it was met by Mr Hancock, in full pontificals, attended by a thurifer and two torch-bearers. The effect was a little marred by the rain, which had extinguished the candles, but the village seemed to look upon it as an excellent show nevertheless. A massive man, dressed with great correctness in a black frock coat and tall hat, and accompanied by a woman in handsome mourning and furs, was sympathetially commented on. This was Haviland Burdock of silk-stocking fame, the younger son of the deceased. A vast number of white wreaths were then handed out, and greeted with murmurs of admiration

118

and approval. The choir struck up a hymn, rather raggedly, and the procession filed away into the church. Polly Flinders shook her head vigorously, and Wimsey, taking this as a signal to be gone, replaced his hat and ambled gently away towards Frimpton.

He followed the main road for about four miles, winding up through finely wooded country to the edge of Frimpton Common. Here the road made a wide sweep, skirting the common and curving gently down into Frimpton village. Wimsey hesitated for a moment, considering that it was growing dark and that both the way and the animal he rode were strange to him. There seemed, however, to be a well-defined bridle-path across the common, and eventually he decided to take it. Polly Flinders seemed to know it well enough, and cantered along without hesitation. A ride of about a mile and a half brought them without adventure into the main road again. Here a fork in the road presented itself confusingly; an electric torch, however, and a signpost solved the problem; after which ten minutes' ride brought the traveller to his goal.

Major Lumsden was a large, cheerful man – none the less cheerful for having lost a leg in the War. He had a large, cheerful wife a large, cheerful house, and a large, cheerful family. Wimsey soon found himself seated before a fire as large and cheerful as the rest of the establishment, exchanging gossip with his hosts over a whisky-and-soda. He described the Burdock funeral with irreverent gusto, and went on to tell the story of the phantom coach. Major Lumsden laughed.

'It's a quaint part of the country,' he said. 'The policeman is just as bad as the rest of them. Do you remember, dear, the time I had to go out and lay a ghost, down at Pogson's farm?'

'I do, indeed,' said his wife emphatically. 'The maids had a wonderful time. Trivett – that's our local constable – came rushing in here and fainted in the kitchen, and they all sat round howling and sustaining him with our best brandy, while Dan went down and investigated.'

'Did you find the ghost?'

'Well, not the ghost, exactly, but we found a pair of boots and half a pork-pie in the empty house, so we put it all down to a tramp. Still, I must say odd things do happen about here. There were those fires on the common last year. They were never explained.'

'Gipsies, Dan.'

'Maybe; but nobody ever saw them, and the fires would start in the most unexpected way, sometimes in the pouring rain; and, before you could get near one, it would be out, and only a sodden wet black mark left behind it. And there's another bit of the common that animals don't like – near what they call the Dead Man's Post. My dogs won't go near it. Funny brutes. I've never seen anything there, but even in broad daylight they don't seem to fancy it. The common's not got a good reputation. It used to be a great place for highwaymen.'

'Is the Burdock coach anything to do with highwaymen?'

'No. I fancy it was some rakehelly dead-and-gone Burdock. Belonged to the Hell-fire Club or something. The usual sort of story. All the people round here believe in it, of course. It's rather a good thing. Keeps the servants indoors at night. Well, let's go and have some grub, shall we?'

'Do you remember,' said Major Lumsden, 'that damned old mill, and the three elms by the pig-sty?'

'Good Lord, yes! You very obligingly blew them out of the landscape for us, I remember. They made us a damned sight too conspicuous.'

'We rather missed them when they were gone.'

'Thank heaven you didn't miss them when they were there. I'll tell you what you did miss, though.'

'What's that?'

'The old sow.'

'By Jove, yes. Do you remember old Piper fetching her in?'

'I'll say I do. That reminds me. You knew Bunthorne . . .'

'I'll say good night,' said Mrs Lumsden, 'and leave you people to it.'

'Do you remember,' said Lord Peter Wimsey, 'that awkward moment when Popham went off his rocker?'

'No. I'd been sent back with a batch of prisoners. I heard about it, though. I never knew what became of him.'

'I got him sent home. He's married now and living in Lincolnshire.'

'Is he? Well, he couldn't help himself, I suppose. He was only a kid. What's happened to Philpotts?'

'Oh, Philpotts . . .'

'Where's your glass, old man?'

'Oh, rot, old man. The night is still young . . .'

'Really? Well but look here, why not stay the night? My wife will be delighted. I can fix you up in no time.'

'No, thanks most awfully. I must be rolling off home. I said I'd be back; and I'm booked to put the chain on the door.'

'As you like, of course, but it's still raining. Not a good night for a ride on an open horse.'

'I'll bring a saloon next time. We shan't hurt. Rain's good for the complexion – makes the roses grow. Don't wake your man up. I can saddle her myself.'

'My dear man, it's no trouble.'

'No, really, old man.'

'Well, I'll came along and lend you a hand.'

A gust of rain and wind blew in through the hall door as they struggled out into the night. It was past one in the morning and pitch-dark. Major Lumsden again pressed Wimsey to stay.

'No, thanks, really. The old lady's feelings might be hurt. It's not so bad, really – wet, but not cold. Come up, Polly, stand over, old lady.'

He put the saddle on and girthed it, while Lumsden held the lantern. The mare, fed and rested, came delicately dancing out of the warm loose-box, head well stretched forward, and nostrils snuffing at the rain.

'Well, so long, old lad. Come and look us up again. It's been great.'

'Rather! By Jove, yes. Best respects to madame. Is the gate open?'

'Yes.'

Well, cheerio!'

'Cheerio!'

Polly Flinders, with her nose turned homewards, settled down to make short work of the nine miles of high-road. Once outside the gates, the night seemed lighter, though the rain poured heavily. Somewhere buried behind the thronging clouds there was a moon, which now and again showed as a pale stain on the sky, a paler reflection on the black road. Wimsey, with a mind full of memories and a skin full of whisky, hummed to himself as he rode.

As he passed the fork, he hesitated for a moment. Should he take the path over the common or stick to the road? On consideration, he decided to give the common a miss – not because of its sinister reputation, but because of ruts and rabbit-holes. He shook the reins, bestowed a word of encouragement on his mount, and continued by the road, having the common on his right hand, and, on the left, fields bounded by high hedges, which gave some shelter from the driving rain.

He had topped the rise, and passed the spot where the bridle-path again joined the high-road, when a slight start and stumble drew his attention unpleasantly to Polly Flinders.

'Hold up, mare,' he said disapprovingly.

Polly shook her head, moved forward, tried to pick up her easy pace again. 'Hullo!' said Wimsey, alarmed. He pulled her to a standstill.

'Lame in the near fore,' he said, dismounting. 'If you've been and gone and strained anything, my girl, four miles from home, father *will* be pleased.' It occurred to him for the first time how curiously lonely the road was. He had not seen a single car. They might have been in the wilds of Africa.

He ran an exploratory hand down the near foreleg. The mare stood quietly enough, without shrinking or wincing. Wimsey was puzzled.

'If these had been the good old days,' he said, 'I'd have thought she'd picked up a stone. But what—'

He lifted the mare's foot, and explored it carefully with fingers and pocket-torch. His diagnosis had been right, after all. A steel nut, evidently dropped from a passing car, had wedged itself firmly between the shoe and the frog. He grunted and felt for his knife. Happily, it was one of that excellent old-fashioned kind which includes, besides blades and corkscrews, an ingenious apparatus for removing foreign bodies from horses' feet.

The mare nuzzled him gently as he stooped over his task. It was a little awkward getting to work; he had to wedge the torch under his arm, so as to leave one hand free for the tool and the other to hold the hoof. He was swearing gently at these difficulties when, happening to glance down the road ahead, he fancied he caught the gleam of something moving. It was not easy to see, for at this point the tall trees stood up on both sides of the road, which dipped abruptly from the edge of the common. It was not a car the light was too faint. A waggon, probably, with a dim lantern. Yet it seemed to move fast. He puzzled for a moment; then bent to work again.

The nut resisted his efforts, and the mare, touched in a tender spot, pulled away, trying to get her foot down. He soothed her with his voice and patted her neck. The torch slipped from his arm. He cursed it impatiently, set down the hoof, and picked up the torch from the edge of the grass, into which it had rolled. As he straightened himself again, he looked along the road and saw.

Up from under the dripping dark of the trees it came, shining with a thin, moony radiance. There was no clatter of hoofs, no rumble of wheels, no ringing of bit or bridle. He saw the white, sleek, shining shoulders with the collar that lay on each, like a faint fiery ring, enclosing nothing. He saw the gleaming reins, their cut ends slipping back and forward unsupported through the ring of the hames. The feet, that never touched the earth, ran swiftly – four times four noiseless hoofs, bearing the pale bodies by like smoke. The driver leaned forward, brandishing his whip. He was faceless and headless, but his whole attitude bespoke desperate haste. The coach was barely visible through the driving rain, but Wimsey saw the dimly spinning wheels and a faint whiteness, still and stiff, at the window. It went past at a gallop – headless driver and headless horses and silent coach. Its passing left a stir, a sound that was less a sound than a vibration – and the wind roared suddenly after it, with a great sheet of water blown up out of the south.

'Good God!' said Wimsey. And then: 'How many whiskies did we have?'

He turned and looked back along the road, straining his eyes. Then suddenly he remembered the mare, and, without troubling further about the torch, picked up her foot and went to work by touch. The nut gave no more trouble, but dropped out into his hand almost immediately. Polly Flinders sighed gratefully and blew into his ear.

Wimsey led her forward a few steps. She put her feet down firmly and strongly. The nut, removed without delay, had left no tenderness. Wimsey mounted, let her go – then pulled her head round suddenly.

'I'm going to see,' he said resolutely. 'Come up, mare! We won't let any headless horses get the better of *us*. Perfectly indecent, goin' about without heads. Get on, old lady. Over the common with you. We'll catch 'em at the cross-roads.'

Without the slightest consideration for his host or his host's property, he put the mare to the bridle-path again, and urged her into a gallop.

At first he thought he could make out a pale, fluttering whiteness, moving away ahead of him on the road. Presently, as high-road and bridle-path diverged, he lost it altogether. But he knew there was no side-road. Bar any accident to his mount, he was bound to catch it before it came to the fork. Polly Flinders, answering easily to the touch of his heel, skimmed over the rough track with the indifference born of familiarity. In less than ten minutes her feet rang out again on the tarmac. He pulled her up, faced round in the direction of little Doddering, and stared down the road. He could see nothing yet. Either he was well ahead of the coach, or it had already passed at unbelievable speed, or else—

He waited. Nothing. The violent rain had ceased, and the moon was struggling out again. The road appeared completely deserted. He glanced over his shoulder. A small beam of light near the ground moved, turned, flashed green, and red, and white again, and came towards him. Presently he made out that it was a policeman wheeling a bicycle.

'A bad night, sir,' said the man civilly, but with a faint note of enquiry in his voice.

'Rotten,' said Wimsey.

'Just had to mend a puncture, to make it all the pleasanter,' added the policeman.

Wimsey expressed sympathy. Have you been here long?' he added.

'Best part o' twenty minutes.'

'Did you see anything pass along this way from Little Doddering?'

'Ain't been nothing along while I've been here. What sort of thing did you mean, sir?'

'I thought I saw –' Wimsey hesitated. He did not care about the idea of making a fool of himself. 'A carriage with four horses,' he said hesitatingly. 'It passed me on this road not a quarter of an hour ago – down at the other end of the common. I – I came back to see. It seemed unusual –' He became aware that his story sounded very lame.

The policeman spoke rather sharply and rapidly.

'There ain't been nothing past here.'

'You're sure?'

'Yes, sir; and, if you don't mind me sayin' so, you'd best be getting home. It's a lonesome bit o' road.'

'Yes, isn't it?' said Wimsey. 'Well, good night, sergeant.'

He turned the mare's head back along the Little Doddering road, going very quietly. He saw nothing, heard nothing, and passed nothing. The night was brighter now, and, as he rode back, he verified the entire absence of side-roads. Whatever the thing was which he had seen, it had vanished somewhere along the edge of the common; it had not gone by the main road, nor by any other.

Wimsey came down rather late for breakfast in the morning, to find his hosts in a state of some excitement.

'The most extraordinary thing has happened,' said Mrs Frobisher-Pym.

'Outrageous!' added her husband. 'I warned Hancock – he can't say I didn't warn him. Still, however much one may disapprove of his goings-on, there is no excuse whatever for such abominable conduct. Once let me get hold of the beggars, whoever they are—'

What's up?' said Wimsey, helping himself to broiled kidneys at the sideboard

'A most scandalous thing,' said Mrs Frobisher-Pym. 'The vicar came up to Tom at once – I hope we didn't disturb you, by the way, with all the excitement. It appears that when Mr Hancock got to the church this morning at 6 o'clock to take the early service—'

'No, no, my dear, you've got it wrong. Let *me* tell it. When Joe Grinch – that's the sexton, you know, and he has to get there first to ring the bell – when he arrived, he found the south door wide open and nobody in the chapel, where they should have been, beside the coffin. He was very much perplexed, of course, but he supposed that Hubbard and young Rawlinson had got sick of it and gone off home. So he went on to the vestry to get the vestments and things ready, and to his amazement he heard women's voice, calling out to him from inside. He was so astonished, didn't know where he was, but he went on and unlocked the door—'

'With his own key?' put in Wimsey.

'The key was in the door. As a rule it's kept hanging up on a nail under a curtain near the organ, but it was in the lock – where it ought not to have been. And inside the vestry he found Mrs Hancock and her daughter, nearly dead with fright and annoyance.'

'Great Scott!'

'Yes, indeed. They had a most extraordinary story to tell. They'd taken over at 2 o'clock from the other pair of watchers, and had knelt down by the coffin in the Lady-chapel, according to plan, to say the proper sort of prayers, whatever they are. They'd been there, to the best of their calculation, about ten minutes, when they heard a noise up by the High Altar, as though somebody was creeping stealthily about. Miss Hancock is a very plucky girl, and she got up and walked up the aisle in the dark, with Mrs Hancock following on behind because, as she said, she didn't want to be left alone. When they'd got as far as the rood-screen, Miss Hancock called out aloud, 'Who's there?' At which they heard a sort of rustling sound, and a noise like something being knocked over.

Miss Hancock most courageously snatched up one of the churchwarden's staffs, which was clipped on to the choir-stalls, and ran forward, thinking, she says, that somebody was trying to steal the ornaments off the altar. There's a very fine fifteenth-century cross—'

'Never mind the cross, Tom. That hasn't been taken, at any rate.'

'No, it hasn't, but she thought it might be. Anyhow, just as she got up to the sanctuary steps, with Mrs Hancock coming close after her and begging her to be careful, somebody seemed to rush out of the choir-stalls, and caught her by the arms and frog's-marched her – that's her expression – into the vestry. And before she could get breath even to shriek, Mrs Hancock was pushed in beside her, and the door locked on them.'

'By jove! You do have exciting times in your village.'

'Well,' said Mr Frobisher-Pym, 'of course they were dreadfully frightened, because they didn't know but what these wretches would come back and murder them, and, in any case, they thought the church was being robbed. But the vestry windows are very narrow and barred, and they couldn't do anything except wait. They tried to listen, but they couldn't hear much. Their only hope was that the four-o'clock watchers might come early and catch the thieves at work. But they waited and waited, and they heard four strike, and five, and nobody came.'

'What happened to what's-his-name and Rawlinson then?'

'They couldn't make out, and nor could Grinch. However, they had a good look round the church, and nothing seemed to be taken or disturbed in any way. Just then the vicar came along, and they told him all about it. He was very much shocked, naturally, and his first thought – when he found the ornaments were safe and the poor-box all right – was that some Kensitite people had been stealing the wafers from the what d'you call it.'

'The tabernacle,' suggested Wimsey.

'Yes, that's his name for it. That worried him very much, and he unlocked it and had a look, but the wafers were all there all right, and, as there's only one key, and that was on his own watch-chain, it wasn't a case of anyone substituting unconsecrated wafers for consecrated ones, or any practical joke of that kind. So he sent Mrs and Miss Hancock home, and had a look round the church outside, and the first thing he saw, lying in the bushes near the south door, was young Rawlinson's motor-cycle.'

'Oho!'

'So his next idea was to hunt for Rawlinson and Hubbard. However, he didn't have to look far. He'd got round the church as far as the furnace-house on the north side, when he heard a terrific hullabaloo going on, and people shouting and thumping on the door. So he called Grinch, and they looked through the little window, and there, if you please, were Hubbard and young Rawlinson, bawling and going on and using the most shocking language. It seems they were set upon in exactly the same way, only before they got inside the church. Rawlinson had been passing the evening with Hubbard, I understand, and they had a bit of a sleep downstairs in the back bar, to avoid disturbing the house early – or so they say, though I dare say if the truth was known they were having drinks; and if that's Hancock's idea of a suitable preparation for going to church and saying prayers, all I can say is, it isn't mine. Anyway, they started off just before four, Hubbard going down on the carrier of Rawlinson's bicycle. They had to get off at the south gate, which was pushed to, and while Rawlinson was wheeling the machine up the path two or three men – they couldn't see exactly – jumped out from the trees. There was a bit of a scuffle, but what with the bicycle, and it's being so unexpected, they couldn't put up a very good fight, and the men dropped blankets over their heads, or something. I don't know all the details. At any rate, they were bundled into the furnace-house and left there. They may be there still, for all I know, if they haven't found the key. There should be a spare key, but I don't know what's become of it. They sent up for it this morning, but I haven't seen it about for a long time.'

'It wasn't left in the lock this time, then?'

'No, it wasn't. They've had to send for the locksmith. I'm going down now to see what's to be done about it. Like to come, if you're ready?'

Wimsey said he would. Anything in the nature of a problem always fascinated him.

'You were back pretty late, by the way,' said Mr Frobisher-Pym jovially, as they left the house. 'Yarning over old times, I suppose.'

'We were, indeed,' said Wimsey.

'Hope the old girl carried you all right. Lonely bit of road, isn't it? I don't suppose you saw anybody worse than yourself, as the saying goes?'

'Only a policeman,' said Wimsey untruthfully. He had not yet decided about the phantom coach. No doubt Plunkett would be relieved to know that he was not the only person to whom the 'warning' had come. But, then, had it really been the phantom coach, or merely a delusion, begotten by whisky upon reminiscence? Wimsey, in the cold light of day, was none too certain.

On arriving at the church, the magistrate and his guest found a little crowd collected, conspicuous among whom were the vicar, in cassock and biretta, gesticulating freely, and the local policeman, his tunic buttoned awry and his dignity much impaired by the small fry of the village, who clustered round his legs. He had just finished taking down the statements of the two men who had been released from the stoke-hole. The younger of these, a fresh-faced, impudent-looking fellow of twenty-five or so, was in the act of starting up his motor-cycle. He greeted Mr Frobisher-Pym pleasantly. 'Afraid they've made us look a bit small, sir. You'll excuse me, won't you? I'll have to be getting back to Herriotting. Mr Graham won't be any too pleased if I'm late for the office. I think some of the bright lads have been having a joke with us.' He grinned as he pushed the throttle-lever over and departed in a smother of unnecessary smoke that made Mr Frobisher-Pym sneeze. His fellow-victim, a large, fat man, who looked the sporting publican that he was, grinned shamefacedly at the magistrate.

'Well, Hubbard,' said the latter, 'I hope you've enjoyed your experience. I must say I'm surprised at a man of your size letting himself be shut up in a coal-hole like a naughty urchin.'

'Yes, sir, I was surprised myself at the time,' retorted the publican, good-humouredly enough. 'When that there blanket came down on my head, I was the most surprised man in this here county. I gave 'em a hack or two on the shins, though, to remember me by,' he added, with a reminiscent chuckle.

'How many of them were there?' asked Wimsey.

'Three or four, I should say, sir. But not 'avin' seen 'em, I can only tell from 'earin' 'em talk. There was two laid 'old of me, I'm pretty sure, and young Rawlinson thinks there was only one 'ad 'old of 'im, but 'e was a wonderful strong 'un.'

'We must leave no stone unturned to find out who these people were,' said the vicar excitedly. 'Ah, Mr Frobisher-Pym, come and see what they have done in the church. It is as I thought – an anti-Catholic protest. We must be most thankful that they have done no more than they have.'

He led the way in. Somebody had lit two or three hanging lamps in the gloomy little chancel. By their light Wimsey was able to see that the neck of the eagle lectern was decorated with an enormous red-white-and-blue bow, and bore a large placard – obviously pinched from the local newspaper offices – 'VATICAN BANS IMMODEST DRESS.' In each of the choir-stalls a teddy-bear sat, lumpishly amiable, apparently absorbed in reading the choir-books upside-down, while on the ledge before them copies of the *Pink 'Un* were obtrusively displayed. In the pulpit, a waggish hand had set up a pantomime ass's head, elegantly arrayed in a nightgown, and crowned wish a handsome nimbus, cut from gold paper.

'Disgraceful, isn't it?' said the vicar.

'Well Hancock,' replied Mr Frobisher-Pym, 'I must say I think you have brought it upon yourself – though I quite agree, of course, that this sort of thing cannot possibly be allowed, and the offenders must be discovered and severely punished. But you must see that many of your practices appear to these people to be papistical nonsense at best, and while that is no excuse . . .'

His reprimanding voice barked on.

'. . . what I really can only look upon as this sacriligious business with old Burdock – a man whose life . . .'

The policeman had by this time shoved away the attendant villagers and was standing beside Lord Peter at the entrance of the rood-screen.

'Was that you was out on the road this morning, sir? Ah! I thought I reckernised your voice. Did you get home all right, sir? Didn't meet nothing?'

There seemed to be a shade more than idle questioning in the tone of his voice. Wimsey turned quickly.

'No, I met nothing – more. Who is it drives a coach with four white horses about this village of a night, sergeant?'

'Not sergeant, sir – I ain't due for promotion yet awhile. Well, sir, as to white horses, I don't altogether like to say. Mr Mortimer over at Abbots Bolton has some nice greys, and he's the biggest horse-breeder about these parts – but, well, there, sir, he wouldn't be driving out in all that rain, sir, would he?'

'It doesn't seem a sensible thing to do, certainly.'

'No, sir. And' – the constable leaned close to Wimsey and spoke into his ear – 'and Mr Mortimer is a man that's got a head on his shoulders – *and, what's more, so have his horses.*'

'Why,' said Wimsey, a little startled by the aptness of this remark, 'did you ever know a horse that hadn't?'

'No, sir,' said the policeman, with emphasis, 'I never knew no *livin'* horse that hadn't. But that's neether here nor there, as the sayin' goes. But as to this church business, that's just a bit of a lark got up among the boys, that's what that is. They don't mean no harm, you know, sir; they likes to be up to their tricks. It's all very well for the vicar to talk, sir, but this ain't no Kensitites nor anythink of that, as you can see with half an eye. Just a bit of fun, that's all it is.'

'I'd come to the same conclusion myself,' said Wimsey, interested, 'but I'd rather like to know what makes you think so.'

'Lord bless you, sir, ain't it plain as the nose on your face? If it had a-bin these Kensitites, wouldn't they have gone for the crosses and the images and the lights and – that there?' He extended a horny finger in the direction of the tabernacle. 'No, sir, these lads what did this ain't laid a finger on the things what you might call sacred images – and they ain't done no harm neether to the communion-table. So I says as it ain't a case of con-*trov*ersy, but more a bit of fun, like. And they've treated Mr Burdock's corpse respectful, sir, you see, too. That shows they wasn't meaning anything wrong at heart, don't you see?'

'I agree absolutely,' said Wimsey. 'In fact, they've taken particular care not to touch anything that a churchman holds really sacred. How long have you been on this job, officer?'

'Three years, sir, come February.'

'Ever had any idea of going to town or taking up the detective side of the business?'

'Well, sir – I have – but it isn't ask and have, as you might say.'

Wimsey took a card from his note-case.

'If ever you think seriously about it,' he said, 'give this card to Chief Inspector Parker, and have a chat with him. Tell him I think you haven't got opportunities enough down here. He's a great friend of mine, and he'll give you a good chance, I know.'

'I've heard of you, my lord,' said the constable, gratified, 'and I'm sure it's very kind of your lordship. Well, I suppose I'd best be getting along now. You leave it to me, Mr Frobisher-Pym, sir; we'll soon get at the bottom of this here.'

'I hope you do,' said the magistrate. 'Meanwhile, Mr Hancock, I trust you will realise the inadvisability of leaving the church doors open at night. Well, come along, Wimsey; we'll leave them to get the church straight for the funeral. What have you found there?'

'Nothing,' said Wimsey, who had been peering at the floor of the Lady-chapel. 'I was afraid you'd got the worm in here, but I see it's only sawdust.' He dusted his fingers as he spoke, and followed Mr Frobisher-Pym out of the building.

When you are staying in a village, you are expected to take part in the interests and amusements of the community. Accordingly, Lord Peter duly attended the funeral of Squire Burdock, and beheld the coffin safely committed to the ground, in a drizzle, certainly, but not without the attendance of a large and reverent congregation. After this ceremony, he was formally introduced to Mr and Mrs Haviland Burdock, and was able to confirm his previous impression that the lady was well, not to say too well, dressed, as might be expected from one whose wardrobe was based upon silk stockings. She was a handsome woman, in a large, bold style, and the hand that clasped Wimsey's was quite painfully encrusted with diamonds. Haviland was disposed to be friendly – and, indeed, silk manufacturers have no reason to be otherwise to rich men of noble birth. He seemed to be aware of Wimsey's reputation as an antiquarian and book-collector, and extended a hearty invitation to him to come and see the old house.

'My brother Martin is still abroad,' he said, 'but I'm sure he would be delighted to have you come and look at the place. I'm told there are some very fine old books in the library. We shall be staying here till Monday – if Mrs Hancock will be good enough to have us. Suppose you come along tomorrow afternoon.'

Wimsey said he would be delighted.

Mrs Hancock interposed and said, wouldn't Lord Peter come to tea at the vicarage first.

Wimsey said it was very good of her.

'Then that's settled,' said Mrs Burdock. 'You and Mr Pym come to tea, and then we'll all go over the house together. I've hardly seen it myself yet.'

'It's very well worth seeing,' said Mr Frobisher-Pym. 'Fine old place, but takes some money to keep up. Has nothing been seen of the will yet, Mr Burdock?'

'Nothing whatever,' said Haviland. 'It's curious, because Mr Graham – the solicitor, you know, Lord Peter – certainly drew one up, just after poor Martin's unfortunate difference with our father. He remembers it perfectly.'

'Can't he remember what's in it?'

'He could, of course, but he doesn't think it etiquette to say. He's one of the crusted old type. Poor Martin always called him an old scoundrel – but then, of course, he never approved of Martin, so Martin was not altogether unprejudiced. Besides, as Mr Graham says, all that was some years ago, and it's quite possible that the governor destroyed the will later, or made a new one in America.'

'"Poor Martin" doesn't seem to have been popular hereabouts,' said Wimsey to Mr Frobisher-Pym, as they parted from the Burdocks and turned homewards.

'N-no,' said the magistrate. 'Not with Graham, any-way. Personally, I rather liked the lad, though he was a bit harum-scarum. I dare say he's sobered up with time – and marriage. It's odd that they can't find the will. But, if it was made at the time of the rumpus, it's bound to be in Haviland's favour.'

'I think Haviland thinks so,' said Wimsey. 'His manner seemed to convey a chastened satisfaction. I expect the discreet Graham made it fairly clear that the advantage was not with the unspeakable Martin.'

The following morning turned out fine, and Wimsey, who was supposed to be enjoying a rest-and-fresh-air cure in Little Doddering, petitioned for a further loan of Polly Flinders. His host consented with pleasure, and only regretted that he could not accompany his guest, being booked to attend a Board of Guardians meeting in connection with the workhouse.

'But you could go up and get a good blow on the common,' he suggested. 'Why not go round by Petering Friars, turn off across the common till you get to Dead Man's Post, and come back by the Frimpton road? It makes a very pleasant round – about nineteen miles. You'll be back in nice time for lunch if you take it easy.'

Wimsey fell in with the plan – the more readily that it exactly coincided with his own inward purpose. He had a reason for wishing to ride over the Frimpton road by daylight.

'You'll be careful about Dead Man's Post,' said Mrs Frobisher-Pym a little anxiously. 'The horses have a way of shying at it. I don't know why. People say, of course—'

'All nonsense,' said her husband. 'The villagers dislike the place and that makes the horses nervous. It's remark-

138

able how a rider's feelings communicate themselves to his mount. *I've* never had any trouble at Dead Man's Post.'

It was a quiet and pretty road, even on a November day, that led to Petering Friars. Jogging down the winding Essex lanes in the wintry sunshine, Wimsey felt soothed and happy. A good burst across the common raised his spirits to exhilaration pitch. He had entirely forgotten Dead Man's Post and its uncanny reputation, when a violent start and swerve, so sudden that it nearly unseated him, recalled him to what he was doing. With some difficulty, he controlled Polly Flinders, and brought her to a standstill.

He was at the highest point of the common, following a bridle-path which was bordered on each side by gorse and dead bracken. A little way ahead of him another bridle-path seemed to run into it, and at the junction of the two was something which he had vaguely imagined to be a decayed sign-post. Certainly it was short and thick for a sign-post, and had no arms. It appeared, however, to bear some sort of inscription on the face that was turned towards him.

He soothed the mare, and urged her gently towards the post. She took a few hesitating steps, and plunged sideways, snorting and shivering.

'Queer!' said Wimsey. 'If this is my state of mind communicating itself to my mount, I'd better see a doctor. My nerves must be in a rotten state. Come up, old lady? What's the matter with you?'

Polly Finders, apologetic but determined, refused to budge. He urged gently with his heel. She sidled away, with ears laid back, and he saw the white of a protesting eye. He slipped from the saddle, and, putting his hand through the bridle, endeavoured to lead her forward.

After a little persuasion, the mare followed him, with stretched neck and treading as though on egg-shells. After a dozen hesitating paces, she stopped again, trembling in all her limbs. He put his hand on her neck and found it wet with sweat.

'Damn it all!' said Wimsey. 'Look here, I'm jolly well going to read what's on that post. If you won't come, will you stand still?'

He dropped the bridle. The mare stood quietly, with hanging head. He left her and went forward, glancing back from time to time to see that she showed no disposition to bolt. She stood quietly enough, however, only shifting her feet uneasily.

Wimsey walked up to the post. It was a stout pillar of ancient oak, newly painted white. The inscription, too, had been recently blacked in. It read:

ON THIS SPOT

GEORGE WINTER

WAS FOULLY MURTHERED

IN DEFENSE OF

HIS MASTER'S GOODS

BY BLACK RALPH

OF HERRIOTTING

WHO WAS AFTERWARD

HANGED IN CHAINS

ON THE PLACE OF HIS CRIME

9 NOVEMBER 1674

FEAR JUSTICE

'And very nice too,' said Wimsey. 'Dead Man's Post without a doubt. Polly Flinders seems to share the local feeling about the place. Well, Polly, if them's your sentiments, I won't do violence to them. But may I ask why, if you're so sensitive about a mere post, you should swallow a death-coach and four headless horses with such hardened equanimity?'

The mare took the shoulder of his jacket gently between her lips and mumbled at it.

'Just so,' said Wimsey. 'I perfectly understand. You would if you could, but you really can't. But those horses, Polly – did they bring with them no brimstone blast from the nethermost pit? Can it be that they really exuded nothing but an honest and familiar smell of stables?'

He mounted, and, turning Polly's head to the right, guided her in a circle, so as to give Dead Man's Post a wide berth before striking the path again.

'The supernatural explanation is, I think, excluded. Not on *a priori* grounds, which would be unsound, but on the evidence of Polly's senses. There remain the alternatives of whisky and jiggery-pokery. Further investigation seems called for.'

He continued to muse as the mare moved quietly forward.

'Supposing I wanted, for some reason, to scare the neighbourhood with the apparition of a coach and headless horses, I should choose a dark, rainy night. Good! It was that kind of night. Now, if I took black horses and painted their bodies white – poor devils! what a state they'd be in. No. How do they do these Maskelyne-and-Devant stunts where they cut off people's heads? White horses, of course – and black felt clothing over their heads. Right! And luminous paint on the harness, with a touch here and there on their bodies, to make good contrast and ensure that the whole show wasn't invisible.

No difficulty about that. But they must go silently. Well, why not? Four stout black cloth bags filled with bran, drawn well up and tied round the fetlocks would make any horse go quietly enough, especially if there was a bit of a wind going. Rags round the bridle-rings to prevent clinking, and round the ends of the traces to keep 'em from squeaking. Give 'em a coachman in a white coat and black mask, hitch 'em to a rubber-tyred fly, picked out with phosphorus and well-oiled at the joints – and I swear I'd make something quite ghostly enough to startle a rather well-irrigated gentleman on a lonely road at half-past two in the morning.'

He was pleased with this thought, and tapped his boot cheerfully with his whip.

'But damn it all! They never passed me again. Where did they go? A coach-and-horses can't vanish into thin air, you know. There must be a side-road after all – or else, Polly Flinders, you've been pulling my leg all the time.'

The bridle-path eventually debouched upon the highway at the now familiar fork where Wimsey had met the policeman. As he slowly ambled homewards, his lordship scanned the left-hand hedgerow, looking for the lane which surely must exist. But nothing rewarded his search. Enclosed fields with padlocked gates presented the only breaks in the hedge, till he again found himself looking down the avenue of trees up which the death-coach had come galloping two nights before.

'Damn!' said Wimsey.

'It occurred to him for the first time that the coach might perhaps have turned round and gone back through Little Doddering. Certainly it had been seen by Little Doddering Church on Wednesday. But on that occasion, also, it had galloped off in the direction of Frimpton. In fact, thinking it over, Wimsey concluded that it had approached from Frimpton, gone round the church – widdershins, naturally – by the Back Lane, and returned by the high-road whence it came. But in that case—

'Turn again, Whittington,' said Wimsey, and Polly Finders rotated obediently in the road. 'Through one of those fields it went, or I'm a Dutchman.'

He pulled Polly into a slow walk, and passed along the strip of grass at the right-hand side, staring at the ground as though he were an Aberdonian who had lost a sixpence.

The first gate led into a ploughed field, harrowed smooth and sown with autumn wheat. It was clear that no wheeled thing had been across it for many weeks. The second gate looked more promising. It gave upon fallow ground, and the entrance was seamed with innumerable wheel-ruts. On further examination, however, it was clear that this was the one and only gate. It seemed unlikely that the mysterious coach should have been taken into a field from which there was no way out. Wimsey decided to seek further.

The third gate was in bad repair. It sagged heavily from its hinges; the hasp was gone, and the gate and post had been secured with elaborate twists of wire. Wimsey dismounted and examined these, convincing himself that their rusty surface had not been recently disturbed.

There remained only two more gates before he came to the cross-roads. One led into plough again, where the dark ridge-and-furrow showed no sign of disturbance, but at sight of the last Wimsey's heart gave a leap.

There was plough-land here also, but round the edge of the field ran a wide, beaten path, rutted and waterlogged. The gate was not locked, but opened simply with a spring catch. Wimsey examined the approach. Among the wide ruts made by farm-waggons was the track of four narrow wheels – the unmistakable prints of rubber tyres. He pushed the gate open and passed through.

The path skirted two sides of the plough; then came another gate and another field, containing a long barrow of mangold wurzels and a couple of barns. At the sound of Polly's hoofs, a man emerged from the nearest barn, with a paint-brush in his hand, and stood watching Wimsey's approach.

' 'Morning!' said the latter genially.

' 'Morning, sir.'

'Fine day after the rain?'

'Yes, it is, sir.'

'I hope I'm not trespassing?'

'Where was you wanting to go, sir?'

'I thought, as a matter of fact – hullo!'

'Anything wrong sir?'

Wimsey shifted in the saddle.

'I fancy this girth's slipped a bit. It's a new one.' (This was a fact.) 'Better have a look.'

The man advanced to investigate, but Wimsey had dismounted and was tugging at the strap, with his head under the mare's belly.

'Yes, it wants taking up a trifle. Oh! Thanks most awfully. Is this a short cut to Abbotts Bolton, by the way?'

'Not to the village, sir, though you can get through this way. It comes out by Mr Mortimer's stables.'

'Ah, yes. This his land?'

'No, sir, it's Mr Topham's land, but Mr Mortimer rents this field and the next for fodder.'

'Oh, yes.' Wimsey peered across the hedge. 'Lucerne, I suppose. Or clover.'

'Clover, sir. And the mangolds is for the cattle.'

'Oh – Mr Mortimer keeps cattle as well as horses?'

'Yes, sir.'

'Very jolly. Have a gasper?' Wimsey had sidled across to the barn in his interest, and was gazing absently into its dark interior. It contained a number of farm implements and a black fly of antique construction, which seemed to be undergoing renovation with black varnish. Wimsey pulled some vestas from his pocket. The box was apparently damp, for, after one or two vain attempts he abandoned it, and struck a match on the wall of the barn. The flame, lighting up the ancient fly, showed it to be incongruously fitted with rubber tyres.

'Very fine stud, Mr Mortimer's, I understand,' said Wimsey carelessly.

'Yes, sir, very fine indeed.'

'I suppose he hasn't any greys, by any chance. My mother – queenly woman, Victorian ideas, and all that – is rather keen on greys. Sports a carriage and pay-ah, don't you know.'

'Yes, sir? Well, Mr Mortimer would be able to suit the lady, I think, sir. He has several greys.'

'No? has he though? I must really go over and see him. Is it far?'

'Matter of five or six miles by the fields, sir.'

Wimsey looked at his watch.

'Oh, dear! I'm really afraid it's too far for this morning. I absolutely promised to get back to lunch. I must come over another day. Thanks *so* much. Is that girth right now? Oh, really, I'm immensely obliged. Get yourself a drink, won't you and tell Mr Mortimer not to sell his greys till I've seen them. Well, *good* morning, and many thanks.'

He set Polly Flinders on the homeward path and trotted gently away. Not till he was out of sight of the barn did he pull up and, stooping from the saddle, thoughtfully examine his boots. They were liberally plastered with bran.

'I must have picked it up in the barn,' said Wimsey. 'Curious, if true. Why should Mr Mortimer be lashing the stuffing out of his greys in an old fly at the dead of night – and with muffled hoofs and no heads, to boot? It's not a kind thing to do. It frightened Plunkett very much. It made me think I was drunk – a thought I hate to think. Ought I to tell the police? Are Mr Mortimer's jokes any business of mine? What do *you* think, Polly?'

The mare, hearing her name, energetically shook her head.

'You think not? Perhaps you are right. Let us say that Mr Mortimer did it for a wager. Who am I to interfere with his amusements? All the same,' added his lordship, 'I'm glad to know it wasn't Lumsden's whisky.'

'This is the library,' said Haviland, ushering in his guests. 'A fine room – and a fine collection of books, I'm told, though literature isn't much in my line. It wasn't much in the governor's line, either, I'm afraid. The place wants doing up, as you see. I don't know whether Martin will take it in hand. It's a job that'll cost money, of course.'

Wimsey shivered a little as he gazed round, more from sympathy than from cold, though a white November fog lay curled against the tall windows, and filtered damply through the frames.

A long, mouldering room, in the frigid neo-classical

146

style, the library was melancholy enough in the sunless grey afternoon, even without the signs of neglect which wrung the book-collector's heart. The walls, panelled to half their height with book-cases, ran up in plaster to the moulded ceiling. Damp had blotched them into grotesque shapes, and here and there were ugly cracks and squamous patches, from which the plaster had fallen in yellowish flakes. A wet chill seemed to ooze from the books, from the calf bindings peeling and perishing, from the stains of greenish mildew which spread horridly from volume to volume. The curious musty odour of decayed leather and damp paper added to the general cheerlessness of the atmosphere.

'Oh, dear, dear!' said Wimsey, peering dismally into this sepulchre of forgotten learning, With his shoulders hunched like the neck-feathers of a chilly bird, with his long nose and half-shut eyes, he resembled a dilapidated heron, brooding over the stagnation of a wintry pool.

'What a freezing-cold place,' exclaimed Mrs Hancock. 'You really ought to scold Mrs Lovall, Mr Burdock. When she was put in here as caretaker, I said to my husband – didn't I, Philip? – that your father had chosen the laziest woman in Little Doddering. She ought to have kept up big fires here, *at least* twice a week! It's really shameful, the way she has let things go.'

'Yes, isn't it?' agreed Haviland.

Wimsey said nothing. He was nosing along the shelves, every now and then taking a volume down and glancing at it.

'It was always rather a depressing room,' went on Haviland. 'I remember, when I was a kid, it used to overawe me rather. Martin and I used to browse about among the books, you know, but I think we were always

147

afraid that something or somebody would stalk out upon us from the dark corners. What's that you've got there, Lord Peter? Oh, *Foxe's Book of Martyrs*. Dear me! How those pictures did terrify me in the old days! And there was a *Pilgrim's Progress*, with a most alarming picture of Apollyon straddling over the whole breadth of the way, which gave me many nightmares. Let me see. It used to live over in this bay, I think. Yes, here it is. How it does bring it all back, to be sure! Is it valuable, by the way?'

'No, not really. But this first edition of Burton is worth money; badly spotted, though – you'd better send it to be cleaned. And this is an extremely fine Boccaccio; take care of it.'

'John Boccace – *The Dance of Machabree*. It's a good title, anyhow. Is that the same Boccaccio that wrote the naughty stories?'

'Yes,' said Wimsey, a little shortly. He resented this attitude towards Boccaccio.

'Never read them,' said Haviland, with a wink at his wife, 'but I've seen 'em in the windows of those surgical shops – so I suppose they're naughty, eh? The vicar's looking shocked.'

'Oh, not at all,' said Mr Hancock, with a conscientious assumption of broad-mindedness. '*Et ego in Arcadia*— that is to say, one doesn't enter the Church without undergoing a classical education, and making the acquaintance of much more worldly authors even than Boccaccio. Those woodcuts are very fine, to my uninstructed eye.'

'Very fine indeed,' said Wimsey.

'There's another old book I remember, with jolly pictures,' said Haviland. 'A chronicle of some sort – what's 'is name – place in Germany – *you* know – where that hangman came from. They published his diary the other day. I read it, but it wasn't very exciting; not half as gruesome as old Harrison Ainsworth. What's the name of the place?'

'Nüremberg?' suggested Wimsey.

'That's it, of course – the *Nüremberg Chronicle*. I wonder if that's still in its old place. It was over here by the window, if I remember rightly.'

He led the way to the end of the bays, which ran up close against a window. Here the damp seemed to have done its worst. A pane of glass was broken, and rain had blown in.

'Now where has it gone to? A big book, it was, with a stamped leather binding. I'd like to see the old *Chronicle* again. I haven't set eyes on it for donkey's years.'

His glance roamed vaguely over the shelves. Wimsey, with the book-lover's instinct, was the first to spot the *Chronicle*, wedged at the extreme end of the shelf, against the outer wall. He hitched his finger into the top edge of the spine, but finding that the rotting leather was ready to crumble at a touch, he dislodged a neighbouring book and drew the *Chronicle* gently out, using his whole hand.

'Here he is – in pretty bad condition, I'm afraid. Hullo!'

As he drew the book away from the wall, a piece of folded parchment came away with it and fell at his feet. He stooped and picked it up.

'I say, Burdock – isn't this what you've been looking for?'

Haviland Burdock, who had been rooting about on one of the lower shelves, straightened himself quickly, his face red from stooping.

'By jove!' he said, turning first redder and then pale with excitement. 'Look at this, Winnie. It's the governor's will. What an extraordinary thing! Whoever would have thought of looking for it here, of all places?'

'Is it really the will?' cried Mrs Hancock.

'No doubt about it, I should say,' observed Wimsey coolly. 'Last Will and Testament of Simon Burdock.' He stood, turning the grimy document over and over in his hands, looking from the endorsement to the plain side of the folded parchment.

'Well, well!' said Mr Hancock. 'How strange! It seems almost providential that you should have taken that book down.'

'What does the will say?' demanded Mrs Burdock, in some excitement.

'I beg your pardon,' said Wimsey, handing it over to her. 'Yes, as you say, Mr Hancook, it does almost seem as if I was meant to find it.' He glanced down again at the *Chronicle*, mournfully tracing with his finger the outline of a damp stain which had rotted the cover and spread to the inner pages, almost obliterating the colophon.

Haviland Burdock meanwhile had spread the will out on the nearest table. His wife leaned over his shoulder. The Hancocks, barely controlling their curiosity, stood near, awaiting the result. Wimsey, with an elaborate pretence of non-interference in this family matter, examined the wall against which the *Chronicle* had stood, feeling its moist surface and examining the damp-stains. They had assumed the appearance of a grinning face. He compared them with the corresponding mark on the book, and shook his head desolately over the damage.

Mr Frobisher-Pym, who had wandered away some time before and was absorbed in an ancient book of farriery, now approached, and enquired what the excitement was about

'Listen to this!' cried Haviland. His voice was quiet, but a suppressed triumph throbbed in it and glittered from his eyes.

'"I bequeath everything of which I die possessed" – there's a lot of enumeration of properties here, which doesn't matter – "to my eldest son, Martin"—'

Mr Frobisher-Pym whistled.

'Listen! "To my eldest son Martin, for so long as my body shall remain above ground. But so soon as I am buried, I direct that the whole of this property shall revert to my younger son Haviland absolutely"—'

'Good God!' said Mr Frobisher-Pym.

'There's a lot more,' said Haviland 'but that's the gist of it.'

'Let me see,' said the magistrate.

He took the will from Haviland, and read it through with a frowning face.

'That's right,' he said. 'No possible doubt about it. Martin has had his property and lost it again. How very curious. Up till yesterday everything belonged to him, though nobody knew it. Now it is all yours, Burdock. This certainly is the strangest will I ever saw. Just fancy that. Martin the heir, up to the time of the funeral. And now – well, Burdock, I must congratulate you.'

'Thank you,' said Haviland. 'It is very unexpected.' He laughed unsteadily.

'But what a queer idea!' cried Mrs Burdock. 'Suppose Martin had been at home. It almost seems a mercy that he wasn't, doesn't it? I mean, it would all have been so awkward. What would have happened if he had tried to stop the funeral, for instance?'

'Yes,' said Mrs Hancock. 'Could he have done anything? Who decides about funerals?'

'The executors, as a rule,' said Mr Frobisher-Pym.

'Who are the executors in this case?' enquired Wimsey.

'I don't know. Let me see.' Mr Frobisher-Pym examined the document again. 'Ah yes! Here we are: "I appoint my two sons, Martin and Haviland, joint executors of this my will." What an extraordinary arrangement.'

'I call it a wicked, un-Christian arrangement,' cried Mrs Hancock. 'It might have caused dreadful mischief if the will hadn't been – quite providentially – lost!'

'Hush, my dear!' said her husband.

'I'm afraid,' said Haviland grimly, 'that that was my father's idea. It's no use my pretending he wasn't spiteful; he was, and I believe he hated both Martin and me like poison.'

'Don't say that,' pleaded the vicar.

'I do say it. He made our lives a burden to us, and he obviously wanted to go on making them a burden after he was dead. If he'd seen us cutting each other's throats, he'd only have been too pleased. Come, vicar, it's no use pretending. He hated our mother and was jealous of us. Everybody knows that. It probably pleased his unpleasant sense of humour to think of us squabbling over his body. Fortunately, he over-reached himself when he hid the will here. He's buried now, and the problem settles itself.'

'Are you quite sure of that?' said Wimsey.

'Why, of course,' said the magistrate. 'The property goes to Mr Haviland Burdock as soon as his father's body is underground. Well, his father was buried yesterday.'

'But are you sure of *that*?' repeated Wimsey. He looked from one to the other, quizzically, his long lips curling into something like a grin.

'Sure of that?' exclaimed the vicar. 'My dear Lord Peter, you were present at the funeral. You saw him buried yourself.'

'I saw his coffin buried,' said Wimsey mildly. 'That the body was in it is merely an unverified inference.'

'I think,' said Mr Frobisher-Pym, 'this is rather an unseemly kind of jest, There is no reason to imagine that the body was not in the coffin.'

'I saw it in the coffin,' said Haviland, 'and so did my wife.'

'And so did I,' said the vicar. 'I was present when it was transferred from the temporary shell in which it crossed over from the States to a permanent lead-and-oak coffin provided by Joliffe. And, if further witnesses are necessary, you can easily get Joliffe himself and his men, who put the body in and screwed it down.'

'Just so,' said Wimsey. 'I'm not denying that the body was in the coffin when the coffin was placed in the chapel. I only doubt whether it was there when it was put in the ground.'

'That is a most unheard-of suggestion to make, Lord Peter,' said Mr Frobisher-Pym, with severity. 'May I ask if you have anything to go upon? And, if the body is not in the grave, perhaps you wouldn't mind telling us where you imagine it to be?'

'Not at all,' said Wimsey. He perched himself on the edge off the table and sat, swinging his legs and looking down at his own hands, as he ticked his points off on his fingers.

'I think,' he said, 'that this story begins with young

Rawlinson. He is a clerk in the office of Mr Graham, who drew up his will, and I fancy he knows something about its conditions. So, of course, does Mr Graham, but I don't somehow suspect *him* of being mixed up in this. From what I can hear, he is not a man to take sides – or not Mr Martin's side, at any rate.

'When the news of Mr Burdock's death was cabled over from the States, I think young Rawlinson remembered the terms of the will, and considered that Mr Martin – being abroad and all that – would be rather at a disadvantage. Rawlinson must be rather attached to your brother, by the way—'

'Martin always had a way of picking up good-for-nothing youths and wasting his time with them,' agreed Haviland sulkily.

The vicar seemed to feel that this statement needed some amendment, and murmured that he had always heard how good Martin was with the village lads.

'Quite so,' said Wimsey. 'Well, I think young Rawlinson wanted to give Martin an equal chance of securing the legacy, don't you see. He didn't like to say anything about the will – which might or might not turn up – and possibly he thought that even if it did turn up there might be difficulties. Well, anyway, he decided that the best thing to do was to steal the body and keep it aboveground till Martin came home to see to things himself.'

'This is an extraordinary accusation,' began Mr Frobisher-Pym.

'I dare say I'm mistaken,' said Wimsey, 'but it's just my idea. It makes a damn good story, anyhow – you see! Well, then, young Rawlinson saw that this was too big a job to carry out alone, so he looked round for somebody to help him. And he pitched on Mr Mortimer.'

'Mortimer?'

'I don't know Mr Mortimer personally, but he seems to be a sportin' sort of customer from what I can hear, with certain facilities which everybody hasn't got. Young Rawlinson and Mortimer put their heads together and worked out a plan of action. Of course, Mr Hancock, you helped them enormously with this lying-in-state idea of yours. Without that, I don't know if they could have worked it.'

Mr Hancock made an embarrassed clucking sound.

'The idea was this. Mortimer was to provide an antique fly and four white horses, made up with luminous paint and black cloth to represent the Burdock death-coach. The advantage of that idea was that nobody would feel inclined to inspect the turn-out too closely if they saw it hangin' round the churchyard at unearthly hours. Meanwhile, young Rawlinson had to get himself accepted as a watcher for the chapel, and to find a sporting companion to watch with him and take a hand in the game. He fixed things up with the publican-fellow, and spun a tale for Mr Hancock, so as to get the vigil from four to six. Didn't it strike you as odd, Mr Hancock, that he should be so keen to come all the way from Herriotting?'

'I am accustomed to find keenness in my congregation,' said Mr Hancock stiffly.

'Yes, but Rawlinson didn't belong to your congregation. Anyway it was all worked out, and there was a dress-rehearsal on the Wednesday night, which frightened your man Plunkett into fits, sir.'

'If I thought this was true –' said Mr Frobisher-Pym.

'On Thursday night,' pursued Wimsey, 'the conspirators were ready, hidden in the chancel at two in the morning. They waited till Mrs and Miss Hancock had taken their places, and then made a row to attract their attention. When the ladies courageously advanced to find out what was up, they popped out and bundled 'em into the vestry.'

'Good gracious!' said Mrs Hancock.

'That was when the death-coach affair was timed to drive up to the south door. It came round the Back Lane, I fancy, though I can't be sure. Then Mortimer and the other two took the embalmed body out of the coffin and filled its place up with bags of sawdust. I know it was sawdust, because I found the remains of it on the Lady-chapel floor in the morning. They put the body in the fly, and Mortimer drove off with it. They passed me on the Herriotting road at half-past two, so they can't have wasted much time over the job. Mortimer may have been alone, or possibly he had someone with him to see to the body while he himself did the headless coachman business in a black mask. I'm not certain about that. They drove through the last gate before you come to the fork at Frimpton, and went across the fields to Mortimer's barn. They left the fly there – I know that, because I saw it, and I saw the bran they used to muffle the horses' hoofs, too. I expect they took it on from there in a car, and fetched the horses up next day – but that's a detail. I don't know, either, where they took the body to, but I expect, if you went and asked Mortimer about it, he would be able to assure you that it was still above ground.'

Wimsey paused. Mr Frobisher-Pym and the Hancocks were looking only puzzled and angry, but Haviland's face was green. Mrs Haviland showed a red, painted spot on each cheek, and her mouth was haggard. Wimsey picked up the *Nüremberg Chronicle* and caressed its covers thoughtfully as he went on.

'Meanwhile, of course, young Rawlinson and his companion were doing the camouflage in the church, to give the idea of a Protestant outrage. Having fixed everything up neat and pretty, all they had to do was to lock themselves up in the furnace-house and chuck the key through the window. You'll probably find it there, Mr Hancock, if you care to look. Didn't you think that story of an assault by two or three men was a bit thin? Hubbard is a hefty great fellow, and Rawlinson's a sturdy lad – and yet, on their own showing, they were bundled into a coal-hole like helpless infants, without a scratch on either of 'em. Look for the men in buckram, my dear sir, look for the men in buckram!'

'Look here, Wimsey, are you sure you're not romancing?' said Mr Frobisher-Pym. 'One would need some very clear proof before—'

'Certainly,' said Wimsey. 'Get a Home Office order. Open the grave. You'll soon see whether it's true or whether it's just my diseased imagination.'

'I think this whole conversation is disgusting,' cried Mrs Burdock. 'Don't listen to it, Haviland. Anything more heartless on the day after father's funeral than sitting here and inventing such a revolting story I simply can't imagine. It is not worth paying a moment's attention to. You will certainly not permit your father's body to be disturbed. It's horrible. It's a desecration.'

'It is very unpleasant indeed,' said Mr Frobisher-Pym gravely, 'but if Lord Peter is seriously putting forward this astonishing theory, which I can scarcely credit—'

Wimsey shrugged his shoulders.

' – then I feel bound to remind you, Mr Burdock, that

your brother, when he returns, may insist on having the matter investigated.'

'But he can't, can he?' said Mrs Burdock.

'Of course he can, Winnie,' snapped her husband savagely. 'He's an executor. He has as much right to have the governor dug up as I have to forbid it. Don't be a fool.'

'If Martin had any decency, he would forbid it, too,' said Mrs Burdock.

'Oh, well!' said Mrs Hancock, 'shocking as it may seem, there's the money to be considered. Mr Martin might think it a duty to his wife, and his family, if he should ever have any—'

'The whole thing is preposterous,' said Haviland decidedly. 'I don't believe a word of it. If I did, naturally I should be the first person to take action in the matter – not only in justice to Martin, but on my own account. But if you ask me to believe that a responsible man like Mortimer would purloin a corpse and desecrate a church – the thing only has to be put into plain words to show how absurd and unthinkable it is. I suppose Lord Peter Wimsey, who consorts, as I understand, with criminals and police officers, finds the idea conceivable. I can only say that I do not. I am sorry that his mind should have become so blunted to all decent feeling. That's all. Good afternoon.'

Mr Frobisher-Pym jumped up.

'Come, come, Burdock, don't take that attitude. I am sure Lord Peter intended no discourtesy. I must say I think he's all wrong, but, 'pon my soul, things have been so disturbed in the village these last few days, I'm not surprised anybody should think there was something behind it. Now, let's forget about it – and hadn't we better be moving out of this terribly cold room? It's nearly dinner-time. Bless me, what will Agatha think of us?'

Wimsey held out his hand to Burdock, who took it reluctantly.

'I'm sorry,' said Wimsey. 'I suffer from hypertrophy of the imagination, y' know. Over-stimulation of the thyroid probably. Don't mind me. I apologise, and all that.'

'I don't think, Lord Peter,' said Mrs Burdock acidly, 'you ought to exercise your imagination at the expense of good taste.'

Wimsey followed her from the room in some confusion. Indeed, he was so disturbed that he carried away the *Nüremberg Chronicle* beneath his arm, which was an odd thing for him to do under the circumstances.

'I am gravely distressed,' said Mr Hancock.

He had come over, after Sunday evening service, to call upon the Frobisher-Pyms. He sat upright on his chair, his thin face flushed with anxiety.

'I could never have believed such a thing of Hubbard. It has been a grievous shock to me. It is not only the great wickedness of stealing a dead body from the very precincts of the church, though that is grave enough. It is the sad hypocrisy of his behaviour – the mockery of sacred things – the making use of the holy services of his religion to further worldly ends. He actually attended the funeral, Mr Frobisher-Pym, and exhibited every sign of grief and respect. Even now he hardly seems to realise the sinfulness of his conduct. I feel it very much, as a priest and as a pastor – very much indeed.'

'Oh, well, Hancock,' said Mr Frobisher-Pym, 'you must make allowances, you know. Hubbard's not a bad fellow, but you can't expect refinement of feeling from a man of his class. The point is, what are we to do about it? Mr Burdock must be told, of course. It's a most awkward situation. Dear me! Hubbard confessed the whole conspiracy, you say? How did he come to do that?'

'I taxed him with it,' said the parson. 'When I came to think over Lord Peter Wimsey's remarks, I was troubled in my mind. It seemed to me – I cannot say why – that there might be some truth in the story, wild as it appeared. I was so worried about it that I swept the floor of the Lady-chapel myself last night, and I found quite a quantity of sawdust among the sweepings. That led me to search for the key of the furnace-house, and I discovered it in some bushes at a little distance – in fact, within a stone's throw – of the furnace-house window. I sought guidance in prayer – and from my wife, whose judgement I greatly respect – and I made up my mind to speak to Hubbard after Mass. It was a great relief to me that he did not present himself at Early Celebration. Feeling as I did, I should have had scruples.'

'Just so, just so,' said the magistrate, a little impatiently. 'Well, you taxed him with it, and he confessed?'

'He did. I am sorry to say he showed no remorse at all. He even laughed. It was a most painful interview.'

'I am sure it must have been,' said Mrs Frobisher-Pym sympathetically.

'We must go and see Mr Burdock,' said the magistrate, rising. 'Whatever old Burdock may or may not have intended by that iniquitous will of his, it's quite evident that Hubbard and Mortimer and Rawlinson were entirely in the wrong. Upon my word, I've no idea whether it's an indictable offence to steal a body. I must look it up.

But I should say it was. If there is any property in a corpse, it must belong to the family or the executors. And in case, it's sacrilege, to say nothing of the scandal in the parish. I must say, Hancock, it won't do us any good in the eyes of the Nonconformists. However, no doubt you realise that. Well, it's an unpleasant job, and the sooner we tackle it the better. I'll run over to the vicarage with you and help you to break it to the Burdocks. How about you, Wimsey? You were right, after all, and I think Burdock owes you an apology.'

'Oh, I'll keep out of it,' said Wimsey. 'I shan't be exactly *persona grata*, don't you know. It's going to mean a deuce of a big financial loss to the Haviland Burdocks.'

'So it is. Most unpleasant. Well, perhaps you're right Come along, vicar.'

Wimsey and his hostess sat discussing the matter by the fire for half an hour or so, when Mr Frobisher-Pym suddenly put his head in and said:

'I say, Wimsey – we're all going over to Mortimer's. I wish you'd come and drive the car. Merridew always has the day off on Sunday, and I don't care about driving at night, particularly in this fog.'

'Right you are,' said Wimsey. He ran upstairs, and came down in a few moments wearing a heavy leather flying-coat, and with a parcel under his arm. He greeted the Burdocks briefly, climbed into the driving-seat, and was soon steering cautiously through the mist along the Herriotting Road.

He smiled a little grimly to himself as they came up under the trees to the spot where the phantom coach had passed him. As they passed the gate through which the ingenious apparition had vanished, he indulged himself by pointing it out, and was rewarded by hearing a snarl from Haviland. At the well-remembered fork, he took the right-hand turning into Frimpton and drove steadily for six miles or so, till a warning shout from Mr Frobisher-Pym summoned him to look out for the turning up to Mortimer's.

Mr Mortimer's house, with its extensive stabling and farm buildings, stood about two miles back from the main road. In the darkness Wimsey could see little of it; but he noticed that the ground-floor windows were all lit up, and, when the door opened to the magistrate's imperative ring, a loud burst of laughter from the interior gave evidence that Mr Mortimer was not taking his misdoings too seriously.

'Is Mr Mortimer at home?' demanded Mr Frobisher-Pym, in the tone of a man not to be trifled with.

'Yes, sir. Will you come in, please?'

They stepped into a large, old-fashioned hall, brilliantly lit, and made cosy with a heavy oak screen across the door. As Wimsey advanced, blinking, from the darkness, he saw a large, thick-set man, with a ruddy face, advancing with hand outstretched in welcome.

'Frobisher-Pym! By Jove! how decent of you to come over! We've got some old friends of yours here. Oh!' (in a slightly altered tone) 'Burdock! Well, well——'

'Damn you!' said Haviland Burdock, thrusting furiously past the magistrate, who was trying to hold him back, 'Damn you, you swine! Chuck this bloody farce. What have you done with the body?'

'The body, eh?' said Mr Mortimer, retreating in some confusion.

'Yes, curse you! Your friend Hubbard's split. It's no good denying it. What the devil do you mean by it?

You've got the body here somewhere. Where is it? Hand it over!'

He strode threateningly round the screen into the lamplight. A tall, thin man rose up unexpectedly from the depths of an armchair and confronted him.

'Hold hard, old man!'

'Good God! said Haviland, stepping heavily back on Wimsey's toes. 'Martin!'

'Sure,' said the other. 'Here I am. Come back like a bad halfpenny. How are you?'

'So *you're* at the bottom of this!' stormed Haviland. 'I might have known it. You damned, dirty hound! I suppose you think it's decent to drag your father out of his coffin and tote him about the country like a circus. It's degrading. It's disgusting. It's abominable. You must be perfectly dead to all decent feeling. You don't deny it, I suppose?'

'I say, Burdock!' expostulated Mortimer.

'Shut up, curse you!' said Haviland. 'I'll deal with you in a minute. Now, look here, Martin, I'm not going to stand any more of this disgraceful behaviour. You'll give up that body, and—'

'Just a moment, just a moment,' said Martin. He stood, smiling a little, his hands thrust into the pockets of his dinner-jacket. 'This *éclaircissement* seems to be rather public. Who are all these people? Oh, it's the vicar, I see. I'm afraid we owe you a little explanation, vicar. And, er—'

'This is Lord Peter Wimsey,' put in Mr Frobisher-Pym, 'who discovered your – I'm afraid, Burdock, I must agree with your brother in calling it your disgraceful plot.'

'Oh, Lord!' said Martin. 'I say, Mortimer, you didn't know you were up against Lord Peter Wimsey, did you?

No wonder the cat got out of the bag. The man's known to be a perfect Sherlock. However, I seem to have got home at the crucial moment, so there's no harm done. Diana, this is Lord Peter Wimsey – my wife.'

A young and pretty woman in a black evening dress greeted Wimsey with a shy smile, and turned deprecatingly to her brother-in-law.

'Haviland, we want to explain—'

He paid no attention to her.

'Now then, Martin, the game's up.'

'I think it is, Haviland. But why make all this racket?'

'Racket! I like that. You take your own father's body out of its coffin—'

'No, no, Haviland. I knew nothing about it. I swear that. I only got the news of his death a few days ago. We were right out in the wilds, filming a show in the Pyrenees, and I came straight back as soon as I could get away. Mortimer here, with Rawlinson and Hubbard, staged the whole show by themselves. I never heard a word about it till yesterday morning in Paris, when I found his letter waiting at my old digs. Honestly, Haviland, I had nothing to do with it. Why should I? I didn't need to.'

'What do you mean?'

'Well, if I'd been here, I should only have had to speak to stop the funeral altogether. Why on earth should I have gone to the trouble of stealing the body? Quite apart from the irreverence and all that. As it is, when Mortimer told me about it, I must say I was a bit revolted at the idea, though I appreciated the kindness and the trouble they'd been to on my account. I think Mr Hancock has most cause for wrath, really. But Mortimer has been as careful as possible, sir – really he has. He has placed the old governor quite reverently and decently in what used to be the chapel, and put flowers round him and so on. You will be quite satisfied, I'm sure.'

'Yes, yes,' said Mortimer. 'No disrespect intended, don't you know. Come and see him.'

'This is dreadful,' said the vicar helplessly.

'They had to do the best they could, don't you see, in my absence,' said Mortimer. 'As soon as I can, I'll make proper arrangements for a suitable tomb – above ground, of course. Or possibly cremation would fit the case.'

'What!' gasped Haviland. 'Do you mean to say you imagine I'm going to let my father stay unburied, simply because of your disgusting greed about money?'

'My dear chap, do you think I'm going to let you put him underground, simply to enable you to grab my property?'

'I'm the executor of his will, and I say he shall be buried whether you like it or not!'

'And *I'm* an executor too – and I say he shan't be buried. He can be kept absolutely decently above ground, and he shall be.'

'But hear me,' said the vicar, distracted between these two disagreeable and angry young men.

'I'll see what Graham says about you,' bawled Haviland.

'Oh, yes – the honest lawyer, Graham,' sneered Martin. '*He* knew what was in the will, didn't he? I suppose he didn't mention it to *you*, by any chance?'

'He did not,' retorted Haviland. 'He knew too well the sort of skunk *you* were to say anything about it. Not content with disgracing us with your miserable, blackmailing marriage—'

'Mr Burdock, Mr Burdock—'

165

'Take care, Haviland!'

'You have no more decency—'

'Stop it!'

'Than to steal your father's body and my money so that you and your damned wife can carry on your loose-living, beastly ways with a parcel of film-actors and chorus-girls—'

'Now then, Haviland. Keep your tongue off my wife and my friends. How about your own? Somebody told me Winnie'd been going the pace pretty well – next door to bankruptcy, aren't you, with the gees and the tables and God knows what! No wonder you want to do your brother out of his money. I never thought much of you, Haviland, but by God—'

'One moment!'

Mr Frobisher-Pym at last succeeded in asserting himself, partly through the habit of authority, and partly because the brothers had shouted themselves breathless.

'One moment, Martin. I will call you so, because I have known you a long time, and your father too. I understand your anger at the things Haviland has said. They were unpardonable, as I am sure he will realise when he comes to his right mind. But you must remember that he has been greatly shocked and upset – as we all have been – by this very very painful business. And it is not fair to say that Haviland has tried to "do you out" of anything. He knew nothing about this iniquitous will, and he naturally saw to it that the funeral arrangements were carried out in the usual way. You must settle the future amicably between you, just as you would have done had the will not been accidentally mislaid. Now, Martin – and Haviland too – think it over. My dear boys, this scene is simply appalling. It really must not happen.

Surely the estate can be divided up in a friendly manner between you. It is horrible that an old man's body should be a bone of contention between his own sons, just over a matter of money.'

'I'm sorry,' said Martin. 'I forgot myself. You're quite right, sir. Look here, Haviland, forget it. I'll let you have half the money—'

'Half the money! But it's all mine. *You'll* let me have half? How damned generous! My own money!'

'No, old man. It's mine at the moment. The governor's not buried yet, you know. That's right, isn't it, Mr Frobisher-Pym?'

'Yes; the money is yours, legally, at this moment. You must see that, Haviland. But your brother offers you half, and—'

'Half! I'm damned if I'll take half. The man's tried to swindle me out of it. I'll send for the police, and have him put in gaol for robbing the Church. You see if I don't. Give me the telephone.'

'Excuse me,' said Wimsey. 'I don't want to butt in on your family affairs any more than I have already, but I really don't advise you to send for the police.'

'*You* don't, eh? What the hell's it got to do with you?'

'Well,' said Wimsey deprecatingly, 'if this will business comes into court, I shall probably have to give evidence, because I was the bird who found the thing, don't you see?'

'Well, then?'

'Well, then. They might ask how long the will was supposed to have been where I found it.'

Haviland appeared to swallow something which obstructed his speech.

'What about it, curse you!'

'Yes. Well, you see, it's rather odd when you come to think of it. I mean, your late father must have hidden that will in the bookcase before he went abroad. That was – how long ago? Three years? Five years?'

'About four years.'

'Quite. And since then your bright caretaker has let the damp get into the library, hasn't she? No fires, and the window getting broken and so on. Ruinous to the books. Very distressin' to anybody like myself, you know. Yes. Well, supposin' they asked that question about the will – and you said it had been there in the damp for four years. Wouldn't they think it a bit funny if I told 'em that there was a big damp stain like a grinning face on the end of the bookshelf, and a big, damp, grinning face on the jolly old *Nüremberg Chronicle* to correspond with it, and no stain on the will which had been sittin' for four years between the two?'

Mrs Haviland screamed suddenly. 'Haviland! You fool! You utter fool!'

'Shut up!'

Haviland snapped round at his wife with a cry of rage, and she collapsed into a chair, with her hand snatched to her mouth.

'Thank you, Winnie,' said Martin. 'No, Haviland – don't trouble to explain. Winnie's given the show away. So you knew – you *knew* about the will, and you deliberately hid it away and let the funeral go on. I'm immensely obliged to you – nearly as obliged as I am to the discreet Graham. Is it fraud or conspiracy or what, to conceal wills? Mr Frobisher-Pym will know.'

'Dear, dear!' said the magistrate. 'Are you certain of your facts, Wimsey?'

'Positive,' said Wimsey, producing the *Nüremberg Chronicle* from under his arm. 'Here's the stain – you can see it yourself. Forgive me for having borrowed your property, Mr Burdock. I was rather afraid Mr Haviland might think this little discrepancy over in the still watches of the night, and decide to sell the *Chronicle*, or give it away, or even think it looked better without its back pages and cover. Allow me to return it to you, Mr Martin – intact. You will perhaps excuse my saying that I don't very much admire any of the rôles in this melodrama. It throws, as Mr Picksniff would say, a sad light on human nature. But I resent extremely the way in which I was wangled up to that bookshelf and made to be the bright little independent witness who found the will. I may be an ass, Mr Haviland Burdock, but I'm not a bloody ass. Good night. I will wait in the car till you are all ready.'

Wimsey stalked out with some dignity.

Presently he was followed by the vicar and by Mr Frobisher-Pym.

'Mortimer's taking Haviland and his wife to the station,' said the magistrate. 'They're going back to town at once. You can send their traps off in the morning, Hancock. We'd better make ourselves scarce.'

Wimsey pressed the self-starter.

As he did so, a man ran hastily down the steps and came up to him. It was Martin.

'I say,' he muttered. 'You've done me a good turn – more than I deserve, I'm afraid. You must think I'm a damned swine. But I'll see the old man decently put away, and I'll share with Haviland. You mustn't judge him too hardly, either. That wife of his is an awful woman. Run him over head and ears in debt. Bust up his business. I'll see it's all squared up. See? Don't want you to think us too awful.'

'Oh, right-ho!' said Wimsey.

He slipped in the clutch, and faded away into the wet, white fog.

THE VINDICTIVE STORY OF THE
FOOTSTEPS THAT RAN

Mr Bunter withdrew his head from beneath the focusing cloth.

'I fancy that will be quite adequate, sir,' he said deferentially, 'unless there are any further patients, if I may call them so, which you would wish put on record.'

'Not today,' replied the doctor. He took the last stricken rat gently from the table, and replaced it in its cage with an air of satisfaction. 'Perhaps on Wednesday, if Lord Peter can kindly spare your services once again—'

'What's that?' murmured his lordship, withdrawing his long nose from the investigation of a number of unattractive-looking glass jars. 'Nice old dog,' he added vaguely. 'Wags his tail when you mention his name, what? Are these monkey-glands, Hartman, or a south-west elevation of Cleopatra's duodenum?'

'You don't know anything, do you?' said the young physician, laughing. 'No use playing your bally-fool-with-an-eyeglass tricks on me, Wimsey. I'm up to them. I was saying to Bunter that I'd be no end grateful if you'd let him turn up again three days hence to register the progress of the specimens – always supposing they do progress, that is.'

'Why ask, dear old thing?' said his lordship. 'Always a pleasure to assist a fellow-sleuth, don't you know. Track-in' down murderers – all in the same way of business and all that. All finished? Good egg! By the way, if you don't

have that cage mended you'll lose one of your patients –
Number 5. The last wire but one is workin' loose –
assisted by the intelligent occupant. Jolly little beasts,
ain't they? No need of dentists – wish I was a rat – wire
much better for the nerves than that fizzlin' drill.'

Dr Hartman uttered a little exclamation.

'How in the world did you notice that, Wimsey? I
didn't think you'd even looked at the cage.'

'Built noticin' – improved by practice,' said Lord Peter,
quietly. 'Anythin' wrong leaves a kind of impression on
the eye; brain trots along afterwards with the warnin'. I
saw that when we came in. Only just grasped it. Can't
say my mind was glued on the matter. Shows the victim's
improvin', anyhow. All serene, Bunter?'

'Everything perfectly satisfactory, I trust, my lord,'
replied the manservant. He had packed up his camera
and plates, and was quietly restoring order in the little
laboratory, whose fittings – compact as those of an ocean
liner – had been disarranged for the experiment.

'Well,' said the doctor, 'I am enormously obliged to
you, Lord Peter, and to Bunter too. I am hoping for a
great result from these experiments, and you cannot
imagine how valuable an assistance it will be to me to
have a really good series of photographs. I can't afford
this sort of thing – yet,' he added, his rather haggard
young face wistful as he looked at the great camera, 'and
I can't do the work at the hospital. There's no time; I've
got to be here. A struggling G.P. can't afford to let his
practice go, even in Bloomsbury. There are times when
even a half-crown visit makes all the difference between
making both ends meet and having an ugly hiatus.'

'As Mr Micawber said,' replied Wimsey, ' "Income
twenty pounds, expenditure nineteen, nineteen, six –

result: happiness; expenditure twenty pounds, ought, six – result: misery." Don't prostrate yourself in gratitude, old bean; nothin' Bunter loves like messin' round with pyro and hyposulphite. Keeps his hand in. All kinds of practice welcome. Finger-prints and process plates spell seventh what-you-may-call-it of bliss, but focal-plane work on scurvy-ridden rodents (good phrase!) acceptable if no crime forthcoming. Crimes have been rather short lately. Been eatin' our heads off, haven't we, Bunter? Don't know what's come over London. I've taken to prying into my neighbour's affairs to keep from goin' stale. Frightened the postman into a fit the other day by askin' him how his young lady at Croydon was. He's a married man, livin' in Great Ormond Street.'

'How did you know?'

'Well, I didn't really. But he lives just opposite to a friend of mine – Inspector Parker; and his wife – not Parker's; he's unmarried; the postman's, I mean – asked Parker the other day whether the flyin' shows at Croydon went on all night. Parker, bein' flummoxed, said "No," without thinkin'. Bit of a giveaway, what? Thought I'd give the poor devil a word in season, don't you know. Uncommonly thoughtless of Parker.'

The doctor laughed. 'You'll stay to lunch, won't' you?' he said. 'Only cold meat and salad, I'm afraid. My woman won't come Sundays. Have to answer my own door. Deuced unprofessional, I'm afraid, but it can't be helped.'

'Pleasure,' said Wimsey, as they emerged from the laboratory and entered the dark little flat by the back door. 'Did you build this place on?'

'No,' said Hartman; 'the last tenant did that. He was an artist. That's why I took the place. It comes in very useful, ramshackle as it is, though this glass roof is a bit sweltering on a hot day like this. Still, I had to have something on the ground floor, cheap, and it'll do till times get better.'

'Till your vitamin experiments make you famous, eh?' said Peter cheerfully. 'You're goin' to be the comin' man, you know. Feel it in my bones. Uncommonly neat little kitchen you've got, anyhow.'

'It does,' said the doctor. 'The lab makes it a bit gloomy, but the woman's only here in the daytime.'

He led the way into a narrow little dining-room, where the table was laid for a cold lunch. The one window at the end farthest from the kitchen looked out into Great James Street. The room was little more than a passage, and full of doors – the kitchen door, a door in the adjacent wall leading into the entrance-hall, and a third on the opposite side, through which his visitor caught a glimpse of a moderate-sized consulting-room.

Lord Peter Wimsey and his host sat down to table, and the doctor expressed a hope that Mr Bunter would sit down with them. That correct person, however, deprecated any such suggestion.

'If I might venture to indicate my own preference, sir,' he said, 'it would be to wait upon you and his lordship in the usual manner.'

'It's no use,' said Wimsey. 'Bunter likes me to know my place. Terrorisin' sort of man, Bunter. Can't call my soul my own. Carry on, Bunter; we wouldn't presume for the world.'

Mr Bunter handed the salad, and poured out the water with a grave decency appropriate to a crusted old tawny port.

It was a Sunday afternoon in that halcyon summer of

174

1921. The sordid little street was almost empty. The ice-cream man alone seemed thriving and active. He leaned luxuriously on the green post at the corner, in the intervals of driving a busy trade. Bloomsbury's swarm of able-bodied and able-voiced infants was still; presumably within-doors, eating steamy Sunday dinners inappropriate to the tropical weather. The only disturbing sounds came from the flat above, where heavy footsteps passed rapidly to and fro.

'Who's the merry-and-bright bloke above?' enquired Lord Peter presently. 'Not an early riser, I take it. Not that anybody is on a Sunday mornin'. Why an inscrutable Providence ever inflicted such a ghastly day on people livin' in town I can't imagine. I ought to be in the country, but I've got to meet a friend at Victoria this afternoon. Such a day to choose. . . . Who's the lady? Wife or accomplished friend? Gather she takes a properly submissive view of woman's duties in the home, either way. That's the bedroom overhead, I take it.'

Hartman looked at Lord Peter in some surprise.

"'Scuse my beastly inquisitiveness, old thing,' said Wimsey. 'Bad habit. Not my business.'

'How did you –?'

'Guesswork,' said Lord Peter, with disarming frankness. 'I heard the squawk of an iron bedstead on the ceiling and a heavy fellow get out with a bump, but it may quite well be a couch or something. Anyway, he's been potterin' about in his stocking feet over these few feet of floor for the last half-hour, while the woman has been clatterin' to and fro, in and out of the kitchen and away into the sittin'-room, with her high heels on, ever since we've been here. Hence deduction as to domestic habits of the first-floor tenants.'

'I thought,' said the doctor, with an aggrieved expression, 'you'd been listening to my valuable exposition of the beneficial effects of Vitamin B, and Lind's treatment of scurvy with fresh lemons in 1755.'

'I was listenin',' agreed Lord Peter hastily, 'but I heard the footsteps as well. Fellow's toddled into the kitchen – only wanted the matches, though; he's gone off into the sittin'-room and left her to carry on the good work. What was I sayin'? Oh, yes! You see, as I was sayin' before, one hears a thing or sees it without knowin' or thinkin' about it. Then afterwards one starts meditatin', and it all comes back, and one sorts out one's impressions. Like those plates of Bunter's. Picture all there, 1 – la – what's the word I want, Bunter?'

'Latent, my lord.'

'That's it. My right-hand man, Bunter; couldn't do a thing without him. The picture's latent till you put the developer on. Same with the brain. No mystery. Little grey books all my respected grandmother! Little grey matter's all you want to remember things with. As a matter of curiosity, was I right about those people above?'

'Perfectly. The man's a gas-company's inspector. A bit surly, but devoted (after his own fashion) to his wife. I mean, he doesn't mind hulking in bed on a Sunday morning and letting her do the chores, but he spends all the money he can spare on giving her pretty hats and fur coats and what not. They've only been married about six months. I was called in to her when she had a touch of flu in the spring, and he was almost off his head with anxiety. She's a lovely little woman, I must say – Italian. He picked her up in some eating-place in Soho, I believe. Glorious dark hair and eyes: Venus sort of figure; proper contours in all the right places; good skin – all that sort of thing. She was a bit of a draw to that restaurant while she was there, I fancy. Lively. She had an old admirer round here one day – awkward little Italian fellow, with a knife – active as a monkey. Might have been unpleasant, but I happened to be on the spot, and her husband came along. People are always laying one another out in these streets. Good for business, of course, but one gets tired of tying up broken heads and slits in the jugular. Still, I suppose the girl can't help being attractive, though I don't say she's what you might call stand-offish in her manner. She's sincerely fond of Brotherton, I think, though – that's his name.'

Wimsey nodded inattentively. 'I suppose life is a bit monotonous here,' he said.

'Professionally, yes. Births and drunks and wife-beatings are pretty common. And all the usual ailments, of course. Just at present. I'm living on infant diarrhoea chiefly – bound to, this hot weather, you know. With the autumn, flu and bronchitis set in. I may get an occasional pneumonia. Legs, of course, and varicose veins – God!' cried the doctor explosively, 'if only I could get away, and do my experiments!'

'Ah!' said Peter, 'where's that eccentric old millionaire with a mysterious disease, who always figures in the novels? A lightning diagnosis – a miraculous cure – "God bless you, doctor, here are five thousand pounds" – Harley Street—'

'That sort doesn't live in Bloomsbury,' said the doctor.

'It must be fascinatin', diagnosin' things,' said Peter thoughtfully. 'How d'you do it? I mean, is there a regular set of symptoms for each disease, like callin' a club to show you want your partner to go no trumps? You don't

177

just say: "This fellow's got a pimple on his nose, therefore he has fatty degeneration of the heart—"'

'I hope not,' said the doctor dryly.

'Or is it more like gettin' a clue to a crime?' went on Peter. 'You see somethin' – a room, or a body, say, all knocked about anyhow, and there's a damn sight of symptoms of somethin' wrong, and you've got just to pick out the ones which tell the story?'

'That's more like it,' said Dr Hartman. 'Some symptoms are significant in themselves – like the condition of the gums in scurvy, let us say – others in conjunction with—'

He broke off, and both sprang to their feet as a shrill scream sounded suddenly from the flat above, followed by a heavy thud. A man's voice cried out lamentably; feet ran violently to and fro; then, as the doctor and his guests stood frozen in consternation, came the man himself – falling down the stairs in his haste, hammering at Hartman's door.

'Help! Help! Let me in! My wife! He's murdered her!'

They ran hastily to the door and let him in. He was a big, fair man, in his shirt-sleeves and stockings. His hair stood up, and his face was set in bewildered misery.

'She is dead – dead. He was her lover,' he groaned. 'Come and look – take her away – Doctor! I have lost my wife! My Maddalena –' He paused, looked wildly for a moment, and then said hoarsely, 'Someone's been in – somehow – stabbed her – murdered her. I'll have the law on him, doctor. Come quickly – she was cooking the chicken for my dinner – Ah-h-h!'

He gave a long, hysterical shriek, which ended in a hiccupping laugh. The doctor took him roughly by the arm and shook him. 'Pull yourself together, Mr Brotherton,' he said sharply. 'Perhaps she is only hurt. Stand out of the way!'

'Only hurt?' said the man, sitting heavily down on the nearest chair. 'No – no – she is dead – little Maddalena – Oh, my God!'

Dr Hartman had snatched a roll of bandages and a few surgical appliances from the consulting-room, and he ran upstairs, followed closely by Lord Peter. Bunter remained for a few moments to combat hysterics with cold water. Then he stepped across to the dining-room window and shouted.

'Well, wot is it? cried a voice from the street.

'Would you be so kind as to step in here a minute, officer?' said Bunter. 'There's been murder done?' ·

When Brotherton and Bunter arrived upstairs with the constable, they found Dr Hartman and Lord Peter in the little kitchen. The doctor was kneeling beside the woman's body. At their entrance he looked up, and shook his head.

'Death instantaneous,' he said. 'Clean through the heart. Poor child. She cannot have suffered at all. Oh, constable, it is very fortunate you are here. Murder appears to have been done – though I'm afraid the man has escaped. Probably Mr Brotherton can give us some help. He was in the flat at the time.'

The man had sunk down on a chair, and was gazing at the body with a face from which all meaning seemed to have been struck out. The policeman produced a notebook.

'Now, sir,' he said, 'don't let's waste any time. Sooner we can get to work the more likely we are to catch our man. Now, you was 'ere at the time, was you?'

Brotherton stared a moment, then, making a violent effort, he answered steadily:

'I was in the sitting-room, smoking and reading the paper. My – *she* – was getting the dinner ready in here. I heard her give a scream, and I rushed in and found her lying on the floor. She didn't have time to say anything. When I found she was dead, I rushed to the window, and saw the fellow scrambling away over the glass roof there. I yelled at him, but he disappeared. Then I ran down—'

''Arf a mo',' said the policeman. 'Now, see, 'ere, sir, didn't you think to go after 'im at once?'

'My first thought was for her,' said the man. 'I thought maybe she wasn't dead. I tried to bring her round –' His speech ended in a groan.

'You say he came in through the window,' said the policeman.

'I beg your pardon, officer,' interrupted Lord Peter, who had been apparently making a mental inventory of the contents of the kitchen. 'Mr Brotherton suggested that the man went *out* through the window. It's better to be accurate.'

'It's the same thing,' said the doctor. 'It's the only way he could have come in. These flats are all alike. The staircase door leads into the sitting-room, and Mr Brotherton was there, so the man couldn't have come that way.'

'And,' said Peter, 'he didn't get in through the bedroom window, or we should have seen him. We were in the room below. Unless, indeed, he let himself down from the roof. Was the door between the bedroom and the sitting-room open?' he asked suddenly, turning to Brotherton.

The man hesitated a moment. 'Yes,' he said finally. 'Yes, I'm sure it was.'

'Could you have seen the man if he had come through the bedroom window?'

'I couldn't have helped seeing him.'

'Come, come, sir,' said the policeman, with some irritation, 'better let *me* ask the questions. Stands to reason the fellow wouldn't get in through the bedroom window in full view of the street.'

'How clever of you to think of that,' said Wimsey. 'Of course not. Never occurred to me. Then it must have been this window, as you say.'

'And, what's more, here's his marks on the window-sill,' said the constable triumphantly, pointing to some blurred traces among the London soot. 'That's right. Down he goes by that drain-pipe, over the glass roof down there – what's that the roof of?'

'My laboratory,' said the doctor. 'Heavens! to think that while we were there at dinner this murdering villain—'

'Quite so, sir,' agreed the constable. 'Well, he'd get away over the wall into the court be'ind. 'E'll 'ave been seen there, no fear; you needn't anticipate much trouble in layin' 'ands on 'im, sir. I'll go round there in 'arf a tick. Now then, sir' – turning to Brotherton – "ave you any idea wot this party might have looked like?'

Brotherton lifted a wild face, and the doctor interposed.

'I think you ought to know, constable,' he said, 'that there was – well, not a murderous attack, but what might have been one, made on this woman before – about eight weeks ago – by a man named Marincetti – an Italian waiter – with a knife.'

'Ah!' The policeman licked his pencil eagerly. 'Do you know this party as 'as been mentioned?' he enquired of Brotherton.

'That's the man,' said Brotherton, with concentrated fury. 'Coming here after my wife – God curse him! I wish to God I had him dead here beside her!'

'Quite so,' said the policeman. 'Now, sir' – to the doctor – ''ave you got the weapon wot the crime was committed with?'

'No,' said Hartman, 'there was no weapon in the body when I arrived.'

'Did *you* take it out?' pursued the constable to Brotherton.

'No,' said Brotherton, 'he took it with him.'

'Took it with 'im,' the constable entered the fact in his notes. 'Phew! Wonderful 'ot it is in 'ere ain't it, sir?' he added, mopping his brow.

'It's the gas-oven, I think,' said Peter mildly. 'Uncommon hot thing, a gas-oven, in the middle of July. D'you mind if I turn it out? There's the chicken inside, but I don't suppose you want—'

Brotherton groaned, and the constable said: 'Quite right, sir. A man wouldn't 'ardly fancy 'is dinner after a thing like this. Thank you, sir. Well now, doctor, wot kind of weapon do you take this to 'ave been?'

'It was a long, narrow weapon – something like an Italian stiletto, I imagine,' said the doctor, 'about six inches long. It was thrust in with great force under the fifth rib, and I should say it had pierced the heart centrally. As you see, there has been practically no bleeding. Such a wound would cause instant death. Was she lying just as she is now when you first saw her, Mr Brotherton?'

'On her back, just as she is,' replied the husband.

'Well, that seems clear enough,' said the policeman. 'This 'ere Marinetti, or wotever 'is name is, 'as a grudge against the poor young lady—'

'I believe he was an admirer,' put in the doctor.

'Quite so,' agreed the constable. 'Of course, these foreigners are like that – even the decentest of 'em. Stabbin' and such-like seems to come nateral to them, as you might say. Well, this 'ere Marinetti climbs in 'ere, sees the poor young lady stendin' 'ere by the table all alone, gettin' the dinner ready; 'e comes in be'ind, catches 'er round the waist, stabs 'er – easy job, you see; no corsets nor nothink – she shrieks out, 'e pulls 'is stiletty out of 'er an' makes tracks. Well, now we've got to find 'im, and by your leave, sir, I'll be gettin' along. We'll 'ave 'im by the 'eels before long, sir, don't you worry. I'll 'ave to put a man in charge 'ere, sir, to keep folks out, but that needn't worry you. Good mornin', gentlemen.'

'May we move the poor girl now?' asked the doctor.

'Certainly. Like me to 'elp you, sir?'

'No. Don't lose any time. We can manage.' Dr Hartman turned to Peter as the constable clattered downstairs. 'Will you help me, Lord Peter?'

'Bunter's better at that sort of thing,' said Wimsey, with a hard mouth.

The doctor looked at him in some surprise, but said nothing, and he and Bunter carried the still form away. Brotherton did not follow them. He sat in a grief-stricken heap, with his head buried in his hands. Lord Peter walked about the little kitchen, turning over the various knives and kitchen utensils, peering into the sink bucket, and apparently taking an inventory of the bread, butter, condiments, vegetables, and so forth which lay about in preparation for the Sunday meal. There were potatoes in the sink, half peeled, a pathetic witness to the quiet domestic life which had been so horribly interrupted. The colander was filled with green peas. Lord Peter turned these things over with an inquisitive finger, gazed into the smooth surface of a bowl of dripping as though it were a divining-crystal, ran his hands several times right through a bowl of flour – then drew his pipe from his pocket and filled it slowly.

The doctor returned, and put his hand on Brotherton's shoulder.

'Come,' he said gently, 'we have laid her in the other bedroom. She looks very peaceful. You must remember that, except for that moment of terror when she saw the knife, she suffered nothing. It is terrible for you, but you must try not to give way. The police—'

'The police can't bring her back to life,' said the man savagely. 'She's dead. Leave me alone, curse you! Leave me alone, I say!'

He stood up, with a violent gesture.

'You must not sit here,' said Hartman firmly. 'I will give you something to take, and you must try to keep calm. Then we will leave you, but if you don't control yourself—'

After some further persuasion, Brotherton allowed himself to be led away.

'Bunter,' said Lord Peter, as the kitchen door closed behind them, 'do you know why I am doubtful about the success of those rat experiments?'

'Meaning Dr Hartman's, my lord?'

'Yes. Dr Hartman has a theory. In any investigation, my Bunter, it is most damnably dangerous to have a theory.'

'I have heard you say so, my lord.'

'Confound you – you know it as well as I do! What is wrong with the doctor's theories, Bunter?'

'You wish me to reply, my lord, that he only sees the facts which fit into the theory.'

'Thought-reader!' exclaimed Lord Peter bitterly.

'And that he supplies them to the police, my lord.'

'Hush!' said Peter, as the doctor returned.

'I have got him to lie down,' said Dr Hartman, 'and I think the best thing we can do is to leave him to himself.'

'D'you know,' said Wimsey, 'I don't cotton to that idea, somehow.'

'Why? Do you think he's likely to destroy himself?'

'That's as good a reason to give as any other, I suppose,' said Wimsey, 'when you haven't got any reason which can be put into words. But my advice is, don't leave him for a moment.'

'But why? Frequently, with a deep grief like this, the presence of other people is merely an irritant. He begged me to leave him.'

'Then for God's sake go back to him,' said Peter.

'Really, Lord Peter,' said the doctor, 'I think I ought to know what is best for my patient.'

'Doctor,' said Wimsey, 'this is not a question of your patient. A crime has been committed.'

'But there is no mystery.'

'There are twenty mysteries. For one thing, when was the window-cleaner here last?'

'The window-cleaner?'

'Who shall fathom the ebony-black enigma of the window-cleaner?' pursued Peter lightly, putting a match to his pipe. 'You are quietly in your bath, in a state of more or less innocent nature, when an intrusive head appears at the window, like the ghost of Hamilton Tighe, and a gruff voice, suspended between earth and heaven, says "Good morning, sir." Where do window-cleaners go between visits? Do they hibernate, like busy bees? Do they –?'

'Really, Lord Peter,' said the doctor, 'don't you think you're going a bit beyond the limit?'

'Sorry you feel like that,' said Peter, 'but I really want to know about the window-cleaner. Look how clear these panes are.'

'He came yesterday, if you want to know,' said Dr Hartman, rather stiffly.

'You are sure?'

'He did mine at the same time.'

'I thought as much,' said Lord Peter. 'In the words of the song:

'I thought as much,
It was a little – window-cleaner.

In that case,' he added, 'it is absolutely imperative that Brotherton should not be left alone for a moment. Bunter! Confound it all, where's that fellow got to?'

The door into the bedroom opened.

'My lord?' Mr Bunter unobtrusively appeared, as he had unobtrusively stolen out to keep an unobtrusive eye upon the patient.

'Good,' said Wimsey. 'Stay where you are.' His lackadaisical manner had gone, and he looked at the doctor as four years previously he might have looked at a refractory subaltern.

'Dr Hartman,' he said, 'something is wrong. Cast your mind back. We were talking about symptoms. Then came the scream. Then came the sound of feet running. *Which direction did they run in?*'

'I'm sure I don't know.'

'Don't you? Symptomatic, though, doctor. They have been troubling me all the time, subconsciously. Now I know why. They ran *from the kitchen.*'

'Well?'

'Well! And now the window-cleaner—'

'What about him?'

'Could you swear that it wasn't the window-cleaner who made those marks on the sill?'

'And the man Brotherton saw—?'

'Have we examined your laboratory roof for his foot-steps?'

'But the weapon? Wimsey, this is madness! Someone took the weapon.'

'I know. But did you think the edge of the wound was clean enough to have been made by a smooth stiletto? It looked ragged to me.'

'Wimsey, what are you driving at?'

'There's a clue here in the flat – and I'm damned if I can remember it. I've seen it – I know I've seen it. It'll come to me presently. Meanwhile, don't let Brotherton—'

'What?'

'Do whatever it is he's going to do.'

'But what is it?'

'If I could tell you that I could show you the clue. Why couldn't he make up his mind whether the bedroom door was open or shut? Very good story, but not quite thought out. Anyhow – I say, doctor, make some excuse, and strip him, and bring me his clothes. And send Bunter to me.'

The doctor stared at him, puzzled. Then he made a

gesture of acquiescence and passed into the bedroom. Lord Peter followed him, casting a ruminating glance at Brotherton as he went. Once in the sitting-room, Lord Peter sat down on a red velvet arm-chair, fixed his eyes on a gilt-framed oleograph, and became wrapped in contemplation.

Presently Bunter came in, with his arms full of clothing. Wimsey took it, and began to search it, methodically enough, but listlessly. Suddenly he dropped the garments, and turned to the manservant.

'No, he said, 'this is a precaution, Bunter mine, but I'm on the wrong tack. It wasn't here I saw – whatever I did see. It was in the kitchen. Now, what was it?'

'I could not say, my lord, but I entertain a conviction that I was also, in a manner of speaking, conscious – not consciously conscious, my lord, if you understand me, but still conscious of an incongruity.'

'Hurray!' said Wimsey suddenly. 'Cheer-oh! for the subconscious what's-his-name! Now let's remember the kitchen. I cleared out of it because I was gettin' obfuscated. Now then. Begin at the door. Fryin'-pans and saucepans on the wall. Gas-stove – oven goin' – chicken inside. Racks of wooden spoons on the wall, gas-lighter, pan-lifter. Stop me when I'm gettin' hot. Mantelpiece. Spice-boxes and stuff. Anything wrong with them? No. Dresser. Plates. Knives and forks, – all clean; flour dredger – milk-jug – sieve on the wall – nutmeg-grater. Three-tier steamer. Looked inside – no grisly secrets in the steamer.'

'Did you look in all the dresser drawers, my lord?'

'No. That could be done. But the point is, I *did* notice somethin'. What did I notice? That's the point. Never mind. On with the dance – let joy be unconfined! Knife-board. Knife-powder. Kitchen table. Did you speak?'

'No,' said Bunter, who had moved from his attitude of wooden deference.

'Table stirs a chord. Very good. On table. Choppin'-board. Remains of ham and herb stuffin'. Packet of suet. Another sieve. Several plates. Butter in a glass dish. Bowl of drippin'—

'Ah!'

'Drippin' –! Yes, there was—'

'Something unsatisfactory, my lord—'

'About the drippin'! Oh, my head! What's that they say in *Dear Brutus*, Bunter? "Hold on to the workbox." That's right. Hold on to the dippin'. Beastly slimy stuff to hold on to – Wait!'

There was a pause.

'When I was a kid,' said Wimsey, 'I used to love to go down into the kitchen and talk to old cookie. Good old soul she was, too. I can see her now, gettin' chicken ready, with me danglin' my legs on the table. *She* used to pluck an' draw 'em herself. I revelled in it. Little beasts boys are, ain't they, Bunter? Pluck it, draw it, wash it, stuff it, tuck its little tail through its little what-you-may-call-it, truss it, grease the dish – Bunter?'

'My lord!'

'Hold on to the dripping!'

'The bowl, my lord—'

'The bowl – visualise it – what was wrong?'

'It was full, my lord!—'

'Got it – got it – *got* it! The bowl was full – smooth surface. Golly! I knew there was something queer about it. Now why shouldn't it be full? Hold on to the—'

'The bird was in the oven.'

'Without dripping!'

'Very careless cookery my lord.'

189

'The bird – in the oven – no dripping. Bunter! Suppose it was never put in till after she was dead? Thrust in hurriedly by someone who had something to hide – horrible!'

'But with what object, my lord?'

'Yes, why? That's the point. One more mental association with the bird. It's just coming. Wait a moment. Pluck, draw, wash, stuff, tuck up, truss – By God!'

'My lord?'

'Come on, Bunter. Thank Heaven we turned off the gas!'

He dashed through the bedroom, disregarding the doctor and the patient, who sat up with a smothered shriek. He flung open the oven door and snatched out the baking-tin. The skin of the bird had just begun to discolour. With a little gasp of triumph, Wimsey caught the iron ring that protruded from the wing, and jerked out – the six-inch spiral skewer.

The doctor was struggling with the excited Brotherton in the doorway. Wimsey caught the man as he broke away, and shook him into the corner with a jiu-jitsu twist.

'Here is the weapon,' he said.

'Prove it, blast you!' said Brotherton savagely,

'I will,' said Wimsey. 'Bunter, call in the policeman whom you will find at the door. Doctor, we shall need your microscope.'

In the laboratory the doctor bent over the microscope. A thin layer of blood from the skewer had been spread upon the slide.

'Well?' said Wimsey impatiently.

'It's all right,' said Hartman. 'The roasting didn't get

anywhere near the middle. My God, Wimsey, yes, you're right – round corpuscles, diameter 1/3621 – mammalian blood – probably human—'

'Her blood,' said Wimsey.

'It was very clever, Bunter,' said Lord Peter, as the taxi trundled along on the way to his flat in Piccadilly. 'If that fowl had gone on roasting a bit longer the blood-corpuscles might easily have been destroyed beyond all hope of recognition. It all goes to show that the unpremeditated crime is usually the safest.'

'And what does your lordship take the man's motive to have been?'

'In my youth,' said Wimsey meditatively, 'they used to make me read the Bible. Trouble was, the only books I ever took to naturally were the ones they weren't over and above keen on. But I got to know the Song of Songs pretty well by heart. Look it up, Bunter; at your age it won't hurt you; it talks sense about jealousy.'

'I have perused the work in question, your lordship,' replied Mr Bunter, with a sallow blush. 'It says, if I remember rightly: "*Jealousy is cruel as the grave.*"'

'*Halte-là! . . . Attention! . . . F———e!*'

The young man in the grey suit pushed his way through the protesting porters and leapt nimbly for the footboard of the guard's van as the Paris-Evreux express steamed out of the Invalides. The guard, with an eye to a tip, fielded him adroitly from among the detaining hands.

'It is happy for monsieur that he is so agile,' he remarked. 'Monsieur is in a hurry?'

'Somewhat. Thank you. I can get through by the corridor?'

'But certainly. The *premières* are two coaches away, beyond the luggage-van.'

The young man rewarded his rescuer, and made his way forward, mopping his face. As he passed the piled-up luggage, something caught his eye, and he stopped to investigate. It was a suit-case, nearly new, of expensive-looking leather, labelled conspicuously:

> LORD PETER WIMSEY,
> Hôtel Saumon d'Or,
> Verneuil-sur-Eure.

and bore witness to its itinerary thus:

> LONDON – PARIS
> (Waterloo) (Gare St Lazare)
> via Southampton-Havre.

The young man whistled, and sat down on a trunk to think it out.

Somewhere there had been a leakage, and they were on his trail. Nor did they care who knew it. There were hundreds of people in London and Paris who would know the name of Wimsey, not counting the police of both countries. In addition to belonging to one of the oldest ducal families in England, Lord Peter had made himself conspicuous by his meddling with crime detection. A label like this was a gratuitous advertisement.

But the amazing thing was that the pursuers were not troubling to hide themselves from the pursued. That argued very great confidence. That he should have got into the guard's van was, of course, an accident, but, even so, he might have seen it on the platform, or anywhere.

An accident? It occurred to him – not for the first time, but definitely now, and without doubt – that it was indeed an accident for them that he was here. The series of maddening delays that had held him up between London and the Invalides presented itself to him with an air of pre-arrangement. The preposterous accusation, for instance, of the woman who had accosted him in Piccadilly, and the slow process of extricating himself at Marlborough Street. It was easy to hold a man up on some trumped-up charge till an important plan had matured. Then there was the lavatory door at Waterloo, which had so ludicrously locked itself upon him. Being athletic, he had climbed over the partition, to find the attendant mysteriously absent. And, in Paris, was it by chance that he had had a deaf taxi-driver, who mistook the direction 'Quai d'Orléans' for 'Gare de Lyon,' and drove a mile and a half in the wrong direction before the shouts of his fare attracted his attention? They were clever, the pursuers, and circumspect. They had accurate information; they would delay him, but without taking any overt step; they knew that, if only they could keep time on their side, they needed no other ally.

Did they know he was on the train? If not, he still kept the advantage, for they would travel in a false security, thinking him to be left, raging and helpless, in the Invalides. He decided to make a cautious reconnaissance.

The first step was to change his grey suit for another of inconspicuous navy-blue cloth, which he had in his small black bag. This he did in the privacy of the toilet, substituting for his grey soft hat a large travelling-cap, which pulled well down over his eyes.

There was little difficulty in locating the man he was in search of. He found him seated in the inner corner of a first-class compartment, facing the engine, so that the watcher could approach unseen from behind. On the rack was a handsome dressing-case, with the initials P. D. B. W. The young man was familiar with Wimsey's narrow, beaky face, flat yellow hair, and insolent dropped eyelids. He smiled a little grimly.

'He is confident,' he thought, 'and has regrettably made the mistake of underrating the enemy. Good! This is where I retire into *a seconde* and keep my eyes open. The next act of this melodrama will take place, I fancy, at Dreux.'

It is a rule on the Chemin de Fer de l'Ouest that all Paris-Evreux trains, whether of Grande Vitesse or what Lord

Peter Wimsey preferred to call Grande Paresse, shall halt for an interminable period at Dreux. The young man (now in navy-blue) watched his quarry safely into the refreshment-room, and slipped unobtrusively out of the station. In a quarter of an hour he was back – this time in a heavy motoring-coat, helmet, and goggles, at the wheel of a powerful hired Peugeot. Coming quietly on to the platform, he took up his station behind the wall of the *lampisterie*, whence he could keep an eye on the train and the buffet door. After fifteen minutes his patience was rewarded by the sight af his man again boarding the express, dressing-case in hand. The porters slammed the doors, crying: 'Next stop Verneuil!' The engine panted and groaned; the long train of grey-green carriages clanked slowly away. The motorist drew a breath of satisfaction, and, hurrying past the barrier, started up the car. He knew that he had a good eighty miles an hour under his bonnet, and there is no speed-limit in France.

Mon Souci, the seat of that eccentric and eremitical genius the Comte de Rueil, is situated three kilometres from Verneuil. It is a sorrowful and decayed château, desolate at the termination of its neglected avenue of pines. The mournful state of a nobility without an allegiance surrounds it. The stone nymphs droop greenly over their dry and mouldering fountains. An occasional peasant creaks with a single waggon-load of wood along the ill-forested glades. It has the atmosphere of sunset at all hours of the day. The woodwork is dry and gaping for lack of paint. Through the jalousies one sees the prim *salon*, with its beautiful and faded furniture. Even the last of its ill-dressed, ill-favoured women has withered away from Mon Souci, with her in-bred, exaggerated features and her long white gloves. But at the rear of the château a chimney smokes incessantly. It is the furnace of the laboratory, the only living and modern thing among the old and dying; the only place tended and loved, petted and spoiled, heir to the long solicitude which counts of a more light-hearted day had given to stable and kennel, portrait-gallery and ballroom. And below, in the cool cellar, lie row upon row the dusty bottles, each an enchanted glass coffin in which the Sleeping Beauty of the vine grows ever more ravishing in sleep.

As the Peugeot came to a standstill in the courtyard, the driver observed with considerable surprise that he was not the count's only visitor. An immense super-Renault, like a *merveilleuse* of the Directoire, all bonnet and no body, had been drawn so ostentatiously across the entrance as to embarrass the approach of any new-comer. Its glittering panels were embellished with a coat of arms, and the count's elderly servant was at that moment staggering beneath the weight of two large and elaborate suit-cases, bearing in silver letters that could be read a mile away the legend: 'LORD PETER WIMSEY.'

The Peugeot driver gazed with astonishment at this display, and grinned sardonically. 'Lord Peter seems rather ubiquitous in this country,' he observed to himself. Then, taking pen and paper from his bag, he busied himself with a little letter-writing. By the time that the suit-cases had been carried in, and the Renault had purred its smooth way to the outbuildings, the document was complete and enclosed in an envelope addressed to the Comte de Rueil. 'The hoist with his own petard touch,' said the young man, and, stepping up to the door, presented the envelope to the manservant.

'I am the bearer of a letter of introduction to monsieur le comte,' he said. 'Will you have the obligingness to present it to him? My name is Bredon – Death Bredon.'

The man bowed, and begged him to enter.

'If monsieur will have the goodness to seat himself in the hall for a few moments. Monsieur le comte is engaged with another gentleman, but I will lose no time in making monsieur's arrival known.'

The young man sat down and waited. The windows of the hall looked out upon the entrance, and it was not long before the château's sleep was disturbed by the hooting of yet another motor-horn. A station taxi-cab came noisily up the avenue. The man from the first-class carriage and the luggage labelled P. D. B. W. were deposited upon the doorstep. Lord Peter Wimsey dismissed the driver and rang the bell.

'Now,' said Mr Bredon, 'the fun is going to begin?' He effaced himself as far as possible in the shadow of a tall *armoire normande*.

'Good evening,' said the new-comer to the manservant, in admirable French. 'I am Lord Peter Wimsey. I arrive upon the invitation of Monsieur le comte de Rueil. Monsieur le comte is at liberty?'

'Milord Peter Wimsey? Pardon, monsieur, but I do not understand. Milord de Wimsey is already arrived and is with monsieur le comte at this moment.'

'You surprise me,' said the other, with complete imperturbability, 'for certainly no one but myself has any right to that name. It seems as though some person more ingenious than honest has had the bright idea of impersonating me.'

The servant was clearly at a loss.

'Perhaps,' he suggested, 'monsieur can show his *papiers d'identité*.'

'Although it is somewhat unusual to produce one's credentials on the doorstep when paying a private visit,' replied his lordship, with unaltered good humour. 'I have not the slightest objection. Here is my passport, here is *a permis de séjour* granted to me in Paris, here my visiting-card, and here a quantity of correspondence addressed to me at the Hôtel Meurice, Paris, at my flat in Piccadilly, London, at the Marlborough Club, London, and at my brother's house at King's Denver. Is that sufficiently in order?'

The servant perused the documents carefully, appearing particularly impressed by the *permis de séjour*.

'It appears there is some mistake,' he murmured dubiously; 'if monsieur will follow me, I will acquaint monsieur le comte.'

They disappeared through the folding doors at the back of the hall, and Bredon was left alone.

'Quite a little boom in Richmonds today,' he observed, 'each of us more unscrupulous than the last. The occasion obviously calls for a refined subtlety of method.'

After what he judged to be a hectic ten minutes in the count's library, the servant reappeared, searching for him.

'Monsieur le comte's compliments, and would monsieur step this way?'

Bredon entered the room with a jaunty step. He had created for himself the mastery of this situation. The count, a thin, elderly man, his fingers deeply stained with chemicals, sat, with a perturbed expression, at his desk. In two arm-chairs sat the two Wimseys. Bredon noted that, while the Wimsey he had seen in the train (whom he mentally named Peter I) retained his unruffled smile, Peter II (he of the Renault) had the flushed and indignant air of an Englishman affronted. The two men were superficially alike – both fair, lean, and long-nosed, with the nondescript, inelastic face which predominates in any assembly of well-bred Anglo-Saxons.

'Mr Bredon,' said the count, 'I am charmed to have the pleasure of making your acquaintance, and regret that I must at once call upon you for a service as singular as it is important. You have presented to me a letter of introduction from your cousin, Lord Peter Wimsey. Will you now be good enough to inform me which of these gentlemen he is?'

Bredon let his glance pass slowly from the one claimant to the other, meditating what answer would best serve his own ends. One, at any rate, of the men in this room was a formidable intellect, trained in the detection of imposture.

'Well?' said Peter II. 'Are you going to acknowledge me, Bredon?'

Peter I extracted a cigarette from a silver case. 'Your confederate does not seem very well up in his part,' he remarked, with a quiet smile at Peter II.

'Monsieur le comte,' said Bredon, 'I regret extremely that I cannot assist you in the matter. My acquaintance with my cousin, like your own, has been made and maintained entirely through correspondence on a subject of common interest. My profession,' he added, 'has made me unpopular with my family.'

There was a very slight sigh of relief somewhere. The false Wimsey – whichever he was – had gained a respite. Bredon smiled.

'An excellent move, Mr Bredon,' said Peter I, 'but it

will hardly explain – Allow me.' He took the letter from the count's hesitating hand. 'It will hardly explain the fact that the ink of this letter of recommendation, dated three weeks ago, is even now scarcely dry – though I congratulate you on the very plausible imitation of my handwriting.'

'If *you* can forge my handwriting,' said Peter II, 'so can this Mr Bredon.' He read the letter aloud over his double's shoulder.

' "Monsieur le comte – I have the honour to present to you my friend and cousin, Mr Death Bredon, who, I understand, is to be travelling in your part of France next month. He is very anxious to view your interesting library. Although a journalist by profession, he really knows something about books." I am delighted to learn for the first time that I have such a cousin. An interviewer's trick, I fancy, monsieur le comte. Fleet Street appears well informed about our family names. Possibly it is equally well informed about the object of my visit to Mon Souci?'

'If,' said Bredon boldly, 'you refer to the acquisition of the de Rueil formula for poison gas for the British Government, I can answer for my own knowledge, though possibly the rest of Fleet Street is less completely enlightened.' He weighed his words carefully now, warned by his slip. The sharp eyes and detective ability of Peter I alarmed him far more than the caustic tongue of Peter II.

The count uttered an exclamation of dismay.

'Gentlemen,' he said, 'one thing is obvious – that there has been somewhere a disastrous leakage of information. Which of you is the Lord Peter Wimsey to whom I should entrust the formula I do not know. Both of you are supplied with papers of identity; both appear completely instructed in this matter; both of your handwritings correspond with the letters I have previously received from Lord Peter, and both of you have offered me the sum agreed upon in Bank of England notes. In addition, this third gentleman arrives endowed with an equal facility in handwritings, an introductory letter surrounded by most suspicious circumstances, and a degree of acquaintance with this whole matter which alarms me. I can see but one solution. All of you must remain here at the château while I send to England for some elucidation of this mystery. To the genuine Lord Peter I offer my apologies, and assure him that I will endeavour to make his stay as agreeable as possible. Will this satisfy you? It will? I am delighted to hear it. My servants will show you to your bedrooms, and dinner will be at half-past seven.'

'It is delightful to think,' said Mr Bredon, as he fingered his glass and passed it before his nostrils with the air of a connoisseur, 'that whichever of these gentlemen has the right to the name which he assumes is assured tonight of a truly Olympian satisfaction.' His impudence had returned to him, and he challenged the company with an air. 'Your callers, monsieur le comte, are as well known among men endowed with a palate as your talents among men of science. No eloquence could say more.'

The two Lord Peters murmured assent.

'I am the more pleased by your commendation,' said the count, 'that it suggests to me a little test which, with your kind co-operation, will, I think, assist us very much in determining which of you gentlemen is Lord Peter Wimsey and which his talented impersonator. Is it not matter of common notoriety that Lord Peter has a palate for wine almost unequalled in Europe?'

'You flatter me, monsieur le comte,' said Peter II modestly.

'I wouldn't like to say unequalled,' said Peter I, chiming in like a well-trained duet; 'let's call it fair to middling. Less liable to misconstruction and all that.'

'Your lordship does yourself an injustice,' said Bredon, addressing both men with impartial deference. 'The bet which you won from Mr Frederick Arbuthnot at the Egotist's Club, when he challenged you to name the vintage years of seventeen wines blindfold, received its due prominence in the *Evening Wire*.'

'I was in extra form that night,' said Peter I.

'A fluke,' laughed Peter II.

'The test I propose, gentlemen, is on similar lines,' pursued the count, 'though somewhat less strenuous. There are six courses ordered for dinner tonight. With each we will drink a different wine, which my butler shall bring in with the label concealed. You shall each in turn give me your opinion upon the vintage. By this means we shall perhaps arrive at something, since the most brilliant forger – of which I gather I have at least two at my table tonight – can scarcely forge a palate for wine. If too hazardous a mixture of wines should produce a temporary incommodity in the morning, you will, I feel sure, suffer it for this once in the cause of truth.'

The two Wimseys bowed.

'*In vino veritas*,' said Mr Bredon, with a laugh. He at least was well seasoned, and foresaw opportunities for himself.

'Accident, and my butler, having placed you at my right hand, monsieur,' went on the count, addressing

Peter I, 'I will ask you to begin by pronouncing, as accurately as may be, upon the wine which you have just drunk.'

'That is scarcely a searching ordeal,' said the other, with a smile. 'I can say definitely that it is a very pleasant and well-matured Chablis Moutonne; and, since ten years is an excellent age for a Chablis – a real Chablis – I should vote for 1916, which was perhaps the best of the war vintages in that district.'

'Have you anything to add to that opinion, monsieur?' enquired the count, deferentially, of Peter II.

'I wouldn't like to be dogmatic to a year or so,' said that gentleman critically, 'but if I must commit myself, don't you know, I should say 1915 – decidely 1915.'

The count bowed, and turned to Bredon.

'Perhaps you, too, monsieur, would be interested to give an opinion,' he suggested, with the exquisite courtesy always shown to the plain man in the society of experts.

'I'd rather not set a standard which I might not be able to live up to,' replied Bredon, a little maliciously. 'I know that it is 1915, for I happened to see the label.'

Peter II looked a little disconcerted.

'We will arrange matters better in future,' said the count. 'Pardon me.' He stepped apart for a few moments' conference with the butler, who presently advanced to remove the oysters and bring in the soup.

The next candidate for attention arrived swathed to the lip in damask.

'It is your turn to speak first, monsieur,' said the count to Peter II. 'Permit me to offer you an olive to cleanse the palate. No haste, I beg. Even for the most excellent political ends, good wine must not be used with disrespect.'

The rebuke was not unnecessary, for, after a preliminary sip, Peter II had taken a deep draught of the heady white richness. Under Peter I's quizzical eye he wilted quite visibly.

'It is – it is Sauterne,' he began, and stopped. Then gathering encouragement from Bredon's smile, he said, with more aplomb, 'Château Yquem, 1911 – ah! the queen of white wines, sir, as what's-his-name says.' He drained his glass defiantly.

The count's face was a study as he slowly detached his fascinated gaze from Peter II to fix it on Peter I.

'If I had to be impersonated by somebody,' murmured the latter gently, 'it would have been more flattering to have had it undertaken by a person to whom all white wine were *not* alike. Well, now, sir, this admirable vintage is, of course, a Montrachet of – let me see' – he rolled the wine delicately upon his tongue – 'of 1911. And a very attractive wine it is, though, with all due deference to yourself, monsieur le comte, I feel that it is perhaps slightly too sweet to occupy its present place in the menu. True, with this excellent *consommé marmite*, a sweetish wine is not altogether out of place, but, in my own humble opinion, it would have shown to better advantage with the *confitures*.'

'There, now,' said Bredon innocently, 'it just shows how one may be misled. Had not I had the advantage of Lord Peter's expert opinion – for certainly nobody who could mistake Montrachet for Sauterne has any claim to the name of Wimsey – I should have pronounced this to be, not the Montrachet-Aîné, but the Chevalier-Montrachet of the same year, which is a trifle sweeter. But no doubt; as your lordship says, drinking it with the soup has caused it to appear sweeter to me than it actually is.'

The count looked sharply at him, but made no comment.

'Have another olive,' said Peter I kindly. 'You can't judge wine if your mind is on other flavours.'

'Thanks frightfully,' said Bredon. 'And that reminds me—' He launched into a rather pointless story about olives, which lasted out the soup and bridged the interval to the entrance of an exquisitely cooked sole.

The count's eye followed the pale amber wine rather thoughtfully as it trilled into the glasses. Bredon raised his in the approved manner to his nostrils, and his face flushed a little. With the first sip he turned excitedly to his host.

'Good God, sir—' he began.

The lifted hand cautioned him to silence.

Peter I sipped, inhaled, sipped again, and his brows clouded. Peter II had by this time apparently abandoned his pretensions. He drank thirstily, with a beaming smile and a lessening hold upon reality.

'Eh bien, monsieur?' enquired the count gently.

'This,' said Peter I, 'is certainly hock, and the noblest hock I have ever tasted, but I must admit that for the moment I cannot precisely place it.'

'No?' said Bredon. His voice was like bean-honey now, sweet and harsh together. 'Nor the other gentleman? And yet I fancy I could place it within a couple of miles, though it is a wine I had hardly looked to find in a French cellar at this time. It is hock, as your lordship says, and at that it is Johannisberger. Not the plebian cousin, but the *echter* Schloss Johannisberger from the castle vineyard itself. Your lordship must have missed it (to your great loss) during the war years. My father laid some down the year before he died, but it appears that the ducal cellars at Denver were less well furnished.'

'I must set about remedying the omission,' said the remaining Peter, with determination.

The *poulet* was served to the accompaniment of an argument over the Lafitte, his lordship placing it at 1878, Bredon maintaining it to be a relic of the glorious 'seventy-fives, slightly over-matured, but both agreeing as to its great age and noble pedigree.

As to the Clos-Vougeôt, on the other hand, there was complete agreement; after a tentative suggestion of 1915, it was pronounced finally by Peter I to belong to the equally admirable though slightly lighter 1911 crop. The *pré-salé* was removed amid general applause and the dessert was brought in.

'Is it necessary,' asked Peter I, with a slight smile in the direction of Peter II – now happily murmuring, 'Damn good wine, damn good dinner, damn good show' – 'is it necessary to prolong this farce any further?'

'Your lordship will not, surely, refuse to proceed with the discussion?' cried the count.

'The point is sufficiently made, I fancy.'

'But no one will surely ever refuse to discuss wine,' said Bredon, 'least of all your lordship, who is so great an authority.'

'Not on this,' said the other. 'Frankly, it is a wine I do not care about. It is sweet and coarse, qualities that would damn any wine in the eyes – the mouth, rather – of a connoisseur. Did your excellent father have this laid down also, Mr Bredon?'

Bredon shook his head.

'No,' he said, 'no. Genuine Imperial Tokay is beyond the opportunities of Grub Street, I fear. Though I agree with you that it is horribly overrated – with all due deference to yourself, monsieur le comte.'

'In that case,' said the count, 'we will pass at once to the liqueur. I admit that I had thought of puzzling these gentlemen with the local product, but, since one competitor seems to have scratched, it shall be brandy – the only fitting close to a good wine-list.'

In a slightly embarrassing silence the huge, round-bellied balloon glasses were set upon the table, and the few precious drops poured gently into each and set lightly swinging to release the bouquet.

'This,' said Peter I, charmed again into amiability, 'is, indeed a woman's old French brandy. Half a century old, I suppose.'

'Your lordship's praise lacks warmth,' replied Bredon. 'This is *the* brandy – the brandy of brandies – the superb – the incomparable – the true Napoleon. It should be honoured like the emperor it is.'

He rose to his feet, his napkin in his hand.

'Sir,' said the count, turning to him, 'I have on my right a most admirable judge of wine, but you are unique.' He motioned to Pierre, who solemnly brought forward the empty bottles, unswathed now, from the humble Chablis to the stately Napoleon, with the imperial seal blown in the glass. 'Every time you have been correct as to growth and year. There cannot be six men in the world with such a palate as yours, and I thought that but one of them was an Englishman. Will you not favour us, this time, with your real name?'

'It doesn't matter what his name is,' said Peter I. He rose. 'Put up your hands, all of you. Count, the formula!'

Bredon's hands came up with a jerk, still clutching the napkin. The white folds spurted flame as his shot struck the other's revolver cleanly between trigger and barrel, exploding the charge, to the extreme detriment of the glass chandelier. Peter I stood shaking his paralysed hand and cursing.

Bredon kept him covered while he cocked a wary eye at Peter II, who, his rosy visions scattered by the report, seemed struggling back to aggressiveness.

'Since the entertainment appears to be taking a lively turn,' observed Bredon, 'perhaps you would be so good, count, as to search these gentlemen for further firearms. Thank you. Now, why should we not all sit down again and pass the bottle round?'

'You – *you* are—' growled Peter I.

'Oh, my name is Bredon all right,' said the young man cheerfully. 'I loathe aliases. Like another fellow's clothes, you know – never seem quite to fit. Peter Death Bredon Wimsey – a bit lengthy and all that, but handy when taken in instalments. I've got a passport and all those things, too, but I didn't offer them, as their reputation here seems a little blown upon, so to speak. As regards the formula, I think I'd better give you my personal cheque for it – all sorts of people seem able to go about flourishing Bank of England notes. Personally, I think all this secret diplomacy work is a mistake, but that's the War Office's pigeon. I suppose we all brought similar credentials. Yes, I thought so. Some bright person seems to have sold himself very successfully in two places at once. But you two must have been having a lively time, each thinking the other was me.'

'My lord,' said the count heavily, 'these two men are, or were, Englishmen, I suppose. I do not care to know what Governments have purchased their treachery. But where they stand, I, alas! stand too. To our venal and corrupt Republic I, as a Royalist, acknowledge no allegiance. But it is in my heart that I have agreed to sell my country to England because of my poverty. Go back to your War Office and say I will not give you the formula. If war should come between our countries – which may God avert! – I will be found on the side of France. That, my lord, is my last word.'

Wimsey bowed.

'Sir,' said he, 'it appears that my mission has, after all, failed. I am glad of it. This trafficking in destruction is a dirty kind of business after all. Let us shut the door upon these two, who are neither flesh nor fowl, and finish the brandy in the library.'

'Uncle Peter!'

'Half a jiff, Gherkins. No, I don't think I'll take the Catullus, Mr Ffolliott. After all, thirteen guineas is a bit steep without either the title or the last folio, what? But you might send me round the Vitruvius and the Satyricon when they come in; I'd like to have a look at them, anyhow. Well, old man, what is it?'

'Do come and look at these pictures, Uncle Peter. I'm sure it's an awfully old book.'

Lord Peter Wimsey sighed as he picked his way out of Mr Ffolliott's dark back shop, strewn with the flotsam and jetsam of many libraries. An unexpected outbreak of measles at Mr Bultridge's excellent preparatory school, coinciding with the absence of the Duke and Duchess of Denver on the Continent, had saddled his lordship with his ten-year-old nephew, Viscount St George, more commonly known as Young Jerry, Jerrykins, or Pickled Gherkins. Lord Peter was not one of those born uncles who delight old nurses by their fascinating 'way with' children. He succeeded, however, in earning tolerance on honorable terms by treating the young with the same scrupulous politeness which he extended to their elders. He therefore prepared to receive Gherkins's discovery with respect, though a child's taste was not to be trusted, and the book might quite well be some horror of woolly mezzotints or an inferior modern reprint adorned with leprous electros. Nothing much better was really to be expected from the 'cheap shelf' exposed to the dust of the street.

'Uncle! there's such a funny man here, with a great long nose and ears and a tail and dogs' heads all over his body. *Monstrum hoc Cracoviæ* – that's a monster, isn't it? I should jolly well think it was. What's *Cracoviæ*, Uncle Peter?'

'Oh,' said Lord Peter, greatly relieved, 'the Cracow monster?' A portrait of that distressing infant certainly argued a respectable antiquity. 'Let's have a look. Quite right, it's a very old book – Munster's *Cosmographia Universalis*. I'm glad you know good stuff when you see it, Gherkins. What's the *Cosmographia* doing out here, Mr Ffolliott, at five bob?"

'Well, my lord,' said the bookseller, who had followed his customers to the door, 'it's in a very bad state, you see; covers loose and nearly all the double-page maps missing. It came in a few weeks ago – dumped in with a collection we bought from a gentleman in Norfolk – you'll find his name in it – Dr Conyers of Yelsall Manor. Of course, we might keep it and try to make up a complete copy when we get another example. But it's rather out of our line, as you know, classical authors being our speciality. So we just put it out to go for what it would fetch in the *status quo*, as you might say.'

'Oh, look!' broke in Gherkins. 'Here's a picture of a man being chopped up in little bits. What does it say about it?'

'I thought you could read Latin.'

'Well, but it's all full of sort of pothooks. What do they mean?'

'They're just contractions,' said Lord Peter patiently.

' "*Solent quoque hujus insulæ cultores*" – It is the custom of the dwellers in this island, when they see their parents stricken in years and of no further use, to take them down into the market-place and sell them to the cannibals, who kill them and eat them for food. This they do also with younger persons when they fall into any desperate sickness.'

'Ha, ha!' said Mr Ffolliott. 'Rather sharp practice on the poor cannibals. They never got anything but tough old joints or diseased meat, eh?'

'The inhabitants seem to have had thoroughly advanced notions of business,' agreed his lordship.

The viscount was enthralled.

'I *do* like this book,' he said; 'could I buy it out of my pocket-money, please?'

'Another problem for uncles,' thought Lord Peter, rapidly ransacking his recollections of the *Cosmographia* to determine whether any of its illustrations were indelicate; for he knew the duchess to be strait-laced. On consideration, he could only remember one that was dubious, and there was a sporting chance that the duchess might fail to light upon it.

'Well,' he said judicially, 'in your place, Gherkins, I should be inclined to buy it. It's in a bad state, as Mr Ffolliott has honourably told you – otherwise, of course, it would be exceedingly valuable; but, apart from the lost pages, it's a very nice clean copy, and certainly worth five shillings to you, if you think of starting a collection.'

Till that moment, the viscount had obviously been more impressed by the cannibals than by the state of the margins, but the idea of figuring next term at Mr Bultridge's as a collector of rare editions had undeniable charm.

'None of the other fellows collect books,' he said; 'they collect stamps, mostly. I think stamps are rather ordinary, don't you, Uncle Peter? I was rather thinking of giving up stamps. Mr Porter, who takes us for history, has got a lot of books like yours, and he is a splendid man at footer.'

Rightly interpreting this reference to Mr Porter, Lord Peter gave it as his opinion that book-collecting could be a perfectly manly pursuit. Girls, he said, practically never took it up, because it meant so much learning about dates and type-faces and other technicalities which called for a masculine brain.

'Besides,' he added, 'it's a very interesting book in itself, you know. Well worth dipping into.'

'I'll take it, please,' said the viscount, blushing a little at transacting so important and expensive a piece of business; for the duchess did not encourage lavish spending by little boys, and was strict in the matter of allowances.

Mr Ffolliott bowed, and took the *Cosmographia* away to wrap it up.

'Are you all right for cash?' enquired Lord Peter discreetly. 'Or can I be of temporary assistance?'

'No, thank you, uncle; I've got Aunt Mary's half-crown and four shillings of my pocket-money, because, you see, with the measles happening, we didn't have our dormitory spread, and I was saving up for that.'

The business being settled in this gentlemanly manner, and the budding bibliophile taking personal and immediate charge of the stout, square volume, a taxi was chartered which, in due course of traffic delays, brought the *Cosmographia* to 110A Piccadilly.

'And who, Bunter, is Mr Wilberforce Pope?'

'I do not think we know the gentleman, my lord. He is

213

asking to see your lordship for a few minutes on business.'

'He probably wants me to find a lost dog for his maiden aunt. What it is to have acquired a reputation as a sleuth! Show him in. Gherkins, if this good gentleman's business turns out to be private, you'd better retire into the dining-room.'

'Yes, Uncle Peter,' said the viscount dutifully. He was extended on his stomach on the library hearthrug, laboriously picking his way through the more exciting-looking bits of the *Cosmographia*, with the aid of Messrs Lewis & Short, whose monumental compilation he had hitherto looked upon as a barbarous invention for the annoyance of upper forms.

Mr Wilberforce Pope turned out to be a rather plump, fair gentleman in the late thirties, with a prematurely bald forehead, horn-rimmed spectacles, and an engaging manner.

'You will excuse my intrusion, won't you?' he began. 'I'm sure you must think me a terrible nuisance. But I wormed your name and address out of Mr Ffolliott. Not his fault, really. You won't blame him, will you? I positively badgered the poor man. Sat down on his doorstep and refused to go, though the boy was putting up the shutters. I'm afraid you will think me very silly when you know what it's all about. But you really mustn't hold poor Mr Ffolliott responsible, now, will you?'

'Not at all,' said his lordship. 'I mean, I'm charmed and all that sort of thing. Something I can do for you about books? You're a collector, perhaps? Will you have a drink or any thing?'

'Well, no,' said Mr Pope, with a faint giggle 'No, not

exactly a collector, Thank you very much, just a spot –
no, no, literally a spot. Thank you; no' – he glanced
round the bookshelves, with their rows of rich old leather
bindings – 'certainly not a collector. But I happen to be –
er, interested – sentimentally interested – in a purchase
you made yesterday. Really, such a very small matter.
You will think it foolish. But I am told you are the
present owner of a copy of Munster's *Cosmographia*,
which used to belong to my uncle, Dr Conyers.'

Gherkins looked up suddenly, seeing that the conversation had a personal interest for him.

'Well, that's not quite correct,' said Wimsey. 'I was
there at the time, but the actual purchaser is my nephew.
Gerald, Mr Pope is interested in your *Cosmographia*. My
nephew, Lord St George.'

'How do you do, young man,' said Mr Pope affably. 'I
see that the collecting spirit runs in the family. A great
Latin scholar, too, I expect, eh? Ready to decline *jusjur-
andum* with the best of us? Ha, ha! And what are you
going to do when you grow up? Be Lord Chancellor, eh?
Now, I bet you think you'd rather be an engine-driver,
what, what?'

'No, thank you,' said the viscount, with aloofness.

'What, not an engine-driver? Well, now, I want you
to be a real business man this time. Put through a book
deal, you know. Your uncle will see I offer you a fair
price, what? Ha, ha! Now, you see, that picture-book
of yours has a great value for me that it wouldn't have
for anybody else. When *I* was a little boy of your age it
was one of my very greatest joys. I used to have it to
look at on Sundays. Ah, dear! the happy hours I used
to spend with those quaint old engravings, and the
funny old maps with the ships and salamanders and

"*Hic dracones*" you know what *that* means, I dare say. What does it mean?'

'Here are dragons,' said the viscount, unwillingly but still politely.

'Quite right. I *knew* you were a scholar.'

'It's a very attractive book,' said Lord Peter. 'My nephew was quite entranced by the famous Cracow monster.'

'Ah yes – a glorious monster, isn't it?' agreed Mr Pope, with enthusiasm. 'Many's the time I've fancied myself as Sir Lancelot or somebody on a white war horse, charging that monster, lance in rest, with the captive princess cheering me on. Ah! childhood! You're living the happiest days of your life, young man. You won't believe me, but you are.'

'Now what is it exactly you want my nephew to do?' enquired Lord Peter a little sharply.

'Quite right, quite right. Well now, you know, my uncle, Dr Conyers, sold his library a few months ago. I was abroad at the time, and it was only yesterday, when I went down to Yelsall on a visit, that I learnt the dear old book had gone with the rest. I can't tell you how distressed I was. I know it's not valuable – a great many pages missing and all that – but I can't bear to think of its being gone. So, purely from sentimental reasons, as I said, I hurried off to Ffolliott's to see if I could get it back. I was quite upset to find I was too late, and gave poor Mr Ffolliott no peace till he told me the name of the purchaser. Now, you see, Lord St George, I'm here to make you an offer for the book. Come, now, double what you gave for it. That's a good offer, isn't it, Lord Peter? Ha, ha! And you will be doing me a very great kindness as well.'

Viscount St George looked rather distressed, and turned appealingly to his uncle.

'Well, Gerald,' said Lord Peter, 'it's your affair, you know. What do you say?'

The viscount stood first on one leg and then on the other. The career of a book collector evidently had its problems, like other careers.

'If you please, Uncle Peter,' he said, with embarrassment, 'may I whisper?'

'It's not usually considered the thing to whisper, Gherkins, but you could ask Mr Pope for time to consider his offer. Or you could say you would prefer to consult me first. That would be quite in order.'

'Then, if you don't mind, Mr Pope, I should like to consult my uncle first.'

'Certainly, certainly; ha, ha!' said Mr Pope. 'Very prudent to consult a collector of greater experience, what? Ah! the younger generation, eh, Lord Peter? Regular little business men, already.'

'Excuse us, then, for one moment,' said Lord Peter, and drew his nephew into the dining-room.

'I say Uncle Peter,' said the collector breathlessly, when the door was shut, '*need* I give him my book? I don't think he's a very nice man. I *hate* people who ask you to decline nouns for them.'

'Certainly you needn't, Gherkins, if you don't want to. The book is yours, and you've a right to it.'

'What would *you* do, uncle?'

Before replying, Lord Peter, the most surprising manner, tiptoed gently to the door which communicated with the library and flung it suddenly open, in time to catch Mr Pope kneeling on the hearthrug intently turning over the pages of the coveted volume, which lay as the owner had left it. He started to his feet in a flurried manner as the door opened.

'Do help yourself, Mr Pope, won't you?' cried Lord Peter hospitably, and closed the door again.

'What is it, Uncle Peter?'

'If you want my advice, Gherkins, I should be rather careful how you had any dealings with Mr Pope. I don't think he's telling the truth. He called those wood-cuts engravings – though, of course, that may be just his ignorance. But I can't believe that he spent all his child-hood's Sunday afternoons studying those maps and pick-ing out the dragons in them, because, as you may have noticed for yourself, old Munster put very few dragons into his maps. They're mostly just plain maps – a bit queer to our ideas of geography, but perfectly straightforward. That was why I brought in the Cracow monster, and, you see, he thought it was some sort of dragon.'

'Oh, I say, uncle! So you said that on purpose!'

'If Mr Pope wants the *Cosmographia*, it's for some reason he doesn't want to tell us about. And, that being so, I wouldn't be in too big a hurry to sell, if the book were mine. See?'

'Do you mean there's something frightfully valuable about the book, which we don't know?'

'Possibly.'

'How exciting! It's just like a story in the *Boys' Friend Library*. What am I to say to him, uncle?'

'Well, in your place I wouldn't be dramatic or any-thing. I'd just say you've considered the matter, and you've taken a fancy to the book and have decided not to sell. You thank him for his offer, of course.'

'Yes – er, won't you say it for me, uncle?'

'I think it would look better if you did it yourself.'

'Yes, perhaps it would. Will he be very cross?'

'Possibly,' said Lord Peter, 'but, if he is, he won't let on. Ready?'

The consulting committee accordingly returned to the library. Mr Pope had prudently retired from the hearth-rug and was examining a distant bookcase.

'Thank you very much for your offer, Mr Pope,' said the viscount, striding stoutly up to him, 'but I have considered it, and I have taken a – a – a fancy for the book and decided not to sell'

'Sorry and all that,' put in Lord Peter, 'but my nephew's adamant about it. No, it isn't the price; he wants the book. Wish I could oblige you, but it isn't in my hands. Won't you take something else before you go? Really? Ring the bell, Gherkins. My man will see you to the lift. *Good* evening.'

When the visitor had gone, Lord Peter returned and thoughtfully picked up the book.

'We were awful idiots to leave him with it, Gherkins, even for a moment. Luckily, there's no harm done.'

'You don't think he found out anything while we were away, do you, uncle?' gasped Gherkins, open-eyed.

'I'm sure he didn't.'

'Why?'

'He offered me fifty pounds for it on the way to the door. Gave the game away. H'm! Bunter.'

'My lord?'

'Put this book in the safe and bring me back the keys. And you'd better set all the burglar alarms when you lock up.'

'Oo-er!' said Viscount St George.

On the third morning after the visit of Mr Wilberforce Pope, the viscount was seated at a very late breakfast in his uncle's flat, after the most glorious and soul-satisfying night that ever boy experienced. He was almost too excited to eat the kidneys and bacon placed before him by Bunter, whose usual impeccable manner was not in the least impaired by a rapidly swelling and blackening eye.

It was about two in the morning that Gherkins – who had not slept very well, owing to too lavish and grown-up a dinner and theatre the evening before – became aware of a stealthy sound somewhere in the direction of the fire-escape. He had got out of bed and crept very softly into Lord Peter's room and woken him up. He had said: 'Uncle Peter, I'm sure there's burglars on the fire-escape.' And Uncle Peter, instead of saying, 'Nonsense, Gherkins, hurry up and get back to bed,' had sat up and listened and said: 'By Jove, Gherkins, I believe you're right.' And had sent Gherkins to call Bunter. And on his return, Gherkins, who had always regarded his uncle as a very top-hatted sort of person, actually saw him take from his handkerchief-drawer an undeniable automatic pistol.

It was at this point that Lord Peter was apotheosed from the state of Quite Decent Uncle to that of Glorified Uncle. He said:

'Look here, Gherkins, we don't know how many of these blighters there'll be, so you must be jolly smart and do anything I say sharp, on the word of command – even if I have to say "Scoot". Promise?'

Gherkins promised, with his heart thumping, and they sat waiting in the dark, till suddenly a little electric bell rang sharply just over the head of Lord Peter's bed and a green light shone out.

'The library window,' said his lordship, promptly silencing the bell by turning a switch. 'If they heard, they may think better of it. We'll give them a few minutes.'

They gave them five minutes, and then crept very quietly down the passage.

'Go round by the dining-room, Bunter,' said his lordship; 'they may bolt that way.'

With infinite precaution, he unlocked and opened the library door, and Gherkins noticed how silently the locks moved.

A circle of light from an electric torch was moving slowly along the bookshelves. The burglars had obviously heard nothing of the counter-attack. Indeed, they seemed to have troubles enough of their own to keep their attention occupied. As his eyes grew accustomed to the dim light, Gherkins made out that one man was standing holding the torch, while the other took down and examined the books. It was fascinating to watch his apparently disembodied hands move along the shelves in the torch-light.

The men muttered discontentedly. Obviously the job was proving a harder one than they had bargained for. The habit of ancient authors of abbreviating the titles on the backs of their volumes, or leaving them completely untitled, made things extremely awkward. From time to time the man with the torch extended his hands into the light. It held a piece of paper, which they anxiously compared with the title-page of a book. Then the volume was replaced and the tedious search went on.

Suddenly some slight noise – Gherkins was sure *he* did not make it; it may have been Bunter in the dining-room – seemed to catch the ear of the kneeling man.

'Wot's that?' he gasped, and his startled face swung round into view.

'Hands up!' said Lord Peter, and switched the light on.

The second man made one leap for the dining-room door, where a smash and an oath proclaimed that he had encountered Bunter. The kneeling man shot his hands up like a marionette.

'Gherkins,' said Lord Peter, 'do you think you can go across to that gentleman by the bookcase and relieve him of the article which is so inelegantly distending the right-hand pocket of his coat? Wait a minute. Don't on any account get between him and my pistol, and mind you take the thing out *very* carefully. There's no hurry. That's splendid. Just point it at the floor while you bring it across, would you? Thanks. Bunter has managed for himself, I see. Now run into my bedroom, and in the bottom of my wardrobe you will find a bundle of stout cord. Oh! I beg your pardon; yes, put your hands down by all means. It must be very tiring exercise.'

The arms of the intruders being secured behind their backs with a neatness which Gherkins felt to be worthy of the best traditions of Sexton Blake, Lord Peter motioned his captives to sit down and despatched Bunter for whisky-and-soda.

'Before we send for the police,' said Lord Peter, 'you would do me a great personal favour by telling me what you were looking for, and who sent you. Ah! thanks, Bunter. As our guests are not at liberty to use their hands, perhaps you would be kind enough to assist them to a drink. Now then, say when.'

'Well, you're a gentleman, guv'nor,' said the First Burglar, wiping his mouth politely on his shoulder, the back of his hand not being available. 'If we'd a known wot a job this wos goin' ter be, blow me if we'd a touched it. The bloke said, ses 'e, "It's takin' candy from a baby," 'e ses. "The gentleman's a reg'lar softie," 'e ses, "one o' these 'ere sersiety toffs wiv a maggot fer old books," that's wot 'e ses, "an' ef yer can find this 'ere old book fer me," 'e ses, "there's a pony fer yer." Well! Sech a job! E didn't mention as 'ow there'd be five 'undred fousand bleedin' ole books all as alike as a regiment o' bleedin' dragoons. Nor as 'ow yer kept a nice little machine-gun like that 'andy by the bedside, *nor* yet as 'ow yer was so bleedin' good at tyin' knots in a bit o' string. No – 'e didn't think ter mention them things.'

'Deuced unsporting of him,' said his lordship. 'Do you happen to know the gentleman's name?'

'No – that was another o' them things wot 'e didn't mention. 'E's a stout, fair party, wiv 'orn rims to 'is goggles and a bald 'ead. One o' these 'ere philanthropists, I reckon. A friend o' mine, wot got inter trouble once, got work froo 'im, and the gentleman comes round and ses to 'im, 'e ses, "Could yet find me a couple o' lads ter do a little job?" 'e ses, an' my friend, finkin' no 'arm, you see, guv'nor, but wot it might be a bit of a joke like, 'e gets 'old of my pal an' me, an' we meets the gentleman in a pub dahn Whitechapel way. W'ich we was ter meet 'im there again Friday night, us 'avin' allowed that time fer ter git 'old of the book.'

'The book being, if I may hazard a guess, the *Cosmographia Universalis?*'

'Sumfink like that, guv'nor. I got its jaw-breakin' name wrote down on a bit o' paper, wot my pal 'ad in 'is 'and. Wot did yer do wiv that 'ere bit o' paper, Bill?'

'Well look here,' said Lord Peter, 'I'm afraid I must send for the police, but I think it likely, if you give us your assistance to get hold of your gentleman, whose name I strongly suspect to be Wilberforce Pope, that you will get off pretty easily. Telephone the police, Bunter, and then go and put something on that eye of yours. Gherkins, we'll give these gentlemen another drink, and then I think perhaps you'd better hop back to bed; the fun's over. No? Well, put a good thick coat on, there's a good fellow, because what your mother will say to me if you catch a cold I don't like to think.'

So the police had come and taken the burglars away, and now Detective-Inspector Parker, of Scotland Yard, a great personal friend of Lord Peter's, sat toying with a cup of coffee and listening to the story.

'But what's the matter with the jolly old book, anyhow, to make it so popular?' he demanded.

'I don't know,' replied Wimsey, 'but after Mr Pope's little visit the other day I got kind of intrigued about it and had a look through it. I've got a hunch it may turn out rather valuable, after all. Unsuspected beauties and all that sort of thing. If only Mr Pope had been a trifle more accurate in his facts, he might have got away with something to which I feel pretty sure he isn't entitled. Anyway, when I'd seen – what I saw, I wrote off to Dr Conyers of Yelsall Manor, the late owner—'

'Conyers, the cancer man?'

'Yes. He's done some pretty important research in his time, I fancy. Getting on now, though; about seventy-eight, I fancy. I hope he's more honest than his nephew, with one foot in the grave like that. Anyway, I wrote (with Gherkin's permission, naturally) to say we had the book and had been specially interested by something we found there, and would he be so obliging as to tell us something of its history. I also—'

'But what did you find in it?'

'I don't think we'll tell him yet, Gherkins, shall we? I

like to keep policemen guessing. As I was saying, when you so rudely interrupted me, I also asked him whether he knew anything about his good nephew's offer to buy it back. His answer has just arrived. He says he knows of nothing specially interesting about the book. It has been in the library untold years, and the tearing out of the maps must have been done a long time ago by some family vandal. He can't think why his nephew should be so keen on it, as he certainly never pored over it as a boy. In fact, the old man declares the engaging Wilberforce has never even set foot in Yelsall Manor to his knowledge. So much for the fire-breathing monsters and the pleasant Sunday afternoons.'

'Naughty Wilberforce!'

'M'm. Yes. So, after last night's little dust-up, I wired the old boy we were tooling down to Yelsall to have a heart-to-heart talk with him about his picture-book and his nephew.'

'Are you taking the book down with you?' asked Parker. 'I can give you a police escort for it if you like.'

'That's not a bad idea,' said Wimsey. 'We don't know where the insinuating Mr Pope may be hanging out, and I wouldn't put it past him to make another attempt.'

'Better be on the safe side,' said Parker. 'I can't come myself, but I'll send down a couple of men with you.'

'Good egg,' said Lord Peter. 'Call up your myrmidons. We'll get a car round at once. You're coming, Gherkins, I suppose? God knows what your mother would say. Don't ever be an uncle, Charles; it's frightfully difficult to be fair to all parties.'

Yelsall Manor was one of those large, decaying country mansions which speak eloquently of times more spacious than our own. The original late Tudor construction had been masked by the addition of a wide frontage in the Italian manner, with a kind of classical portico surmounted by a pediment and approached by a semicircular flight of steps. The grounds had originally been laid out in that formal manner in which grove nods to grove and each half duly reflects the other. A late owner, however, had burst out into the more eccentric sort of landscape gardening which is associated with the name of Capability Brown. A Chinese pagoda, somewhat resembling Sir William Chambers's erection in Kew Gardens, but smaller, rose out of a grove of laurustinus towards the eastern extremity of the house, while at the rear appeared a large artificial lake, dotted with numerous islands, on which odd little temples, grottos, tea-houses, and bridges peeped out from among clumps of shrubs, once ornamental, but now sadly overgrown. A boat-house, with wide eaves like the designs on a willow-pattern plate, stood at one corner, its landing-stage fallen into decay and wreathed with melancholy weeds.

'My disreputable old ancestor, Cuthbert Conyers, settled down here when he retired from the sea in 1732,' said Dr Conyers, smiling faintly. 'His elder brother died childless, so the black sheep returned to the fold with the determination to become respectable and found a family. I fear he did not succeed altogether. There were very queer tales as to where his money came from. He is said to have been a pirate, and to have sailed with the notorious Captain Blackbeard. In the village, to this day, he is remembered and spoken of as Cut-throat Conyers. It used to make the old man very angry, and there is an unpleasant story of his slicing the ears off a groom who had been heard to call him "Old Cut-throat". He was not an uncultivated person, though. It was he who did the landscape-gardening round at the back, and he built the pagoda for his telescope. He was reputed to study the Black Art, and there were certainly a number of astrological works in the library with his name on the fly-leaf, but probably the telescope was only a remembrance of his seafaring days.

'Anyhow, towards the end of his life he became more and more odd and morose. He quarrelled with his family, and turned his younger son out of doors with his wife and children. An unpleasant old fellow.

'On his deathbed he was attended by the parson – a good, earnest, God-fearing sort of man, who must have put up with a deal of insult in carrying out what he firmly believed to be the sacred duty of reconciling the old man to this shamefully treated son. Eventually, "Old Cut-throat" relented so far as to make a will, leaving to the younger son "My treasure which I have buried in Munster." The parson represented to him that it was useless to bequeath a treasure unless he also bequeathed the information where to find it, but the horrid old pirate only chuckled spitefully, and said that, as he had been at the pains to collect the treasure, his son might well be at the pains of looking for it. Further than that he would not go, and so he died, and I dare say went to a very bad place.

'Since then the family has died out, and I am the sole representative of the Conyers, and heir to the treasure, whatever and wherever it is, for it was never discovered. I do not suppose it was very honestly come by, but, since it would be useless now to try and find the original owners, I imagine I have a better right to it than anybody living.

'You may think it very unseemly, Lord Peter, that an old, lonely man like myself should be greedy for a hoard of pirate's gold. But my whole life has been devoted to studying the disease of cancer, and I believe myself to be very close to a solution of one part at least of the terrible problem. Research costs money, and my limited means are very nearly exhausted. The property is mortgaged up to the hilt, and I do most urgently desire to complete my experiments before I die, and to leave a sufficient sum to found a clinic where the work can be carried on.

'During the last year I have made very great efforts to solve the mystery of "Old Cut-throat's" treasure. I have been able to leave much of my experimental work in the most capable hands of my assistant, Dr Forbes, while I pursued my researches with the very slender clue I had to go upon. It was the more expensive and difficult that Cuthbert had left no indication in his will whether Münster in Germany or Munster in Ireland was the hiding-place of the treasure. My journeys and my search in both places cost money and brought me no further on my quest. I returned, disheartened, in August, and found myself obliged to sell my library, in order to defray my expenses and obtain a little money with which to struggle on with my sadly delayed experiments.'

'Ah!' said Lord Peter. 'I begin to see light.'

The old physician looked at him enquiringly. They had finished tea, and were seated around the great fireplace in the study. Lord Peter's interested questions about the beautiful, dilapidated old house and estate had led the conversation naturally to Dr Conyers's family, shelving for the time the problem of the *Cosmographia*, which lay on a table beside them.

'Everything you say fits into the puzzle,' went on Wimsey, 'and I think there's not the smallest doubt what

Mr Wilberforce Pope was after, though how he knew that you had the *Cosmographia* here I couldn't say.'

'When I disposed of the library, I sent him a catalogue,' said Dr Conyers. 'As a relative, I thought he ought to have the right to buy anything he fancied. I can't think why he didn't secure the book then, instead of behaving in this most shocking fashion.'

Lord Peter hooted with laughter.

'Why, because he never tumbled to it till afterwards,' he said. 'And oh, dear, how wild he must have been! I forgive him everything. Although,' he added, 'I don't want to raise your hopes too high, sir, for, even when we've solved old Cuthbert's riddle, I don't know that we're very much nearer to the treasure.'

'To the *treasure*?'

'Well, now, sir. I want you first to look at this page, where there's a name scrawled in the margin. Our ancestors had an untidy way of signing their possessions higgledy-piggledy in margins instead of in a decent, Christian way in the fly-leaf. This is a handwriting of somewhere about Charles I's reign: "Jac: Coniers." I take it that goes to prove that the book was in the possession of your family at any rate as early as the first half of the seventeenth century, and has remained there ever since. Right. Now we turn to page 1099, where we find a description of the discoveries of Christopher Columbus. It's headed, you see, by a kind of map, with some of Mr Pope's monsters swimming about in it, and apparently representing the Canaries, or, as they used to be called, the Fortunate Isles. It doesn't look much more accurate than old maps usually are, but I take it the big island on the right is meant for Lanzarote, and the two nearest to it may be Teneriffe and Gran Canaria.'

Liber V.

DE NOVIS INSVLIS,
quomodo, quando, & per quem
illæ inuentæ sint.

Hristophorus Columbus natione Genuensis, cùm diu in aula regis Hispan-
rum deuersatus fuisset, animum induxit, ut hactenus inaccessas orbis partes p
agrarer. Petit præterea à rege itruaro suo non deesset, futuris sibi & toti Hisp

'But what's that writing in the middle?'

'That's just the point. The writing is later than "Jac: Coniers's" signature; I should put it about 1700 – but, of course, it may have been written a good deal later still. I mean, a man who was elderly in 1730 would still use the style of writing he adopted as a young man, especially if, like your ancestor the pirate, he had spent the early part of his life in outdoor pursuits and hadn't done much writing.'

'Do you mean to say, Uncle Peter,' broke in the viscount excitedly, 'that that's "Old Cut-throat's" writing?'

'I'd be ready to lay a sporting bet it is. Look here, sir, you've been scouring round Münster in Germany and Munster in Ireland – but how about good old Sebastian Munster here in the library at home?'

'God bless my soul! Is it possible?'

'It's pretty nearly certain, sir. Here's what he says, written, you see, round the head of that sort of sea-dragon:

> Hic in capite draconis ardet perpetuo Sol.
> Here the sun shines perpetually upon the Dragon's Head.

Rather doggy Latin – sea-dog Latin, you might say, in fact.'

'I'm afraid,' said Dr Conyers, 'I must be very stupid, but I can't see where that leads us.'

'No; "Old Cut-throat" was rather clever. No doubt he thought that, if anybody read it, they'd think it was just an allusion to where it says, further down, that "the islands were called *Fortunatæ* because of the wonderful temperature of the air and the clemency of the skies." But the cunning old astrologer up in his pagoda had a meaning of his own. Here's a little book published in 1678 – Middleton's *Practical Astrology* – just the sort of popular handbook an amateur like "Old Cut-throat" would use. Here you are: "If in your figure you find Jupiter or Venus or *Dragon's head*, you may be confident there is Treasure in the place supposed. . . . If you find *Sol* to be the Significator of the hidden Treasure, you may conclude there is Gold, or some jewels." You know, sir, I think we may conclude it.'

'Dear me!' said Dr Conyers. 'I believe, indeed, you must be right. And I am ashamed to think that if anybody had suggested to me that it could ever be profitable to me to learn the terms of astrology, I should have replied in my vanity that my time was too valuable to waste on such foolishness. I am deeply indebted to you.'

'Yes,' said Gherkins, 'but where *is* the treasure, uncle?'

'That's just it,' said Lord Peter. 'The map is very vague; there is no latitude or longitude given; and the directions, such as they are, seem not even to refer to any spot on the islands, but to some place in the middle of the sea. Besides, it is nearly two hundred years since the treasure was hidden, and it may already have been found by somebody or other.'

Dr Conyers stood up.

'I am an old man,' he said, 'but I still have some strength. If I can by any means get together the money for an expedition, I will not rest till I have made every possible effort to find the treasure and to endow my clinic.'

'Then, sir, I hope you'll let me give a hand to the good work,' said Lord Peter.

Dr Conyers had invited his guests to stay the night, and, after the excited viscount had been packed off to bed, Wimsey and the old man sat late, consulting maps and diligently reading Munster's chapter '*De Novis Insulis*', in the hope of discovering some further clue. At length, however, they separated, and Lord Peter went up upstairs, the book under his arm. He was restless, however, and, instead of going to bed, sat for a long time at his window, which looked out upon the lake. The moon, a few days past the full, was riding high among small, windy clouds, and picked out the sharp eaves of the Chinese tea-houses and the straggling tops of the unpruned shrubs. 'Old Cut-throat' and his landscape-gardening! Wimsey could have fancied that the old pirate was sitting now beside his telescope in the preposterous pagoda, chuckling over his riddling testament and counting the craters of the moon. 'If *Luna*, there is silver.' The water of the lake was silver enough; there was a great smooth path across it, broken by the sinister wedge of the boat-house, the black shadows of the islands, and, almost in the middle of the lake, a decayed fountain, a writhing Celestial dragon-shape, spiny-backed and ridiculous.

Wimsey rubbed his eyes. There was something strangely familiar about the lake; from moment to moment it assumed the queer unreality of a place which one recognises without having ever known it. It was like one's first sight of the Leaning Tower of Pisa – too like its picture to be quite believable. Surely, thought Wimsey, he knew that elongated island on the right, shaped rather like a winged monster, with its two little clumps of buildings. And the island to the left of it, like the British Isles, but warped out of shape. And the third island, between the others, and nearer. The three formed a triangle, with the Chinese fountain in the centre, the moon shining steadily upon its dragon head. '*Hic in capite draconis ardet perpetuo—*'

Lord Peter sprang up with a loud exclamation, and flung open the door into the dressing-room. A small figure wrapped in an eiderdown hurriedly uncoiled itself from the window-seat.

'I'm sorry, Uncle Peter,' said Gherkins. 'I was so *dreadfully* wide awake, it wasn't any good staying in bed.'

'Come here,' said Lord Peter, 'and tell me if I'm mad or dreaming. Look out of the window and compare it with the map – Old Cut-throat's "New Islands". He made 'em, Gherkins; he put 'em here. Aren't they laid out just like the Canaries? Those three islands in a triangle, and the fourth down here in the corner? And the boat-house where the big ship is in the picture? And the dragon fountain where the dragon's head is? Well, my son, that's where your hidden treasure's gone to. Get your things on, Gherkins, and damn the time when all good little boys should be in bed! We're going for a row on the lake, if there's a tub in that boat-house that'll float.'

'Oh, Uncle Peter! This is a *read* adventure!'

'All right,' said Wimsey. 'Fifteen men on the dead man's chest, and all that! Yo-ho-ho, and a bottle of Johnny Walker! Pirate expedition fitted out in dead of night to seek hidden treasure and explore the Fortunate Isles! Come on, crew!'

Lord Peter hitched the leaky dinghy to the dragon's knobbly tail and climbed out carefully, for the base of the fountain was green and weedy.

'I'm afraid it's your job to sit there and bail, Gherkins,' he said. 'All the best captains bag the really interesting jobs for themselves. We'd better start with the head. If the old blighter said head, he probably meant it.' He passed an arm affectionately round the creature's neck for support, while he methodically pressed and pulled the various knobs and bumps of its anatomy. 'It seems beastly solid, but I'm sure there's a spring somewhere. You won't forget to bail, will you? I'd simply hate to turn round and find the boat gone. Pirate chief marooned on island and all that. Well, it isn't its back hair, anyhow. We'll try its eyes. I say, Gherkins, I'm sure I felt something move, only it's frightfully stiff. We might have thought to bring some oil. Never mind; it's dogged as does. It's coming. It's coming. Booh! Pah!'

A fierce effort thrust the rusted knob inwards, releasing a huge spout of water into his face from the dragon's gaping throat. The fountain, dry for many years, soared rejoicingly heavenwards, drenching the treasure-hunters, and making rainbows in the moonlight.

'I suppose this is "Old Cut-throat's" idea of humour,' grumbled Wimsey, retreating cautiously round the dragon's neck. 'And now I can't turn it off again. Well, dash it all, let's try the other eye.'

He pressed for a few moments in vain. Then, with a grinding clang, the bronze wings of the monster clapped down to its. sides, revealing a deep square hole, and the fountain ceased to play.

'Gherkins!' said Lord Peter, 'we've done it. (But don't neglect bailing on that account!) There's a box here. And it's beastly heavy. No; all right, I can manage. Gimme the boathook. Now I do hope the old sinner really did have a treasure. What a bore if it's only one of his little jokes. Never mind – hold the boat steady. There, Always remember, Gherkins, that you can make quite an effective crane with a boat-hook and a stout pair of braces. Got it? That's right. Now for home and beauty . . . Hullo! what's all that?'

As he paddled the boat round, it was evident that something was happening down by the boat-house. Lights were moving about, and a sound of voices came across the lake.

'They think we're burglars, Gherkins. Always misunderstood. Give way, my hearties—

'A-roving, a-roving, since roving's been my ru-i-in,
I'll go no more a-roving with you, fair maid.'

'Is that you, my lord?' said a man's voice as they drew
into the boat-house.

'Why, it's our faithful sleuths!' cried his lordship.
'What's the excitement?'

'We found this fellow sneaking round the boat-house,'
said the man from Scotland Yard. 'He says he's the old
gentleman's nephew. Do you know him, my lord?'

'I rather fancy I do,' said Wimsey. 'Mr Pope, I think.
Good evening. Were you looking for anything? Not a
treasure, by any chance? Because we've just found one.
Oh! don't say that. *Maxima reverentia*, you know. Lord
St George is of tender years. And, by the way, thank you
so much for sending your delightful friends to call on me
last night. Oh, yes, Thompson, I'll charge him all right.
You there, doctor? Splendid. Now, if anybody's got a
spanner or anything handy, we'll have a look at Great-
grandpapa Cuthbert. And if he turns out to be old iron,
Mr Pope, you'll have had an uncommonly good joke for
your money.'

An iron bar was produced from the boat-house and
thrust under the hasp of the chest. It creaked and burst.
Dr Conyers knelt down tremulously and threw open the
lid.

There was a little pause.

'The drinks are on you, Mr Pope,' said Lord Peter. 'I
think, doctor, it ought to be a jolly good hospital when
it's finished.'

'What in the world,' said Lord Peter Wimsey, 'is that?'

Thomas Macpherson disengaged the tall jar from its final swathings of paper and straw and set it tenderly upright beside the coffee-pot.

'That,' he said, 'is Great-Uncle Joseph's legacy.'

'And who is Great-Uncle Joseph?'

'He was my mother's uncle. Name of Ferguson. Eccentric old boy. I was rather a favourite of his.'

'It looks like it. Was that all he left you?'

'Imph'm. He said a good digestion was the most precious thing a man could have.'

'Well, he was right there. Is this his? Was it a good one?'

'Good enough. He lived to be ninety-five, and never had a days' illness.'

Wimsey looked at the jar with increased respect.

'What did he die of?'

'Chucked himself out of a sixth-story window. He had a stroke, and the doctors told him – or he guessed for himself – that it was the beginning of the end. He left a letter. Said he had never been ill in his life and wasn't going to begin now. They brought it in temporary insanity, of course, but I think he was thoroughly sensible.'

'I should say so. What was he when he was functioning?'

'He used to be in business – something to do with shipbuilding, I believe, but he retired long ago. He was what the papers call a recluse. Lived all by himself in a little top flat in Glasgow, and saw nobody. Used to go off by himself for days at a time, nobody knew where or why. I used to look him up about once a year and take him a bottle of whisky.'

'Had he any money?'

'Nobody knew. He ought to have had – he was a rich man when he retired. But, when we came to look into it, it turned out he only had a balance of about five hundred pounds in the Glasgow Bank. Apparently he drew out almost everything he had about twenty years ago. There were one or two big bank failures round about that time, and they thought he must have got the wind up. But what he did with it, goodness only knows.'

'Kept it in an old stocking, I expect.'

'I should think Cousin Robert devoutly hopes so.'

'Cousin Robert?'

'He's the residuary legatee. Distant connection of mine, and the only remaining Ferguson. He was awfully wild when he found he'd only got five hundred. He's rather a bright lad, is Robert, and a few thousands would have come in handy.'

'I see. Well, how about a bit of brekker? You might stick Great-Uncle Joseph out of the way somewhere. I don't care about the looks of him.'

'I thought you were rather partial to anatomical specimens.'

'So I am, but not on the breakfast-table. "A place for everything and everything in its place," as my grandmother used to say. Besides, it would give Maggie a shock if she saw it.'

Macpherson laughed, and transferred the jar to a cupboard.

'Maggie's shock-proof. I brought a few odd bones and things with me, by way of a holiday task. I'm getting near my final, you know. She'll just think this is another of them. Ring the bell, old man, would you? We'll see what the trout's like.'

The door opened to admit the housekeeper, with a dish of grilled trout and a plate of fried scones.

'These look good, Maggie,' said Wimsey, drawing his chair up and sniffing appreciatively.

'Aye, sir, they're gude, but they're awfu' wee fish.'

'Don't grumble at them,' said Macpherson. 'They're the sole result of a day's purgatory up on Loch Whyneon. What with the sun fit to roast you and an east wind, I'm pretty well flayed alive. I very nearly didn't shave at all this morning.' He passed a reminiscent hand over his red and excoriated face. 'Ugh! It's a stiff pull up that hill, and the boat was going wallop, wallop all the time, like being in the Bay of Biscay.'

'Damnable, I should think. But there's a change coming. The glass is going back. We'll be having some rain before we're many days older.'

'Time, too,' said Macpherson. 'The burns are nearly dry, and there's not much water in the Fleet.' He glanced out of the window to where the little river ran tinkling and skinkling over the stones at the bottom of the garden. 'If only we get a few days' rain now, there'll be some grand fishing.'

'It *would* come just as I've got to go, naturally,' remarked Wimsey.

'Yes; can't you stay a bit longer? I want to have a try for some sea-trout.'

'Sorry, old man, can't be done. I must be in Town on Wednesday. Never mind. I've had a fine time in the fresh air and got in some good rounds of golf.'

'You must come up another time. I'm here for a month – getting my strength up for the exams and all that. If you can't get away before I go, we'll put it off till August and have a shot at the grouse. The cottage is always at your service, you know, Wimsey.'

'Many thanks. I may get my business over quicker than I think, and, if I do, I'll turn up here again. When did you say your great-uncle died?'

Macpherson stared at him.

'Some time in April as far as I can remember. Why?'

'Oh, nothing – I just wondered. You were a favourite of his, didn't you say?'

'In a sense. I think the old boy liked my remembering him from time to time. Old people are pleased by little attentions, you know?'

'M'm. Well, it's a queer world. What did you say his name was?'

'Ferguson – Joseph Alexander Ferguson, to be exact. You seem extraordinarily interested in Great-Uncle Joseph.'

'I thought, while I was about it, I might look up a man I know in the ship-building line, and see if he knows anything about where the money went to.'

'If you can do that, Cousin Robert will give you a medal. But, if you really want to exercise your detective powers on the problem, you'd better have a hunt through the flat in Glasgow.'

'Yes – what is the address, by the way?'

Macpherson told him the address.

'I'll make a note of it, and, if anything occurs to me, I'll communicate with Cousin Robert. Where does he hang out?'

'Oh, he's in London, in a solicitor's office. Crosbie & Plump, somewhere in Bloomsbury. Robert was studying for the Scottish Bar, you know, but he made rather a mess of things, so they pushed him off among the Sassenachs. His father died a couple of years ago – he was a Writer to the Signet in Edinburgh – and I fancy Robert has rather gone to the bow-wows since then. Got among a cheerful crowd down there, don't you know, and wasted his substance somewhat.'

'Terrible! Scotsmen shouldn't be allowed to leave home. What are you going to do with Great-Uncle?'

'Oh, I don't know. Keep him for a bit, I think. I liked the old fellow, and I don't want to throw him away. He'll look rather well in my consulting-room, don't you think, when I'm qualified and set up my brass plate. I'll say he was presented by a grateful patient on whom I performed a marvellous operation.'

'That's a good idea. Stomach-grafting. Miracle of surgery never before attempted. He'll bring sufferers to your door in flocks.'

'Good old Great-Uncle – he may be worth a fortune to me after all.'

'So he may. I don't suppose you've got such a thing as a photograph of him, have you?'

'A photograph?' Macpherson stared again. 'Great-Uncle seems to be becoming a passion with you. I don't suppose the old man had a photograph taken these thirty years. There was one done then – when he retired from business. I expect Robert's got that.'

'Och aye,' said Wimsey, in the language of the country.

*   *   *

Wimsey left Scotland that evening, and drove down through the night towards London, thinking hard as he went. He handled the wheel mechanically, swerving now and again to avoid the green eyes of rabbits as they bolted from the roadside to squat fascinated in the glare of his head-lamps. He was accustomed to say that his brain worked better when his immediate attention was occupied by the incidents of the road.

Monday morning found him in town with his business finished and his thinking done. A consultation with his ship-building friend had put him in possession of some facts about Great-Uncle Joseph's money, together with a copy of Great-Uncle Joseph's photograph, supplied by the London representative of the Glasgow firm to which he had belonged. It appeared that old Ferguson had been a man of mark in his day. The portrait showed a fine, dour old face, long-lipped and high in the cheek-bones – one of those faces which alter little in a lifetime. Wimsey looked at the photograph with satisfaction as he slipped it into his pocket and made a bee-line for Somerset House.

Here he wandered timidly about the wills department, till a uniformed official took pity on him and enquired what he wanted.

'Oh, thank you,' said Wimsey effusively, 'thank you so much. Always feel nervous in these places. All these big desks and things, don't you know, so awe-inspiring and business-like. Yes, I just wanted to have a squint at a will. I'm told you can see anybody's will for a shilling. Is that really so?'

'Yes, sir, certainly. Anybody's will in particular, sir?'

'Oh, yes, of course – how silly of me. Yes. Curious, isn't it, that when you're dead any stranger can come and snoop round your private affairs – see how much you cut up for and who your lady friends were, and all that. Yes. Not at all nice. Horrid lack of privacy, what?'

The attendant laughed.

'I expect it's all one when you're dead, sir.'

'That's awfully true. Yes, naturally, you're dead by then and it doesn't matter. May be a bit trying for your relations, of course, to learn what a bad boy you've been. Great fun annoyin' one's relations. Always do it myself. Now, what were we sayin'? Ah! yes – the will. (I'm always so absent-minded.) Whose will, you said? Well, it's an old Scots gentleman called Joseph Alexander Ferguson that died at Glasgow – you know Glasgow, where the accent's so strong that even Scotsmen faint when they hear it – in April, this last April as ever was. If it's not troubling you too much, may I have a bob's-worth of Joseph Alexander Ferguson?'

The attendant assured him that he might, adding the caution that he must memorise the contents of the will and not on any account take notes. Thus warned, Wimsey was conducted into a retired corner, where in a short time the will was placed before him.

It was a commendably brief document, written in holograph, and was dated the previous January. After the usual preamble and the bequest of a few small sums and articles of personal ornament to friends, it proceeded somewhat as follows:

'And I direct that, after my death, the alimentary organs be removed entire with their contents from my body, commencing with the oesophagus and ending with the anal canal, and that they be properly secured at both ends with a suitable ligature, and be enclosed in a proper preservative medium in a glass vessel and given to my great-nephew Thomas Macpherson of the Stone Cottage, Gatehouse-of-the-Fleet, in Kirkcudbrightshire, now studying medicine in Aberdeen. And I bequeath him these my alimentary organs with their contents for his study and edification, they having served me for ninety-five years without failure, or defect, because I wish him to understand that no riches in the world are comparable to the riches of a good digestion. And I desire of him that he will, in the exercise of his medical profession, use his best endeavours to preserve to his patients the blessing of good digestion unimpaired, not needlessly filling their stomachs with drugs out of concern for his own pocket, but exhorting them to a sober and temperate life agreeably to the design of Almighty Providence.'

After this remarkable passage, the document went on to make Robert Ferguson residuary legatee without particular specification of any property, and to appoint a firm of lawyers in Glasgow executors of the will.

Wimsey considered the bequest for some time. From the phraseology he concluded that old Mr Ferguson had drawn up his own will without legal aid, and he was glad of it, for its wording thus afforded a valuable clue to the testator's mood and intention. He mentally noted three points: the 'alimentary organs with their contents' were mentioned twice over, with a certain emphasis; they were to be ligatured top and bottom; and the legacy was accompanied by the expression of a wish that the legatee should not allow his financial necessities to interfere with the conscientious exercise of his professional duties

Wimsey chuckled. He felt he rather liked Great-Uncle Joseph.

He got up, collected his hat, gloves, and stick, and advanced with the will in his hand to return it to the attendant. The latter was engaged in conversation with a young man, who seemed to be expostulating about something.

'I'm sorry, sir,' said the attendant, 'but I don't suppose the other gentleman will be very long. Ah!' He turned and saw Wimsey. 'Here is the gentleman.'

The young man, whose reddish hair, long nose, and slightly sodden eyes gave him the appearance of a dissipated fox, greeted Wimsey with a disagreeable stare.

'What's up? Want me?' asked his lordship airily.

'Yes, sir. Very curious thing, sir; here's a gentleman enquiring for that very same document as you've been studying, sir. I've been in this department fifteen years, and I don't know as I ever remember such a thing happening before.'

'No,' said Wimsey, 'I don't suppose there's much of a run on any of your lines as a rule.'

'It's a very curious thing indeed,' said the stranger, with marked displeasure in his voice.

'Member of the family?' suggested Wimsey.

'I *am* a member of the family,' said the foxy-faced man. 'May I ask whether *you* have any connection with us?'

'By all means,' replied Wimsey graciously.

'I don't believe it. I don't know you.'

'No, no – I meant you might ask, by all means.'

The young man positively showed his teeth.

'Do you mind telling me who you are, anyhow, and why you're so damned inquisitive about my great-uncle's will?'

Wimsey extracted a card from his case and presented it with a smile. Mr Robert Ferguson changed colour.

'If you would like a reference as to my respectability,' went on Wimsey affably, 'Mr Thomas Macpherson will, I am sure, be happy to tell you about me. I am inquisitive,' said his lordship – 'a student of humanity. Your cousin mentioned to me the curious clause relating to your esteemed great-uncle's – er – stomach and appurtenances. Curious clauses are a passion with me. I came to look it up and add it to my collection of curious wills. I am engaged in writing a book on the subject – *Clauses and Consequences*. My publishers tell me it should enjoy a ready sale. I regret that my random jottings should have encroached upon your doubtless far more serious studies. I wish you a very good morning.'

As he beamed his way out, Wimsey, who had quick ears, heard the attendant informing the indignant Mr Ferguson that he was 'a very funny gentleman – not quite all there, sir.' It seemed that his criminological fame had not penetrated to the quiet recesses of Somerset House. 'But,' said Wimsey to himself, 'I am sadly afraid that Cousin Robert has been given food for thought.'

Under the spur of this alarming idea, Wimsey wasted no time, but took a taxi down to Hatton Garden, to call upon a friend of his. This gentleman, rather curly in the nose and fleshy about the eyelids, nevertheless came under Mr Chesterton's definition of a nice Jew, for his name was neither Montagu nor McDonald, but Nathan Abrahams, and he greeted Lord Peter with a hospitality amounting to enthusiasm.

'So pleased to see you. Sit down and have a drink. You

have come at last to select the diamonds for the future Lady Peter, eh?'

'Not yet,' said Wimsey.

'No? That's too bad. You should make haste and settle down. It is time you became a family man. Years ago we arranged I should have the privilege of decking the bride for the happy day. That is a promise, you know. I think of it when the fine stones pass through my hands. I say "That would be the very thing for my friend Lord Peter." But I hear nothing, and I sell them to stupid Americans who think only of the price and not of the beauty.'

'Time enough to think of the diamonds when I've found the lady.'

Mr Abrahams threw up his hands.

'Oh, yes! And then everything will be done in a hurry! "Quick, Mr Abrahams! I have fallen in love yesterday and I am being married tomorrow." But it may take months – years – to find and match perfect stones. It can't be done between today and tomorrow. Your bride will be married in something ready-made from the jeweller's.'

'If three days are enough to choose a wife,' said Wimsey, laughing, 'one day should surely be enough for a necklace.'

'That is the way with Christians,' replied the diamond-merchant resignedly. 'You are so casual. You do not think of the future. Three days to choose a wife! No wonder the divorce-courts are busy. My son Moses is being married next week. It has been arranged in the family these ten years. Rachel Goldstein, it is. A good girl, and her father is in a very good position. We are all very pleased, I can tell you. Moses is a good son, a very good son, and I am taking him into partnership.'

'I congratulate you,' said Wimsey heartily. 'I hope they will be very happy.'

'Thank you, Lord Peter. They will be happy, I am sure. Rachel is a sweet girl and very fond of children. And she is pretty, too. Prettiness is not everything, but it is an advantage for a young man in these days. It is easier for him to behave well to a pretty wife.'

'True,' said Wimsey. 'I will bear it in mind when my time comes. To the health of the happy pair, and may you soon be an ancestor. Talking of ancestors, I've got an old bird here that you may be able to tell me something about.'

'Ah, yes! Always delighted to help you in any way, Lord Peter.'

'This photograph was taken some thirty years ago, but you may possibly recognise it.'

Mr Abrahams put on a pair of horn-rimmed spectacles, and examined the portrait of Great-Uncle Joseph with serious attention.

'Oh, yes, I know him quite well. What do you want to know about him, eh?' He shot a swift and cautious glance at Wimsey.

'Nothing to his disadvantage. He's dead, anyhow. I thought it just possible he had been buying precious stones lately.'

'It is not exactly business to give information about a customer,' said Mr Abrahams.

'I'll tell you what I want it for,' said Wimsey. He lightly sketched the career of Great-Uncle Joseph, and went on: 'You see, I looked at it this way. When a man gets a distrust of banks, what does he do with his money? He puts it into property of some kind. It may be land, it may be houses – but that means rent, and more money to put into banks. He is more likely to keep it in gold or notes, or to put it into precious stones. Gold and notes are comparatively bulky; stones are small. Circumstances in this case led me to think he might have chosen stones. Unless we can discover what he did with the money, there will be a great loss to his heirs.'

'I see. Well, if it is as you say, there is no harm in telling you. I know you to be an honourable man, and I will break my rule for you. This gentleman, Mr Wallace—'

'Wallace, did he call himself?'

'That was not his name? They are funny, these secretive old gentlemen. But that is nothing unusual. Often, when they buy stones, they are afraid of being robbed, so they give another name. Yes, yes. Well, this Mr Wallace used to come to see me from time to time, and I had instructions to find diamonds for him. He was looking for twelve big stones, all matching perfectly and of superb quality. It took a long time to find them, you know.

'Of course.'

'Yes. I supplied him with seven altogether, over a period of twenty years or so. And other dealers supplied him also. He is well known in this street. I found the last one for him – let me see – in last December, I think. A beautiful stone – beautiful! He paid seven thousand pounds for it.'

'Some stone. If they were all as good as that, the collection must be worth something.'

'Worth anything. It is difficult to tell how much. As you know, the twelve stones, all matched together, would be worth far more than the sum of the twelve separate prices paid for the individual diamonds.'

'Naturally they would. Do you mind telling me how he was accustomed to pay for them?'

'In Bank of England notes – always – cash on the nail. He insisted on discount for cash,' added Mr Abrahams, with a chuckle.

'He was a Scotsman,' replied Wimsey. 'Well, that's clear enough. He had a safe-deposit somewhere, no doubt. And, having collected the stones, he made his will. That's clear as daylight, too.'

'But what has become of the stones?' enquired Mr Abrahams, with professional anxiety.

'I think I know that too,' said Wimsey. 'I'm enormously obliged to you, and so, I fancy, will his heir be.'

'If they should come into the market again—' suggested Mr Abrahams.

'I'll see you get the handling of them,' said Wimsey promptly.

'That is kind of you,' said Mr Abrahams. 'Business is business. Always delighted to oblige you. Beautiful stones – beautiful. If you thought of being the purchaser, I would charge you a special commission, as my friend.'

'Thank you,' said Wimsey, 'but as yet I have no occasion for diamonds, you know.'

'Pity, pity,' said Mr Abrahams. 'Well, very glad to have been of service to you. You are not interested in rubies? No? Because I have something very pretty here.'

He thrust his hand casually into a pocket, and brought out a little pool of crimson fire like a miniature sunset.

'Look nice in a ring, now, wouldn't it?' said Mr Abrahams. 'An engagement ring, eh?'

Wimsey laughed, and made his escape.

He was strongly tempted to return to Scotland and attend personally to the matter of Great-Uncle Joseph, but the thought of an important book sale next day deterred him. There was a manuscript of Catullus which he was passionately anxious to secure, and he never entrusted his interests to dealers. He contented himself with sending a wire to Thomas Macpherson:

'Advise opening up Greatuncle Joseph immediately.'

The girl at the post-office repeated the message aloud and rather doubtfully. 'Quite right,' said Wimsey, and dismissed the affair from his mind.

He had great fun at the sale next day. He found a ring of dealers in possession, happily engaged in conducting a knock out. Having lain low for an hour in a retired position behind a large piece of statuary, he emerged, just as the hammer was falling upon the Catullus for a price representing the tenth part of its value, with an overbid so large, prompt, and sonorous that the ring gasped with a sense of outrage. Skrymes – a dealer who had sworn an eternal enmity to Wimsey, on account of a previous little encounter over a Justinian – pulled himself together and offered a fifty-pound advance. Wimsey promptly doubled his bid. Skrymes overbid him fifty again. Wimsey instantly jumped another hundred, in the tone of a man prepared to go on till Doomsday. Skrymes scowled and was silent. Somebody raised it fifty more; Wimsey made it guineas and the hammer fell. Encouraged by his success, Wimsey, feeling that his hand was in, romped happily into the bidding for the next lot, a *Hypnerotomachia* which he already possessed, and for which he felt no desire whatever. Skrymes, annoyed by his defeat, set his teeth, determining that, if Wimsey was in the bidding mood, he should pay through the nose for his rashness. Wimsey, entering into the spirit of the thing, skied the bidding with enthusiasm. The dealers, knowing his reputation as a collector, and fancying that there must be some special excellence about the book that they had failed to observe, joined in whole-heartedly, and the fun became fast and furious. Eventually they all dropped out again, leaving Skrymes and Wimsey in together. At which point Wimsey, observing a note of hesitation in the dealer's voice, neatly extricated himself and left Mr Skrymes with the baby. After this disaster, the ring became sulky and demoralised and refused to bid at all, and a timid little outsider, suddenly flinging himself into the arena, became the owner of a fine fourteenth-century missal at bargain price. Crimson with excitement and surprise, he paid for his purchase and ran out of the room like a rabbit, hugging the missal as though he expected to have it snatched from him. Wimsey thereupon set himself seriously to acquire a few fine early printed books, and, having accomplished this, retired, covered with laurels and hatred.

After this delightful and satisfying day, he felt vaguely hurt at receiving no ecstatic telegram from Macpherson. He refused to imagine that his deductions had been wrong, and suppposed rather that the rapture of Macpherson was too great to be confined to telegraphic expression and would come next day by post. However, at eleven next morning the telegram arrived. It said:

'Just got your wire what does it mean greatuncle stolen last night burglar escaped please write fully.'

Wimsey committed himself to a brief comment in language usually confined to the soldiery. Robert had undoubtedly got Great-Uncle Joseph, and, even if they could trace the burglary to him, the legacy was by this time gone for ever. He had never felt so furiously helpless. He even cursed the Catullus, which had kept him from going north and dealing with the matter personally.

While he was meditating what to do, a second telegram was brought in, It ran:

> 'Greatuncle's bottle found broken in fleet dropped by burglar in flight contents gone what next.'

Wimsey pondered this.

'Of course,' he said, 'if the thief simply emptied the bottle and put Great-Uncle in his pocket, we're done. Or if he's simply emptied Great-Uncle and put the contents in his pocket, we're done. But "dropped in flight" sounds rather as though Great-Uncle had gone overboard lock, stock, and barrel. Why can't the fool of a Scotsman put a few more details into his wire? It'd only cost him a penny or two. I suppose I'd better go up myself. Meanwhile a little healthy occupation won't hurt him.'

He took a telegraph form from his desk and despatched a further message:

> 'Was greatuncle in bottle when dropped if so drag river if not pursue burglar probably Robert Ferguson spare no pains starting for Scotland tonight hope arrive early tomorrow urgent important put your back into it will explain.'

The night express decanted Lord Peter Wimsey at Dumfries early the following morning, and a hired car deposited him at the Stone Cottage in time for breakfast. The door was opened by Maggie, who greeted him with hearty cordiality:

'Come awa' in, sir. All's ready for ye, and Mr Macpherson will be back in a few minutes, I'm thinkin'. Ye'll be tired with your long journey, and hungry, maybe? Aye. Will ye tak' a bit parritch to your eggs and bacon? There's nae troot the day, though yesterday was a gran' day for the fush. Mr Macpherson has been up and doun, and up and doun the river wi' my Jock, lookin' for ane of his specimens, as he ca's them, that was dropped by the thief that cam' in. I dinna ken what the thing may be – my Jock says it's like a calf's pluck to look at, by what Mr Macpherson tells him.'

'Dear me!' said Wimsey. 'And how did the burglary happen, Maggie?'

'Indeed, sir, it was a vera' remarkable circumstance. Mr Macpherson was awa' all day Monday and Tuesday, up at the big loch by the viaduct, fishin'. There was a big rain Saturday and Sunday, ye may remember, and Mr Macpherson says, "There'll be grand fishin' in the morn, Jock," says he. "We'll go up to the viaduct if it stops rainin' and we'll spend the nicht at the keeper's lodge." So on Monday it stoppit rainin' and was a grand warm, soft day, so aff they went together. There was a telegram come for him Tuesday mornin', and I set it up on the mantelpiece, where he'd see it when he cam' in, but it's been in my mind since that maybe the telegram had something to do wi' the burglary.'

'I wouldn't say but you might be right, Maggie,' replied Wimsey gravely.

'Aye, sir, that wadna' surprise me.' Maggie set down a generous dish of eggs and bacon before the guest and took up her tale again.

'Well, I was sittin' in my kitchen the Tuesday nicht, waitin' for Mr Macpherson and Jock to come hame, and sair I pitied them, the puir souls, for the rain was peltin' down again, and the nicht was sae dark I was afraid they micht ha' tummelt into a bog-pool. Weel, I was listenin' for the sound o' the door-sneck when I heard something movin' an the front room. The door wanna lockit, ye ken, because Mr Macpherson was expectit back. So I up from my chair and I thocht they had mebbe came in and I not heard them. I waited a meenute to set the kettle on the fire, and then I heard a crackin' sound. So I cam' out and I called "Is't you, Mr Macpherson?" And there was nae answer, only anither big crackin' noise, so I ran forrit, and a man cam' quickly oot o' the front room, brushin' past me an' puttin' me aside wi' his hand, so, and oot o' the front door like a flash o' lightnin'. So, wi, that, I let oot a skelloch, an' Jock's voice answered me fra' the gairden gate. "Och!" I says "Jock! here's a burrglar been i' the hoose!" An' I heard him rennin' across the gairden, doun toe the river, tramplin' down a' the young kail and the stra'berry beds, the blackguard!'

Wimsey expressed his sympathy.

'Aye, that was a bad business. An' the next thing, there was Mr Macpherson and Jock helter-skelter after him. If Davie Murray's cattle had brokken in, they couldna ha' done mair deevastation. An' then there was a big splasin' an' crashin', an', after a bit, back comes Mr Macpherson an' he says. "He's jumpit intil the Fleet," he says, "an' he's awa'. What has he taken?" he says. "I dinna ken," says I, "for it all happened sae quickly I couldna see onything." "Come awa' ben," says he, "an' we'll see what's missin'." So we lookit high and low, an' all we could find was the cupboard door in the front room broken open, and naething taken but this bottle wi' the specimen.'

'Aha!' said Wimsey.

'Ah! an' they baith went oct tegither wi' lichts, but

naething could they see of the thief. Sae Mr Macpherson comes back, and "I'm gaun to ma bed," says he, "for I'm that tired I can die nae mair the nicht," says he. "Oh!" I said, "I daurna gae bed; I'm frichtened,' An' Jock said, "Hoots, wumman, dinna fash yersel'. There'll be nae mair burglars the nicht, wi' the fricht we've gied 'em." So we lockit up a' the doors an' windies an' gaed to oor beds, but I couldna sleep a wink.'

'Very natural,' said Wimsey.

'It wasna till the next mornin',' said Maggie, 'that Mr Macpherson opened yon telegram. Eh! but he was in a taking. An' then the telegrams startit. Back an' forrit, back and' forrit atween the house an' the post-office. An' then they fund the bits o' the bottle that the specimen was in, stuck between twa stanes i' the river. And aff goes Mr Macpherson an' Jock wi' their warders on an' a couple o' gaffs, huntin' in a' the pools an' under the stanes to find the specimen. An' they're still at it.'

At this point three heavy thumps sounded on the ceiling.

'Gude save us!' ejaculated Maggie, 'I was forgettin' the puir gentleman.'

'What gentleman?' enquired Wimsey.

'Him that was feshed out o' the Fleet,' replied Maggie. 'Excuse me juist a moment, sir.'

She fled swiftly upstairs. Wimsey poured himself out a third cup of coffee and lit a pipe.

Presently a thought occurred to him. He finished the coffee – not being a man to deprive himself of his pleasures – and walked quietly upstairs in Maggie's wake. Facing him stood a bedroom door, half open – the room which he had occupied during his stay at the cottage. He pushed it open. In the bed lay a red-haired gentleman, whose long, foxy countenance was in no way beautified by a white bandage, tilted rakishly across the left temple. A breakfast-tray stood on a table by the bed. Wimsey stepped forward with extended hand.

'Good morning, Mr Ferguson,' said he. 'This is an unexpected pleasure.'

'Good morning,' said Mr Ferguson snappishly.

'I had no idea, when we last met,' pursued Wimsey, advancing to the bed and sitting down upon it, 'that you were thinking of visiting my friend Macpherson.'

'Get off my leg,' growled the invalid. 'I've broken my knee-cap.'

'What a nuisance! Frightfully painful, isn't it? And they say it takes years to get right – if it ever does get right. Is it what they call a Potts fracture? I don't know who Potts was, but it sounds impressive. How did you do it? Fishing?'

'Yes. A slip in that damned river.'

'Beastly. Sort of thing that might happen to anybody. A keen fisher, Mr Ferguson?'

'So-so.'

'So am I, when I get the opportunity. What kind of fly do you fancy for this part of the country. I rather like a Greenaway's Gadget myself. Ever tried it?'

'No,' said Mr Ferguson briefly.

'Some people find a Pink Sisket better, so they tell me. Do you use one? Have you got your fly-book here?'

'Yes – no,' said Mr Ferguson. 'I dropped it.'

'Pity. But do give me your opinion of the Pink Sisket.'

'Not so bad,' said Mr Ferguson. 'I've sometimes caught trout with it.'

'You surprise me,' said Wimsey, not unnaturally, since

he had invented the Pink Sisket on the spur of the moment, and had hardly expected his improvisation to pass muster. 'Well, I suppose this unlucky accident has put a stop to your sport for the season. Damned bad luck. Otherwise, you might have helped us to have a go at the Patriarch.'

'What's that? A trout?'

'Yes – a frightfully wily old fish. Lurks about in the Fleet. You never know where to find him. Any moment he may turn up in some pool or other. I'm going out with Mac to try for him today. He's a jewel of a fellow. We've nicknamed him Great-Uncle Joseph. Hi! don't joggle about like that – you'll hurt that knee of yours. Is there anything I can get for you?'

He grinned amiably, and turned to answer a shout from the stairs.

'Hullo! Wimsey! is that you?'

'It is. How's sport?'

Macpherson came up the stairs four steps at a time, and met Wimsey on the landing as he emerged from the bedroom.

'I say, d'you know who that is? It's Robert.'

'I know. I saw him in town. Never mind him. Have you found Great-Uncle?'

'No, we haven't, What's all this mystery about? And what's Robert doing here? What did you mean by saying he was the burglar? And why is Great-Uncle Joseph so important?'

'One thing at a time. Let's find the old boy first. What have you been doing?'

'Well, when I got your extraordinary messages I thought, of course, you were off your rocker.' (Wimsey groaned with impatience.) 'But then I considered what a funny thing it was that somebody should have thought Great-Uncle worth stealing, and thought there might be some sense in what you said, after all.' ('Dashed good of you,' said Wimsey.) 'So I went out and poked about a bit, you know. Not that I think there's the faintest chance of finding anything, with the river coming down like this. Well, I hadn't got very far – by the way, I took Jock with me. I'm sure he thinks I'm mad, too. Not that he says anything; these people here never commit themselves—'

'Confound Jock! Get on with it.'

'Oh – well, before we'd got very far, we saw a fellow wading about in the river with a rod and creel. I didn't pay much attention, because, you see, I was wondering what you – Yes. Well! Jock noticed him and said to me, "Yon's a queer kind of fisherman, I'm thinkin'." So I had a look, and there he was, staggering about among the stones with his fly floating away down the stream in front of him; and he was peering into all the pools he came to, and poking about with a gaff. So I hailed him, and he turned round, and then he put the gaff away in a bit of a hurry and started to reel in his line. He made an awful mess of it,' added Macpherson appreciatively.

'I can believe it,' said Wimsey. 'A man who admits to catching trout with a Pink Sisket would make a mess of anything.'

'A pink what?'

'Never mind. I only meant that Robert was no fisher. Get on.'

'Well, he got the line hooked round something, and he was pulling and hauling, you know, and splashing about, and then it came out all of a sudden, and he waved it all over the place and got my hat. That made me pretty wild, and I made after him, and he looked round again, and I yelled out, "Good God, it's Robert!" And he dropped his rod and took to his heels. And of course he slipped on the stones and came down an awful crack. We rushed forward and scooped him up and brought him home. He's got a nasty bang on the head and a fractured patella. Very interesting. I should have liked to have a shot at setting it myself, but it wouldn't do, you know, so I sent for Strachan. He's a good man.'

'You've had extraordinary luck about this business so far,' said Wimsey. 'Now the only thing left is to find Great-Uncle. How far down have you got?'

'Not very far. You see, what with getting Robert home and setting his knee and so on, we couldn't do much yesterday.'

'Damn Robert! Great-Uncle may be away out to sea by this time. Let's get down to it.'

He took up a gaff from the umbrella-stand ('Robert's,' interjected Macpherson), and led the way out. The little river was foaming down in a brown spate, rattling stones and small boulders along in its passage. Every hole, every eddy might be a lurking-place for Great-Uncle Joseph. Wimsey peered irresolutely here and there – then turned suddenly to Jock.

'Where's the nearest spit of land where things usually get washed up?' he demanded.

'Eh, well! there's the Battery Pool, about a mile doon the river. Ye'll whiles find things washed up there. Aye, Imph'm. There's a pool and a bit sand, where the river mak's a bend. Ye'll mebbe find it there, I'm thinkin'. Mebbe no. I couldna say.'

'Let's have a look, anyway.'

Macpherson, to whom the prospect of searching the stream in detail appeared rather a dreary one, brightened a little at this.

'That's a good idea. If we take the car down to just above Gatehouse, we've only got two fields to cross.'

The car was still at the door; the hired driver was enjoying the hospitality of the cottage. They pried him loose from Maggie's scones and slipped down the road to Gatehouse.

'Those gulls seem rather active about something,' said Wimsey, as they crossed the second field. The white wings swooped backwards and forwards in narrowing circles over the yellow shoal. Raucous cries rose on the wind. Wimsey pointed silently with his hand. A long, unseemly object, like a drab purse, lay on the shore. The gulls, indignant, rose higher, squawking at the intruders. Wimsey ran forward, stooped, rose again with the long bag dangling from his fingers.

'Great-Uncle Joseph, I presume,' he said, and raised his hat with old-fashioned courtesy.

'The gulls have had a wee peck at it here and there,' said Jock. 'It'll be tough for them. Aye. They havena done so vera much with it.'

'Aren't you going to open it?' said Macpherson impatiently.

'Not here,' said Wimsey. 'We might lose something.' He dropped it into Jock's creel. 'We'll take it home first and show it to Robert.?'

Robert greeted them with ill-disguised irritation.

'We've been fishing,' said Wimsey cheerfully. 'Look at our bonny wee fush.' He weighed the catch in his hand. 'What's inside this wee fush, Mr Ferguson?'

'I haven't the faintest idea,' said Robert.

'Then why did you go fishing for it?' asked Wimsey pleasantly. 'Have you got a surgical knife there, Mac?'

'Yes – here. Hurry up.'

'I'll leave it to you. Be careful I should begin with the stomach.'

Macpherson laid Great-Uncle Joseph on the table, and slit him with a practised hand.

'Gude be gracious to us!' cried Maggie, peering over his shoulder. 'What'll that be?'

Wimsey inserted a delicate finger and thumb into the cavities of Uncle Joseph. 'One – two – three –' The stones glittered like fire as he laid them on the table. 'Seven – eight – nine. That seems to be all. Try a little further down, Mac.'

Speechless with astonishment, Mr Macpherson dissected his legacy.

'Ten – eleven,' said Wimsey. 'I'm afraid the sea-gulls have got number twelve. I'm sorry, Mac.'

'But how did they get there?' demanded Robert foolishly.

'Simple as shelling peas. Great-Uncle Joseph makes his will, swallows his diamonds—'

'He must ha' been a grand man for a pill,' said Maggie, with respect.

'– and jumps out of the window. It was as clear as crystal to anybody who read the will. He told you, Mac, that the stomach was given you to study.'

Robert Ferguson gave a deep groan.

'I knew there was something in it,' he said. 'That's why I went to look up the will. And when I saw *you* there, I knew I was right. (Curse this leg of mine!) But I never imagined for a moment—'

His eyes appraised the diamonds greedily.

'And what will the value of these same stones be?' enquired Jock.

'About seven thousand pounds apiece, taken separately. More than that, taken together.'

'The old man was mad,' said Robert angrily. 'I shall dispute the will.'

'I think not,' said Wimsey. 'There's such an offence as entering and stealing, you know.'

'My God!' said Macpherson, handling the diamonds like a man in a dream. 'My God!'

'Seven thousan' pund,' said Jock. 'Did I unnerstan' ye richtly to say that one o' they gulls is gaun aboot noo wi' seven thousan' pund's worth o' diamonds in his wane? Ech! it's just awfu' to think of. Guid day to you, sirs. I'll be gaun round to Jimmy McTaggart to ask will he lend me the loan o' a gun.'

'And what would *you* say, sir,' said the stout man, 'to this here business of the bloke what's been found down on the beach at East Felpham?'

The rush of travellers after the Bank Holiday had caused an overflow of third-class passengers into the firsts, and the stout man was anxious to seem at ease in his surroundings. The youngish gentleman whom he addressed had obviously paid full fare for a seclusion which he was fated to forgo. He took the matter amiably enough, however, and replied in a courteous tone:

'I'm afraid I haven't read more than the headlines. Murdered, I suppose, wasn't he?'

'It's murder, right enough,' said the stout man, with relish. 'Cut about he was, something shocking.'

'More like as if a wild beast had done it,' chimed in the thin, elderly man opposite. 'No face at all he hadn't got, by what my paper says. It'll be one of these maniacs, I shouldn't be surprised, what goes about killing children.'

'I wish you wouldn't talk about such things,' said his wife, with a shudder. 'I lays awake at nights thinking what might 'appen to Lizzie's girls, till my head feels regular in a fever, and I has such a sinking in my inside I has to get up and eat biscuits. They didn't ought to put such dreadful things in the papers.'

'It's better they should, ma'am,' said the stout man, 'then we're warned, so to speak, and can take our measures accordingly. Now, from what I can make out, this unfortunate gentleman had gone bathing all by himself in a lonely spot. Now, quite apart from cramps, as is a thing that might 'appen to the best of us, that's a very foolish thing to do.'

'Just what I'm always telling my husband,' said the young wife. The young husband frowned and fidgeted. 'Well, dear, it really isn't safe, and you with your heart not strong—'Her hand sought his under the newspaper. He drew away, self-consciously, saying, 'That'll do, Kitty.'

'The way I look at it is this,' pursued the stout man. 'Here we've been and had a war, what has left 'undreds o'men in what you might call a state of unstable ekilibrium. They've seen all their friends blown up or shot to pieces. They've been through five years of 'orrors and bloodshed, and it's given 'em what you might call a twist in the mind towards 'orrors. They may seem to forget it and go along as peaceable as anybody to all outward appearance, but it's all artificial, if you get my meaning. Then, one day something 'appens to upset them – they 'as words with the wife, or the weather's extra hot, as it is today – and something goes pop inside their brains and makes raving monsters of them. It's all in the books. I do a good bit of reading myself of an evening, being a bachelor without encumbrances.'

'That's all very true,' said a prim little man, looking up from his magazine, 'very true indeed – too true. But do you think it applies in the present case? I've studied the literature of crime a good deal – I may say I make it my hobby – and it's my opinion there's more in this than meets the eye. If you will compare this murder with some of the most mysterious crimes of late years – crimes which, mind you, have never been solved, and, in my opinion, never will be – what do you find?' He paused and looked round. 'You will find many features in common with this case. But especially you will find that the face – and the face only, mark you – has been disfigured, as though to prevent recognition. As though to blot out the victim's personality from the world. And you will find that, in spite of the most thorough investigation, the criminal is never discovered. Now what does all that point to? To organisation. Organisation. To an immensely powerful influence at work behind the scenes. In this very magazine that I'm reading now' – he tapped the page impressively – 'there's an account – not a faked-up story, but an account extracted from the annals of the police – of the organisation of one of these secret societies, which mark down men against whom they bear a grudge, and destroy them. And, when they do this, they disfigure their faces with the mark of the Secret Society, and they cover up the track of the assassin so completely – having money and resources at their disposal – that nobody is ever able to get at them.'

'I've read of such things, of course,' admitted the stout man, 'but I thought as they mostly belonged to the medeevial days. They had a thing like that in Italy once. What did they call it now? A Gomorrah, was it? Are there any Gomorrahs nowadays?'

'You spoke a true word, sir, when you said Italy,' replied the prim man. 'The Italian mind is made for intrigue. There's the Fascisti. That's come to the surface now, of course, but it started by being a secret society. And, if you were to look below the surface, you would be amazed at the way in which that country is honey-combed with hidden organisations of all sorts. Don't you agree with me, sir?' he added, addressing the first-class passenger.

'Ah!' said the stout man, 'no doubt this gentleman has been in Italy and knows all about it. Should you say this murder was the work of a Gomorrah, sir?'

'I hope not, I'm sure,' said the first-class passenger. 'I mean, it rather destroys the interest, don't you think? I like a nice, quiet, domestic, murder myself, with the millionaire found dead in the library. The minute I open a detective story and find a Camorra in it, my interest seems to dry up and turn to dust and ashes – a sort of Sodom and Camorra, as you might say.'

'I agree with you there,' said the young husband, 'from what you might call the artistic standpoint. But in this particular case I think there may be something to be said for this gentleman's point of view.'

'Well,' admitted the first-class passenger, 'not having read the details—'

'The details are clear enough,' said the prim man. 'This poor creature was found lying dead on the beach at East Felpham early this morning, with his face cut about in the most dreadful manner. He had nothing on him but his bathing-dress—'

'Stop a minute. Who was he, to begin with?'

'They haven't identified him yet. His clothes had been taken—'

'That looks more like robbery, doesn't it?' suggested Kitty.

'If it was just robbery,' retorted the prim man, 'why should his face have been cut up in that way? No – the clothes were taken away, as I said, to prevent identification. That's what these societies always try to do.'

'Was he stabbed?' demanded the first-class passenger.

'No,' said the stout man. 'He wasn't. He was strangled.'

'Not a characteristically Italian method of killing,' observed the first-class passenger.

'No more it is,' said the stout man. The prim man seemed a little disconcerted.

'And if he went down there to bathe,' said the thin, elderly man, 'how did he get there? Surely somebody must have missed him before now, if he was staying at Felpham. It's a busy spot for visitors in the holiday season.'

'No,' said the stout man, 'not East Felpham. You're thinking of West Felpham, where the yacht-club is. East Felpham is one of the loneliest spots on the coast. There's no house near except a little pub all by itself at the end of a long road, and after that you have to go through three fields to get to the sea. There's no real road, only a cart-track, but you can take a car through. I've been there.'

'He came in a car,' said the prim man. 'They found the track of the wheels. But it had been driven away again.'

'It looks as though the two men had come there together,' suggested Kitty.

'I think they did,' said the prim man. 'The victim was probably gagged and bound and taken along in the car to the place, and then he was taken out and strangled and—'

'But why should they have troubled to put on his bathing-dress?' said the first-class passenger.

'Because,' said the prim man, 'as I said, they didn't want to leave any clothes to reveal his identity.'

'Quite; but why not leave him naked? A bathing-dress seems to indicate an almost excessive regard for decorum, under the circumstances.'

'Yes, yes,' said the stout man impatiently, 'but you 'aven't read the paper carefully. The two men couldn't have come there in company, and for why? There was only one set of footprints found, and they belonged to the murdered man.'

'Only one set of footprints, eh?' said the first-class passenger quickly. 'This looks interesting. Are you sure?'

'It says so in the paper. A single set of footprints, it says, made by bare feet, which by a careful comparison 'ave been shown to be those of the murdered man, lead from the position occupied by the car to the place where the body was found. What do you make of that?'

'Why,' said the first-class passenger, 'that tells one quite a lot, don't you know. It gives one a sort of a bird's eye view of the place, and it tells one the time of the murder, besides castin' quite a good bit of light on the character and circumstances of the murderer – or murderers.'

'How do you make that out, sir?' demanded the elderly man.

'Well, to begin with – though I've never been near the place, there is obviously a sandy beach from which one can bathe.'

'That's right,' said the stout man.

'There is also, I fancy, in the neighbourhood, a spur of rock running out into the sea, quite possibly with a handy diving-pool. It must run out pretty far; at any rate, one can bathe there before it is high water on the beach.'

'I don't know how you know that, sir, but it's a fact. There's rocks and a bathing-pool, exactly as you describe, about a hundred yards farther along. Many's the time I've had a dip off the end of them.'

'And the rocks run right back inland, where they are covered with short grass.'

'That's right.'

'The murder took place shortly before high tide, I fancy, and the body lay just about at high-tide mark.'

'Why so?'

'Well, you say there were footsteps leading right up to the body. That means that the water hadn't been up beyond the body. But there no other marks. Therefore the murderer's footprints must have been washed away by the tide. The only explanation is that the two men were standing together just below the tide-mark. The murderer came up out of the sea. He attacked the other man – maybe he forced him back a little on his own tracks – and there he killed him. Then the water came up and washed out any marks the murderer may have left. One can imagine him squatting there, wondering if the sea was going to come up high enough?'

'Ow!' said Kitty, 'you make me creep all over.'

'Now, as to these marks on the face,' pursued the first-class passenger. 'The murderer, according to the idea I get of the thing, was already in the sea when the victim came along. You see the idea?'

'I get you,' said the stout man. 'You think as he went in off them rocks what we was speaking of, and came up through the water, and that's why there weren't no footprints.'

'Exactly. And since the water is deep round those rocks, as you say, he was presumably in a bathing-dress too.'

'Looks like it.'

'Quite so. Well, now – what was the face-slashing done with? People don't usually take knives out with them when they go for a morning dip.'

'That's a puzzle,' said the stout man.

'Not altogether. Let's say, either the murderer had a knife with him or he had not. If he had—'

'If he had,' put in the prim man eagerly, 'he must have laid wait for the deceased on purpose. And, to my mind, that bears out my idea of a deep and cunning plot.'

'Yes. But, if he was waiting there with the knife, why didn't he stab the man and have done with it? Why strangle him, when he had a perfectly good weapon there to hand? No – I think he came unprovided, and, when he saw his enemy there, he made for him with his hands in the characteristic British way.'

'But the slashing?'

'Well, I think that when he had got his man down, dead before him, he was filled with a pretty grim sort of fury and wanted to do more damage. He caught up something that was lying near him on the sand – it might be a bit of old iron, or even one of those sharp shells you sometimes see about, or a bit of glass – and he went for him with that in a desperate rage of jealousy or hatred.'

'Dreadful, dreadful!' said the elderly woman.

'Of course, one can only guess in the dark, not having seen the wounds. It's quite possible that the murderer dropped his knife in the struggle and had to do the actual killing with his hands, picking the knife up afterwards. If the wounds were clean knife-wounds, that is probably what happened, and the murder was premeditated. But if they were rough, jagged gashes, made by an impromptu weapon, then I should say it was a chance encounter, and that the murderer was either mad or—'

'Or?'

'Or had suddenly come upon somebody whom he hated very much.'

What do you think happened afterwards?'

'That's pretty clear. The murderer, having waited, as I said, to see that all his footprints were cleaned up by the tide, waded or swam back to the rock where he had left his clothes, taking the weapon with him. The sea would wash away any blood from his bathing-dress or body. He then climbed out upon the rocks, walked with bare feet, so as to leave no tracks on any seaweed or anything, to the short grass of the shore, dressed, went along to the murdered man's car, and drove it away.'

'Why did be do that?'

'Yes, why? He may have wanted to get somewhere in a hurry. Or he may have been afraid that if the murdered man were identified too soon it would cast suspicion on him. Or it may have been a mixture of motives. The point is, where did he come from? How did he come to be bathing at that remote spot, early in the morning? He didn't get there by car, or there would be a second car to be accounted for. He may have been camping near the spot; but it would have taken him a long time to strike camp and pack all his belongings into the car, and he might have been seen. I am rather inclined to think he had bicycled there, and that he hoisted the bicycle into the back of the car and took it away with him.'

'But, in that case, why take the car?'

'Because he had been down at East Felpham longer than he expected, and he was afraid of being late. Either he had to get back to breakfast at some house, where his absence would be noticed, or else he lived some distance off, and had only just time enough for the journey home. I think, though, he had to be back to breakfast.'

'Why?'

'Because, if it was merely a question of making up time

on the road, all he had to do was to put himself and his bicycle on the train for part of the way. No; I fancy he was staying in a smallish hotel somewhere. Not a large hotel, because there nobody would notice whether he came in or not. And not, I think, in lodgings, or somebody would have mentioned before now that they had a lodger who went bathing at East Felpham. Either he lives in the neighbourhood, in which case he should be easy to trace, or was staying with friends who have an interest in concealing his movements. Or else – which I think is more likely – he was in a smallish hotel, where he would be missed from the breakfast-table, but where his favourite bathing-place was not a matter of common knowledge.'

'That seems feasible,' said the stout man.

'In any case,' went on the fast-class passenger,' he must have been staying within easy bicycling distance of East Felpham, so it shouldn't be too hard to trace him. And then there is the car.'

'Yes. Where is the car, on your theory?' demanded the prim man, who obviously still had hankerings after the Camorra theory.

'In a garage, waiting to be called for,' said the first-class passenger promptly.

'Where?' persisted the prim man.

'Oh! somewhere on the other side of wherever it was the murderer was staying. If you have a particular reason for not wanting it to be known that you were in a certain place at a specified time, it's not a bad idea to come back from the opposite direction. I rather think I should look for the car at West Felpham, and the hotel in the nearest town on the main road beyond where the two roads to East and West Felpham join. When you've found the car, you've found the name of the victim, naturally. As for the murderer, you will have to look for an active man, a good swimmer and ardent bicyclist – probably not very well off, since he cannot afford to have a car – who has been taking a holiday in the neighbourhood of the Felphams, and who has a good reason for disliking the victim, whoever he may be.'

'Well, I never,' said the elderly woman admiringly. 'How beautiful you do put it all together. Like Sherlock Holmes, I do declare.'

'It's a very pretty theory,' said the prim man, 'but, all the same, you'll find it's a secret society. Mark my words. Dear me! We're just running in. Only twenty minutes late. I call that very good for holiday-time. Will you excuse me? My bag is just under your feet.'

There was an eighth passenger in the compartment, who had remained throughout the conversation apparently buried in a newspaper. As the passengers decanted themselves upon the platform, this man touched the first-class passenger upon the arm.

'Excuse me, sir,' he said. 'That was a very interesting suggestion of yours. My name is Winterbottom, and I am investigating this case. Do you mind giving me your name? I might wish to communicate with you later on.'

'Certainly,' said the first-class passenger. 'Always delighted to have a finger in any pie, don't you know. Here is my card. Look me up any time you like.'

Detective-Inspector Winterbottom took the card and read the name:

LORD PETER WIMSEY,
110A Piccadilly.

*   *   *

The *Evening Views* vendor outside Piccadilly Tube Station arranged his placard with some care. It looked very well, he thought.

MAN WITH
NO FACE
IDENTIFIED

It was, in his opinion, considerably more striking than that displayed by a rival organ, which announced, unimaginatively:

BEACH MURDER
VICTIM
IDENTIFIED

A youngish gentleman in a grey suit who emerged at that moment from the Criterion Bar appeared to think so too, for he exchanged a copper for the *Evening Views*, and at once plunged into its perusal with such concentrated interest that he bumped into a hurried man outside the station and had to apologise.

The *Evening Views*, grateful to murderer and victim alike for providing so useful a sensation in the dead days after the Bank Holiday, had torn Messrs Negretti & Zambra's rocketing thermometrical statistics from the 'banner' position which they had occupied in the lunch edition, and substituted:

FACELESS VICTIM OF BEACH OUTRAGE IDENTIFIED

———

MURDER OF PROMINENT
PUBLICITY ARTIST

———

POLICE CLUES

'The body of a middle-aged man who was discovered, attired only in a bathing-costume and with his face horribly disfigured by some jagged instrument, on the beach at East Felpham last Monday morning, has been identified as that of Mr Coraggio Plant, studio manager of Messrs Crichton Ltd, the well-known publicity experts of Holborn.

'Mr Plant, who was forty-five years of age and a bachelor, was spending his annual holiday in making a motoring tour along the West Coast. He had no companion with him and had left no address for the forwarding of letters, so that, without the smart work of Detective-Inspector Winterbottom of the Westshire police, his disappearance might not in the ordinary way have been noticed until he became due to return to his place of business in three weeks' time. The murderer had no doubt counted on this, and had removed the motor-car, containing the belongings of his victim, in the hope of covering up all traces of this dastardly outrage so as to gain time for escape.

'A rigorous search for the missing car, however, eventuated in its discovery in a garage at West Felpham, where it had been left for decarbonisation and repairs to the magneto. Mr Spiller, the garage proprietor, himself saw the man who left the car, and has furnished a description of him to the police. He is said to be a small, dark man of foreign appearance. The police hold a clue to his identity, and an arrest is confidently expected in the near future.'

'Mr Plant was for fifteen years in the employment of Messrs Crichton, being appointed Studio Manager the latter years of the war. He was greatly liked by all his colleagues, and his skill in the lay-out and designing of advertisements did much to justify the truth of Messrs Crichton's well-known slogan: "Crichton's for Admirable Advertising."

'The funeral of the victim will take place tomorrow at Golders Green Cemetery.

'(Pictures on Back Page.)'

Lord Peter Wimsey turned to the back page. The portrait of the victim did not detain him long; it was one of the characterless studio photographs which establish nothing except that the sitter has a tolerable set of features. He noted that Mr Plant had been thin rather than fat, commercial in appearance rather than artistic, and that the photographer had chosen to show him serious rather than smiling. A picture of East Felpham beach, marked with a cross where the body was found, seemed to arouse in him rather more than a casual interest. He studied it intently for some time, making little surprised noises. There was no obvious reason why he should have been surprised, for the photograph bore out in every detail the deductions he had made in the train. There was the curved line of sand, with a long spur of rock stretching out behind it into deep water, and running back it mingled with the short, dry turf. Nevertheless, he looked at it for several minutes with close attention, before folding the newspaper and hailing a taxi; and when he was in the taxi he unfolded the paper and looked at it again.

'Your lordship having been kind enough,' said Inspector Winterbottom, emptying his glass rather too rapidly for true connoisseurship, 'to suggest I should look you up in Town, I made bold to give you a call in passing. Thank you, I won't say no. Well, as you've seen in the papers by now, we found that car all right.'

Wimsey expressed his gratification at this result.

'And very much obliged I was to your lordship for the hint,' went on the Inspector generously, 'not but what I wouldn't say but what I should have come to the same conclusion myself, given a little more time. And, what's more, we're on the track of the man.'

'I see he's supposed to be foreign-looking. Don't say he's going to turn out to be a Camorrist after all!'

'No, my lord.' The Inspector winked. 'Our friend in the corner had got his magazine stories a bit on the brain, if you ask me. And *you* were a bit out too, my lord, with your bicyclist idea.'

'Was I? That's a blow.'

'Well, my lord, these here theories *sound* all right, but half the time they're too fine-spun altogether. Go for the facts – that's our motto in the Force – facts and motive, and you won't go far wrong.'

'Oh! you've discovered the motive, then?'

The Inspector winked again.

'There's not many motives for doing a man in,' said he. 'Women or money – or women *and* money – it mostly comes down to one or the other. This fellow Plant went in for being a bit of a lad, you see. He kept a little cottage down Felpham way, with a nice little skirt to furnish it and keep the love-nest warm for him – see?'

'Oh! I thought he was doing a motor-tour.'

'Motor-tour your foot!' said the Inspector, with more energy than politeness. 'That's what the old [epithet] told 'em at the office. Handy reason, don't you see, for leaving no address behind him. No, no. There was a lady in it all right. I've seen her. A very taking piece too, if you like 'em skinny, which I don't. I prefer 'em better upholstered myself.'

'That chair is really more comfortable with a cushion,' put in Wimsey, with anxious solicitude. 'Allow me.'

'Thanks, my lord, thanks. I'm doing very well. It seems that this woman – by the way, we're speaking in confidence, you understand. I don't want this to go further till I've got my man under lock and key.'

Wimsey promised discretion.

'That's all right, my lord, that's all right. I know I can rely on you. Well, the long and the short is, this young woman had another fancy man – a sort of an Italiano, whom she'd chucked for Plant, and this same dago got wind of the business and came down to East Felpham on the Sunday night, looking for her. He's one of these professional partners in a Palais de Danse up Cricklewood way, and that's where the girl comes from, too. I suppose she thought Plant was a cut above him. Anyway, down he comes, and busts in upon them Sunday night when they were having a bit of supper – and that's when the row started.'

Didn't you know about this cottage and the goings-on there?'

'Well, you know, there's such a lot of these weekenders nowadays. We can't keep tabs on all of them, so long as they behave themselves and don't make a disturbance. The woman's been there – so they tell me – since last June, with him coming down Saturday to Monday; but it's a lonely spot, and the constable didn't take much notice. He came in the evenings, so there wasn't anybody much to recognise him, except the old girl who did the slops and things, and she's half-blind.

And of course, when they found him, he hadn't any face to recognise. It'd be thought he'd just gone off in the ordinary way. I dare say the dago fellow reckoned on that. As I was saying, there was a big row, and the dago was kicked out. He must have lain in wait for Plant down by the bathing-place, and done him in.'

'By strangling?'

'Well, he *was* strangled.'

'Was his face cut up with a knife, then?'

'Well, no – I don't think it was a knife. More like a broken bottle, I should say, if you ask me. There's plenty of them come in with the tide.'

'But then we're brought back to our old problem. If this Italian was lying in wait to murder Plant, why didn't he take a weapon with him, instead of trusting to the chance of his hands and a broken bottle?'

The Inspector shook his head.

'Flighty,' he said. 'All these foreigners are flighty. No headpiece. But there's our man and there's our motive, plain as a pikestaff. You don't want more.'

'And where is the Italian fellow now?'

'Run away. That's pretty good proof of guilt in itself. But we'll have him before long. That's what I've come to Town about. He can't get out of the country. I've had an all-stations call sent out to stop him. The dance-hall people were able to supply us with a photo and a good description. I'm expecting a report in now any minute. In fact, I'd best be getting along. Thank you very much for your hospitality, my lord.'

'The pleasure is mine,' said Wimsey, ringing the bell to have the visitor shown out. 'I have enjoyed our little chat immensely.'

*   *   *

Sauntering into the Falstaff at twelve o'clock the following morning, Wimsey, as he had expected, found Salcombe Hardy supporting his rather plump contours against the bar. The reporter greeted his arrival with a heartiness amounting almost to enthusiasm, and called for two large Scotches immediately. When the usual skirmish as to who should pay had been honourably settled by the prompt disposal of the drinks and the standing of two more, Wimsey pulled from his pocket the copy of last night's *Evening Views*.

'I wish you'd ask the people over at your place to get hold of a decent print of this for me,' he said, indicating the picture of East Felpham beach.

Salcombe Hardy gazed limpid enquiry at him from eyes like drowned violets.

'See here, you old sleuth,' he said, 'does this mean you've got a theory about the thing? I'm wanting a story badly. Must keep up the excitement, you know. The police don't seem to have got any further since last night.'

'No; I'm interested in this from another point of view altogether. I did have a theory – of sorts – but it seems it's all wrong. Bally old Homer nodding, I suppose. But I'd like a copy of the thing.'

'I'll get Warren to get you one when we come back. I'm just taking him down with me to Crichton's. We're going to have a look at a picture. I say, I wish you'd come too. Tell me what to say about the damned thing.'

'Good God! I don't know anything about commercial art.'

' 'Tisn't commercial art. It's supposed to be a portrait of this blighter Plant. Done by one of the chaps an his studio or something. Kid who told me about it says it's clever. I don't know. Don't suppose she knows, either. You go in for being artistic, don't you?'

'I wish you wouldn't use such filthy expressions, Sally. Artistic! Who is this girl?'

'Typist in the copy department.'

'Oh, Sally!'

'Nothing of that sort. I've never met her. Name's Gladys Twitterton. I'm sure that's beastly enough to put anybody off. Rang us up last night and told us there was a bloke there who'd done old Plant in oils and was it any use to us? Drummer thought it might be worth looking into. Make a change from that everlasting syndicated photograph.'

'I see. If you haven't got an exclusive story, an exclusive picture's better than nothing. The girl seems to have her wits about her. Friend of the artist's?'

'No – said he'd probably be frightfully annoyed at her having told me. But I can wangle that. Only I wish you'd come and have a look at it. Tell me whether I ought to say it's an unknown masterpiece or merely a striking likeness.'

'How the devil can I say if it's a striking likeness of a bloke I've never seen?'

'I'll say it's that, in any case. But I want to know if it's well painted.'

'Curse it, Sally, what's it matter whether it is or not? I've got other things to do. Who's the artist, by the way? Anybody one's ever heard of?'

'Dunno. I've got the name here somewhere.' Sally rooted in his hip-pocket and produced a mass of dirty correspondence, its angles blunted by constant attrition. 'Some comic name like Buggle or Snagtooth – wait a bit – here it is. Crowder. Thomas Crowder. I knew it was something out of the way.'

'Singularly like Buggle or Snagtooth. All right, Sally. I'll make a martyr of myself. Lead me to it.'

'We'll have another quick one. Here's Warren. This is Lord Peter Wimsey. This is on me.'

'On me,' corrected the photographer, a jaded young man with a disillusioned manner. 'Three large White Labels, please. Well, here's all the best. Are you fit, Sally? Because we'd better make tracks. I've got to be up at Golders Green by two for the funeral.'

Mr Crowder of Crichton's appeared to have had the news broken to him already by Miss Twitterton, for he received the embassy in a spirit of gloomy acquiescence.

'The directors won't like it,' he said, 'but they've had to put up with such a lot that I suppose one irregularity more or less won't give 'em apoplexy.' He had a small, anxious, yellow face like a monkey. Wimsey put him down as being in his late thirties. He noticed his fine, capable hands, one of which was disfigured by a strip of sticking-plaster.

'Damaged yourself?' said Wimsey pleasantly, as they made their way upstairs to the studio. 'Mustn't make a practice of that, what? An artist's hands are his livelihood – except, of course, for Armless Wonders and people of that kind! Awkward job, painting with your toes.'

'Oh, it's nothing much,' said Crowder, 'but it's best to keep the paint out of surface scratches. There's such a thing as lead-poisoning. Well, here's this dud portrait, such as it is. I don't mind telling you that it didn't please the sitter. In fact, he wouldn't have it at any price.'

'Not flattering enough?' asked Hardy.

'As you say.' The painter pulled out a four by three canvas from its hiding-place behind a stack of poster cartoons, and heaved it up on to the easel.

'Oh!' said Hardy, a little surprised. Not that there was

any reason for surprise as far as the painting itself was concerned. It was a straightforward handling enough; the skill and originality of the brushwork being of the kind that interests the painter without shocking the ignorant.

'Oh!' said Hardy. 'Was he really like that?'

He moved closer to the canvas, peering into it as he might have peered into the face of the living man, hoping to get something out of him. Under this microscopic scrutiny, the portrait, as is the way of portraits, dis-limned, and became no more than a conglomeration of painted spots and streaks. He made the discovery that, to the painter's eye, the human face is full of green and purple patches.

He moved back again, and altered the form of his question:

'So that's what he was like, was he?'

He pulled out the photograph of Plant from his pocket, and compared it with the portrait. The portrait seemed to sneer at his surprise.

'Of course, they touch these things up at these fashion-able photographers,' he said. 'Anyway, that's not my business. This thing will make a jolly good eye-catcher, don't you think so, Wimsey? Wonder if they'd give us a two-column spread on the front page? Well, Warren, you'd better get down to it.'

The photographer, bleakly unmoved by artistic or journalistic considerations, took silent charge of the canvas, mentally resolving it into a question of pan-chromatic plates and coloured screens. Crowder gave him a hand in shifting the easel into a better light. Two or three people from other departments, passing through the studio on their lawful occasions, stopped, and lingered in the neighbourhood of the disturbance, as though it were a street accident. A melancholy, grey-haired man, temporary head of the studio, vice Coreggio Plant, deceased, took Crowder aside, with a muttered apology, to give him some instructions about adapting a whole quad to an eleven-inch treble. Hardy turned to Lord Peter.

'It's damned ugly,' he said. 'Is it good?'

'Brilliant,' said Wimsey. 'You can go all out. Say what you like about it.'

'Oh, splendid! Could we discover one of our neglected British masters?'

'Yes; why not? You'll probably make the man the fashion and ruin him as an artist, but that's his pigeon.'

'But, I say – do you think it's a good likeness? He's made him look a most sinister sort of fellow. After all, Plant thought it was so bad be wouldn't have it.'

'The more fool he. Ever heard of the portrait of a certain statesman that was so revealing of his inner emptiness that he hurriedly bought it up and hid it to prevent people like you from getting hold of it?'

Crowder came back.

'I say,' said Wimsey, 'whom does that picture belong to? You? Or the heirs of the deceased, or what?'

'I suppose it's back on my hands,' said the painter. 'Plant – well, he more or less commissioned it, you see, but—'

'How more or less?'

'Well, he kept on hinting, don't you know, that he would like me to do him, and, as he was my boss, I thought I'd better. No price actually mentioned. When he saw it, he didn't like it, and told me to alter it.'

'But you didn't.'

'Oh – well, I put it aside and said I'd see what I could do with it. I thought he'd perhaps forget about it.'

'I see. Then presumably it's yours to dispose of.'

'I should think so. Why?'

'You have a very individual technique, haven't you?' pursued Wimsey. 'Do you exhibit much?'

'Here and there. I've never had a show in London.'

'I fancy I once saw a couple of small sea-scapes of yours somewhere. Manchester, was it? or Liverpool? I wasn't sure of your name, but I recognised the technique immediately.'

'I dare say. I did send a few things to Manchester about two years ago.'

'Yes – I felt sure I couldn't be mistaken. I want to buy the portrait. Here's my card, by the way. I'm not a journalist; I collect things.'

Crowder looked from the card to Wimsey and from Wimsey to the card, a little reluctantly.

'If you want to exhibit it, of course,' said Lord Peter, 'I should be delighted to leave it with you as long as you liked.'

'Oh, it's not that,' said Crowder. 'The fact is, I'm not altogether keen on the thing. I should like to – that is to say, it's not really finished.'

'My dear man, it's a bally masterpiece.'

'Oh, the painting's all right. But it's not altogether satisfactory as a likeness.'

'What the devil does the likeness matter? I don't know what the late Plant looked like and I don't care. As I look at the thing it's a damn fine bit of brush-work, and if you tinker about with it you'll spoil it. You know that as well as I do. What's biting you? It isn't the price, is it? You know I shan't boggle about that. I can afford my modest

286

pleasures, even in these thin and piping times. You don't want me to have it? Come now – what's the real reason?'

'There's no reason at all why you shouldn't have it if you really want it, I suppose,' said the painter, still a little sullenly. 'If it's really the painting that interests you.'

'What do you suppose it is? The notoriety? I can have all I want of *that* commodity, you know, for the asking – even without asking. Well, anyhow, think it over, and when you've decided, send me a line and name your price.'

Crowder nodded without speaking, and the photographer having by this time finished his job, the party took their leave.

As they left the building, they became involved in the stream of Crichton's staff going out to lunch. A girl, who seemed to have been loitering in a semi-intentional way in the lower hall, caught them as the lift descended.

'Are you the *Evening Views* people? Did you get your picture all right?'

'Miss Twitterton?' said Hardy interrogatively. 'Yes, rather – thank you so much for giving us the tip. You'll see it on the front page this evening.'

'Oh! that's splendid! I'm frightfully thrilled. It has made an excitement here – all this business. Do they know anything yet about who murdered Mr Plant? Or am I being horribly indiscreet?'

'We're expecting news of an arrest any minute now,' said Hardy. 'As a matter of fact, I shall have to buzz back to the office as fast as I can, to sit with one ear glued to the telephone. You will excuse me, won't you? And, look here – will you let me come round another day, when things aren't so busy, and take you out to lunch?'

'Of course. I should love to.' Miss Twitterton giggled. 'I do so want to hear about all the murder cases.'

'Then here's the man to tell you about them, Miss Twitterton,' said Hardy, with mischief in his eye. 'Allow me to introduce Lord Peter Wimsey.'

Miss Twitterton offered her hand in an ecstasy of excitement which almost robbed her of speech.

'How do you do?' said Wimsey. 'As this blighter is in such a hurry to get back to his gossip-shop, what do you say to having a spot of lunch with me?'

'Well, really –' began Miss Twitterton.

'He's all right,' said Hardy; 'he won't lure you into any gilded dens of infamy. If you look at him, you will see he has a kind, innocent face.'

'I'm sure I never thought of such a thing,' said Miss Twitterton. 'But you know – really – I've only got my old things on. It's no good wearing anything decent in this dusty old place.'

'Oh, nonsense!' said Wimsey. 'You couldn't possibly look nicer. It isn't the frock that matters – it's the person who wears it. *That's* all right, then. See you later, Sally! Taxi! Where shall we go? What time do you have to be back, by the way?'

'Two o'clock,' said Miss Twitterton regretfully.

'Then we'll make the Savoy do,' said Wimsey; 'it's reasonably handy.'

Miss Twitterton hopped into the waiting taxi with a little squeak of agitation.

'Did you see Mr Crichton?' she said. 'He went by just as we were talking. However, I dare say he doesn't really know me by sight. I hope not – or he'll think I'm getting too grand to need a salary.' She rooted in her hand-bag. 'I'm sure my face is getting all shiny with excitement.

What a silly taxi. It hasn't got a mirror – and I've bust mine.'

Wimsey solemnly produced a small looking-glass from his pocket.

'How wonderfully competent of you!' exclaimed Miss Twitterton. 'I'm afraid, Lord Peter, you are used to taking girls about.'

'Moderately so,' said Wimsey. He did not think it necessary to mention that the last time he had used that mirror it had been to examine the back teeth of a murdered man.

'Of course,' said Miss Twitterton, 'they had to say he was popular with his colleagues. Haven't you noticed that murdered people are always well dressed and popular?'

'They have to be,' said Wimsey. 'It makes it more mysterious and pathetic. Just as girls who disappear are always bright and home-loving and have no men friends.'

'Silly, isn't it?' said Miss Twitterton, with her mouth full of roast duck and green peas. 'I should think everybody was only too glad to get rid of Plant – nasty, rude creature. So mean, too, always taking credit for other people's work. All those poor things in the studio, with all the spirit squashed out of them. I always say, Lord Peter, you can tell if a head of a department's fitted for his job by noticing the atmosphere of the place as you go into it. Take the copy-room, now. We're all as cheerful and friendly as you like, though I must say the language that goes on there is something awful, but these writing fellows are like that, and they don't mean anything by it. But then, Mr Ormerod is a real gentleman – that's our copy-chief, you know – and he makes them all take an interest in the work, for all they grumble about the cheese-bills and the department-store bilge they have to turn out. But it's quite different in the studio. A sort of dead-and-alive feeling about it, if you understand what I mean. We girls notice things like that more than some of the high-up people think. Of course, I'm very sensitive to these feelings – almost psychic, I've been told.'

Lord Peter said there was nobody like a woman for sizing up character at a glance. Women, he thought, were remarkably intuitive.

'That's a fact,' said Miss Twitterton. 'I've often said, if I could have a few frank words with Mr Crichton, I could tell him a thing or two. There are wheels within wheels beneath the surface of a place like this that these brass-hats have no idea of.'

Lord Peter said he felt sure of it.

'The way Mr Plant treated people he thought were beneath him,' went on Miss Twitterton, 'I'm sure it was enough to make your blood boil. I'm sure, if Mr Ormerod sent me with a message to him, I was glad to get out of the room again. Humiliating, it was, the way he'd speak to you. I don't care if he's dead or not; being dead doesn't make a person's past behaviour any better, Lord Peter. It wasn't so much the rude things he said. There's Mr Birkett, for example; *he's* rude enough, but nobody minds him. He's just like a big, blundering puppy – rather a lamb, really. It was Mr Plant's nasty sneering way we all hated so. And he was always running people down.'

'How about this portrait?' asked Wimsey. 'Was it like him at all?'

'It was a lot too like him,' said Miss Twitterton

emphatically. 'That's why he hated it so. He didn't like Crowder, either. But, of course, he knew he could paint, and he made him do it, because he thought he'd be getting a valuable thing cheap. And Crowder couldn't very well refuse, or Plant would have got him sacked.'

'I shouldn't have thought that would have mattered much to a man of Crowder's ability.'

'Poor Mr Crowder! I don't think he's ever had much luck. Good artists don't always seem able to sell their pictures. And I know he wanted to get married – otherwise he'd never have taken up this commercial work. He's told me a good bit about himself. I don't know why – but I'm one of the people men seem to tell things to.'

Lord Peter filled Miss Twitterton's glass.

'Oh, please! No, really! Not a drop more! I'm talking a lot too much as it is. I don't know what Mr Ormerod will say when I go in to take his letters. I shall be writing down all kinds of funny things. Ooh! I really must be getting back. Just look at the time!'

'It's not really late. Have a black coffee – just as a corrective.' Wimsey smiled. 'You haven't been talking at all too much. I've enjoyed your picture of office life enormously. You have a very vivid way of putting things, you know. I see now why Mr Plant was not altogether a popular character.'

'Not in the office, anyway – whatever he may have been elsewhere,' said Miss Twitterton darkly.

'Oh?'

'Oh! he was a one,' said Miss Twitterton. 'He certainly was a one. Some friends of mine met him one evening up in the West End, and they came back with some nice stories. It was quite a joke in the office – old Plant and his rosebuds, you know. Mr Cowley – he's *the* Cowley, you know, who rides in the motor-cycle races – he always said he knew what to think of Mr Plant and his motor-tours. That time Mr Plant pretended he'd gone touring in Wales, Mr Cowley was asking him about the roads, and he didn't know a thing about them. Because Mr Cowley really had been touring there, and he knew quite well Mr Plant hadn't been where he said he had; and, as a matter of fact, Mr Cowley knew he'd been staying the whole time in a hotel at Aberystwyth, in very attractive company.'

Miss Twitterton finished her coffee and slapped the cup down defiantly.

'And now I really *must* run away, or I shall be most dreadfully late. And thank you ever so much.'

'Hullo!' said Inspector Winterbottom, 'you've bought that portrait, then?'

'Yes,' said Wimsey. 'It's a fine bit of work.' He gazed thoughtfully at the canvas. 'Sit down, inspector; I want to tell you a story.'

'And I want to tell *you* a story,' replied the inspector.

'Let's have yours first,' said Wimsey, with an air of flattering eagerness.

'No, no, my lord. You take precedence. Go ahead.'

He snuggled down with a chuckle into his arm-chair.

'Well!' said Wimsey. 'Mine's a sort of a fairy-story. And, mind you, I haven't verified it.'

'Go ahead, my lord, go ahead.'

'Once upon a time –' said Wimsey, sighing.

'That's the good old-fashioned way to begin a fairy-story,' said Inspector Winterbottom.

'Once upon a time,' repeated Wimsey, 'there was a painter. He was a good painter, but the bad fairy of

Financial Success had not been asked to his christening – what?'

'That's often the way with painters,' agreed the inspector.

'So he had to take up a job as a commercial artist, because nobody would buy his pictures and, like so many people in fairy-tales, he wanted to marry a goose-girl.'

'There's many people want to do the same,' said the inspector.

'The head of his department,' went on Wimsey, 'was a man with a mean, sneering soul. He wasn't even really good at his job, but he had been pushed into authority during the war, when better men went to the Front. Mind you, I'm rather sorry for the man. He suffered from an inferiority complex' – the inspector snorted – 'and he thought the only way to keep his end up was to keep other people's end down. So he became a little tin tyrant and a bully. He took all the credit for the work of the men under his charge, and he sneered and harassed them till they got inferiority complexes even worse than his own.'

'I've known that sort,' said the inspector, 'and the marvel to me is how they get away with it.'

'Just so,' said Wimsey. 'Well, I dare say this man would have gone on getting away with it all right, if he hadn't thought of getting this painter to paint his portrait.'

'Damn silly thing to do,' said the inspector. 'It was only making the painter-fellow conceited with himself.'

'True. But, you see, this tin tyrant person had a fascinating female in tow, and he wanted the portrait for the lady. He thought that, by making the painter do it, he would get a good portrait at starvation price. But unhappily he'd forgotten that, however much an artist will put up with in the ordinary way, he is bound to be sincere with his art. That's the one thing a genuine artist won't muck about with.'

'I dare say,' said the inspector. 'I don't know much about artists.'

'Well, you can take it from me. So the painter painted the portrait as he saw it, and he put the man's whole creeping, sneering, paltry soul on the canvas for everybody to see.'

Inspector Winterbottom stared at the portrait, and the portrait sneered back at him.

'It's not what you'd call a flattering picture, certainly,' he admitted.

'Now, when a painter paints a portrait of anybody,' went on Wimsey, 'that person's face is never the same to him again. It's like – what shall I say? Well, it's like the way a gunner, say, looks at a landscape where he happens to be posted. He doesn't see it as a landscape. He doesn't see it as a thing of magic beauty, full of sweeping lines and lovely colour. He sees it as so much cover, so many landmarks to aim by, so many gun-emplacements. And when the war is over and he goes back to it, he will still see it as cover and landmarks and gun-emplacements. It isn't a landscape any more. It's a war map.'

'I know that,' said Inspector Winterbottom. 'I was a gunner myself.'

'A painter gets just the same feeling of deadly familiarity with every line of a face he's once painted,' pursued Wimsey. 'And, if it's a face he hates, he hates it with a new and more irritable hatred. It's like a defective barrel-organ, everlastingly grinding out the same old maddening tune, and making the same damned awful wrong note every time the barrel goes round.'

'Lord! how you can talk!' ejaculated the inspector.

'That was the way the painter felt about this man's hateful face. All day and every day he had to see it. He couldn't get away because he was tied to his job, you see.'

'He ought to have cut loose,' said the inspector. 'It's no good going on like that, trying to work with uncongenial people.'

'Well, anyway, he said to himself, he could escape for a bit during his holidays. There was a beautiful little quiet spot he knew on the West Coast, where nobody ever came. He'd been there before and painted it. Oh! by the way, that reminds me – I've got another picture to show you.'

He went to a bureau and extracted a small panel in oils from a drawer.

'I saw that two years ago at a show in Manchester, and I happened to remember the name of the dealer who bought it.'

Inspector Winterbottom gaped at the panel.

'But that's East Felpham!' he exclaimed.

'Yes. It's only signed T.C., but the technique is rather unmistakable, don't you think?'

The inspector knew little about technique, but initials he understood. He looked from the portrait to the panel and back at Lord Peter.

'The painter—'

'Crowder?'

'If it's all the same to you, I'd rather go on calling him the painter. He packed up his traps on his push-bike carrier, and took his tormented nerves down to this beloved and secret spot for a quiet weekend. He stayed

295

at a quiet little hotel in the neighbourhood, and each morning he cycled off to this lovely little beach to bathe. He never told anybody at the hotel where he went, because it was *his* place, and he didn't want other people to find it out.'

Inspector Winterbottom set the panel down on the table, and helped himself to whisky.

'One morning – it happened to be the Monday morning' – Wimsey's voice became slower and more reluctant – 'he went down as usual. The tide was not yet fully in, but he ran out over the rocks to where he knew there was a deep bathing-pool. He plunged in and swam about, and let the small noise of his jangling troubles be swallowed up in the innumerable laughter of the sea.'

'Eh?'

'κυμάτων ανήριθμον γέλασμα – quotation from the classics. So people say it means the dimpled surface of the waves in the sunlight – but how could Prometheus, bound upon his rock, have seen it? Surely it was the chuckle of the incoming tide among the stones that came up to his ears on the lonely peak where the vulture fretted at his heart. I remember arguing about it with old Philpotts in class, and getting rapped over the knuckles for contradicting him. I didn't know at the time that he was engaged in producing a translation on his own account, or doubtless I should have contradicted him more rudely and been told to take my trousers down. Dear old Philpotts!'

'I don't know anything about that,' said the inspector.

'I beg your pardon. Shocking way I have of wandering. The painter – well! he swam round the end of the rocks, for the tide was nearly in by that time; and, as he came up from the sea, he saw a man standing on the beach – that beloved beach, remember, which he thought was his own sacred haven of peace. He came wading towards it, cursing the Bank Holiday rabble who must needs swarm about everywhere with their cigarette-packets and their kodaks and their gramophones – and then he saw that it was a face he knew. He knew every hated line in it, on that clear sunny morning. And, early as it was, the heat was coming up over the sea like a haze?'

'It was a hot weekend,' said the Inspector.

'And then the man hailed him, in his smug, mincing voice. "Hullo!" he said, "you here? How did you find my little bathing-place?" And that was too much for the painter. He felt as if his last sanctuary had been invaded. He leapt at the lean throat – it's rather a stringy one, you may notice, with a prominent Adam's apple – an irritating throat. The water chuckled round their feet as they swayed to and fro. He felt his thumbs sink into the flesh he had painted. He saw, and laughed to see, the hateful familiarity of the features change and swell into an unrecognisable purple. He watched the sunken eyes bulge out and the thin mouth distort itself as the blackened tongue thrust through it – I am not unnerving you, I hope?'

The inspector laughed.

'Not a bit. It's wonderful, the way you describe things. You ought to write a book.'

> 'I sing but as the throstle sings,
> Amid the branches dwelling,'

replied his lordship negligently, and went on without further comment.

'The painter throttled him. He flung him back on the sand. He looked at him, and his heart crowed within him. He stretched out his hand, and found a broken bottle, with a good jagged edge. He went to work with a will, stamping and tearing away every trace of the face he knew and loathed. He blotted it out and destroyed it utterly.

'He sat beside the thing he had made. He began to be frightened. They had staggered back beyond the edge of the water, and there were the marks of his feet on the sand. He had blood on his face and on his bathing-suit, and he had cut his hand with the bottle. But the blessed sea was still coming in. He watched it pass over the bloodstains and the footprints and wipe the story of his madness away. He remembered that this man had gone from his place, leaving no address behind him. He went back, step by step, into the water, and as it came up to his breast, he saw the red stains smoke away like a faint mist in the brown-blueness of the tide. He went – wading and swimming and plunging his face and arms deep in the water, looking back from time to time to see what he had left behind him. I think that when he got back to the point and drew himself out, clean and cool, upon the rocks, he remembered that he ought to have taken the body back with him and let the tide carry it away, but it was too late. He was clean, and could not bear to go back for the thing. Besides, he was late, and they would wonder at the hotel if he was not back in time for breakfast. He ran lightly over the bare rocks and the grass that showed no footprint. He dressed himself, taking care to leave no trace of his presence. He took the car, which would have told a story. He put his bicycle in the back seat, under the rugs, and he went – but you know as well as I do where he went.'

Lord Peter got up with an impatient movement, and

went over to the picture, rubbing his thumb meditatively over the texture of the painting.

'You may say, if he hated the face so much, why didn't he destroy the picture? He couldn't. It was the best thing he'd ever done. He took a hundred guineas for it. It was cheap at a hundred guineas. But then – I think he was afraid to refuse me. My name is rather well known. It was a sort of blackmail, I suppose. But I wanted that picture.'

Inspector Winterbottom laughed again.

'Did you take any steps, my lord, to find out if Crowder has really been staying at East Felpham?'

'No.' Wimsey swung round abruptly. 'I have taken no steps at all. That's your business. I have told you the story, and, on my soul, I'd rather have stood by and said nothing.'

'You needn't worry.' The inspector laughed for the third time. 'It's a good story, my lord, and you told it well. But you're right when you say it's a fairy-story. We've found this Italian fellow – Francesco, he called himself, and he's the man all right.'

'How do you know? Has he confessed?'

'Practically. He's dead. Killed himself. He left a letter to the woman, begging for forgiveness, and saying that when he saw her with Plant he felt murder come into his heart. "I have revenged myself," he says, "on him who dared to love you."' I suppose he got the wind up when he saw we were after him – I wish these newspapers wouldn't be always putting these criminals on their guard – so he did away with himself to cheat the gallows. I may say it's been a disappointment to me.'

'It must have been,' said Wimsey. 'Very unsatisfactory, of course. But I'm glad my story turned out to be only a fairy-tale after all. You're not going?'

'Got to get back to my duty,' said the inspector, heaving himself to his feet. 'Very pleased to have met you, my lord. And I mean what I say – you ought to take to literature.'

Wimsey remained after he had gone, still looking at the portrait.

'"What is Truth?" said jesting Pilate. No wonder, since it is so completely unbelievable. . . . I could prove it . . . if I liked . . . but the man had a villainous face, and there are few good painters in the world.'

THE ADVENTUROUS EXPLOIT OF THE
CAVE OF ALI BABA

In the front room of a grim and narrow house in Lambeth a man sat eating kippers and glancing through the *Morning Post*. He was smallish and spare, with brown hair rather too regularly waved and a strong, brown beard, cut to a point. His double-breasted suit of navy-blue and his socks, tie, and handkerchief, all scrupulously matched, were a trifle more point-device than the best taste approves, and his boots were slightly too bright a brown. He did not look a gentleman, not even a gentleman's gentleman, yet there was something about his appearance which suggested that he was accustomed to the manner of life in good families. The breakfast-table, which he had set with his own hands, was arrayed with the attention to detail which is exacted of good-class servants. His action, as he walked over to a little side-table and carved himself a plate of ham, was the action of a superior butler; yet he was not old enough to be a retired butler; a footman, perhaps, who had come into a legacy.

He finished the ham with good appetite, and, as he sipped his coffee, read through attentively a paragraph which he had already noticed and put aside for consideration.

BEQUEST TO VALET

£10,000 TO CHARITIES

'The will of Lord Peter Wimsey, who was killed last December while shooting big game in Tanganyika, was proved yesterday at £500,000. A sum of £10,000 was left to various charities, including [here followed a list of bequests]. To his valet, Mervyn Bunter, was left an annuity of £500 and the lease of the testator's flat in Piccadilly. [Then followed a number of personal bequests.] The remainder of the estate, including the valuable collection of books and pictures at 110a Piccadilly, was left to the testator's mother, the Dowager Duchess of Denver.

_____

'Lord Peter Wimsey was thirty-seven at the time of his death. He was the younger brother of the present Duke of Denver, who is the wealthiest peer in the United Kingdom. Lord Peter was distinguished as a criminologist and took an active part in the solution of several famous mysteries. He was a well-known book collector and man-about-town.'

The man gave a sigh of relief.

'No doubt about that,' he said aloud. 'People don't give their money away if they're going to come back again. The blighter's dead and buried right enough. I'm free.'

He finished his coffee, cleared the table, and washed up the crockery, took his bowler hat from the hall-stand, and went out.

A bus took him to Bermondsey. He alighted, and plunged into a network of gloomy streets, arriving after a quarter of an hour's walk at a seedy-looking public-house in a low quarter. He entered and called for a double whisky.

The house had only just opened, but a number of customers, who had apparently been waiting on the doorstep for this desirable event, were already clustered about the bar. The man who might have been a footman reached for his glass, and in doing so jostled the elbow of a flash person in a check suit and regrettable tie.

'Here!' expostulated the flash person, 'what d'yer mean by it? We don't want your sort here. Get out!'

He emphasised his remarks with a few highly coloured words, and a violent push in the chest.

'Bar's free to everybody, isn't it?' said the other, returning the shove with interest.

'Now then!' said the barmaid, 'none o' that. The gentleman didn't do it intentional, Mr Jukes.'

'Didn't he?' said Mr Jukes. 'Well, I *did*.'

'And you ought to be ashamed of yourself,' retorted the young lady, with a toss of the head. 'I'll have no quarrelling in my bar – not this time in the morning.'

'It was quite an accident,' said the man from Lambeth. 'I'm not one to make a disturbance, having always been used to the best houses. But if any gentleman *wants* to make trouble—'

'All right, all right,' said Mr Jukes, more pacifically. 'I'm not keen to give you a new face. Not but what any alteration wouldn't be for the better. Mind your manners another time, that's all. What'll you have?'

'No, no,' protested the other, 'this one must be on me. Sorry I pushed you. I didn't mean it. But I didn't like to be taken up so short.'

'Say no more about it,' said Mr Jukes generously. 'I'm standing this. Another double whisky, miss, and one of the usual. Come over here where there isn't so much of a crowd, or you'll be getting yourself into trouble again.'

He led the way to a small table in the corner of the room.

'That's all right,' said Mr Jukes. 'Very nicely done. I don't think there's any danger here, but you can't be too careful. Now, what about it, Rogers? Have you made up your mind to come in with us?'

'Yes,' said Rogers, with a glance over his shoulder, 'yes, I have. That is, mind you, if everything seems all right. I'm not looking for trouble, and I don't want to get let in for any dangerous games. I don't mind giving you information, but it's understood as I take no active part in whatever goes on. Is that straight?'

'You wouldn't be allowed to take an active part if you wanted to,' said Mr Jukes. 'Why, you poor fish, Number One wouldn't have anybody but experts on his jobs. All you have to do is to let us know where the stuff is and how to get it. The Society does the rest. It's some organisation, I can tell you. You won't even know who's doing it, or how it's done. You won't know anybody, and nobody will know you – except Number One, of course. He knows everybody.'

'And you,' said Rogers.

'And me, of course. But I shall be transferred to another district. We shan't meet again after today, except at the general meetings, and then we shall all be masked.'

'Go on!' said Rogers incredulously.

'Fact. You'll be taken to Number One – he'll see you, but you won't see him. Then, if he thinks you're any good, you'll be put on the roll, and after that you'll be told where to make your reports to. There is a divisional meeting called once a fortnight, and every three months there's a general meeting and share-out. Each member is called up by number and has his whack handed over to him. That's all.'

'Well, but suppose two members are put on the same job together?'

'If it's a daylight job, they'll be so disguised their mothers wouldn't know 'em. But it's mostly night work.'

'I see. But, look here – what's to prevent somebody following me home and giving me away to the police?'

'Nothing, of course. Only I wouldn't advise him to try it, that's all. The last man who had that bright idea was fished out of the river down Rotherhithe way, before he had time to get his precious report in. Number One knows everybody, you see.'

'Oh! – and who is this Number One?'

'There's lots of people would give a good bit to know that.'

'Does nobody know?'

'Nobody. He's a fair marvel, is Number One. He's a gentleman, I can tell you that, and a pretty high-up one, from his ways. *And* he's got eyes all round his head. *And* he's got an arm as long as from here to Australia. *But* nobody knows anything about him, unless it's Number Two, and I'm not even sure about her.'

'There are women in it, then?'

'You can bet your boots there are. You can't do a job without 'em nowadays. But that needn't worry you. The women are safe enough. They don't want to come to a sticky end, no more than you and me.'

'But look here, Jukes – how about the money? It's a big risk to take. Is it worth it?'

'Worth it?' Jukes leant across the little marble-topped table and whispered.

'Cool!' gasped Rogers. 'And how much of that would I get, now?'

'You'd share and share alike with the rest, whether you'd been in that particular job or not. There's fifty members, and you'd get one-fiftieth, same as Number One and same as me.'

'Really? No kidding?'

'See that wet, see that dry!' Jukes laughed. 'Say, can you beat it? There's never been anything like it. It's the biggest thing ever been known. He's a great man, is Number One.'

'And do you pull off many jobs?'

'Many? Listen. You remember the Carruthers necklace, and the Gorleston Bank robbery? And the Faversham burglary? And the big Rubens that disappeared from the National Gallery? And the Frensham pearls? All done by the Society. And never one of them cleared up.'

Rogers licked his lips.

'But now, look here,' he said cautiously. 'Supposing I was a spy, as you might say, and supposing I was to go straight off and tell the police about what you've been saying?'

'Ah!' said Jukes, 'suppose you did, eh? Well, supposing something nasty didn't happen to you on the way there – which I wouldn't answer for, mind—'

'Do you mean to say you've got me watched?'

'You can bet your sweet life we have. Yes. Well,

supposing nothing happened on the way there, and you was to bring the slops to this pub, looking for yours truly—'

'Yes?'

'You wouldn't find me, that's all. I should have gone to Number Five.'

'Who's Number Five?'

'Ah! I don't know. But he's the man that makes you a new face while you wait. Plastic surgery, they call it. And new fingerprints. New everything. We go in for up-to-date methods in our show.'

Rogers whistled.

'Well, how about it?' asked Jukes, eyeing his acquaintance over the rim of his tumbler.

'Look here – you've told me a lot of things. Shall I be safe if I say "no"?'

'Oh, yes – if you behave yourself and don't make trouble for us.'

'H'm, I see. And if I say "yes"?'

'Then you'll be a rich man in less than no time, with money in your pocket to live like a gentleman. And nothing to do for it, except to tell us what you know about the houses you've been to when you were in service. It's money for jam if you act straight by the Society.'

Rogers was silent, thinking it over.

'I'll do it!' he said at last.

'Good for you. Miss! The same again, please. Here's to it, Rogers! I knew you were one of the right sort the minute I set eyes on you. Here's to money for jam, and take care of Number One! Talking of Number One, you'd better come round and see him tonight. No time like the present.'

'Right you are. Where'll I come to? Here?'

'Nix. No more of this little pub for us. It's a pity, because it's nice and comfortable, but it can't be helped. Now, what you've got to do is, this. At ten o'clock tonight exactly, you walk across Lambeth Bridge.' (Rogers winced at this intimation that his abode was known), 'and you'll see a yellow taxi standing there, with the driver doing something to his engine. You'll say to him, "Is your bus fit to go?" and he'll say, "Depends where you want to go to." And you'll say, "Take me to Number One, London." There's a shop called that, by the way, but he won't take you there. You won't know where he *is* taking you, because the taxi-windows will be covered up, but you mustn't mind that. It's the rule for the first visit. Afterwards, when you're regularly one of us, you'll be told the name of the place. And when you get there, do as you're told and speak the truth, because, if you don't, Number One will deal with you. See?'

'I see.'

'Are you game? You're not afraid?'

'Of course I'm not afraid.'

'Good man! Well, we'd better be moving now. And I'll say good-bye, because we shan't see each other again. Good-bye – and good luck!'

'Good-bye.'

They passed through the swing-doors, and out into the mean and dirty street.

The two years subsequent to the enrolment of the ex-footman Rogers in a crook society were marked by a number of startling and successful raids on the houses of distinguished people. There was the theft of the great diamond tiara from the Dowager Duchess of Denver; the burglary at the flat formerly occupied by the late Lord Peter Wimsey, resulting in the disappearance of £7,000 worth of silver and gold plate; the burglary at the country mansion of Theodore Winthrop, the millionaire – which, incidentally, exposed that thriving gentleman as a confirmed Society blackmailer and caused a reverberating scandal in Mayfair; and the snatching of the famous eight-string necklace of pearls from the neck of the Marchioness of Dinglewood during the singing of the Jewel Song in *Faust* at Covent Garden. It is true that the pearls turned out to be imitation, the original string having been pawned by the noble lady under circumstances highly painful to the Marquis, but the coup was nevertheless a sensational one.

On a Saturday afternoon in January, Rogers was sitting in his room in Lambeth, when a slight noise at the front door caught his ear. He sprang up almost before it had ceased, dashed through the small hallway, and flung she door open. The street was deserted. Nevertheless, as he turned back to the sitting-room, he saw an envelope lying on the hat-stand. It was addressed briefly to 'Number Twenty-one'. Accustomed to this time to the somewhat dramatic methods used by the Society to deliver its correspondence, he merely shrugged his shoulders, and opened the note.

It was written in cipher, and, when transcribed, ran thus:

> 'Number Twenty-one, – An Extraordinary General Meeting will be held tonight at the house of Number One at 11.30. You will be absent at your peril. The word is FINALITY.'

Rogers stood for a little time considering this. Then he

made his way to a room at the back of the house, in which there was a tall safe, built into the wall. He manipulated the combination and walked into the safe, which ran back for some distance, forming, indeed, a small strong-room. He pulled out a drawer marked 'Correspondence', and added the paper he had just received to the contents.

After a few moments he emerged, re-set the lock to a new combination, and returned to the sitting-room.

'Finality,' he said. 'Yes – I think so.' He stretched out his hand to the telephone – then appeared to alter his mind.

He went upstairs to an attic, and thence climbed into a loft close under the roof. Crawling among the rafters, he made his way into the farthest corner; then carefully pressed a knot on the timber-work. A concealed trap-door swung open. He crept through it, and found himself in the corresponding loft of the next house. A soft cooing noise greeted him as he entered. Under the skylight stood three cages, each containing a carrier pigeon.

He glanced cautiously out of the skylight, which looked out upon a high blank wall at the back of some factory or other. There was nobody in the dim little courtyard, and no window within sight. He drew his head in again, and, taking a small fragment of thin paper from his pocket-book, wrote a few letters and numbers upon it. Going to the nearest cage, he took out the pigeon and attached the message to its wing. Then he carefully set the bird on the window-ledge. It hesitated a moment, shifted its pink feet a few times, lifted its wings, and was gone. He saw it tower up into the already darkening sky over the factory roof and vanish into the distance.

He glanced at his watch and returned downstairs. An

hour later he released the second pigeon, and in another hour the third. Then he sat down to wait.

At half-past nine he went up to the attic again. It was dark, but a few frosty stars were shining, and a cold air blew through the open window. Something pale gleamed faintly on the floor. He picked it up – it was warm and feathery. The answer had come.

He ruffled the soft plumes and found the paper. Before reading it, he fed the pigeon and put it into one of the cages. As he was about to fasten the door, he checked himself.

'If anything happens to me,' he said, 'there's no need for you to starve to death, my child.'

He pushed the window a little wider open and went down-stairs again. The paper in his hand bore only the two letters, 'O.K.' It seemed to have been written hurriedly, for there was a long smear of ink in the upper left-hand corner. He noted this with a smile, put the paper in the fire, and, going out into the kitchen, prepared and ate a hearty meal of eggs and corned beef from a new tin. He ate it without bread, though there was a loaf on the shelf near at hand, and washed it down with water from the tap, which he let run for some time before venturing to drink it. Even then he carefully wiped the tap, both inside and outside, before drinking.

When he had finished, he took a revolver from a locked drawer, inspecting the mechanism with attention to see that it was in working order, and loaded it with new cartridges from an unbroken packet. Then he sat down to wait again.

At a quarter before eleven, he rose and went out into the street. He walked briskly, keeping well away from the wall, till he came out into a well-lighted thoroughfare.

Here he took a bus, securing the corner seat next the conductor, from which he could see everybody who got on and off. A succession of buses eventually brought him to a respectable residential quarter of Hampstead. Here he alighted and, still keeping well away from the walls, made his way up to the Heath.

The night was moonless, but not altogether black, and, as he crossed a deserted part of the Heath, he observed one or two other dark forms closing in upon him from various directions. He paused in the shelter of a large tree, and adjusted to his face a black velvet mask, which covered him from brow to chin. At its base the number 21 was clearly embroidered in white thread.

At length a slight dip in the ground disclosed one of those agreeable villas which stand, somewhat isolated, among the rural surroundings of the Heath. One of the windows was lighted. As he made his way to the door, other dark figures, masked like himself, pressed forward and surrounded him. He counted six of them.

The foremost man knocked on the door of the solitary house. After a moment, it was opened slightly. The man advanced his head to the opening; there was a murmur, and the door opened wide. The man stepped in, and the door was shut.

When three of the men had entered, Rogers found himself to be the next in turn. He knocked, three times loudly, then twice faintly. The door opened to the extent of two or three inches, and an ear was presented to the chink. Rogers whispered 'Finality'. The ear was with-drawn, the door opened, and he passed in.

Without any further word of greeting, Number Twenty-one passed into a small room on the left, which was furnished like an office, with a desk, a safe, and a couple of chairs. At the desk sat a massive man in evening dress, with a ledger before him. The new arrival shut the door carefully after him; it clicked to, on a spring lock. Advancing to the desk, he announced, 'Number Twenty-one, sir,' and stood respectfully waiting. The big man looked up, showing the number 1 startlingly white on his mask. His eyes, of a curious hard blue, scanned Rogers attentively. At a sign from him, Rogers removed his mask. Having verified his identity with care, the President said, 'Very well, Number Twenty-one,' and made an entry in the ledger. The voice was hard and metallic, like his eyes. The close scrutiny from behind the immovable black mask seemed to make Rogers uneasy; he shifted his feet, and his eyes fell. Number One made a sign of dismissal, and Rogers, with a faint sigh as though of relief, replaced his mask and left the room. As he came out, the next comer passed in in his place.

The room in which the Society met was a large one, made by knocking the two largest of the first-floor rooms into one. It was furnished in the standardised taste of twentieth-century suburbia and brilliantly lighted. A gramophone in one corner blared out a jazz tune, to which about ten couples of masked men and women were dancing, some in evening dress and others in tweeds and jumpers.

In one corner of the room was an American bar. Rogers went up and asked the masked man in charge for a double whisky. He consumed it slowly, leaning on the bar. The room filled. Presently somebody moved across to the gramophone and stopped it. He looked round. Number One had appeared on the threshold. A tall woman in black stood beside him. The mask, embroidered with a white 2, covered hair and face completely; only her fine bearing and her white arms and bosom and the dark eyes shining through the eye-slits proclaimed her a woman of power and physical attraction.

'Ladies and gentlemen.' Number One was standing at the upper end of the room. The woman sat beside him; her eyes were cast down and betrayed nothing, but her hands were clenched on the arms of the chair and her whole figure seemed tensely aware.

'Ladies and gentlemen. Our numbers are two short tonight.' The masks moved; eyes were turned, seeking and counting. 'I need not inform you of the disastrous failure of our plan for securing the plans of the Court-Windlesham helicopter. Our courageous and devoted comrades, Number Fifteen and Number Forty-eight, were betrayed and taken by the police.'

An uneasy murmur arose among the company.

'It may have occurred to some of you that even the well-known steadfastness of these comrades might give way under examination. There is no cause for alarm. The usual orders have been issued, and I have this evening received the report that their tongues have been effectually silenced. You will, I am sure, be glad to know that these two brave men have been spared the ordeal of so great a temptation to dishonour, and that they will not be called upon to face a public trial and the rigours of a long imprisonment.'

A hiss of intaken breath moved across the assembled members like the wind over a barley-field.

'Their dependants will be discreetly compensated in the usual manner. I call upon Numbers Twelve and Thirty-four to undertake this agreeable task. They will attend me in my office for their instructions after the meeting. Will the Numbers I have named kindly signify that they are able and willing to perform this duty?'

Two hands were raised in salute. The President continued, looking at his watch:

'Ladies and gentlemen, please take your partners for the next dance.'

The gramophone struck up again. Rogers turned to a girl near him in a red dress. She nodded, and they slipped into the movement of a fox-trot. The couples gyrated solemnly and in silence. Their shadows were flung against the blinds as they turned and stepped to and fro.

'What has happened?' breathed the girl in a whisper, scarcely moving her lips. 'I'm frightened, aren't you? I feel as if something awful was going to happen.'

'It does take one a bit short, the President's way of doing things,' agreed Rogers, 'but it's safer like that.'

'Those poor men—'

A dancer, turning and following on their heels, touched Rogers on the shoulder.

'No talking, please,' he said. His eyes gleamed sternly; he twirled his partner into the middle of the crowd and was gone. The girl shuddered.

The gramophone stopped. There was a burst of clapping.

The dancers again clustered before the President's seat.

'Ladies and gentlemen. You may wonder why this extraordinary meeting has been called. The reason is a serious one. The failure of our recent attempt was no accident. The police were not on the premises that night by chance. We have a traitor among us.'

Partners who had been standing close together fell distrustfully apart. Each member seemed to shrink, as a snail shrinks from the touch of a finger.

'You will remember the disappointing outcome of the Dinglewood affair,' went on the President, in his harsh voice. 'You may recall other smaller matters which have not turned out satisfactorily. All these troubles have been traced to their origin. I am happy to say that our minds can now be easy. The offender has been discovered and will be removed. There will be no more mistakes. The misguided member who introduced the traitor to our Society will be placed in a position where his lack of caution will have no further ill-effects. There is no cause for alarm.'

Every eye roved about the company, searching for the traitor and his unfortunate sponsor. Somewhere beneath the black masks a face must have turned white; somewhere under the stifling velvet there must have been a brow sweating, not with the heat of the dance. But the masks hid everything.

'Ladies and gentlemen, please take your partners for the next dance.'

The gramophone struck into an old and half-forgotten tune: 'There ain't nobody loves me.' The girl in red was claimed by a tall mask in evening dress. A hand laid on Rogers's arm made him start. A small, plump woman in a green jumper slipped a cold hand into his. The dance went on.

When it stopped, amid the usual applause, everyone stood, detached, stiffened in expectation. The President's voice was raised again.

'Ladies and gentlemen, please behave naturally. This is a dance, not a public meeting.'

Rogers led his partner to a chair and fetched her an ice. As he stooped over her, he noticed the hurried rise and fall of her bosom.

'Ladies and gentlemen.' The endless interval was over. 'You will no doubt wish to be immediately relieved from suspense. I will name the persons involved. Number Thirty-seven!'

A man sprang up with a fearful, strangled cry.

'Silence!'

The wretch choked and gasped.

'I never – I swear – I never – I'm innocent.'

'Silence. You have failed in discretion. You will be dealt with. If you have anything to say in defence of your folly, I will hear it later. Sit down.'

Number Thirty-seven sank down upon a chair. He pushed his handkerchief under the mask to wipe his face. Two tall men closed in upon him. The rest fell back, feeling the recoil of humanity from one stricken by mortal disease.

The gramophone struck up.

'Ladies and gentlemen, I will now name the traitor. Number Twenty-one, stand forward.'

Rogers stepped forward. The concentrated fear and loathing of forty-eight pairs of eyes burned upon him. The miserable Jukes set up a fresh wail.

'Oh, my God! Oh! my God!'

'Silence! Number Twenty-one, take off your mask.'

The traitor pulled the thick covering from his face. The intense hatred of the eyes devoured him.

'Number Thirty-seven, this man was introduced here by you, under the name of Joseph Rogers, formerly second footman in the service of the Duke of Denver, dismissed for pilfering. Did you take steps to verify that statement?'

'I did – I did! As God's my witness, it was all straight. I had him identified by two of the servants. I made enquiries. The tale was straight – I'll swear it was.'

The President consulted a paper before him, then he looked at his watch again.

'Ladies and gentlemen, please take your partners . . .'

Number Twenty-one, his arms twisted behind him and bound, and his wrists handcuffed, stood motionless, while the dance of doom circled about him. The clapping, as it ended, sounded like the clapping of the men and women who sat, thirsty-lipped beneath the guillotine.

'Number Twenty-one, your name has been given as Joseph Rogers, footman, dismissed for theft. Is that your real name?'

'No.'

'What is your name?'

'Peter Death Bredon Wimsey.'

'We thought you were dead.'

'Naturally. You were intended to think so.'

'What has become of the genuine Joseph Rogers?'

'He died abroad. I took his place. I may say that no real blame attaches to your people for not having realised who I was. I not only took Rogers's place; I *was* Rogers. Even when I was alone, I walked like Rogers, I sat like Rogers, I read Rogers's books, and wore Rogers's clothes. In the end, I almost thought Rogers's thoughts. The only way to keep up a successful impersonation is never to relax.'

'I see. The robbery of your own flat was arranged?'

'Obviously.'

'The robbery of the Dowager Duchess, your mother, was connived at by you?'

'It was. It was a very ugly tiara – no real loss to anybody with decent taste. May I smoke, by the way?'

'You may not. Ladies and gentlemen . . .'

The dance was like the mechanical jigging of puppets. Limbs jerked, feet faltered. The prisoner watched with an air of critical detachment.

'Numbers Fifteen, Twenty-two, and Forty-nine. You have watched the prisoner. Has he made any attempts to communicate with anybody?'

'None.' Number Twenty-two was the spokesman. 'His letters and parcels have been opened, his telephone tapped, and his movements followed. His water-pipes have been under observation for Morse signals.'

'You are sure of what you say?'

'Absolutely.'

'Prisoner, have you been alone in this adventure? Speak the truth, or things will be made somewhat more unpleasant for you than they might otherwise be.'

'I have been alone. I have taken no unnecessary risks.'

'It may be so. It will, however, be as well that steps should be taken to silence the man at Scotland Yard – what is his name? – Parker. Also the prisoner's man-servant, Mervyn Bunter, and possibly also his mother and sister. The brother is a stupid oaf, and not, I think, likely to have been taken into the prisoner's confidence. A precautionary watch will, I think, meet the necessities of his case.'

The prisoner appeared, for the first time, to be moved.

'Sir, I assure you that my mother and sister know nothing which could possibly bring danger on the Society.'

'You should have thought of their situation earlier. Ladies and gentlemen, please take—'

'No – no!' Flesh and blood could endure the mockery no longer. 'No! Finish with him. Get it over. Break up the meeting. It's dangerous. The police—'

'Silence!'

The President glanced round at the crowd. It had a dangerous look about it. He gave way.

'Very well. Take the prisoner away and silence him. He will receive Number 4 treatment. And be sure you explain it to him carefully first.'

'Ah!'

The eyes expressed a wolfish satisfaction. Strong hands gripped Wimsey's arms.

'One moment – for God's sake let me die decently.'

'You should have thought this over earlier. Take him away. Ladies and gentlemen, be satisfied – he will not die quickly.'

'Stop! Wait!' cried Wimsey desperately. 'I have something to say. I don't ask for life – only for a quick death. I – I have something to sell.'

'To sell?'

'Yes.'

'We make no bargains with traitors.'

'No – but listen! Do you think I have not thought of this? I am not so mad. I have left a letter.'

'Ah! now it is coming. A letter. To whom?'

'To the police. If I do not return tomorrow—'

'Well?'

'The letter will be opened.'

'Sir,' broke in Number Fifteen. 'This is bluff. The prisoner has not sent any letter. He has been strictly watched for many months.'

'Ah! but listen. I left the letter before I came to Lambeth.'

'Then it can contain no information of value.'

'Oh, but it does.'

'What?'

'The combination of my safe.'

'Indeed? Has this man's safe been searched?'

'Yes, sir.'

'What did it contain?'

'No information of importance, sir. An outline of our organisation – the name of this house – nothing that cannot be altered and covered before morning.'

Wimsey smiled.

'Did you investigate the inner compartment of the safe?'

There was a pause.

'You hear what he says,' snapped the President sharply. 'Did you find this inner compartment?'

'There was no inner compartment, sir. He is trying to bluff.'

'I hate to contradict you,' said Wimsey, with an effort at his ordinary pleasant tone, 'but I really think you must have over-looked the inner compartment.'

'Well,' said the President, 'and what do you say is in this inner compartment, if it does exist?'

'The names of every member of this Society, with their addresses, photographs, and finger-prints.'

'What?'

The eyes round him now were ugly with fear. Wimsey kept his face steadily turned towards the President.

'How do you say you have contrived to get this information?'

'Well, I have been doing a little detective work on my own, you know.'

'But you have been watched.'

'True. The finger-prints of my watchers adorn the first page of the collection.'

'This statement can be proved?'

'Certainly. I will prove it. The name of Number Fifty, for example—'

'Stop!'

A fierce muttering arose. The President silenced it with a gesture.

'If you mention names here, you will certainly have no hope of mercy. There is a fifth treatment – kept specially for people who mention names. Bring the prisoner to my office. Keep the dance going.'

'The President took an automatic from his hip-pocket and faced the tightly fettered prisoner across the desk.

'Now speak!' he said.

'I should put that thing away, if I were you,' said Wimsey contemptuously. 'It would be a much pleasanter form of death than treatment Number 5, and I might be tempted to ask for it.'

'Ingenious,' said the President, 'but a little too ingenious. Now, be quick; tell me what you know.'

'Will you spare me if I tell you?'

'I make no promises. Be quick.'

Wimsey shrugged his bound and aching shoulders.

'Certainly. I will tell you what I know. Stop me when you have heard enough.'

He leaned forward and spoke low. Overhead the noise of the gramophone and the shuffling of feet bore witness that the dance was going on. Stray passers-by crossing the Heath noted that the people in the lonely house were making a night of it again.

'Well,' said Wimsey, 'am I to go on?'

From beneath the mask the President's voice sounded as though he were grimly smiling.

'My lord,' he said, 'your story fills me with regret that

you are not, in fact, a member of our Society. Wit, courage, and industry are valuable to an association like ours. I fear I cannot persuade you? No – I supposed not.'

He touched a bell on his desk.

'Ask the members kindly to proceed to the supper-room,' he said to the mask who entered.

The 'supper-room' was on the ground-floor, shuttered and curtained. Down its centre ran a long, bare table, with chairs set about it.

'A Barmecide feast, I see,' said Wimsey pleasantly. It was the first time he had seen this room. At the far end, a trap-door in the floor gaped ominously.

The President took the head of the table.

'Ladies and gentlemen,' he began, as usual – and the foolish courtesy had never sounded so sinister – 'I will not conceal from you the seriousness of the situation. The prisoner has recited to me more than twenty names and addresses which were thought to be unknown, except to their owners and to me. There has been great carelessness' – his voice rang harshly – 'which will have to be looked into. Finger-prints have been obtained – he has shown me the photographs of some of them. How our investigators came to overlook the inner door of this safe is a matter which calls for enquiry.'

'Don't blame them,' put in Wimsey. 'It was meant to be overlooked, you know. I made it like that on purpose.'

The President went on, without seeming to notice the interruption.

'The prisoner informs me that the book with the names and addresses is to be found in this inner compartment, together with certain letters and papers stolen from the houses of members, and numerous objects bearing authentic finger-prints. I believe him to be telling the truth. He offers the combination of the safe in exchange for a quick death. I think the offer should be accepted. What is your opinion, ladies and gentlemen?'

'The combination is known already,' said Number Twenty-two.

'Imbecile! This man has told us, and has proved to me, that he is Lord Peter Wimsey. Do you think he will have forgotten to alter the combination? And then there is the secret of the inner door. If he disappears tonight and the police enter his house—'

'I say,' said a woman's rich voice, 'that the promise should be given and the information used – and quickly. Time is getting short.'

A murmur of agreement went round the table.

'You hear,' said the President, addressing Wimsey. 'The Society offers you the privilege of a quick death in return for the combination of the safe and the secret of the inner door.'

'I have your word for it?'

'You have.'

'Thank you. And my mother and sister?'

'If you in your turn will give us your word – you are a man of honour – that these women know nothing that could harm us, they shall be spared.'

'Thank you, sir. You may rest assured, upon my honour, that they know nothing. I should not think of burdening any woman with such dangerous secrets – particularly those who are dear to me.'

'Very well. It is agreed – yes?'

The murmur of assent was given, though with less readiness than before.

'Then I am willing to give you the information you want. The word of the combination is UNRELIABILITY.'

'And the inner door?'

'In anticipation of the visit of the police, the inner door – which might have presented difficulties – is open.'

'Good! You understand that if the police interfere with our messenger—'

'That would not help me, would it?'

'It is a risk,' said the President thoughtfully, 'but a risk which I think we must take. Carry the prisoner down to the cellar. He can amuse himself by contemplating apparatus Number 5. In the meantime, Numbers Twelve and Forty-six—'

'No, no!'

A sullen mutter of dissent arose and swelled threateningly.

'No,' said a tall man with a voice like treacle. 'No – why should any members be put in possession of this evidence? We have found one traitor among us tonight and more than one fool. How are we to know that Numbers Twelve and Forty-six are not fools and traitors also?'

The two men turned savagely upon the speaker, but a girl's voice struck into the discussion, high and agitated.

'Hear, hear! That's right, I say. How about us? We ain't going to have our names read by somebody we don't know nothing about. I've had enough of this. They might sell the 'ole lot of us to the narks.'

'I agree,' said another member. 'Nobody ought to be trusted, nobody at all.'

The President shrugged his shoulders.

'Then what, ladies and gentlemen, do you suggest?'

There was a pause. Then the same girl shrilled out again:

'I say Mr President oughter go himself. He's the only

one as knows all the names. It won't be no cop to him. Why should we take all the risk and trouble and him sit at home and collar the money? Let him go himself, that's what I say.'

A long rustle of approbation went round the table.

'I second that motion,' said a stout man who wore a bunch of gold seals at his fob. Wimsey smiled as he looked at the seals; it was that trifling vanity which had led him directly to the name and address of the stout man, and he felt a certain affection for the trinkets on that account.

The President looked round.

'It is the wish of the meeting, then, that I should go?' he said, in an ominous voice.

Forty-five hands were raised in approbation. Only the woman known as Number Two remained motionless and silent, her strong white hands clenched on the arm of the chair.

The President rolled his eyes slowly round the threatening ring till they rested upon her.

'Am I to take it that this vote is unanimous?' he enquired.

The woman raised her head.

'Don't go,' she gasped faintly.

'You hear,' said the President, in a faintly derisive tone. 'This lady says, don't go.'

'I submit that what Number Two says is neither here nor there,' said the man with the treacly voice. 'Our own ladies might not like us to be going, if they were in madam's privileged position.' His voice was an insult.

'Hear, hear!' cried another man. 'This is a democratic society, this is. We don't want no privileged classes.'

'Very well,' said the President. 'You hear, Number

Two. The feeling of the meeting is against you. Have you any reasons to put forward in favour of your opinion?'

'A hundred. The President is the head and soul of our Society. If anything should happen to him – where should we be? You' – she swept the company magnificently with her eyes – 'you have all blundered. We have your carelessness to thank for all this. Do you think we should be safe for five minutes if the President were not here to repair your follies?'

'Something in that,' said a man who had not hitherto spoken.

'Pardon my suggesting,' said Wimsey maliciously, 'that, as the lady appears to be in a position peculiarly favourable for the reception of the President's confidences, the contents of my modest volume will probably be no news to her. Why should not Number Two go herself?'

'Because I say she must not,' said the President sternly, checking the quick reply that rose to his companion's lips. 'If it is the will of the meeting, I will go. Give me the key of the house.'

One of the men extracted it from Wimsey's jacket-pocket and handed it over.

'Is the house watched?' he demanded of Wimsey.

'No.'

'That is the truth?'

'It is the truth.'

The President turned at the door.

'If I have not returned in two hours' time,' he said, 'act for the best to save yourselves, and do what you like with the prisoner. Number Two will give orders in my absence.'

He left the room. Number Two rose from her seat with a gesture of command.

'Ladies and gentlemen. Supper is now considered over. Start the dancing again.'

Down in the cellar the time passed slowly, in the contemplation of apparatus Number 5. The miserable Jukes, alternately wailing and raving, at length shrieked himself into exhaustion. The four members guarding the prisoners whispered together from time to time.

'An hour and a half since the President left,' said one.

Wimsey glanced up. Then he returned to his examination of the room. There were many curious things in it, which he wanted to memorise.

Presently the trap-door was flung open. 'Bring him up!' cried a voice. Wimsey rose immediately, and his face was rather pale.

The members of the gang were again seated round the table. Number Two occupied the President's chair, and her eyes fastened on Wimsey's face with a tigerish fury, but when she spoke it was with a self-control which roused his admiration.

'The President has been two hours gone,' she said. 'What has happened to him? Traitor twice over – what has happened to him?'

'How should I know?' said Wimsey. 'Perhaps he has looked after Number One and gone while the going was good!'

She sprang up with a little cry of rage, and came close to him.

'Beast! liar!' she said, and struck him on the mouth. 'You know he would never do that. He is faithful to his friends. What have you done with him? Speak – or I will make you speak. You two, there – bring the irons. He *shall* speak!'

'I can only form a guess, madame,' replied Wimsey, 'and I shall not guess any the better for being stimulated with hot irons, like Pantaloon at the circus. Calm yourself, and I will tell you what I think. I think – indeed, I greatly fear – that Monsieur le Président in his hurry to examine the interesting exhibits in my safe may, quite inadvertently, no doubt, have let the door of the inner compartment close behind him. In which case—'

He raised his eyebrow, his shoulders being too sore for shrugging, and gazed at her with a limpid and innocent regret.

'What do you mean?'

Wimsey glanced round the circle.

'I think,' he said, 'I had better begin from the beginning by explaining to you the mechanism of my safe. It is rather a nice safe,' he added plaintively. 'I invented the idea myself – not the principle of its working, of course; that is a matter for scientists – but just the idea of the thing.

'The combination I gave you is perfectly correct as far as it goes. It is a three-alphabet thirteen-letter lock by Bunn & Fishett – a very good one of its kind. It opens the outer door, leading into the ordinary strong-room, where I keep my cash and my Froth Blower's cuff-links and all that. But there is an inner compartment with two doors, which open in a quite different manner. The outermost of these two inner doors is merely a thin steel skin, painted to look like the back of the safe and fitting closely, so as not to betray any join. It lies in the same plane as the wall of the room, you understand, so that if you were to measure the outside and the inside of the safe you would discover no discrepancy. It opens outwards with an ordinary key, and, as I truly assured the President, it was left open when I quitted my flat.'

'Do you think,' said the woman sneeringly, 'that the President is so simple as to be caught in a so obvious trap? He will have wedged open that inner door undoubtedly.'

'Undoubtedly, madame. But the sole purpose of that outer inner door, if I may so express myself, is to appear to be the only inner door. But hidden behind the hinge of that door is another door, a sliding panel, set so closely in the thickness of the wall that you would hardly see it unless you knew it was there. This door was also left open. Our revered Number One had nothing to do but to walk straight through into the inner compartment of the safe, which, by the way, is built into the chimney, of the old basement kitchen, which runs up the house at that point. I hope I make myself clear?'

'Yes, yes – get on. Make your story short.'

Wimsey bowed, and, speaking with even greater deliberation than ever, resumed:

'Now, this interesting list of the Society's activities, which I have had the honour of compiling, is written in a very large books – bigger, even, than Monsieur le Président's ledger which he uses downstairs. (I trust, by the way, madame, that you have borne in mind the necessity of putting that ledger in a safe place. Apart from the risk of investigation by some officious policeman, it would be inadvisable that any junior member of the Society should get hold of it. The feeling of the meeting would, I fancy, be opposed to such an occurrence.)'

'It is secure,' she answered hastily. '*Mon dieu!* get on with your story.'

'Thank you – you have relieved my mind. Very good. This big book lies on a steel shelf at the back of the inner compartment. Just a moment. I have not described this inner compartment to you. It is six feet high, three feet wide, and three feet deep. One can stand up in it quite comfortably, unless one is very tall. It suits me nicely – as you may see, I am not more than five feet eight and a half. The President has the advantage of me in height; he might be a little cramped, but there would be room for him to squat if he grew tired of standing. By the way, I don't know if you know it, but you have tied me up rather tightly.'

'I would have you tied till your bones were locked together. Beat him, you! He is trying to gain time.'

'If you beat me,' said Wimsey, 'I'm damned if I'll speak at all. Control yourself, madame; it does not do to move hastily when your king is in check.'

'Get on!' she cried again, stamping with rage.

'Where was I? Ah! the inner compartment. As I say, it is a little snug – the more so that it is not ventilated in any way. Did I mention that the book lay on a steel shelf?'

'You did.'

'Yes. The steel shelf is balanced on a very delicate concealed spring. When the weight of the book – a heavy one, as I said – is lifted, the shelf rises almost imperceptibly. In rising it makes an electrical contact. Imagine to yourself, madame; our revered President steps in – propping the false door open behind him – he sees the book – quickly he snatches it up. To make sure that it is the right one, he opens it – he studies the pages. He looks about for the other objects I have mentioned, which bear the marks of fingerprints. And silently, but very, very quickly – you can imagine it, can you not? – the secret panel, released by the rising of the shelf, leaps across like a panther behind him. Rather a trite simile, but apt, don't you think?'

'My God! oh, my God!' Her hand went up as though to tear the choking mask from her face. 'You – you devil – devil! What is the word that opens the inner door? Quick! I will have it torn out of you – the word!'

'It is not a hard word to remember, madame – though it has been forgotten before now. Do you recollect, when you were a child, being told the tale of "Ali Baba and the Forty Thieves"? When I had that door made, my mind reverted, with rather a pretty touch of sentimentality, in my opinion, to the happy hours of my childhood. The words that open the door are – "Open Sesame."'

'Ah! How long can a man live in this devil's trap of yours?'

'Oh,' said Wimsey cheerfully, 'I should think he might hold out a few hours if he kept cool and didn't use up the available oxygen by shouting and hammering. If we went there at once, I dare say we should find him fairly all right.'

'I shall go myself. Take this man and – do your worst with him. Don't finish him till I come back. I want to see him die!'

'One moment,' said Wimsey, unmoved by this amiable wish. 'I think you had better take me with you.'

'Why – why?'

'Because, you see, I'm the only person who can open the door.'

'But you have given me the word. Was that a lie?'

'No – the word's all right. But, you see, it's one of these new-style electric doors. In fact, it's really the very latest thing in doors. I'm rather proud of it. It opens to the words "Open Sesame" all right – *but to my voice only*.'

'Your voice? I will choke your voice with my own hands. What do you mean – your voice only?'

'Just what I say. Don't clutch my throat like that, or you may alter my voice so that the door won't recognise it. That's better. It's apt to be rather pernickety about voices. It got stuck up for a week once, when I had a cold and could only implore it in a hoarse whisper. Even in the ordinary way, I sometimes have to try several times before I hit on the exact right intonation.'

She turned and appealed to a short, thick-set man standing beside her.

'Is this true? Is it possible?'

'Perfectly, ma'am, I'm afraid,' said the man civilly. From his voice Wimsey took him to be a superior workman of some kind – probably an engineer.

'Is it an electrical device? Do you understand it?'

'Yes, ma'am. It will have a microphone arrangement somewhere, which converts the sound into a series of vibrations controlling an electric needle. When the needle has traced the correct pattern, the circuit is completed and the door opens. The same thing can be done by light vibrations equally easily.'

'Couldn't you open it with tools?'

'In time, yes, ma'am. But only by smashing the mechanism, which is probably well protected.'

'You may take that for granted,' interjected Wimsey reassuringly.

She put her hands to her head.

'I'm afraid we're done in,' said the engineer, with a kind of respect in his tone for a good job of work.

'No – wait! Somebody must know – the workmen who made this thing?'

'In Germany,' said Wimsey briefly.

'Or – yes, yes, I have it – a gramophone. This – this – *he*

– shall be made to say the word for us. Quick – how can it be done?'

'Not possible, ma'am. Where should we get the apparatus at half-past three on a Sunday morning? The poor gentleman would be dead long before—'

There was a silence, during which the sounds of the awakening day came through the shuttered windows. A motor-horn sounded distantly.

'I give in,' she said. 'We must let him go. Take the ropes off him. You will free him, won't you?' she went on, turning piteously to Wimsey. 'Devil as you are, you are not such a devil as that! You will go straight back and save him!'

'Let him go, nothing!' broke in one of the men. 'He doesn't go to peach to the police, my lady, don't you think it. The President's done in, that's all, and we'd all better make tracks while we can. It's all up, boys. Chuck this fellow down the cellar and fasten him in, so he can't make a row and wake the place up. I'm going to destroy the ledgers. You can see it done if you don't trust me. And you, Thirty, you know where the switch is. Give us a quarter of an hour to clear, and then you can blow the place to glory.'

'No! You can't go – you can't leave him to die – your President – your leader – my – I won't let it happen. Set this devil free. Help me, one of you, with the ropes—'

'None of that, now,' said the man who had spoken before. He caught her by the wrists, and she twisted, shrieking, in his arms, biting and struggling to get free.

'Think, think,' said the man with the treacly voice. 'It's getting on to morning. It'll be light in an hour or two. The police may be here any minute.'

'The police!' She seemed to control herself by a violent

effort. 'Yes, yes, you are right. We must not imperil the safety of all for the sake of one man. *He* himself would not wish it. That is so. We will put this carrion in the cellar where it cannot harm us, and depart, every one to his own place, while there is time.'

'And the other prisoner?'

'He? Poor fool – he can do no harm. He knows nothing. Let him go,' she answered contemptuously.

In a few minutes' time Wimsey found himself bundled unceremoniously into the depths of the cellar. He was a little puzzled. That they should refuse to let him go, even at the price of Number One's life, he could understand. He had taken the risk with his eyes open. But that they should leave him as a witness against them seemed incredible.

The men who had taken him down strapped his ankles together and departed, switching the lights out as they went.

'Hi! Kamerad!' said Wimsey. 'It's a bit lonely sitting here. You might leave the light on.'

'It's all right, my friend,' was the reply. 'You will not be in the dark long. They have set the time-fuse.'

The other man laughed with rich enjoyment, and they went out together. So that was it. He was to be blown up with the house. In that case the President would certainly be dead before he was extricated. This worried Wimsey; he would rather have been able to bring the big crook to justice. After all, Scotland Yard had been waiting six years to break up this gang.

He waited, straining his ears. It seemed to him that he heard footsteps over his head. The gang had all crept out by this time. . . .

There was certainly a creak. The trap-door had

335

opened; he felt, rather than heard, somebody creeping into the cellar.

'Hush!' said a voice in his ear. Soft hands passed over his face, and went fumbling about his body. There came the cold touch of steel on his wrists. The ropes slackened and dropped off. A key clicked in the handcuffs. The strap about his ankles was unbuckled.

'Quick! quick! they have set the time-switch. The house is mined. Follow me as fast as you can. I stole back – I said I had left my jewellery. It was true. I left it on purpose. *He* must be saved – only you can do it. Make haste!'

Wimsey, staggering with pain, as the blood rushed back into his bound and numbed arms, crawled after her into the room above. A moment, and, she had flung back the shutters and thrown the window open.

'Now go! Release him! You promise?'

'I promise. And I warn you, madame, that this house is surrounded. When my safe-door closed it gave a signal which sent my servant to Scotland Yard. Your friends are all taken—'

'Ah! But you go – never mind me – quick! The time is almost up.'

'Come away from this!'

He caught her by the arm, and they went running and stumbling across the little garden. An electric torch shone suddenly in the bushes.

'That you, Parker?' cried Wimsey. 'Get your fellows away. Quick! the house is going up in a minute.'

The garden seemed suddenly full of shouting, hurrying men. Wimsey, floundering in the darkness, was brought up violently against the wall. He made a leap at the coping, caught it, and hoisted himself up. His hands groped for the woman; he swung her up beside him. They jumped; everyone was jumping; the woman caught her foot and fell with a gasping cry. Wimsey tried to stop himself, tripped over a stone, and came down headlong. Then, with a flash and a roar, the night went up in fire.

Wimsey picked himself painfully out from among the débris of the garden wall. A faint moaning near him proclaimed that his companion was still alive. A lantern was turned suddenly upon them.

'Here you are!' said a cheerful voice. 'Are you all right, old thing? Good lord! what a hairy monster!'

'All right,' said Wimsey. 'Only a bit winded. Is the lady safe? H'm – arm broken, apparently – otherwise sound. What's happened?'

'About half a dozen of 'em got blown up; the rest we've bagged.' Wimsey became aware of a circle of dark forms in the wintry dawn. 'Good Lord, what a day! What a come-back for a public character! You old stinker – to let us go on for two years thinking you were dead! I bought a bit of black for an armband. I did, really. Did anybody know, besides Bunter?'

'Only my mother and sister. I put it in a secret trust – you know, the thing you send to executors and people. We shall have an awful time with the lawyers, I'm afraid, proving I'm me. Hullo! Is that friend Sugg?'

'Yes, my lord,' said Inspector Sugg, grinning and nearly weeping with excitement. 'Damned glad to see your lordship again. Fine piece of work, your lordship. They're all wanting to shake hands with you, sir.'

'Oh, Lord! I wish I could get washed and shaved first. Awfully glad to see you all again, after two years' exile in Lambeth. Been a good little show, hasn't it?'

'Is he safe?'

Wimsey started at the agonised cry.

'Good Lord!' he cried. 'I forgot the gentleman in the safe. Here, fetch to car, quickly. I've got the great big top Moriarty of the whole bunch quietly asphyxiating at home. Here – hop in, and put the lady in too. I promised we'd get back and save him – though' (he finished the sentence in Parker's ear) 'there may be murder charges too, and I wouldn't give much for his chance at the Old Bailey. Whack her up. He can't last much longer shut up there. He's the bloke you've been wanting, the man at the back of the Morrison case and the Hope-Wilmington case, and hundreds of others.'

The cold morning had turned the streets grey when they drew up before the door of the house in Lambeth. Wimsey took the woman by the arm and helped her out. The mask was off now, and showed her face, haggard and desperate, and white with fear and pain.

'Russian, eh?' whispered Parker in Wimsey's ear.

'Something of the sort. Damn! the front door's blown shut, and the blighter's got the key with him in the safe. Hop through the window, will you?'

Parker bundled obligingly in, and in a few seconds threw open the door to them. The house seemed very still. Wimsey led the way to the back room, where the strong-room stood. The outer door and the second door stood propped open with chairs. The inner door faced them like a blank green wall.

'Only hope he hasn't upset the adjustment with thumping at it,' muttered Wimsey. The anxious hand on his arm clutched feverishly. He pulled himself together, forcing his tone to one of cheerful commonplace.

'Come on, old thing,' he said, addressing himself conversationally to the door. 'Show us your paces. Open Sesame, confound you. Open Sesame!'

The green door slid suddenly away into the wall. The woman sprang forward and caught in her arms the humped and senseless thing that rolled out from the safe. Its clothes were torn to ribbons, and its battered hands dripped blood.

'It's all right,' said Wimsey, 'it's all right! He'll live – to stand his trial.'

I.1.   VIRGO: The sign of the zodiac between LEO (strength) and LIBRA (justice). Allusion to parable of The Ten Virgins.

I.3.   R.S.: Royal Society, whose 'fellows' are addicted to studies usually considered dry-as-dust.

IV.3.   TESTAMENT (or will); search is to be directed to the Old Testament. Ref. to parable of New Cloth and Old Garment.

XIV.3.   HI: 'He would answer to Hi!
                     Or to any loud cry.'
                        The Hunting of the Snark.

I.5.   TRANS.: Abbreviation of Translation; ref. to building of Babel.

XI.5.   SCENT: 'Even the scent of roses
                 Is not what they supposes,
                 But more than mind discloses
                 And more than men believe.'
                 G. K. Chesterton:
                 The Song of Quoodle.

VI.7.   ICTUS: Blow, add V (five) and you get VICTUS (vanquished); the ictus is the stress in a foot of verse; if the stress be misplaced the line goes lamely.

I.8.   SPINOZA: He wrote on the properties of optical glasses; also on metaphysics.

IV.13.   THIRTY-ONE: Seven (months) out of the twelve

of the sun's course through the heavens have thirty-one days.

XIV.13. ET: Conjunction. In astrology an aspect of the heavenly bodies. That Cicero was the master of this word indicates that it is a Latin one.

X.14. BEZOAR: The bezoar stone was supposed to be a prophylactic against poison.

11.I. PLAUD: If you would laud, then plaud (var. of applaud); Plaud-it also means 'cheer.'

10.II. ALIENA: *As You Like It*. II.1.130.

1.III. R.D.: 'Refer to Drawer.'

4.III. CANTICLES: The Magnificat and Nunc Dimittis are known as the Canticles, but the Book of Canticles (the Vulgate name for the Song of Songs, in which the solution is found) occurs earlier in the Bible.

2.VI. EST: 'ον και μη 'ον = est and *non est* – the problem of being and not-being. Ref. Marlowe: *Doctor Faustus* I.1.

12.X. TOB.: Add IT to get Tobit; the tale of Tobit and the Fish is in the Apocrypha (the book of hidden things).

1.XI. MANES: 'Un lion est une mâchoire et non pas une criniere': Emile Faguet: *Lit. du XVIIe siècle*. Manes: benevolent spirits of the dead.

1.XV. SAINT: Evidence of miraculous power is required for canonisation.

THE SOLUTION OF THE CROSS-WORD PUZZLE
IN "UNCLE MELEAGER'S WILL"

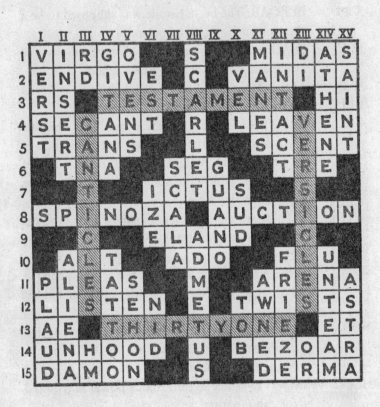